MY UNCLE WAS A W

At least that's wh him part an impas believe him. But t my own parents had been leading a double life, raising me on Earth yet sneaking off to Mom's kingdom whenever Dad was needed to be the Hero of Varay, defending the realm against invaders of all sorts, from humans to trolls, elves, and the occasional hungry dragon. That was just a little too much to take in all at once.

But now I'm in Varay myself. I got there by stepping through a magical door I found in my basement back home in Kentucky, so I guess I have to accept what my uncle told me. And the most important thing he said was that my parents are in big trouble and it's up to me to find and rescue them. The only things standing between me and success are a conquering army and a wizard with powers far beyond any my uncle could conjure up.

What he didn't tell me was that rescuing my family was just the beginning. . . .

THE VARAYAN MEMOIR
1

SON OF THE HERO

A FANTASY NOVEL BY

RICK SHELLEY

A ROC BOOK

ROC
Published by the Penguin Group
Penguin Books USA Inc., 375 Hudson Street, New York, New York 10014, U.S.A.
Penguin Books Ltd, 27 Wrights Lane, London W8 5TZ, England
Penguin Books Australia Ltd, Ringwood, Victoria, Australia
Penguin Books Canada Ltd, 2801 John Street, Markham, Ontario,
Canada L3R 1B4
Penguin Books (N.Z.) Ltd, 182-190 Wairau Road, Auckland 10, New Zealand

Penguin Books Ltd, Registered Offices: Harmondsworth, Middlesex, England

First published by Roc, an imprint of New American Library, a division of Penguin
Books USA. Inc.

First Printing, August, 1990
10 9 8 7 6 5 4 3 2 1

 Roc is a trademark of Penguin Books USA Inc.

Printed in the United States of America

1

The Cellar Room

I wasn't sure that I had enough cash to pay for the cab ride. I'd never expected to need a taxi. My folks had planned to meet me at the airport, the way they normally did when I came home from college. This time, I was coming home for my last spring vacation. In another six weeks I would have my B.S. in computer science. I was also coming home to celebrate my twenty-first birthday. Dad had promised something unusual for my "coming of age"—not my eighteenth birthday when I could vote and all, but number twenty-one. Dad wouldn't say what he had in mind, just that he wasn't being old-fashioned about twenty-one being "of age." I was a little edgy about the surprise. The one he'd hit me with when I turned eighteen was unusual enough. He dumped me in the Colorado Rockies with a light backpack and a few essentials and told me that I had three days to cover fifty miles of rough mountainous forest. He would meet me on the other side. But then, Dad was always a little strange. For years I worried that he was completely loony. Some of his habits were hard to accept as rational. And Mom wasn't a whole lot better. But it was a fun kind of crazy, and I guess I had a better childhood than most kids I knew. Even being dumped out in the wilderness wasn't *that* rough. Dad and I had done a lot of camping, and I knew how to take care of myself. Dad called it a test. I passed without much trouble, even enjoyed it.

"Here you are, kid," the cabbie said when we pulled up to the curb in front of the house. "That'll be twenty-fifty."

Searching for the money and worrying that I might not have that much on me kept me from getting too upset at being called a "kid." I even had to give him the ten quarters I had left from the video arcade at O'Hare. There was nothing left for a tip—but then, I wouldn't have tipped anyone who called me "kid" on my twenty-first birthday anyway. I got my suitcase and overnight bag out and shut the door. The cabbie screeched away to let me know how he felt about not getting a tip.

I stood out front and looked at the only home I had ever known. It looked old-fashioned and was. Even when the house was new it must have looked out of place, out of time—limestone blocks in a development of brick, wood, and aluminum; two stories with high-peaked roof and gables among ranchers; nearly hidden behind a stone wall and thick bushes instead of neat white picket or chain-link fencing with sparse, carefully manicured landscaping. Dad had designed the place. He liked to say that it was sometimes worth being different just to be different. From the street, the house was almost hidden. Twelve-foot privet hedges surrounded it. Windows peeped out. Thick ivy clung to the walls. The walk curved back and forth through two decades of transplanted Christmas trees. Lilacs bloomed everywhere, giving the place an overwhelming sweetness for a few weeks every spring. —Home.

I carried my bags toward the front door slowly, savoring the lilacs and the feeling of being home. The house sits 120 feet from the road, and the ground rises five feet from curb to porch. Ten acres of land—most of it looks wild, though there was reason, rationale, behind the layout . . . at least Dad claimed there was.

No one came out to greet me, but I didn't start to worry until I saw three newspapers on the porch. *Three days' papers.* Both locks on the front door were locked. When I opened the door, I had to push a stack of mail out of the way.

"Mom? Dad?" I didn't get any answer. I brought the papers in, set them and the mail on the little table in the entryway. I headed for the kitchen then, my mother's private kingdom. There were no dirty dishes piled up. There was also no birthday cake waiting. The milk in the fridge smelled sour. A package of hamburger had turned a peculiar gray color. A quick tour told me that there was no one in the house but me. The search was a frenzied formality. After seeing what was in the fridge, I knew that no one else was home. But both cars were in the garage.

It was time to start worrying.

I went through the house again, more slowly, more carefully, looking for notes. There was nothing in the living room, dining room, or kitchen—places Mom was likely to leave word. Nor was there anything in Dad's office or in any of the bedrooms or bathrooms upstairs. I even unraveled a couple of feet off every roll of toilet paper looking for a message. I know that sounds crazy, but in my family, it's not enough to merely be logical.

That left the garage, basement, and yard. I checked the garage first. I looked through Dad's Citroën and Mom's Dodge van, and then under them. Nothing. The yard—all ten acres—would need hours to search thoroughly; it's not as though we just had grass and a few tame trees—it's a jungle out there. So I headed for the basement.

The cellar was always taboo for me while I was growing up. The door leading down from the kitchen was always locked. On the few occasions when I *was* allowed down there, it was to get something out of the larger of the two cellar rooms. The smaller room was Dad's private preserve, and I was *never* allowed into it. Well, when I was very young, before I started school, there may have been a few times when I went in there with Mom and Dad, but those memories were impossibly vague, connected somehow to memories of visits to relatives.

The door leading from the kitchen down to the cellar was unlocked. I turned on the lights and went down the steps—slowly. My stomach started to churn. I hesitated and wondered if I should call the police. I decided to wait until I finished my search. There were some other calls I could make too—back to the dorm to see if a letter had come for me, to Dad's agent and a couple of people my folks sometimes did things with. I didn't think that the calls would do any good, though, not with both cars in the garage, rotten food in the fridge, no note, and the pile of papers and mail. My folks were much too organized for that.

The main part of the basement—furnace, central air,

water heater, an old sofa and chair that had been exiled
when I was ten, three bicycles (my "wheels" from ages
seven to fifteen), and other odds and ends you might find
in any cellar—was as I remembered it. Back in the farthest corner, the door to my father's *sanctum sanctorum*
was propped open with the snow shovel. I stopped at the
bottom of the stairs and stared at that open door, reluc-
tant to cross the cellar and look inside that room. I was
afraid of what I might find. That door was always secured
by two combination locks and a heavy deadbolt.

I held my breath and listened to silence for a couple
of minutes, crazy fears racing through my mind. Had
someone broken in and killed them? Had they run off on
my twenty-first birthday? Murder-suicide? Was the old
man really as crazy as I sometimes thought he was?

After a long hesitation, I walked slowly toward the
open door, wishing I had a weapon. I stopped at the door
and reached inside for the light switch. It took a bit of
fumbling. The switch was set farther from the door than
the rest of the switches in the house.

Bright light. Nothing jumped out. I looked in, then
stepped inside . . . maybe with my jaw hanging open.

The Room. There were swords, knives, maces, shields,
pennants, and other medieval goodies hanging on the
walls. A suit of chain mail was arranged on a dummy in
one corner. There was a huge rolltop desk and a work-
table in the center of the room. I saw a pile of stuff on
the table with several sheets of my mother's lilac-colored-
and-scented stationery on top, but I didn't run right for
that. I was, momentarily, flabbergasted at what else the
room held—seven extra doors spaced around the four
walls. Two doors flanked the door I had entered through,
on the wall between Dad's room and the rest of the basement, doors that weren't there on the other side. I shook
my head, almost forgetting the search that had brought
me to the room. The weaponry was no surprise. There
was more of that all over the house. But those doors!
Then I went to the table and picked up mother's stationery.

One mystery at a time. I told myself.

Mother's stationery was an off-size, six inches by

twelve, made of heavy paper that felt like parchment. She had written the note. Her ornate script and the royal-blue ink were quite distinctive. The note was dated Wednesday, three days back.

"Dear Gilbert," it started. Mom never called me "son" or Gil,—well, almost never, certainly not in writing—and *I* never admitted to Gilbert.

"Your father is overdue from a trip. I'm going after him. I fear he may be in trouble. This is certainly an awkward time. I hope we get home before you arrive—of course, if we do, you won't see this note—but if your father *has* gotten himself into a sticky situation, it might not be possible for us to get home before you do.

"Awkward. We intended to have a long talk with you while you were home this time, to tell you about our family history and to initiate you into some of our—shall we say—family mysteries. Your heritage."

Mother has never been able to write a *short* note. Once, while I was in high school, I came home one afternoon and found a note that boiled down to "Ride down to the grocery store and get a loaf of bread." It was 130 words long. I counted.

I took a moment to look through the rest of the stuff piled on the table, hoping it would help me understand what the hell she was getting at. My sword was there. Yes, *my sword*, one of them. Fencing was one of Dad's obsessions. I started taking fencing lessons when I was six—not to mention judo, karate, savate, boxing, and a half-dozen other varieties of martial mayhem. The shooting lessons, guns and bows, didn't start until I was eight. My favorite sword was there on the table—heavy, double-edged blade, simple cross-hilt—plus a twelve-inch stiletto, weapon belt, camouflage fatigues (I had refused to continue wearing a Robin Hood costume when I was fourteen), compound bow, quiver of razor-headed hunting arrows, small pack, full canteen, and about thirty pounds of other Sherwood Forest–type equipment. Okay, I was looking at some kind of trip again, apparently wilder than my survival trek of three years before. There was also a small leather-bound book—four by six, and three inches thick—held closed by a cracked leather strap. I went back to the note.

"I certainly don't have time to tell you everything you need to know right now. If I tried, I would still be writing when you got home and I don't dare wait that long to go after your father. Three days are too many if he *is* in trouble. Some of it I might even get wrong, and that would be worse than leaving you ignorant of certain possibilities. Knight-errantry is your father's area anyway, not mine. But I have to give you what help I can. Among the gear I've left for you is my grandmother's *Tower Chapbook*. It's filled with odds and ends of lore and whatnot, things she wrote down during the years she was imprisoned. You may find it useful if you have time to consult it at need. The short index is one I added when I was a young girl. It's not complete. I fear that I grew bored long before it was finished."

I didn't even know that I *had* a great-grandmother who had been imprisoned for years. I opened the book and flipped through some of the pages. The script was even more convoluted than Mother's, and I couldn't read a single word of it. The language didn't look the least bit familiar, though it seemed to use our alphabet. Back to the letter.

"The best advice I can offer if you have to come looking for us is to be as paranoid as you can about *everything* and *everyone.*" I shook my head. Dear old Mother was starting to sound as wacky as father, and she'd always seemed more sensible. Of course, her relatives, the few I had met, all seemed peculiar. Maybe it was a family thing, like in *Arsenic and Old Lace*.

"Looking back over this," the note continued, "I see that I really haven't told you anything that you need to know. Your father went off to answer a call for help from my Uncle Parthet (not *Parker,* dear, that's just the name he uses in this world). Your father should have been home by last weekend at the very latest. It is hard to pin this kind of thing down to a rigid timetable because you never know precisely what sort of trouble a Hero will run into along the way, but last weekend by the latest. He still hasn't shown, so I fear he may have run into something too big for him to handle. Maybe I won't be in time to help, maybe my help won't be enough if I do, but I have to make the attempt.

"You'll have to go to Uncle Parthet for details, and yes, I know you've never gone calling on him, that you don't know exactly where he lives. That's one of the things your father and I could never explain, part of what you would have learned on this vacation.

"Really, it is quite simple. You just have to know which door to use and where to go after you step through." I stopped and looked around at the batch of doors again. It didn't make sense yet, but I don't know that *anything* would have made sense just then.

"Oh dear, the *doors!* You've never operated them, have you?"

"No, Mother," I said. "I didn't even know about them. I still don't." Too bad she couldn't hear and answer. I looked back to her note.

"You just need the rings. I hope they fit. If your fingers haven't swollen up since last summer, they ought to. The rings are in a small box in one of the side pockets of your pack. Always wear the eagle on your left hand and the signet on the right. You touch the rings to the silver tracing on each side of the doors to operate them. A sword in your right hand will serve in place of the signet, though, as long as you're wearing both rings."

I glanced at the nearest door but didn't see anything that looked like silver tracing, so I went to the door and pulled it open. The tracing was inside, all the way around the jamb, but there was a concrete wall behind the door. Time to read on.

"The door to Parthet's place is the one with the green trout on it (a private joke; your father says that Parthet drinks like a fish). On the other side of the door, you just follow the path. Bear left at the fork and you'll come to Parthet's cottage.

"I don't even know for sure what to warn you about. Once you go through the door, almost anything *could* happen. I mean that in the most literal way possible. You've led such a sheltered life in such a civilized world. Not all places are so tame or predictable. If you can imagine something, it's probably possible somewhere, and many things you could *never* imagine.

"If you have to come after us, expect the worst at every turn. Even then, what you find may be worse than the worst you can expect. I don't suppose that makes much sense now. It will, I fear, if you come through the door. Deadly danger. *Always*. That's why I have so few living relatives.

"Eat hearty before you leave. Never miss a chance for a safe meal—if there is such a thing beyond the door.

"If I can get to your father and make it straight back, we'll be home sometime Saturday afternoon. If we're not there by sunset, we probably both need help."

The note was signed, "Love, Mother," as if I might not know who wrote it. I folded the papers and put them in my hip pocket. I did another slow spin to look at the doors. Then I made the circuit and opened every one of them. They all opened on concrete blocks except the door I had come in through, and *that* door didn't have the silver tracing.

Back at the table, I dug the two rings out of the pack. I had seen the rings before, or their mates. My parents each wore a set. "A custom," they called it. I slipped them on the way the note said, eagle on the left, signet on the right. The signet was a simplified version of our coat of arms. That was all over the house—on tapestries, on a shield in the living room, carved into the front and back doors, even stamped into the silverware and embossed on the dishes, the good service that only came out on special occasions. The design was quartered, diagonal lines in the upper-left and lower-right quadrants, a bird that looked something like a penguin in the other two sections.

I went back to the door with the green trout and touched the rings to the silver tracing on either side . . . and almost browned out. The blank concrete wall disappeared and showed me what looked like the interior of a cave, dim, with a hint of distant light off to the left. I jumped back and the wall returned. I tried again and jumped back just as quickly.

"Holy shit!" I shouted. I went out through the regular

door and up to the kitchen. I had spotted a six-pack of Michelob in the fridge. I opened two and started drinking one with each hand—much too quickly. But the bottles were half empty before I could make myself stop.

"The whole family's crazy," I said, looking at the bottles. "I'm as loony as the rest." But that explanation didn't sit well. I went back down to the basement room with one way in and eight ways out. Crossing the main part of the cellar, I picked up a baseball—teenage memorabilia. I took the ball to the door with the green trout and put my rings against the silver tracing. The cave was still there. I dropped the baseball, bounced it off my knee, and watched it bounce twice on the floor of the cave, then roll away. When I pulled my hands away from the silver tracing, the wall returned and there was no hint of the baseball.

I stared at the door, at the bare concrete wall, for several minutes before I worked up the nerve to open the passage again. I took away just my right hand. The portal remained open. When I took the other hand away, the wall returned. I started over, reversing the order. Same result. Opening the way needed both rings on the tracing, but one hand would hold it open.

"If this is crazy," I started, but I didn't know how to finish. I went back to the table and looked through the pack—two changes of clothing (including one of those silly Robin Hood outfits), cigarette lighter and matches (and I don't smoke), water-purification tablets, aspirin, fishing lines and hooks, six freeze-dried meals (just add water and heat). It looked like an assortment Dad would prepare.

"Dad, if this is a joke, you're sure going to hear about it," I said. An answer would have been comforting, but there was none.

According to my watch, sunset was about an hour off. I didn't figure on hopping through that doorway any sooner than that, if then. But I really didn't want to do my waiting in that screwy room, so I went back upstairs. After a futile search for something decent to eat, I settled on a peanut butter sandwich. The bread was stale but didn't show any mold. It was passable, since I washed it down with the rest of the beer in my two open bottles. Then I went through the entire house, room by room, looking at all of the doors. The door to Dad's office had silver tracing. Looking in from the hallway, I put the rings against the silver, but nothing happened. I went into the office and tried from that side. Looking out, the hallway changed. It was still a hall, but the walls were made of large stones. There was a torch burning smokily in a bracket on the other side. The door between the master bedroom and its bath had the silver. Looking into the bathroom and touching the tracing, I saw what seemed to be a closet full of rough brooms and mops. Looking out from the bathroom, I saw a different bedroom with a huge canopied bed, torch brackets on stone walls, and a tatty-looking forest tapestry with unicorns and dragons. Two closet doors were also gimmicked.

After I finished my look-around, I went to the living room and turned on the TV to try to find something normal. I flipped through the channels—German soccer, American golf, baseball, a newly colorized Errol Flynn movie, a crafts show, news, news, *Andy Griffith, Leave It to Beaver.* Some things hadn't changed.

After twenty-one years of living with my parents, I shouldn't have been surprised by *anything,* but those doors in the basement weren't just against the rules, they weren't even within the range of cheating. It was as if somebody had added a phony CHANCE card to the Monopoly set. *"You have been abducted by aliens from another planet. Go straight to Arcturus III."*

I turned off the TV. It wasn't doing the job. "Allen Funt, where are you when I need you?" I asked. Nobody answered. A second peanut butter sandwich didn't do anything but convince me that beer and peanut butter don't mix.

As the day's light started to fade, I locked the front door and went back to the basement. I put on the fatigues and combat boots, strapped on the belt with my sword, knife, and quiver, slipped on the backpack, and picked up my bow. There was no hat with the outfit, at least none I would wear. Mother had provided only a long green thing with a feather, part of the Robin Hood costume. So I went upstairs for one of my Chicago Cubs caps. That was in my room on the second floor. I looked at myself in the full-length mirror on my closet door.

"You look like a jackass, Gil Tyner," I said. I felt like one too.

"There's only one thing missing." I nodded at my reflection. "No, besides your sanity. A gun. If you're going into trouble, a gun might do more good than the rest of this garbage."

Mom didn't like guns—though she had nothing against swords, spears, battle-axes, halberds, bows, or similar pointed and edged weapons. For Dad, weapons were weapons—tools. He made me practice with all of them. The gun cabinet was in Dad's office. The cabinet was locked, but I knew the combination to his safe, and the keys to the gun cabinet were kept in there. Two guns were missing from the collection, an HK-91 assault rifle and a Smith & Wesson automatic pistol. Dad's sword was missing from its pegs on the wall as well.

"He did expect trouble," I said. Somewhere along the line, I guess I had decided that it *might* not all be an elaborate and strange put-on.

I took the other Smith & Wesson 9mm automatic with the double-column clip, filled two fourteen-shot magazines, stuck one in the gun and the other in a pouch on my belt. I also packed a full box of ammo. The pistol went under my shirt in a clip-on holster. I decided against taking a rifle on practical grounds. I already had enough weight to carry.

Sunset was gone. I shut off lights on my way to the basement; I grabbed a flashlight from the kitchen cabinet, checked the batteries, and stuck it in my pack. There wasn't much room left, but I managed to cram in the last four bottles of beer. I thought I might need them before the night was over.

Down to the basement—nothing had changed there. The green-trout door was still open. I looked through Mom's note again: ". . . just follow the path. Bear left at the fork and you'll come to Parthet's cottage." A hint about how far I had to follow the path might have been nice. I shoved the note into my shirt pocket and buttoned

it. I left the room light on when I went to the open door
with the green trout on it.

"Time for your grand entrance, fool," I mumbled. No
more hesitating. I slipped my bow over my shoulder, then
put my hands up so the rings touched the silver tracing.
There was still a little light in the cave beyond, not much.
I took a deep breath, and stepped forward . . .

2

Parthet

. . . and fell flat on my face in the damp cave.

I didn't try to get to my feet right away. That wasn't
because I felt foolish or anything like that—at least, not
entirely. One of Dad's early lessons for me was to *not*
jump right up after a fall but to stay down and take stock
first to make sure that I wasn't badly hurt—unless staying
down risked greater injury, as in a fight. I wasn't hurt,
except maybe in the ego. My fall just knocked the air out
of me. There was a difference in level between the basement and the cave, or the doorway was placed above the
ground in the cave. I hadn't noticed. Banging my head
on the rock floor of the cave didn't help. It wasn't the
most auspicious start to my rescue mission.

After a moment the cave stopped spinning and I could
breathe again. I became aware of a sore spot on my head
and noticed the sound of water dripping nearby.

Then I heard something else, sort of a soft scraping
sound. The first time, it came and went so quickly that
it might have been my imagination. But it certainly got
my attention.

"What the hell's going on?" I mumbled as I stood. I
looked around quickly while I dug out my flashlight. My
heart seemed to be thumping around a little crazily. It
didn't help at all to see that I was certainly in a cave, not
just in some part of the basement I had never known
about. I could see a faint light—still off to my left—and
guessed that it was coming from the mouth of the cave.

Then I got the flashlight turned on and discovered that I wasn't alone in the cave. The flashlight started shaking as if I had a bad case of coffee nerves, like after pulling an all-nighter to get ready for finals. Deeper in the cave— on the side away from the faint glow—maybe twenty feet from me, beyond a small pool of water, there was a lizard staring at me. Some lizard. It was seven feet from nose to tail, two feet high, as close as I could make out under the circumstances—the circumstances being that I was scared a lot worse than I like to admit. A long forked tongue flicked in my direction. The eyes blinked once. It was no Komodo dragon, and I couldn't think of any other lizards that could be so big.

I thought it looked hungry, but that might easily have been my imagination.

For a long moment I stood frozen in place, not daring to move an inch, though that didn't stop the beam of my flashlight from continuing to wobble all over the place. I wondered how much time I would have to react if the lizard decided to charge. I had both hands full, bow and flashlight. I couldn't use the bow one-handed, and I couldn't do much of anything without the flashlight. I ruled out running for the cave's exit. First of all, I didn't know if I would be able to outrun the lizard. Secondly, I wanted to make sure that I could find the doorway back to the basement before I moved too far from where I was. I didn't know any other route home, and it looked all too certain that I was going to want to find my way back, maybe pretty damn fast.

Drop the bow, switch the flashlight to the left hand, pull the pistol, and shoot the damn thing, I told myself. Then I realized that I hadn't jacked a cartridge into the chamber.

"You're not scoring points for being prepared," I told myself as softly as I could.

The lizard's tongue kept flicking in and out. It blinked again. I glanced at the wall but didn't see any trace of the doorway at first, and that pumped another load of adrenaline through my system. When I finally caught a glimpse of badly tarnished silver, I breathed a little easier.

Pop back through the basement, get the gun ready, and shoot the damn thing from the doorway.

That sounded like an excellent plan. I could even run upstairs and get more firepower to bolster my courage.

That's the ticket, I decided. I counted three in my head and made my move. But the second I started to move, the lizard moved too—in my direction. It didn't move fast, but I wasn't waiting to find out for sure if it had "hostile intent." I threw my bow to the ground, more or less in the direction of the lizard, and started fumbling to get my pistol out and ready.

I was slow—*way* too slow. If that lizard had really been determined, I'd have been supper before I got a shell jacked into the chamber. But when my bow clattered on the stone, the lizard turned and scuttled off deeper into the cave. I could hear it moving farther off even after I lost sight of it.

I looked down at my hands. They were trembling. A deep breath helped, but for a bit all I could do was stand there. That lizard didn't have any business being there—or anywhere.

Finally, I realized that I wasn't accomplishing anything and that the damn lizard might come back. I took another deep breath and then took a long, close look at the wall until I could follow enough of the silver tracing to locate the door mentally. When I touched the silver with my rings, I could see into the basement room, and that reassured me.

I stepped right through then, just to assure myself that I could. Back in that strange-but-familiar basement room, I took my hand away from the door and breathed deeply, several times. There was a crazy jumble of thoughts bouncing around in my head, and "crazy" was still the operative word. I dearly wanted to dig out the rest of those beers and polish them off . . . but I remembered why I was in the cave in the first place.

"You're going to have to go back through there," I told myself. I may even have nodded. But after my encounter with that damn lizard, I had to make a quick trip upstairs. Somehow, my bladder managed to avoid letting go when I saw the lizard, but it was clamoring for attention—and it gave me an excuse to put off my return for a few more minutes.

Then, reluctantly, I stepped back through into the cave and let the doorway close behind me. This time, I had the pistol in my hand, cocked, with the safety off. At least I knew that if I could get back to the cave, I could get home.

If I could get by the lizard again.

I picked up my bow and started toward the mouth of the cave, counting my steps going out so I would know how far I had to come in to reach the door tracing.

Although I didn't waste a lot of thought on it (I had enough on my mind without that), the cave didn't look altogether natural. Dad and I had done a little spelunking. There wasn't much that we hadn't sampled over the years. Dad was gone so often on his "business trips" that he always wanted to spend a lot of time with me when he was home. For Dad, that meant *doing* things like hiking, camping, and exploring caves, not just watching ballgames or parades—though we did that too. This cave had been altered. Low spots in the ceiling had been hacked out. The floor was flat and met the walls almost at right angles. Most of the passage was room-high and eight feet wide.

Twenty paces from the tracing I didn't need the flashlight any longer. A few steps beyond that, the cave widened into a chamber about twenty feet square. In the center of the chamber, an altar—a large cube of rock with arcane symbols chiseled into its surfaces—had been erected. The cave walls around it were painted with exaggerated nudes, fat-bottomed women with huge breasts, like the fertility goddesses of the ancient Mideast.

Beyond that chamber, the cave narrowed down again, but the mouth wasn't far off. The last few steps I had to take hunched over. I stayed inside the mouth of the cave long enough to let my eyes adjust to the outside light. I had had one surprise too many already.

It seemed to be about mid-afternoon, not thirty minutes past dark—wherever I was. It had to be afternoon (rather than morning) because there had been light visible in the cave when I first looked through the green-trout door. I saw a lot of green outside the cave, even wilder and more disorganized than our backyard. The hillside around me was covered with something like Scottish heather, except for a few large bushes and trees. The cave mouth was some feet above the path. I could see it running off into the forest. The path didn't come directly to the cave but went around the base of the hill to my right. It was a well-defined track, wide enough for a subcompact car, but rough enough that I'd want four-wheel drive to try it. In the ten minutes that I watched, I didn't see any traffic.

"None of this is real," I told myself. "It can't be." There was no tract of land like this anywhere near our house. It wasn't in our yard, and that cave hadn't been long enough to get me clear of our subdivision.

I wasn't too crazy about continuing, but I also wasn't quite ready to go back and risk facing that lizard again. Well, I *knew* what was behind me, and I *didn't* know what was in front of me. That may have made the difference. I moved out of the cave, put the safety on my pistol and holstered it, then stretched. The hill rose two hundred feet behind me. I considered climbing to get a better look at the land, but that scratchy heather wasn't very inviting. It was knee-deep, stiff and prickly. It smelled vaguely like lilacs.

Mother's note didn't say which way to follow the path, just to bear left at the fork. I didn't see the fork. I assumed—initial hypothesis—that I wanted to head toward the forest. The temperature was comfortable, the breeze perfect. "Nice day for a hike," I mumbled as I started. Sometimes I can't help being sarcastic even when I'm my only audience.

I don't know what I expected. After the lizard, I don't think anything would have surprised me. I felt relieved that the forest looked so normal when I got into it. The bottom twenty or thirty feet of the trees were bare trunk, giving it the air of a pillared hall with a thick canopy. Firs, some oaks, other types I didn't recognize. From the new green, I assumed it was spring there too. Birds sang somewhere. I didn't recognize the calls, but I only know about half-dozen. A flaw in my education as an outdoorsman. The only birds I've ever been interested in watching are beyond singing—usually brown and steaming, on their backs on a platter on the dining-room table . . . or in one of the Colonel's boxes or buckets.

There was a heavy earth smell of recent rain in the air. The path was soft, spongy but not muddy. Part of the time, I moved slowly, observing, checking out the scenery. The rest of the time, I stepped out smartly, trying to cover ground fast since I didn't know how far I had to go—and I might have to backtrack to try the path in the other direction.

It was a pleasant place to walk. It gave my nerves a chance to unwind a little, gave me time to start breathing normally. I might almost have been down in the Land Between the Lakes, or any of a dozen other places where Dad and I had gone hiking and camping over the years.

I had walked about a quarter of a mile before I saw any animal life on the ground in the forest—another one of the damn lizards. It disappeared too quickly for me to be positive, but with the better light, the lizard appeared to have rudimentary wings folded back along its sides. Crazy—there's that word again, but it's hard to avoid. I stopped and listened, not nearly as nervous as I had been when I stumbled on the lizard in the cave. I was out in the open and this one was farther off than the first had been. The beast wasn't very quiet. I drew my pistol again and kept it ready until I was long past where the animal crossed the path. I've never liked reptiles.

The fork in the path was about three-quarters of a mile from the cave. The track to the left was the less well traveled, no more than a footpath. There were thick brambles, knotty vines, along both sides for quite a distance. The trees seemed shorter, meaner. Low branches needed ducking under. Uncle Parker—Parthet—evidently didn't get a lot of company.

The farther I went, the more disorganized the forest became. It made me think of a PBS show a long time back that showed the crazy webs spun by spiders on drugs. Smaller, twisted trees forced the path to detour back and forth. The underbrush got thicker, thornier.

Stickers reached out to poke me. I was glad I was wearing good fatigues. Those thorns would have shredded the leggings of a Robin Hood costume.

I almost missed the cottage. It was concealed better than our house, almost invisible among the trees and brambles. The cottage was small (well, cottages are *supposed* to be small, aren't they?) and had a thatched roof with new greenery growing out of it. I was surprised that Dad hadn't tried for that effect at home. It would have been the crowning touch. The two windows I saw had no glass. Warped wooden shutters stuck out and creaked in the light breeze.

"Uncle Parker?" I called. "Uncle Parker?"

"Is that you, Carl? Are you back? Did Avedell find you?" The questions tripped over each other before the door opened and Uncle Parker—Parthet—came out. Carl was my father, Avedell my mother.

"It's me, Gil," I said. Parthet squinted up at me. He was barely five feet tall and had acquired a stoop since I last saw him.

"Gil?" He came closer and squinted so tightly that his eyes seemed to be closed. "How'd you get here?"

"Mother left a note. What's going on?"

"What's going on? *What's going on?*" He snorted and shook his head. "Come in, lad, and I'll try to explain."

The cottage was even bleaker on the inside than it was from out front. Everything was wood, gray with age. The planks in a small table were all warped differently. Some of the wall planks were missing completely. The floor was dirt. A fireplace at one end of the room provided the only contrast to the ash gray—soot black. A single door led to another room—a bedroom, I guessed, since there didn't seem to be much chance that the cottage had indoor plumbing. Parthet sat me on a bench at the table. I found a splinter immediately, the hard way.

"Young Gil, is it?" He sat across the table from me and leaned across it—as far as he reached.

"It's me, Uncle Parker. Mom left a note that said Dad was overdue and she was going after him, and she told me how to find you."

"Ah, yes, she would." Parthet nodded. "And what do you propose to do?"

Good question. I'd been asking myself the same thing. "I don't know what the hell's going on," I said. "I don't even know where I am."

"You're in my home, not that I use it all that much. This is the Forest of Precarra in the Kingdom of Varay."

That didn't help much.

"I didn't think it was Kentucky. Nobody gave me a script to this madness. Those doors in our basement. All this nonsense. What the hell is it all about?" I may have started sputtering. It was so insane that I wasn't even sure what questions to ask.

"Your father was going to tell you soon," Parthet said.

"All I know is what was in Mom's note." I dug it out of my pocket and handed it to him. Parthet looked at the paper, sniffed at it, turned it over, then handed it back to me.

"Unfortunately, I seem to have misplaced my spectacles and I haven't been able to find them," he said.

"Don't you have a spare set?"

"I have trouble enough keeping track of one pair, let alone two."

I read the note to him, with some difficulty. There wasn't much light in the place. Parthet listened and nodded a lot. The nodding continued after I finished.

"It's so hard to know where to begin," he said.

"Well, let's not go back all the way to Adam and Eve." It was meant to be a joke, but it didn't sound that way, even to me. "I didn't mean that the way it sounded, Uncle Parker." I couldn't call him Parthet yet. He had always been Uncle Parker, and the habit was hard to break.

"That's all right, lad," he said. "I was never much of a storyteller. I could never remember which bits go where." He shrugged, a peculiar gesture the way he was stooped. "I was never even that much of a wizard."

"Hold it! Time out! What do you mean, wizard?"

"Well, yes, I think that's still the word." He paused a moment, then said, "Conjuring, spells, potions, the odd bit of magic. That sort of lot."

And I'm the King of Siam, I thought. Okay, the whole

family *was* crazy. That was the obvious explanation. And I just happened to pick my twenty-first birthday to join the club.

"My eyesight's always been bad, and getting worse all the time," Parthet continued. "Weak eyes are a terrible handicap to a wizard. So much of the craft depends on being able to see what you're doing. A wizard who can't see the end of his nose isn't worth much." He sighed, rather theatrically, I thought. "I was so glad when spectacles were invented. It gave me the chance to do a spot of business now and again."

"Uncle Parker, I think glasses were invented more than six hundred years ago, back in the Middle Ages."

He looked toward the ceiling for a moment, then nodded. "That sounds about right. As soon as I heard about this newfangled invention, I went and had a pair made for me. I got this last pair—wherever they've gotten themselves off to—while I was visiting the World's Fair in St. Louis in your world."

"More than eighty years ago?"

"Why, yes, I suppose it was. My, how time flies. I'm due for a new pair, but I never seem to find the time."

We were getting way off track, drifting farther off into Never-Never Land. "Mom said you called Dad for help. What kind of help?"

"Well, there was a job of work to be done, the kind of to-do your father has handled for us for the last twenty-odd years. He wasn't much older than you are now the first time he came to Varay." Parthet licked his lips. "This will be thirsty work. Would you care for a flagon of wine with me?" I was beginning to see where Mom's discursive notes came from.

"I'd prefer beer if you've got it," I said.

"Ah, me, so would I, but I don't have any to hand, and it would take time to fetch some in."

Then I remembered. "I have some with me." I stripped off my pack—which shows how distracted I had been; all that time and I still had it on—and took out two bottles. Good thing I'd fallen forward in the cave. None of my bottles had broken. "It's not as cold as it could be, but I think it'll do." I handed one bottle to Parthet.

"It will indeed." He held the bottle close to his eyes. "Did you remember to fetch along an opener?"

"Don't need one. Just twist the cap." I demonstrated with mine and he managed his.

"Now, *that's* convenient." He almost drowned the last word by pouring beer all over it. He took a long swallow, smacked his lips, and held the bottle close to his eyes again. The afternoon was getting late and the inside of the cottage was getting darker by the minute. It hardly mattered that Uncle Parthet was more than half blind and I had perfect eyesight. Neither of us could see much.

"The doorways are a bit of family magic," Parthet said after a second pull on his Michelob. I wasn't sure if that was a non sequitur or a good place to begin whatever he had to tell me. "Been in the family for ages." He paused for a moment.

"I guess this story really starts when I went looking for a Hero, two, maybe three years before you were born. Your mother had been kidnapped by the Etevar of Dorthin, the neighboring kingdom. To the east. Her grandfather, your great-grandfather Pregel, is King of Varay. The Etevar wanted to marry his son to your mother to unite the two kingdoms. King Pregel didn't want any part of the union on general principles, and he couldn't stand the old Etevar anyway, so he absolutely refused—rather less than diplomatically, not that diplomacy would have mattered. That's why the Etevar kidnapped your mother, to force the marriage, but Pregel still refused to countenance the union. We had to rescue your mother, but open war wasn't considered a smart response. While Dorthin wasn't strong enough to invade and conquer us as we were, if *we* invaded Dorthin to try to rescue Avedell, our losses might easily have weakened us enough to make us vulnerable. And my magic wasn't enough, even though I did have my glasses then. The Etevar's wizard was a tad bit better than me even when I was at my best. I counseled that we find ourselves a Hero. That's the traditional method. It took a bit of doing—it always does—but we ended up with your father. He had no family of his own and he had most of the necessary skills after serving in Vietnam."

Parthet fell quiet then. His face was lost in the shadows. Maybe that's where his mind was too—not to mention mine. I brought out my last two beers and we started on them. After a couple of minutes, Parthet resumed his tale.

"How your father rescued your mother and gave the old Etevar and his wizard their just reward is too long a story to tell just now. And modesty forbids me telling my own part in that adventure. For a time afterward, your father lived here in Varay. He married Avedell. They didn't go to your world until Avedell was expecting you. Since then, Carl has returned whenever we've needed our Hero. Varay is generally a peaceful little kingdom, but we have need for a Hero more often than you might imagine. That's the way of things here."

"What about this time?" I asked.

"The young Etevar—oh, not so young as you, lad, more your father's age—has been causing trouble, more than usual. He's always looking for ways to avenge his father's death. His army took a small castle on the march between our lands, a fief belonging to a Varayan knight, a distant cousin of yours, I believe. His Majesty was angry, but there were other complications, a dispute with the elflord on our nothern border. Our army, such as it is, is fully occupied with that. Since it didn't appear that the Etevar would leave much of a garrison to hold Castle Thyme, His Majesty thought that your father might be able to handle the incident with such modest help as we could give."

I sat there and tried to soak it all in. No matter how it sounded, I had to accept everything as real until proved otherwise. Sure, it all sounded like the premise for an arcade game, but just *maybe* we weren't all crazy. I wasn't sure about this Hero jazz, but it would explain all of Dad's scars, and the way new ones appeared now and then. While I was on my James Bond kick, I thought Dad was a spy, off on dangerous missions with beautiful lady spies.

"What did Mother think *she* could do?" I asked.

Parthet chuckled. "Well, she's not all that helpless, lad. She's really deadly with a bow. I've seen her skewer a hot dog—the *long* way—from fifty yards. And she does control a wee bit of magic of her own. Nothing major, you understand, but a little, a little.''

''So what do I do?''

''I'm not sure.'' He shook his head a couple of times. ''If your father and mother didn't succeed, there may be more to this than I thought. There may be wizardry involved.''

''It's getting dark,'' I said, since Parthet didn't seem to have noticed. ''You have any candles or anything?'' The shadows were so deep that I could do no more than make out Parthet's outline.

''There's a lamp, if there's any fuel left. Hold on, I'll try to find it.'' He got up and went to the end of the fireplace, right to the lantern. He shook it gently and brought it back. ''There seems to be a bit of kerosene left.'' When the light came on, I was surprised to see that it was a Coleman lantern, not some primitive local thingie.

''Ah, yes, that is better.'' Parthet sat across from me again. ''Now, where were we?''

''You said there might be wizardry involved.''

''Yes, certainly there might be. A wizard with better eyesight than mine. You may have a touch of the gift yourself, lad, like your mother. Your father was going to bring you around so I could make some tests. Should have done years ago, but your parents didn't want to expose you to any of this until you grew up.''

''So I gather. Still, I have to do something. I guess that means I have to go to this castle and see if I can find them.''

''I suppose you do, lad.'' He steepled his fingers and rested his chin on them. ''And I suppose I need to go along. Not that I'll be much use. I can't even see well enough to conjure up a meal in the field.''

''Then we'll do it the old-fashioned way,'' I said, glad to have any company at all. I was feeling way out of my depth. ''There is game around, isn't there?''

''Plenty of game and fish, but it takes so long that way.''

"Well, you have any idea where you might have lost your glasses?"

"I expect they're around here somewhere. Perhaps a packrat grabbed them."

"Wonderful," I mumbled under my breath. Louder: "Maybe I can find them. I've got a good flashlight and I can see well enough." I didn't give him much chance to answer. I just got busy. The cottage was so small that I knew it wouldn't take long to give it the once-over, even if I had to do it two or three times.

"How long's it been?" I asked.

"I'm not rightly sure. Maybe a month or two."

"How do you get by?"

"Oh, I know where 'most everything I need is at. And I'm truly not here all that much."

I only needed ten minutes to find the glasses, but finding them at all was a fluke. I happened to glance up at the ceiling at the right place. The glasses were stuck in the thatch over the front door. The halogen beam of my flashlight glinted off a lens. The glasses were absolutely cruddy and the left lens was badly starred. I cleaned them as well as I could, then handed them to Uncle Parthet.

"How in the world did they get up there?" he asked as he slipped the wires over his ears.

"Somebody had to put them there, and I doubt it was your packrat."

"Much better." He looked at me—still squinting.

"How much difference do those glasses really make?" I asked.

"Oh, worlds, worlds. I still couldn't read anything but very large letters, but *oh,* this is *so* much better." He came right over to me. "You look more and more like your mother, lad—the jaw line, the nose, the—"

"When do we leave?" I asked, cutting off the comparisons.

"First thing in the morning. No good starting out this time of the day."

I nodded. That made sense. Anyway, I was ready for sleep. I took the thermal blanket from my pack and looked for an area light on the cobwebs to spread it.

"Just one more question for now," I said. "Where's the john?" That beer was screaming to get out.

3

Pregel

I curled up in the back corner, next to the fireplace, and wrapped my blanket around me. I hoped that Uncle Parker's packrat wouldn't get too chummy. It had been a long day full of more shocks and surprises than any day has had a right to. Still, I got to sleep without much trouble, and that's rare enough for me even when things are normal. It might be dramatic to say that I had a bunch of weird or frightening dreams, but if I did, I slept right through them and didn't recall a one. What did wake me was a nasty cramp in my left leg. I woke with a painful jerk as the muscles knotted up, then sat up and massaged the leg. It was three in the morning by my watch, but that was Louisville time. Judging from the difference in sunsets, it was probably midnight or one in the morning in Varay, wherever Varay was.

Sitting in the dark rubbing my leg gave me time to do some thinking without getting sidetracked. My parents were missing and maybe in great danger. My Uncle Parker—actually my mother's Uncle Parthet—claimed to have been wearing, or at least needing, glasses for more than six centuries. He also claimed to be a half-baked wizard. What was worse, I was starting to accept the whole damn fairy tale: those doors in our cellar, the lizards, this place that wasn't Kentucky. Having survived a crazy childhood and adolescence helped, I guess. All the survival rigmarole Dad insisted on made sense if he was leading up toward making me assistant Hero—or whatever he planned to spring on me for my twenty-first birthday. And it did fit in with a lot of the things I had always written off as testaments to Dad's general nuttiness.

The difficulty with accepting the major premise was that I also had to accept the minor premise, the likelihood that my parents were in mortal danger, or worse. It took forever to get back to sleep. I still didn't dream, but I woke several times before I heard Parthet stirring in the other room. When he came out and lit the Coleman lantern, I was up and folding my blanket.

"Ah, good lad, you're an early riser." He peered at me more or less through his glasses.

"Not when I can help it," I said. "When I can get away with it, I like to sleep till a more civilized hour, like noon."

Parthet clucked over that. "Still, you're up early today, and that's what matters. We can get an early start."

"We *are* going to wait for sunup, aren't we?" I rubbed at my leg again. It was still a little tender.

"Hmmm. I guess that would simplify matters."

"Do we have time for a little breakfast?" It had been a long time since those peanut butter sandwiches.

"We don't want to spoil our appetites, do we, lad? We'll have a fine meal when we get to Pregel's castle, as much as you can possibly eat."

"I thought we were going to this border castle, the one that was captured by the whoozis."

"By the Etevar of Dorthin." Parthet nodded. "Of course we're going there. First, however, we must drop by the palace to see if they have any news. *And* for a good meal." It sounded as though the meal was the more important reason. "I take most of my meals there."

"So how far is it from here to the king's place?"

"How far?" He stopped bustling around and stared at me. "Why, I think it's about twenty miles. I've never paid much attention. Why?"

Twenty miles before breakfast? I stifled my groan. "I was just wondering how far we had to hike on empty stomachs."

Parthet's mouth dropped open. "Hike? You mean as in walk?" A dazed sound. "Who said anything about walking?" He seemed to gather his thoughts then. "Oh." He blinked several times. "I forgot. You're new to this. We won't walk at all. We'll just pop straight through. The doorway there." He pointed at his bedroom door.

I felt foolish, and then I felt even more foolish for

feeling foolish. I wasn't used to thinking in terms of magic doors to anywhere. I wasn't used to not having the faintest idea what was going on. I'm not stupid, but I certainly felt that way then.

"There'll be a grand meal awaiting when we get there," Parthet said. "Always a fine table in the hall of Pregel He sets great store by it." So, obviously, did Parthet.

A good meal close at hand made me feel better. I looked at the doorway. The silver tracing was almost as tarnished as on the doorway in the cave. Then I checked the front door and saw tracing there too.

"Where does this one lead?" I asked.

"To Basil," Parthet said.

"Who's Basil?"

"Not who, what. Or where. Basil is our market town, just below Pregel's castle, which is also called Basil. That door"—the bedroom door—"goes to the castle, the other to the town."

"Does everybody use magic doors here?"

"Oh, no, lad. Only a few people have the key. Most folks don't even know they exist. A family affair." Yeah, I forgot.

I started to ask what "most folks" thought when people popped in and out, but the lantern sputtered out of fuel just then. Parthet said, "Thunderation!" quite loudly, and thunder rumbled in the distance.

"Did you do that?" I asked, jumping.

"Do what?" Parthet looked at me, then at the front door. "Oh. I don't know. Perhaps." He shook his head, then went outside. I followed. Parthet looked at the sky, but it wasn't light enough for him to see much, not with *his* eyes.

"I don't see any clouds," I said. Dawn wasn't far off. There was just enough light to silhouette the upper reaches of the trees.

"Good, good," Parthet said. "Then we won't have to worry about rain." Maybe he forgot what we had been talking about.

I had a lot of questions left over from the previous evening, but there were so many that I couldn't think of a good place to start. Besides, I didn't want to clutter my mind with a lot of stuff that wouldn't help in the immediate crisis. With luck, there would be plenty of time after we pulled my folks out of whatever mess they were in.

Parthet went back inside. Not having a light didn't seem to bother him. If he had been functioning without glasses for a month or two, it might not. I stayed outside awhile longer, watching the sky lighten.

"You ready to go, lad?" Parthet called finally.

"I guess." I went in, strapped on my pack and weapon belt, and hung my bow over my shoulder. "You don't think anyone'll say anything if I show up for breakfast armed, do you?"

"Why should they?" He shook his head when I put on my Cubs cap. "But we've really got to get you a decent hat, something properly jaunty." *Jaunty?* He was dressed like a contender for King of the Hobos—threadbare green work pants, red-and-black-plaid flannel shirt with the elbows out, and a greasy leather vest held closed by an old shoelace. He didn't seem to be taking anything in the way of supplies either, just a metal-tipped walking stick—too long to be a cane, too short to be a proper staff.

"Light enough now," Parthet said, staring at the silver tracing on his bedroom door from a nose away. "Stay close, lad." He touched both sides. I saw familiar-looking gray stone. I had my rings on the tracing before Parthet let go and stepped through right behind him—cautiously, in case the floor level was different again. It wasn't. Parthet turned to make sure I was with him.

"Beats hiking through the forest," he said.

We were in a small stone room, rounded enough to let me guess that it was in a narrow tower. Beyond the door was a circular stairway—stone, not one of those tight metal things. We went down two levels. There were armed guards at the bottom, scruffy types who would have been right at home with the *Wizard of Id*.

"Must be breakfast time," one guard said. "Here's our wizard." The guards both wore chain mail and leather, conical helmets with nose guards. Their weapons were halberds and broadswords.

"He has someone with him this morning," the other guard said.

"A little respect!" Parthet's voice had more temper to it than I had heard before. "This is young Gil, the son of Carl and Avedell."

I don't think I can adequately describe the change that came over the guards. They stared at me and lost the look of bantering good humor. There was *respect* in their eyes, maybe something close to awe. They backed off and damn near bowed.

"The son of the Hero?" one of them asked. I could hear the capital letter in the tone. I noticed something peculiar too. The guard's mouth and voice were out of sync, like in a dubbed movie. I looked to Parthet, but he was watching the guards. He nodded, then started off too fast for me to ask questions. We crossed a large paved courtyard with high gray walls all around. Maybe my uncle had a magic doorway into the castle, but it sure didn't open on the dining room.

"Hold up a second," I called and Parthet waited for me. "What was that all about?"

"The churls forgot themselves. I merely upbraided them for it. More gently than they deserved."

"That's not what I mean. When you told them who I am, they did everything but kiss my feet."

"Your parents are held in high respect here. Avedell is Princess Royal and Carl is King's Champion, Hero of Varay."

"And what's wrong with their mouths? The words didn't match the way their lips were moving."

That slowed Parthet for a second. "English isn't the language of Varay, but part of the magic of the seven kingdoms lets everyone hear his own language, no matter what is spoken."

"You're in sync, though."

"I speak English as much as anything, I suppose."

"Another question. Since you've got a magical doorway into the castle, why not to a more convenient location? Like the great hall, for instance."

Parthet started walking again, more leisurely. "It wouldn't do to have such a doorway into a critical place inside all the defenses. There is a chance that an enemy might gain access to a doorway, and perhaps to the keys. And my cottage is open to anyone." We walked on, and he shook his head. "Actually, there *are* ways into the keep, but not from my place. It doesn't matter. I'm close enough for meals." He bashed his staff against a small door twenty feet left of a huge set of double doors, and another guard opened it.

"Good morning, Parthet," this guard said, nodding respectfully.

"Good morning, Lesh," Parthet replied cheerfully. "Is the table ready?"

"At the crack of dawn, as always, Lord Wizard." There was no mockery in Lesh's voice. I got the impression he liked Parthet.

"You might announce my companion," Parthet said. "Gil, son of Carl and Avedell."

Lesh's face went funny like the others', but only for an instant. He recovered quickly. "Of course." He gave us each a half-bow and led the way through a small anteroom into the great hall of Castle Basil. At the inner door, Parthet held me back. Lesh went on in.

"The Lord Wizard of Varay, and His Highness Prince Gil Tyner." The words really boomed out.

"Am I hearing thing?" I asked Parthet.

"Unless your ears have quit working." He chuckled, then grinned widely. "Come on, lad. Let's make a proper entrance."

The great hall was eighty feet long, thirty wide, and twenty high at the edges, rising to an arched ceiling supported by massive timbers about forty feet above the floor along the center ridge. There were tapestries and sconces on the walls, several immense fireplaces, bunches of weapons, both long and short. People were sitting at two rough tables that met in a T. Other people loitered about. Even a few animals. The tables were the focus of the room, with the smaller table at the head of the T raised a couple of feet above the other, on a dais. The head table was sparsely populated, but the lower had some thirty people sitting at it, waiting for the food that was just then being hauled in.

People turned to look at us. A young boy, maybe nine or ten years old, hurried toward us and bowed.

"Good morning, my lords," he said, his voice shaking as if we were the Lords High Executioner.

"Good morning, lad," Parthet said. I managed a greeting of my own—almost as shaky as the boy's.

"This way, my lords." He led us toward the head table.

"Uncle Parker?" I asked under my breath.

"Not now," he whispered. "Not now."

We were seated near the center of the high table, facing the lower. I was placed next to what had to be the king's chair—not a proper throne perhaps, but the fanciest seat around, higher and wider and decorated with fancy carvings. I sat down and Parthet leaned close.

"Tell everyone to sit," he whispered. Everyone at the lower table was standing.

"Sit down, please," I said, feeling very self-conscious. "Don't let me interrupt." They sat, but there wasn't the same murmur of conversation that I had heard from the doorway. The meal wasn't in full swing yet either. Servants were still toting in food.

Food. There was plenty: whole hams, huge bowls of steaming scrambled eggs, greasy fried potatoes, mountains of sausage and bacon, buckets of hot cereal, whole tomatoes and melons, pitchers of juice and coffee, long loaves of still-hot bread.

"I told you they set a good table," Parthet said.

"Looks like." My stomach grumbled in anticipation. I had everything but the mush. Two pages served me larger portions than I would have dreamed of taking myself, and I didn't leave a scrap. I even had seconds on some things. Everything was greasy and highly seasoned except the bread, tomatoes, and melons. The juice was orange and tart. The coffee was bitter and strong. Parthet ate a lot more than I did. He even shoveled in two bowls of mush.

"Where's the king?" I asked.

"Probably sleeping," Parthet whispered. "The last decade he hasn't been nearly as spry as he once was."

"Is he as old as you?"

"Oh, my, no, not by a long patch. He's—let's see— he's my brother's umpty-something-great-grandson. He must be getting close to one hundred and twenty-five, though, and that's pushing it for him, I fear."

"Why is one hundred and twenty-five pushing it for him if you're six hundred and something?"

"I'm a wizard." He stuffed in a couple of mouthfuls of food and dealt with them before he added, "A *lot* more than six hundred. There are *some* benefits to the craft, even if you're not very good at it. Initiation confers certain magics that you don't have to muck about with yourself."

I would have continued, but Parthet busied himself loading his platter again, with just as much food as the first time. *He* had to serve himself, but all *I* had to do was glance toward a serving tray and those two kids, the pages, rushed to transfer heaping portions to my plate. I was hungry enough not to get too upset by the attention. I didn't even have time to be surprised at how much food I was shoveling in. Finally though, I was filled ready to burst. I pushed my platter away and started to push my chair away from the table. Parthet quickly reached over and stopped me.

"Don't get up or everyone'll think that the meal is over," he said around his food.

I nodded and settled down again. More coffee. A little more of the hot bread. The coffee was rotten enough to make anyone want to fight. I watched the people at the lower table but tried to be inconspicuous about it. I wanted a better feel for this world, wherever it was— whatever it was. Most of the people at the table had to be guards, soldiers, minor court functionaries. Maybe knights. None of them looked very fancy, not like in the movies—you know, King Arthur and Camelot, Robin Hood and Sherwood Forest, that sort of thing. Some of these jokers looked like common thugs, men that street cops would roust just on general principles. Others looked like winos at a skid-row mission. It was a while before I found out that I wasn't far wrong.

Parthet quit eating, sat up bolt straight, and stared toward the side of the hall. I turned to see what had captured his attention.

"I guess that's it for breakfast," he said, and he sighed.

"Why? Who is it?"

"Baron Kardeen, Lord High Chamberlain." The baron came right to us. Someone had given him the word, because he wasn't surprised to see me.

"Your Highness," he said with a gesture that was more nod than bow. "It's good to finally see you back at court." *Back?*

"Baron," I said with a nod that was carefully just a fraction less than his. *That* came naturally.

"Parthet, I see that you can still surprise us on occasion."

"I try. Has His Majesty risen yet?"

"He's up and anxious to see his grandson."

"That's good," Parthet said. "We're anxious to see His Majesty." That seemed to be a proper cue. I stood. So did Parthet—and everyone else.

"Go ahead, keep eating," I said, waving toward the people at the lower table. A few sat down quickly. Others were slower, but by the time Parthet and I left the room, most of the people had returned to their victuals.

We went out a side door, down a corridor, up a broad stairway. There were narrow window openings on the courtyard and on the great hall until we got above the rafters. The stairway climbed another thirty steps before we got to a landing and went along another corridor. This one was lit only by a large window at the far end. We went halfway down the hall before the chamberlain turned to double doors on our right and pushed them open.

Kardeen gestured us through. Inside, no introductions were needed. Parthet went to where Pregel was sitting on the edge of the largest bed I've ever seen and went down on one knee. So did I.

"Get up, get up," Pregel said. His voice was reedy but strong. He did look old, but nothing like one hundred twenty-five. I would have guessed seventy-ish. But what good were my guesses when Parthet claimed to be a lot more than six hundred years old and didn't look much older than fifty?

"It's been a long time, Gil," Pregel said. "I haven't seen you since you were so small you couldn't see across the top of this bed." He glanced at Parthet, then back at me. "You may have been four or five, no more. Your parents thought you were getting too old to bring back all the time without your asking a lot of questions." He shrugged and stood. He was a little taller than me. "They wanted to wait until you were grown to tell you of your heritage. I still think it was the wrong choice, but it was theirs to make. And how you've grown!" He took my by the arm, and we started toward the door. His grip was strong, and he didn't move like one hundred twenty-five and ailing. Parthet and the chamberlain followed us.

"I still know almost nothing about it, Your Majesty," I said. "This crisis. All I had was a note from Mother saying that she thought Dad might be in trouble and she was going to try to rescue him."

"Avedell has always been headstrong," Pregel said. "It runs in the family. Gallops. I wish I could say that the crisis is past, that they've made it back from Castle Thyme, but we've had no word from either of them."

"I think that's why I'm here. I guess it's my turn. And I really don't know where to start."

"If I were a bit younger, I'd saddle up and lead the army after them, or ride along with you myself. But the army, such as it is, is fully occupied in the north, trying to hold back magic with metal. It doesn't work as well as a good wizard would." He didn't raise his voice or look back, but I couldn't miss the rebuke he was directing at Parthet. Neither could Parthet.

"When this is over," I said, "perhaps I can take Parthet back to my world to let an eye doctor fit him with proper glasses."

"Anything to help," Pregel said. Parthet kept silent.

We crossed to a room on the other side of the hall.

"My private dining room," Pregel said, "for days when I don't feel like going up and down steps." The room was thirty feet square. A long table bisected the room. There was a fancy chair at one end and six plainer chairs along each side. As soon as the king arrived, servants started hauling in food through a door in the back corner.

"Will you join me in a little breakfast?" the king asked. I had a notion that it wouldn't be proper etiquette to refuse even though I was stuffed. I didn't need Parthet's discreet throat-clearing behind me.

"I'd be honored," I said.

"It never hurts to fill up the corners," Parthet said.

"We did have a bite downstairs," I said.

Just the three of us sat, with Parthet across the table from me. Pages served us. Kardeen stood at the king's right elbow. He didn't eat, but he didn't seem to be lacking for nourishment. Pregel started on a large platter of food. So did Parthet. The wizard ate as if it had been twenty days since his last meal, not twenty minutes. I ate just a little, and had trouble with that.

"We've had no news at all from Castle Thyme," Pregel said after he had made serious inroads on breakfast. "Your father went some two weeks ago, taking just his squire and two men-at-arms. Your mother came through four days back and set off at once. She didn't even stop to eat. Of course, there really hasn't been time for her to get to Thyme and back. Or scarcely enough. It's two days each way, and that wouldn't leave her time to do anything."

"Her note said she expected to be home yesterday afternoon," I said.

Pregel frowned. "Peculiar. She knows how long the journey takes."

"Could she have planned to use magic doors to get there and back?"

"There are none in or near Castle Thyme. Too risky."

"Perhaps she merely wanted to ensure that Gil would follow as soon as possible," Parthet suggested.

"Could be," I said. "She always used to say it was later than it really was when she was trying to get me up for school."

"Or perhaps she thought the situation would be beyond her ability to handle alone," Parthet said.

"Then I should hurry."

The king nodded. "Parthet, you *do* plan to accompany him, don't you?"

"Of course, Your Majesty. He knows nothing of our country."

"I don't like this one bit. Turning a stranger loose on such a perilous mission." Pregel stared at me. "I don't like risking my heir like this."

I looked from him to Parthet. Neither was paying any attention to me at the moment. His *heir?*

"The lad hasn't proved himself," Parthet said. "Much as I like him, you can't know that he will be the heir you need."

"He is my heir," Pregel said firmly.

"You know, Your Majesty," I said, just to remind everyone that I was still in the room, "I still don't know what the hell anyone's talking about."

Three pairs of eyes turned to me.

"You are my only direct male descendant," the king said. "Heir apparent to the throne of Varay."

I don't think anyone heard the muted "Holy shit!" that I just couldn't restrain.

4

Chamberlain

Pregel groused and pouted by turn. His face got red. He left food on his plate, shoved it away, got up and went to one of the four tall, narrow windows in the room. I got up from the table with relief, Parthet with reluctance. We waited for His Majesty. Baron Kardeen remained as he had been. Waiting seemed to be his natural function. The wait wasn't long, but as usual in uncomfortable situations, it seemed eternal.

"We have to do what we can for my grandson," Pregel

finally said without turning away from the window. "I won't risk him alone on this."

"Your Majesty, delay might put my parents at greater risk," I said.

"I know. Don't worry, we'll get you out of here quickly, as fast as may be. I think we can still find horses."

"Yes, Your Majesty," the chamberlain said. Neither of them bothered to ask if I could ride. Maybe they took it for granted, or maybe my parents had talked about my riding—sometime in the past I knew nothing about.

"A page to attend him and at least one soldier," Pregel said, his voice starting to sound almost bitter. "The heir of Varay need an entourage, poor though it might be. And perhaps you can spare an hour to brief the prince and equip him properly."

"At once, Your Majesty," Kardeen said.

We waited some more. "Then get about it, man, while I dress," Pregel said. He came over to me. "When this is over, we'll have to spend some time together, get to know each other while we may."

"I hope to have that opportunity," I said, meaning it.

"I'll see you in an hour then, in the throne room."

I nodded, and the king left the room alone.

There was a moment of silence and then Parthet looked at Kardeen and said, "His health seems much improved."

The baron nodded. "When I told him his grandson was here, he virtually leaped out of bed." Kardeen smiled wanly. "It feels wonderful to give him good news for a change. He's been so besieged by worry lately, especially since the young Etevar seized Castle Thyme."

"If we've only got an hour, shouldn't we get busy?" I asked. I was getting increasingly annoyed at being discussed in the third person all the time, but there was no decent way to make the point. all I could do was toss in my two cents' worth now and then to remind everyone that I was there.

"You're right, of course," Kardeen said easily. "Let's go down to my office."

It was quite a walk, down the stairs we had come up,

along the broad corridor past the great hall, through a left turn and along a short corridor, up a shorter flight of steps, thirty yards along another corridor, up another short flight of steps into yet another—but much narrower—short corridor. By my reckoning, we had left the keep and had to be in what I had thought was just a curtain wall, or maybe we were in the large tower at the southeast corner of the courtyard. We went through one office where a clerk was writing—using a long quill on a sheet of parchment the size of a Monopoly board—into a smaller office with a large desk and several chairs. Kardeen indicated chairs and seated himself behind the desk. When he rang a bell, his clerk raced in from the outer office.

"I need the Master of Pages and the guard commander, as quickly as possible," Kardeen said. "Also the armorer." The clerk bowed and left.

Kardeen stared at me. I stared at him. He was just under six feet tall, about my height, and built solidly enough to be an athlete or warrior. He looked to be in his late thirties, but by that time I didn't put any trust at all in age estimates. Age was apparently a very nebulous quality in Varay. The baron was clean-shaven, had inky black hair with just the slightest trace of gray, and had deep-set black eyes, a hooded look. His desk was large, unpolished. There were a number of scrolls on it, rolled-up, held by ribbons or rubber bands. A desk set held a pair of felt-tip markers.

"I think that the first thing I need is basic data," I said. "Background information. How big is Varay? How far is it to Castle Thyme? What's the trouble in the north that keeps the army busy? What's the basis of the current dispute with the Etevar?" I could have asked questions all week and still had more waiting, but that wouldn't do much good, so I wrapped up the abbreviated recital with a reminder. "I don't know anything at all about this place."

"I know that your parents planned to wait until you turned twenty-one before they told you about the buffer zone. You might be surprised to know how often you have been the topic of discussion here at court.'' Kardeen glanced at Parthet before he continued.

"Varay is one of seven buffer kingdoms that lie between the domains of Man and Fairy. This is a particularly narrow place in the zone, with the unscalable Titans to our south and the Mist, also called the Sea of Fairy, and the Isthmus of Xayber to the north. Xayber is the only land passage to Fairy. We have often stood at the van in struggles with the elflords. Dorthin lies to our east, and Mauroc beyond it. Belorz is our western neighbor. Both of our immediate neighbors are much larger, more populous, and stronger than Varay—mostly because we are always the first to feel the wrath of the elflords of Fairy. Belorz has given us no trouble in many generations, but Dorthin is a recurrent plague.''

"Just where in the world *is* Varay located, though?'' The time difference would seem to put it on the west coast of the United States or Canada, and while it wouldn't surprise me to find something as screwy as Varay in California, I didn't think it was there. *Somebody* would have mentioned it.

"It isn't located anywhere in your world, or in the world of Fairy either,'' Kardeen said. "The buffer zone partakes of both but is part of neither.''

"I don't understand,'' I said, "but go ahead. We can't waste time on details now.''

"Logic and science contend with chaos and magic in the seven kingdoms,'' Parthet said. "Logic and science don't always win. Perhaps that is essential. The worlds balance each other across our fulcrum. Neither side can be confident of victory in any particular clash. The rules are liable to change without notice.''

"In Varay, and to some extent in the other kingdoms, we stand between the forces of the two polar realms, mortal and Fairy,'' Kardeen said. "Walking the edge of that precipice is our key to survival. Tradition is our only measure. In the buffer zone, neither mortality nor immortality can be taken for granted. A gain in strength by one side calls forth renewed efforts by the other, trying to redress the imbalance.''

"Complete domination by either side would likely destroy both," Parthet said. "And any major swing in either realm is reflected all too quickly here in the center. Jerked back and forth like a pull of taffy."

"And your army is tied up by trouble with Fairy," I said, trying to direct the conversation to more practical considerations.

"Off and on for decades now," Kardeen said. "And whenever our troubles in the north increase, the Etevar of Dorthin tries to take advantage."

"Why?"

"Our most ancient legends tell of a time when the seven kingdoms were united in an empire strong enough to enforce an era when the buffer zone was just as potent as either Fairy or the mortal realm—our Golden Age, with prosperity and contentment. The Etevar wants to recreate that empire with himself as ruler."

"The title Etevar means "emperor" in the old language," Parthet said. "The renewal of this legendary empire is a recurrent disease in their family. Generation after generation of Etevar holds the same goal, strives after it whenever he can, thirsts after it always."

The Master of Pages arrived. Kardeen and Parthet wrangled with him over the selection of a page for me. It sounded like nonsense, but I was in no position to gripe after the king said I was to have a page. I told myself to go with the flow until I doped out enough of the situation to assert myself. The discussion did give me time for a little mental digestion. All I really got out of the previous discussion was that we were the good guys and everybody else was the bad guys, especially the Etevar of Dorthin and anyone out of Fairy.

By the time the Master of Pages was dismissed, the guard commander and the armorer were waiting. I couldn't ignore this discussion.

"How many soldiers can you find to accompany the prince, right away, this morning?" Kardeen asked the guard commander—one of the thug-types I had seen in the great hall at breakfast. He was several inches shorter than me and built solid, like a side of beef.

"We don't have enough men for garrison duty now," the commander said. His voice was a throaty growl that sounded like the harbinger of serious health problems in the near future.

"At His Majesty's direction," Kardeen said.

The guard commander looked as if he wanted to growl, but didn't.

"Someone who knows the land between here and Castle Thyme," I suggested. A half-blind wizard might not be the most reliable pathfinder. "What about that man we talked to this morning, Uncle Parthet? What was his name, Lesh?" Parthet nodded.

"I believe Lesh is from the eastern marches," the guard commander said. "But perhaps someone a bit younger might serve you better."

"Or not," I said. "If Lesh is willing to go, I'll have him." Parthet looked pleased by my choice.

"As you wish, my lord," the commander said, bowing.

"*If* he's willing," I emphasized. "I don't want draftees."

"Is there anyone else you'd also like?" Kardeen asked.

"Lesh is the only one I really had a chance to meet," I said. "Look, I know this is difficult, but time seems to be in short supply. One man or six won't make much difference unless I take a whole army, and the more time we waste finding people, the longer it will take. I appreciate the concern, but I'm worried about my folks. Lesh, Uncle Parthet, and the page. That's entourage enough for now. Truly." Kardeen looked relieved. He dismissed the guard commander with instructions to get Lesh and four horses ready to go, fully equipped for a week in the field. Then it was the armorer's turn.

"We need equipment for His Highness," Kardeen told him, "Mail shirt, buckler, helmet."

"I have my own weapons," I said. Everything but the pistol was in plain sight. I didn't bring the gun out.

"If I might examine them, Highness?" The armorer studied my bow, sword, and knife critically. The compound bow didn't throw him for an instant. "Excellent weapons, lord." I though so. Dad always insisted on the best.

"I think it's time for us to see His Majesty," I said, checking my watch.

"We still have a few minutes to spare," Kardeen said without looking at a timepiece. "Batheus, we'll need the shield and other items quickly." As the armorer left, Kardeen's clerk came in and whispered to the chamberlain.

"And *now* it's time for us to attend His Majesty," Kardeen said with a soft smile in my direction.

"One more thing before I forget," I said. "Do you have a map of the area between here and Castle Thyme?"

"We have maps of the seven kingdoms around somewhere," Kardeen said. "My clerk will sketch you a copy of the appropriate portion if he can find them in time."

The clerk nodded quickly. "Immediately, Your Highness."

The throne room was an office scarcely larger than the chamberlain's. The throne was set on a dais two feet above the floor, but it sat behind a desk as cluttered as Kardeen's. Pregel was apparently a working monarch when the mood struck him. When Kardeen, Parthet, and I entered, there were already a couple of dozen people in the room. But the king hadn't arrived yet. He came in just a minute after we did. Everyone bowed—not too deeply—from the time the herald announced Pregel until the king climbed on his throne and told us to rise.

"Come here, Gil," Pregel said. "Stand on my right."

I climbed up on the dais and stood next to the throne, feeling nervous as everyone in the room stared at me.

"My loyal subjects." The king's voice carried well in the small room. "This young man is Gil Tyner, son of my granddaughter Avedell and her husband, Carl, King's Champion, Hero of Varay. Gil departs today on a mission as fraught with peril as any ever attempted by a Hero. We name him our heir for all to hear, King of Varay when I am no more. Our prayers and magics go with him today and always."

I had a fleeting moment to wish that someone had taught me the proper etiquette for occasions of that sort. I would have settled for a simple warning of what was going to happen. I didn't have the faintest idea what I was supposed to do. All of the people down in front of the dais bowed deeply and held it.

"What do I do now?" I whispered to the king when I had figured out that the people were going to hold the position.

He grinned, then whispered back, "A simple 'Thank you, Your Majesty,' loud enough for everyone to hear, should do it."

I bowed and said exactly what he'd told me to say and everyone straightened up and started staring at me again.

"You have everything you need?" the king asked me, softly, but not in a whisper.

"It's all been arranged, I think," I said.

"Our prayers and magics do go with you, Gil," he said. He gripped my arm—very tightly. "That's not completely an empty formula here. And if you can keep Parthet from losing his spectacles, he can actually help." Pregel smiled. "Go now, and I wish you luck."

I bowed again and climbed down from the dais, wishing I hadn't lost all those years with Pregel. I had only the faintest memories of him from when I was little, and I had found myself liking him right from the start that morning. Kardeen, Parthet, and I left the throne room together while people continued to stare.

"I wish somebody had warned me what to expect in there," I said when we were out in the corridor. "Remember, I'm a stranger here. I don't know the right things to do and say."

"I'm sorry, Highness." Kardeen sounded like he meant it. "I keep forgetting."

Lesh and a boy who said his name was Timon met us in the antechamber beyond the great hall. Timon looked to be about eight or nine years old. He said he was to be my page. The armorer and Kardeen's clerk joined us a moment later. The armorer was carrying a real load.

"I'm supposed to wear all that?" I asked.

"Just the necessities, Your Highness," the armorer said. He held up the mail shirt, small chain links attached to a heavy leather foundation. Timon and Lesh took off my pack and sword belt. The armorer draped the mail over my fatigue shirt and I gained a quick twenty pounds or more. When he tried to clap a steel-and-leather skull-cap on me though, I rebelled.

"I have my own headgear," I said. I whipped the Cubs cap from my back pocket and slipped it on.

"But . . ." Lesh started. I cut him short.

"No way! I'm not even real crazy about this steel straitjacket. The tin pot is out." Lesh didn't argue in front of the others, but he handed the helmet to Timon, who held on to it as if it were the Grail.

The shield was round and two feet in diameter. A wood core was sandwiched between layers of sheet metal and leather, with scores of rivets holding the whole thing together and adding their own measure of protection. In the center there was a raised boss with a six-inch spike protruding. That shield was meant as much for offense as defense. I slipped my arm through the one loop on the back and gripped the wooden handle. It was heavy, but it felt good.

"I hope I can hang this thing on the horse when I don't need it," I said. The armorer assured me that the saddle had provision for the shield.

"How about food?" I asked. "I don't recall anyone mentioning food."

"Taken care of, Highness," Lesh said. "I've been on a campaign or two. I saw to it myself."

"And here's the map you wanted," Kardeen said, taking a bulky scroll from his clerk. I untied the leather thong and unrolled the scroll, an eighteen-by-thirty-six-inch sheet of parchment. For a rush job, it looked damn good. Roads, towns, villages, castles, and streams were marked for all of Varay and the nearer portions of Dorthin and the Isthmus of Xayber; mountains in the south, sea and isthmus in the north. There was even a large forested area north of the route to Castle Thyme marked with the warning "Here there be dragons." What more could I ask for?

"Admirable work," I said, smiling at the clerk. He smiled back and bowed.

We went out to the horses. Walking in chain mail, with the shield and everything else, was something like wading through Jell-O. I'd have to shed some of the weight if I wanted to accomplish anything. Putting my pack in a saddlebag was a start. Hanging my shield from the skirt of the saddle was even better. I got light enough to mount without help.

The horses were a mixed lot. I had a decent-looking stallion the size of a Clydesdale. Lesh's charger might have been the sire of mine. It looked old, but still fit. Timon's pony looked like a runt even without comparing it to the big animals. And Parthet—well, someone had dug up an old swaybacked nag that looked as if it came from a Three Stooges short. Someone had a sick sense of humor, I thought—putting a hunchback on a sway-back.

"She's a fine animal," Parthet said as I was about to blow some steam. It was almost as if he had read my mind. "I've ridden Glory here before, lad. We're comfortable with each other."

I still needed a moment to cool off. "Then I guess we're ready," I said. I hadn't done any riding since the previous summer, but I didn't expect that I would have any difficulty. I learned how to ride a horse before I got my first tricycle. We all got mounted. I did manage to get aboard without help, even with all the extra weight.

"I wish you every luck," Baron Kardeen said, standing next to my horse—Gold—and holding the pommel of my saddle. "Your coming has meant a lot to His Majesty. Come back safely."

"I'll try. Thanks for your help."

Kardeen bowed and backed off. I nodded—regally, I hoped—and clicked at my horse. Gold started up and I aimed him at the gate. Parthet moved into place at my left, about two feet below me on his smaller horse. Lesh and Timon got into line behind us.

I didn't look back.

5

Precarra

Castle Basil was located on a prominence that looked remarkably like the Rock of Gibraltar in the insurance commercials. The rock was stained by water and waste that had dripped from the castle over the ages. There was only one road into or out of the castle. It wound back and forth through a series of wicked switchbacks down a steep slope to Basil Town. The town was more a village, maybe three hundred buildings—homes, shops, and whatnot. According to Parthet, there were two good inns. "They both brew a decent enough beer" was how he phrased it. The River Tarn came from the north, past the east side of the castle's rock, and wrapped around the south end of the town. "It bends north again farther west to finally empty into the Mist," Parthet said.

Basil Town was aromatic, but it didn't smell like the herb. Smell? Stench. I guess all towns must have smelled like that before indoor plumbing and municipal sewage works. At least no one emptied a chamber pot into the street while we rode through.

People stared openly at us as we passed. Craftsmen worked in their open-front shops and directed apprentices. I saw a cooper assembling a barrel, a miller hauling flour bags to a small cart that was hitched to two dogs who didn't look far removed from their lupine ancestry. There were women sweeping out their homes, a lot of them. They might almost have had a union schedule that said, "Sweep the dirt out the front door at such and such a time."

We passed one of the pubs, stared at it with longing, but didn't stop. Maybe we could have afforded time for a single drink, but I didn't know how we would pay. I didn't have any local currency, and I didn't expect that

Parthet did. I couldn't impose on Lesh or the boy, even assuming that one or the other might have a coin or two.

A few minutes after we passed the pub, our horses clomped across a rickety wooden bridge over the Tarn into the Forest of Precarra. The bridge shimmied and shuddered as if ready to fall into the river, but none of my companions showed the slightest apprehension about using it, so I kept my worries to myself. The river wasn't much of a stream, about forty feet wide and shallow. But the bank was steep and high on the town side.

The transition from town to forest was abrupt. There were only a few small farms on the east side of the river. Most of the Basiliers' farms lay west of town, according to Parthet. We crossed the narrow strip of cleared fields and entered the forest.

"Precarra covers about a fifth of the kingdom," Parthet said, "from the southwest corner to the middle of our border with Dorthin—a rough horn shape with the bell flat against the Titans and the mouthpiece sticking into the Etevar's domain. Southeast of the forest the land is wrinkled with foothills and long valleys. It's an area for sheep, cattle, and grapes, but mostly it's left to wilderness. There are some evil places there. Northwest of Precarra is where most of our farmland is, and a few fishing villages along the Mist. Then there's Battle Forest toward the isthmus, north and northeast of here. Few Varayans live in that quarter."

Lesh snorted. "There are farms everywhere," he said. "The forest isn't a blanket. There are gaps all around, some natural, more made by folks who need space to plant their beans and taters. Peasants can't wait for strangers to send them food from someplace else."

Our ride was no mad gallop. We let the horses stick to a fast walk most of the time, a gait that would allow them to keep going for the five or six days we might need to get to Thyme and back. During the hottest part of the first day, we stopped to rest the animals and get ourselves out of the sun for a few minutes every hour or so. We had a long way to go. When we talked, it wasn't about Castle Thyme or what might have happened to my parents. I couldn't fully accept the danger yet, not on a gut

level. We talked about Varay and Fairy, and about ourselves. Mostly, I listened and let the others talk. I was
the new kid on the block and I had a lot to learn.

"Tell me about yourself, Lesh," I said, early in the
ride.

"What's to tell, lord? I'm a soldier. I've always been
a soldier."

"Where were you raised? What was it like at home?
Even a soldier has a history."

"I was born in County Gemma, somewhat south of
Castle Thyme. My folks farmed a small clay patch. Of
six children, only four of us made it out of the cradle. I
worked on the farm until I was old enough to join the
King's Guard. I've been a soldier ever since, nigh on
thirty years. Like I said, what's to tell?"

I looked back at him: a bored face, uncomfortable
talking about himself.

"Are you married? Do you have children of your
own?"

He shrugged. "I've never been married formal-like.
As to brats, who can tell?"

The willows and birches that flanked a creek alongside
the path gave way to oaks, chestnuts, and firs. The air
cooled a little in the shade.

"Do you know Castle Thyme?" I asked.

"I've been there, lord," Lesh admitted. "It's not much
of a castle, not nearly so grand or strong as Castle Basil.
Thyme is little more than a single tower with a puny
curtain wall behind a dry ditch."

"Not much to the eye but important," Parthet contributed. "It has been fought over so often that the magics around it are quite unpredictable."

"Let's leave that till tomorrow," I suggested. I didn't
want to cram my head full of porcupines yet. *Magic.* So
far, all I had seen was the doorways, and while *I* couldn't
explain them logically, that didn't mean that there was
no logical explanation—something out of science fiction
maybe, something like folded space.

"How far have we traveled?" Timon asked when we
took our first break. The boy was dressed in forest green,
in an outfit that looked as though it had been handed

down several times. He wore a long dagger on his belt. Timon was skinny but nearly as tall as Parthet. The boy's voice was still childish, high-pitched. His hair was lopped off simply at the sides and back.

"About seven miles," Parthet said.

"I've never been *this* far before." Timon didn't seem nearly as awed by being assigned to serve the heir of Varay as he was at being seven miles from home.

"And what's your life been like, Timon?" I asked. I was sitting on the ground, leaning back against a cedar, trying to put my weight on parts of my butt that the saddle hadn't chafed. A difficult quest.

"My mam works in the kitchen at the castle. I've been scrubbing pots as far back as I know."

"You get any schooling?"

"I can read a little, and write my name," Timon said proudly.

"Education is a practical matter here," Parthet said. "Children learn what they need to know by doing it, by apprenticeship and imitation."

"No need to sound so defensive, Uncle," I said, not even glancing his way. "I wasn't going to criticize. It's a good way to learn practical affairs. As long as you're not building computers or H-bombs."

"We have no need of those things here," Parthet said.

"No H-bombs?" No kidding, I thought. "That may be the best news I've heard since I left school. What would happen to the buffer zone if my world blew itself to hell in a nuclear war?" Parthet sat next to me. I was confident that he knew what I was talking about. He had visited us often enough in Louisville.

"I've wondered about that more often than you might imagine," he said. "I don't have an answer, though." He looked off into the trees, and his voice got reflective. "It frightens me when I think about it. I fear that Fairy would overflow us and move into the void. What might happen then, I can't even guess. I don't think it's something I'd care to experience."

Timon looked back and forth between us, his eyes wide with wonder. It may have sounded like gibberish to him. Or maybe he simply assumed that we were discussing magics beyond his capacity. Maybe we were, come to think of it. Nuclear winter sounds beyond the limits of objective possibility to me too, like witches and wizards and elflords out of Fairy. I wondered how the buffer zone's translation magic had rendered ''H-bombs'' and ''nuclear war.''

''Whenever your world is at war, Fairy grows stronger here,'' Parthet said. He shrugged. ''Of course, there is always war of one dimension or another going on there, but major war is what I'm talking about. I remember your Second World War. I think that's what your father called it. Before he was born. The seven kingdoms were all hard pressed to hold their own against a series of invasions out of Fairy—that's when your mother's parents were killed— and we're still trying to clear out the last of the dragons and a few outlaw bands of elves.''

I missed something in that at the time, the bit about my mother's parents being killed during the Second World War, which meant that she was also older than I'd thought. I didn't recall what Parthet had said until much later.

''Shouldn't we be moving on?'' Lesh asked.

I looked up and nodded. We had taken more of a break than I had planned. It was maybe an hour later before I brought up the subject of the dragons again. I described the lizards I had seen the day before.

''Is that what you call a dragon?'' I asked.

''You saw one of those near *my* cottage?'' Parthet asked, a bit stridently.

''Two of them, one in the forest and another in the cave where I came through from our basement. Were those dragons?''

''Dragonkind, but not dragons. Bad enough if you're not careful. You saw one of those near my cottage?'' he asked again.

''Yes, not too far off. What's wrong with that?''

''There shouldn't be any of those creatures within fifty miles of my home, that's what's wrong. They usually don't stray far from Battle Forest.''

''They didn't look all that dangerous,'' I said, crossing

my fingers mentally. The one in the cave had looked dangerous enough at the time.

"Those beasts can bite you in two like that." Parthet slapped his hands together. Timon's pony shied at the noise. The heavier chargers didn't pay any mind. And Parthet's Glory just pointed his ears, as if he didn't have the energy to get upset at the noise. I swallowed, remembering my first encounter with one of the lizards.

"They can be hunted at least," Lesh said before I could wander too far down memory lane. "But they make foul eating, nothing you'd care to taste if you had any choice." He looked at the sky. "They can be hunted, not like a real dragon. A real dragon hunts you."

"How big?" I asked, not at all certain that I wanted to know. I looked at the sky myself.

"Like a castle with wings," Lesh said.

"Try thinking of something like a 747 with bigger wings and a badly swollen gut," Parthet suggested. "A pregnant 747. That would make a small dragon. They're hungry all the time. The four of us and our horses wouldn't make a decent bedtime snack for a dragon." After that, there were three of us looking at the sky. Only Parthet didn't bother.

"How many dragons are there?" I asked.

"One's too many," Lesh said.

"They don't exactly fill out census questionnaires," Parthet said. "But there can't be many or the buffer kingdoms would soon be totally barren. I doubt there's a half-dozen that come across our skies."

"Where do they live?"

"Anywhere they want to," Lesh said with an explosive laugh.

Parthet scowled at him but nodded. "Sometimes they come in from the Mist. Sometimes they seem to nest in the Titan Mountains. They can fly from Mist to mountains in an hour."

"What does it take to kill one?"

"A bigger dragon." That was Lesh's contribution. The subject of dragons really pushed all his buttons.

"They *have* been killed by mortals," Parthet said.

"Can you show me one who did and lived to tell about

it?'' Lesh challenged. ''Introduce us and I'll buy his beer for ten years.''

The way Parthet tried to fade into his saddle, I knew he couldn't.

Precarra seemed to change its nature every few miles. It wasn't a homogenous forest at all, more like a number of different forests tacked together. For a time it would look tame around us, like a city park, and then the forest would go suddenly berserk in a mass of tangled underbrush. Groves of oak gave way to soaring fir trees, which gave way to willow and birch every time we came to a waterway. Creeks, some of them looking more like drainage ditches in a drought, were common. There were no bridges out in the country, only traces where generations of Varayans had forded each stream. The road—the others insisted on calling the rutted cart path we followed a road—wound through the forest from one ford to the next. So, though we were heading generally east, we might be moving in almost any direction at any given moment. Several times we saw smaller paths leading away from the road, narrow tracks as overgrown as the path to Uncle Parthet's cottage. Once I spotted a field of young corn in a clearing ringed by burned stumps.

''We should be coming to the village of Nushur soon,'' Lesh said about mid-afternoon. My watch said five-fifty, but that was still Louisville time. ''The last time I was over this way, the innkeeper had a potent brew for his guests. I could sure use a flagon or two.''

''So could I,'' I said, ''but I don't think anyone thought to equip us with ready cash.''

''The crown's credit is good,'' Parthet said. ''His Majesty's bursar pays every reckoning promptly. Whatever our problems, poverty isn't one of them.''

''You mean all I have to do is charge it?'' I asked.

''It's not American Express, but you wear the family rings. No one will refuse you service in Varay,'' Parthet said.

''We could have an early supper, and a drink or two, and ride on a few more miles before sunset,'' I said. There were no dissenting votes.

The anticipation of refreshments made the miles to Nushur seem longer. It took us an hour to reach the village—thirty homes and two larger buildings in the center. "The inn and the home of the local magistrate," Parthet said.

"Do we need to stop to see the magistrate?" I asked.

"No need at all," Parthet said. "Once he hears that you're in his village, he'll come to pay his respects. You outrank him."

We rode straight into the courtyard of the inn. It looked as though the walls were made of adobe, but the region didn't seem dry enough for that. A herd of young boys came to care for our horses and to guide us to the inn's public room. As we entered, the innkeeper came up, bowing and scraping. Lesh and I both had to duck our heads to avoid hitting the lintel over the doorway. The ceiling wasn't much higher. The innkeeper led us to his largest table—there were only three in the room—and carried on at length about how honored he was to serve us and how excellent his kitchen and beers were. When Parthet "announced" me, the innkeeper got positively slobbering in his attempts to serve us. We were seated and served our first steins of beer before we knew what was going on. I was surprised that Timon was given beer, but nobody else was. Timon certainly didn't object. He took a sip and smacked his lips.

The beer was good even if it was just cool, not cold. Supper was a thick, gritty stew served in large wooden bowls. The bread was gritty too. I didn't know if the grit was dirt or poor milling. I was too hungry to get overly fastidious. The stew meat was some kind of game; I didn't ask what. But there were also potatoes, carrots, and loads of onion. The bread was in flat, rounded loaves like hamburger buns for the Jolly Green Giant, thick-crusted and chewy. Sopping up gravy was the best way to eat the bread.

Except for Timon, we emptied our beers quickly even though the mugs must have held more than a quart, and the landlord brought a second round. And a third while we dredged up the last traces of gravy from our second large bowls of stew with the last crusts of bread. It was a satisfying meal.

The landlord asked if we wanted lodging for the night. Rather than approach me directly, he asked Lesh, who looked to Parthet, who looked to me.

"We have to travel on, I'm afraid," I said. "There's still sun in the sky. But this has been an excellent meal, most satisfying."

The landlord's head bobbed up and down at the compliment, but I think he was just as happy to see us move on. He was a nervous sort, and we were obviously not his usual trade. Parthet asked how much we owed, then dug a BIC pen and a three-by-five spiral notebook from some recess of his clothing, wrote out an IOU, and signed it. "The magistrate will make sure you get your money," Parthet told the innkeeper. "By the way, we expected to see him. Is he out of town?"

The innkeeper cackled and nodded. He started to explain but changed his mind after a glance my way. Whatever the juicy gossip was, we weren't going to hear it.

I felt more loaded down than ever as we walked back to the courtyard. Two and a half huge meals in one day, probably more food than I ate in a full week at college. A burger and fries or a couple of slices of pizza for lunch, maybe a decent supper three nights a week, junk food taken on the run the rest of the time, with a snack thrown in whenever my stomach complained that it was empty—that was my school diet.

Our horses had been fed and groomed. They actually seemed eager to get started again.

Past Nushur, the road tended to head northeast rather than east. I spent a few minutes studying the map that Kardeen's clerk had prepared. Nushur was marked, and so was the road's change of direction. The map didn't show every nip and tuck, but it had the general layout fairly well. Varay east of Nushur got decidedly seedy-looking. The trees were shorter and scraggly with gnarled, knotty trunks and vegetation that looked wasted, more like the heat of summer than the bloom of spring. For long stretches, the road became a single trace scarcely wide enough for a rider, with branches hanging low enough over the path to be a serious hazard.

"You sure we didn't miss a turn or something?" I asked.

"This is the road," Lesh said. Since dinner, he had cut back on the number of lords and highnesses he used. "It gets better a ways ahead, as I recall. Another four miles perhaps." A long four miles. A couple of times Lesh and I had to dismount to lead our horses through the worst spots. The afternoon wore on.

"We should make camp before it gets dark," I said as I remounted at the end of the worst of the worst stretches.

"That would be wise," Parthet said. He hadn't needed to dismount for any of the bad patches. "I need light for my camping magics."

"Camping magics?" I asked.

"There are a few things I can do to make a camp more comfortable, but I have to be able to see to do them."

Two hours later he decided that we had to find a spot soon if he was going to have enough light to work. "Well off the road would be wise," he added. "There's not much traffic hereabout, I'll warrant, but any traffic that does happen past would likely be someone we'd rather not meet."

"What if Dad and Mother come by on their way back?" I asked.

"If they do, I'll know," Parthet said.

"Whatever you say." I looked to both sides of the road. The landscape was in one of its most tangled moods. For the last half hour we had been riding between what seemed to be briar patches woven between the trees. The undergrowth had completely overgrown one rivulet.

"We're going to need a tank to get into that, and anyone who happened along would be able to follow in a second," I said.

Parthet chuckled as if I'd just told a brand-new dirty joke. He pushed his glasses up on his nose and said, "I learned this one from your Cecil B. deMille. Just watch, and when I start through, the rest of you follow closely, nose to rump, nose to rump."

He started making a whooshing noise, blowing in and

out. Once in a while, a whistle crept into the sound effects, like a winter wind. At first I didn't see anything happening, but after a few minutes Parthet started to sway from side to side in his saddle. The whooshing got louder and louder. About the time I thought that it had become much too loud for one little old man to make, I realized that it wasn't all him any longer. There was a new wind swirling about the legs of our horses, raising dust from the road. And the thorny underbrush on the north side of the road started to sway in time with Uncle Parthet.

DeMille. *The Ten Commandments*. Parthet was parting the Red Sea, without the sea. The brush opened up in front of him and he started Glory forward into the swaying bramble patch. I followed him. Timon followed me. Lesh brought up the rear. The underbrush bent away from the horses and closed in again behind us, leaving no evidence of our passing. It was extremely slow going at first, but Parthet and the briars seemed to gather momentum. After thirty yards, Glory was walking as fast as she had out on the road.

Parthet aimed for a copse of willows two hundred yards from the road. Willows would provide shelter and probably meant that water was near.

I watched silently. I couldn't have spoken if I had to. Magic doorways might be future or alien science, something I just didn't know about. This snake dance had to be Magic with a capital M. Maybe I still wasn't the King of Siam (I certainly wasn't going to shave my head!), but heir designate to the crown of Varay was almost as outré. Good old Uncle Parker, always handy with a dirty joke when we happened to be alone together—once I got into my teens. This wasn't *that* Uncle Parker. This was Parthet the Wizard of Varay—somebody entirely different.

He had to bend over in the saddle to get under the hanging branches of the weeping willows, and the rest of us had trouble clearing them even lying flat against our horses' necks. Parthet kept going, kept whooshing, until the rest of us got out of the brambles into the clear ground right under the trees. When he stopped swaying and making noises, the brambles also quit swaying. I dismounted and looked back the way we had come. There was no hint that anyone had *ever* ridden through that mess.

"You see," Parthet said, grinning at me, "there is a bit of magic left in me yet."

I nodded, not up to a wisecrack for a change. I looked at Parthet differently than I ever had before, I think. What choice did I have? "The king said there was."

"He did?" That seemed to please him more than the deed.

"As long as we could keep you from losing your glasses again."

"Ah, yes, there is that," Parthet said. It didn't seem to bother him. "I told you I need to see to do most of my magics."

"Well, if you've got any more to spring, you'd better get cracking. It's going to be dark in another half hour."

"Yes. To work, to work, not a time to shirk."

A wizard maybe, but not much of a poet.

6

Thyme

Parthet's only other contribution was a shield that was supposed to keep out bugs and small animals that might otherwise disturb our comfort. It may have worked. There was nothing visible about this magic, but I wasn't nibbled by mosquitos and nobody woke up with a snake or skunk in his bedding. Parthet offered to whip up a campfire, but we decided that we would be better off without it.

Under the willows, night followed posthaste upon sunset. The dark was complete. We arranged our bedrolls and settled in. There was a little soft talk at first, but the conversation languished quickly and all that remained was the murmur of the creek that flowed past the edge of our camp.

Occasionally a horse moved around or drank. The animals were tied to a picket line, more to keep them from stumbling over us than to keep them from wandering off. They had no place to wander, not even along the creek. Brambles had overgrown it, making it impassable. Only right under the willows were the brambles missing.

I slept poorly. During the day I had managed to keep from wasting a lot of energy worrying. With the night, though, the worries pecked at the edges of my mind until I paid attention. The soft breathing of the others couldn't hold off thoughts of what the morrow might bring. Castle Thyme was drawing members of the family like a magnet. Dad had gone first, to try to take the castle back from the soldiers of the Etevar of Dorthin almost single-handedly. He had a couple of soldiers, men like Lesh, and his squire. No more. Then Mom took off to see what was taking him so long, and she *had* gone alone. To rescue Dad. We hadn't met along the road, so she too was overdue and likely in trouble. If she happened by in the dark, while we were camped, we might or might not hear her. Parthet said he would know. I had a feeling he was right, but it was still something extra to worry about.

Now Uncle Parthet and I were going to Castle Thyme too. That would damn near complete the reunion. I knew less about the situation, about the whole damn world, than either of my parents. Everybody treated me like a big shot, son of the Hero, great-grandson and heir of the King of Varay. But I really didn't know what was going on, and that may have bothered me more than the rest. I still thought that there was at least an even chance that my brain had jumped the rails. Maybe the pressures of trying to finish my last year of college *had* snapped my sanity, shattered it into little bitty bits. I had seen cases of sheepskin syndrome. The pressure got to be too much and they went crackers. Or maybe I would wake up and find that it was all a dream, like *Dallas*.

Wake up? I couldn't even get to sleep.

I was toting around a bunch of weapons that I had practiced with for most of my life but had never used in a real fight, or even in serious competition. "It's not a game," Dad told me while he taught me how to kill and maim in every conceivable way. "It's survival. If you ever need the skills, you have to know that: *it's not a game.''* Sometimes he screamed it. ''You can't play by anybody's rules, can't wait for a referee to call a foul on the other guy or worry that he might call a foul on you. If you get into a situation where your life's on the line, the only rule is that the winner walks away and the loser doesn't.'' When I wasn't practicing those fighting skills, Dad had me studying military tactics on every level from squad to full army. In high school, I could map out and re-create nearly every landmark battle from Marathon and Thermopylae to Tarawa, Arnhem, and the Israelis' Six-Day War. Dad had dozens of army field manuals, technical manuals, and other military reference books. By the time I was seventeen, I had gone through most of the practical curriculum of the Army War College. And although Dad disapproved, that training made me a wicked competitor in simulation games at school.

''It's not a game,'' I whispered a couple of times that night in Precarra. ''It's not a game.'' I started to get scared, so maybe I was really starting to believe the whole scam. I was going to rescue my parents if I could, if they needed rescuing—and they probably did. I might have to capture a castle to do it, a fortress whose defenders had already faced or were facing similar puny attacks. Surprise wasn't likely, and I didn't have any other advantages—unless Parthet could come up with something even fancier than his Red Sea trick, and I wasn't counting on that. Okay, Castle Thyme was a small castle surrounded by a low wall and a dry ditch. Given a dark enough night and a lot of luck, we might scale the wall and sneak inside. If Lesh had a long rope and a quiet grapple in one of the saddlebags.

It's not a game. One more full day on the road, maybe a few hours the following morning before we reached Castle Thyme and a kill-or-be-killed situation. I had never been in that kind of position before. I had never been in any spot that looked so dangerous going in.

Eventually, I dozed off. I don't know how long I slept; not long enough, by half. The soft hooting of an owl in the distance woke me. Sometime later, I heard thrashing noises in the underbrush, frenzied sounds of some small animal crying in its final agony. The owl apparently found dinner. I strained to hear any other sounds, but there were none around our camp. Inside, soft snoring, the horses shifting position. When my watch reached seven-fifteen, I woke the others even though it was still dark.

"Let's do what we have to do and leave as soon as there's enough light to get back to the road," I said.

"A good idea," Lesh said after a noisy routine of stretches and yawns.

"Let's start a fire," I said, an impulsive decision. "I've got instant coffee. We can heat water and have that much to get us moving. That and whatever kind of breakfast we can put together." I needed something. I felt more tired than I had been when we made camp. I got out my flashlight and Lesh assembled enough dry wood for a decent little cooking fire.

"I've never tried to conjure by flashlight," Parthet warned while Lesh was assembling the wood.

"Never mind, I've got a lighter." The disposable Mom had packed was still in its cardboard-and-plastic package. I set the flashlight on the ground next to the twigs and branches and got the lighter right down in the shavings Lesh provided with his dagger. I spun the wheel of the lighter, but nothing happened. There was a spark from the flint but no fire. I tried again with the same lack of result. I kept flicking the lighter. There was butane in it. I could hear it hissing when I held the lighter next to my ear and held the lever down. But it wouldn't light.

"It looks like magic *is* needed," Parthet said.

"I've got matches. *They* should work," I said. They did. I started to toss the lighter away but ended up sticking it back in my pack. There was no call to start littering.

Hot instant coffee, day-old bread, salted beef jerky—eating was exercise enough for anyone's morning. By the time we finished, there was light in the east. Saddling up and getting loaded gave dawn time to sneak across the sky. I made one change in my attire. I put the chain mail under my fatigue shirt. That made it easier to get at the pistol holstered at my waist. None of the others noticed the gun during the instant it was visible.

"There's light enough now," Parthet said. He hoisted himself aboard Glory. "Remember, stay close to me."

The magic was just as impressive the second time. The brambles swayed and parted in front and closed behind us. When we reached the road, we stopped and looked back across the brambles. There was no trace of our passage.

I took the lead and we started off single-file for Castle Thyme. Not long after we started, the road widened enough for us to ride two abreast again. The road turned a little more toward the north too. We were able to move faster on the better track. I was edgy after my uneasy night, so I picked up the pace to the fastest the horses were comfortable with.

"We're getting closer to the marches," Lesh said near noon. "We're maybe ten or twelve miles from the border now, due east of here. A little farther on, we'll hit a spot where the road forks coming down from the north. The other branch runs south past my home village on to the other two marcher castles."

"Three castles to guard the entire border?" I asked.

"Four if you include Coriander in Battle Forest," Parthet said. "There aren't many decent routes between the two kingdoms, certainly not fit to take a sizable force across. There's no use building castles to guard passages no enemy can make."

It still sounded like scanty protection for a border that stretched 250 or 300 miles.

"From the fork, it's five hours to Castle Thyme, maybe six," Lesh said ignoring the interruption.

That morning, I had arbitrarily set my watch to six o'clock when I caught my first glimpse of the sun—very roughly, since the forest didn't allow for close accuracy. It still wasn't the right time, but it had to be closer than before. Minutes and hours seemed to mean less in Varay than they did in Louisville or Evanston, but *I* still thought in those terms and I liked the comfort of being able to look at my wrist and knowing the time.

Thirty minutes later, a shadow blocked the sun—too abruptly for a cloud. We all looked up. The horses got skittish.

"There's a dragon for you," Parthet said tightly. I didn't get much of a look. The creature moved past the sun, and the sudden glare put spots in front of my eyes. I couldn't see anything for a few seconds. "This time of day, he's probably already eaten and is on his way home to nest for a long sleep. Even so, it's better to hope that he doesn't see us, and best to make sure that he can't. Don't bother me for a bit."

Parthet started mumbling and humming, a different kind of sound from the one he used to part the brambles. He turned in his saddle and leaned back to keep the dragon in sight as much as possible while he conjured. When my eyes cleared, I could see the huge form in the sky, but it was too high for me to see any real detail. The body looked bulky, fat in the middle, tapering off quickly in front and back to serpentine neck and tail. The wings were massive and moved stiffly. They didn't look like bat wings, but more like the wings of some large bird of prey. The legs had to be tucked up close to the body. I didn't see any trace of them.

The sky started to shimmer like heat mirages on the highway, and the dragon became even more indistinct.

"He won't see us through that," Parthet said. I couldn't be positive that this was magic, but neither could I be positive that it wasn't. After seeing the deMille act, I was inclined to accept Parthet at his word. We kept riding and the shimmering sky stayed between us and the dragon.

"If he does see us, will that stop him?" I asked.

"If he saw us, castle walls might not stop him," Parthet said, "but he won't see us."

I got a stiff neck looking over my shoulder though. The dragon disappeared to the south within a couple of minutes, but I kept looking that way, wondering if he might decide to come back. Parthet's shimmering sky calmed down gradually. Not long after it cleared completely, we reached the fork in the road and stopped for a rest. I dismounted and walked fifty yards along the road to the south. It didn't seem any different from the road we had been on. I saw no sign of recent traffic.

"Not many folks live in these parts," Lesh said when

I came back from my short walk. "Too much war. Those who do live along the marches stay close to their villages and farms, where they have some little feeling of safety. Maybe months go by without anyone but a royal messenger or tax collector coming to visit. Maybe a peddler now and then. Not often." Stay-at-homes with a vengeance. It gave me an empty feeling.

"I suppose we should start figuring out what we're going to do when we reach this castle," I said.

"We don't know yet what we're going to face," Parthet pointed out.

"Can't you find out?" I asked. "You've shown a couple of nifty magics. Haven't you got some way to get in touch with my parents or to look over the scene before we get there?" I hadn't noticed a crystal ball, but I guess that's what I was hoping for.

"Not from this distance. Not for a long while yet," Parthet said. "When the castle is in sight I might be able to penetrate its more superficial secrets. *Might.* Now"— he paused for a moment—"by bending my thoughts her way, I can just barely perceive something of Avedell's presence. Nothing more."

"What about Dad?"

A shrug. "He isn't blood kin to me. I'm not nearly so aware of his mind's signatures. Carl's mind isn't easy to touch even when we're standing next to each other. Nor is yours. With your father, it's part of the magic of being Hero of Varay—a protection. With you, I'm not certain. You *are* blood kin. I should be able to sense you."

"You read minds?"

"No!" Very forcefully, that. "No," he repeated. "I can't truly read anyone's mind, not even my own. But, with some people, sometimes, I can sense things, occasionally share a perception. It's not a simple matter."

"Let me know when we're close enough for something definite."

"Of course." Parthet looked around. "We're making better time than I expected. We might come within an hour's ride of Castle Thyme by sunset."

"Maybe that's a good thing," I said. "We may have

a chance to look around before anyone knows we've arrived. Lesh, how high is the wall around the castle?''

''No more'n twenty feet,'' he said after a moment's reflection.

''Can it be scaled?''

''Not if it's defended, lord.''

''How about at night, with no moon?''

He shook his head. ''Two guards can cover the entire wall. They'd hear or see a grapple by the watchfires.''

''Parthet, could you help with this?'' I was still groping in the dark, but Dad *had* made me study all that military jazz. I knew the words, the concepts, even if I had never had to apply them in real life.

''If the circumstances are right. I need light to work, but the more light, the more difficult the problem. I'll study on it while we ride.''

We rode. Precarra Forest thinned out. There were occasional areas where the scrub brush held trees in isolation from each other, patches of rocky soil that supported only a little grass. We took advantage of one clearing to eat an early supper and rest the horses. The meal was more hard bread and harder beef jerky. The stream we dipped our water from was clear, the water cool and refreshing, coming from a spring on the side of a low ridge that paralleled the road. Lesh climbed to the top of the ridge with me.

''That deeper line of green in the distance.'' Lesh pointed and moved his arm to show the line he meant. ''Unless I'm mistaken, that's the Borerun. The river bends our way, then returns to Dorthin. It runs north to the Eastern Sea east of Xayber. We fought a battle at the bend over this way when I was just a young soldier. My first campaign it were. We had to retreat when the old Etevar's wizard turned the river out of its banks against us.''

''Maybe we'll get something back on the new Etevar tonight or tomorrow,'' I said, starting back down the slope.

''Maybe we will, lord,'' Lesh said.

I shook my head, very casually. None of my companions had expressed any reservations about the sanity of our mission or the fact that an utter rookie was going in to attempt something that the seasoned veterans had apparently failed to manage. Maybe there was nothing remarkable about the situation in the buffer zone. Parthet had told me that Dad had regularly done "Hero work" through the years, that there was more call for it than I might imagine. And half the time, I accepted the idea that it was natural for me to be doing this. That was enough to send ominous shivers up my spine the other half of the time.

Lesh was solid, ready to take on any challenge. Timon seemed eager for the adventure, whatever it might involve. And Uncle Parthet—when he showed any feeling at all about it—seemed to regard our mission as a chance for his own vindication as a wizard. If he worried about Mom and Dad, and I'm not saying that he didn't, he hid it well.

We rode on again into an area of old primary forest, straight, tall trees with little undergrowth. The canopy overhead filtered the light, casting deep greens. The occasional shaft of late-afternoon sunlight stood out in sharp relief like a spotlight beam. Parthet seemed buried inside himself. His horse followed mine without guidance. Glory was an old campaigner. Parthet didn't even respond to my questions, so I finally quit trying. I guessed that he was deep in some magic, probably trying to contact Mother. Either that or he was dozing.

"Another hour to sunset," Lesh said when we reached the end of the tall timber. "If we're going on to Thyme tonight, maybe we should rest our horses a bit now. And maybe have another bite." I nodded, and we dismounted, Parthet last. He didn't seem to notice that we stopped at first.

"You look troubled," I said when Parthet finally got down from Glory. Parthet wouldn't meet my eyes at first. "You've learned something," I said. What is it?"

"Nothing certain, lad," he whispered, none too calmly. "I still can't make firm contact with your mother, but there is an agony in the air that eats at my mind. It's too vague to know what it means." He turned to look north. According to Lesh, Thyme was almost directly due north of us now.

"I fear the worst," Parthet said, "but I fear my fears even more."

Lesh and Timon tended the horses. I stared at Parthet's back. He walked a few steps toward the final rank of lofty trees.

"If my fears were true, there could be no way for me to catch them. But if they aren't true, there's a rare deception in the wind, a more powerful magic than my own."

"At Castle Thyme?"

"Somewhere near for it to be so strong." He turned and stared blankly at me. He was far enough away that my features were probably only a blur to him. "Why are we stopped?" He looked around and blinked, coming back from wherever his mind had wandered.

"To rest the horses so we can push on this evening," I said.

Lesh came to us. "In two miles or so, the road turns east and climbs toward higher ground, bending back north. Castle Thyme sits atop a low mound on the west side of the road, perhaps four miles altogether from here."

"Can we cut cross-country and come from a way they won't expect?" I asked.

"The land around the castle offers little concealment up close," Lesh said. "There's naught but fields right around it."

"But they might have sentries watching this road at a distance, almost anywhere now," I said.

"The way overland is difficult at any time. It might take extra hours in the dark," Lesh said.

"Time, lad," Parthet whispered. His arms started to tremble. "We must make time now." He turned away before he added, "If time remains." I don't think he meant for me to hear that, but my hearing is quite sharp.

"We'll make time, but we still need a few minutes now," I said. Lesh handed me a strip of beef, and I started chewing on it. There was no stream handy, so we had to settle for the tepid water in our canteens—leather pouches that gave the water a bitter taste. We ate and stretched and took care of the other things that needed doing. I checked my weapons. I even turned away from the others to make sure that there was a shell in the chamber of my pistol. I think only Timon noticed the gun, and he might not have known what it was. Timon had the metal skullcap out. He offered it to me.

"Not yet," I told him. "I've got my lucky hat." I adjusted the blue Cubs cap, pulling the brim a little lower.

"Lucky?" Parthet asked from behind. I turned. The old man could sure move silently enough when he wanted to. "Lucky? How many championships have they won in the last fifty years?"

I hate questions like that. "What happened to the last guy who wore this tin pot?" I asked. Parthet didn't have the answer, but Lesh did.

"He got an arrow through the throat."

"I rest my case," I said.

"Pardon me, Highness," Lesh said, "but cloth won't turn a sword blade. I think you should wear the helmet." He rapped his knuckles against his own. "It might save your life."

"We'll see when we get there," I said, to cut off the discussion. I had no intention of wearing another five pounds. Dad and I always emphasized speed, movement, for defense. Every ounce of weight slowed me. The mail shirt. The shield I hadn't toted since I tried it on, back in Castle Basil.

After our short break, we hit the road at a trot. Riding back home, I always hated the trot. On an English saddle, that meant posting, going up and down like a yo-yo, meeting the horse in the middle. With a Western saddle, it meant sitting there and having your spine hammered. I was surprised to find the trot fairly comfortable on the huge charger Gold. All four horses seemed to find the change of pace refreshing. When we got into the clear, we even stretched them into an easy canter for a time, covering ground nicely. Then we slowed to a walk, changing the pace every couple of hundred yards.

We caught our first glimpse of Castle Thyme just be-

fore sunset. It was still some distance off, visible briefly
through a long valley. The road became wider, more
traveled. A number of trails led off from it.

Then Parthet called, "Hold!" and reined in Glory.

The rest of us stopped and looked to the wizard for an
explanation. Lesh had his spear at the ready, searching
the land around us for any threat. Parthet stood in the
saddle and looked off into a distance he couldn't see with
his eyes. "This way," he said after a moment. He led
the way off the road, west of north, cross-country after
all.

"What is it?" I asked, moving Gold up alongside
Glory. We were riding through tall prairie grass, a plain
broken only by solitary trees, easy going for the horses
unless there was something to trip them up in the grass.
And with twilight, we wouldn't be able to see anything
low.

"Ride!" Parthet said harshly. "To your mother.
Ride!"

I looked ahead, trying to see what Parthet was aiming
for, but I didn't see anything but more of the stuff we
were in. There was a low hill across our path at an angle
from southeast to northwest. Parthet changed course
enough to hit the northern end of the ridge. He pushed
Glory to a gallop. Lesh and I had no problem keeping
up, but Timon's pony was outclassed, even by old, swaybacked Glory. Or maybe Timon just wasn't an experienced enough rider for that kind of terrain. He couldn't
have done much riding scrubbing pots. I tried to keep an
eye on him, but I had to watch Gold and our course too.
I held on, hoping there were no gopher holes to trip us.

Parthet led us across the shoulder of the long hill, down
into another valley. The trees disappeared and the grass
became sparser in rocky soil. The footing was more difficult. Now and then a horseshoe sparked off stone. There
was a track along the flank of one of the bordering hills,
and Parthet angled up to that. Glory started to tire and
slow. Parthet's eyes remained fixed on the horizon. He
seemed to strain forward, either trying to see something
that was still out of sight or trying to urge more speed
from his animal. I had to rein back on Gold to keep from

running over Glory. I could hear Lesh right behind me, and see him too, when I turned to look for Timon. The boy was fifty yards behind Lesh, but he wasn't losing any more ground. Glory's slower pace made it possible for Timon to keep us in sight.

The evening shadows were getting thick and long. Soon it would be impossible to see anything well enough to continue this mad dash.

"How much farther?" I shouted. Parthet didn't answer. Perhaps he was too deep in magic or concentration to hear. All I could do was follow and hope that our horses could still find footing.

At the end of that valley, Parthet cut left across a low pass between two neighboring hills—neither more than about thirty feet high—then went north again into the next valley. This one widened out quickly, and the bottom was flat. I could see a thick patch of trees ahead—moderate-sized trees with rounded shapes. When we got closer, I could see that it was apples and pears in an orchard. There was a cottage at the far end of the orchard, between two garden-sized fields.

Parthet headed straight for the cottage.

We were a hundred yards off when I saw a brief glint that had to be the cottage door opening and closing. A figure moved in front of the doorway and notched arrow to bow. We were a lot closer before I could tell that it was my mother, dressed in a Robin Hood costume without the cap, her black hair pulled back and tied behind her head. She didn't ease the tension on her bowstring until we were reining in our horses.

I was the first out of the saddle, but Parthet was less than a step behind me. Mother had been crying. She looked at me, then at Parthet.

"I was too late," she said, her voice wavering.

7

The Hero

My insides seemed to lock up on me. I knew what she was saying. There was no point in questioning it. Even the blind instinct to repeat bad news was blocked. I don't think I had ever seen Mother cry before. Parthet and Lesh stood with us. The four of us remained silent for a time and a time. Timon arrived, dismounted, gathered up the reins of all our horses, and took them off to the side without saying anything, while the rest of us remained locked in tableau. Timon must have felt the grief. When I finally spoke, the words seemed to isolate themselves in the air one at a time, like crystal bubbles, fragile explosive charges.

"Where is he?" I asked.

"Inside," Mother said, without any hint of gesture.

I looked at the door behind her, walked to it—very slowly. I hesitated before I pulled it open, and hesitated again between the dim twilight outside and the blackness within. As my eyes started to adjust, as well as they could, to the internal darkness, I saw a few vague shapes inside. I felt a tap on my shoulder. When I turned, Parthet handed me my flashlight. I nodded and he backed off, leaving the moment to me.

I turned on the flashlight and stepped into the cottage. It was as simple and mean a hovel as Parthet's. Dad was lying on a bench at the side of the room, over to my right. Carl Tyner, King's Champion, Hero of Varay. Dad.

Dead.

He was dressed for the outdoors, leather tunic over fatigue trousers like mine, Robin Hood cap on his head. His head rested on a small shield with a piece of fabric, something like burlap, folded over it into a thin pillow. His hands were clasped on his chest, over the hilt of his sword. I stared, looking for some trace of his chest rising and falling as he breathed, but there was no movement, no breath. I knew that there wouldn't be, but that impossible hope nagged at my mind. His eyes were closed. His face looked serene, at peace. I saw no sign of wounds.

An emptiness swelled up inside and reached out to engulf me, a series of sensations that I had no precedents for. My throat got tight. My heart seemed to flutter. But even those commonplaces were somehow different, *strange*. The pain was there, but something bottled it up tight, sealed it off in a cold chamber somewhere to wait for a more appropriate time. My mind tried to reject the reality. Maybe I was trapped in a fairy-tale world with dragons and wizards, but no matter how hard I tried, I couldn't con myself into believing that death was any less final because of that. I looked at the body at the side of the room. I had never let myself dwell on this possibility. Deep down, I guess I had never been able to completely shake the feeling that Varay was some kind of mental aberration, that none of my adventures were real.

Too late the waking. I walked across the room and stood next to the bench. I played the light along the supine form and kept staring. Death was real, and reality was an ulcer's fire in my gut. Closing my eyes didn't make the pain go away, and opening them didn't alter the reality.

I heard a slight shuffling behind me. Mother and Uncle Parthet had come in together. I turned around while Mother lit two candles.

"How did it happen?" I whispered instinctively.

"Nine days ago," Mother said, answering a different question. I turned to look at the body again, another question leaping to my mouth. Mother answered this one before I could get it out. "He was Hero of Varay. The magic of his initiation protects him now, more than it could in life. His flesh will remain whole until he is properly interred."

"But no magic can bring him back," I said. It wasn't a question.

"No magic can bring him back," Parthet agreed softly.

I moved between Mother and Parthet and walked outside, flicking off my flashlight. An appropriately chilled breeze did what grief had been unable to do, bring tears to my eyes, blur my vision. When I blinked my eyes clear, I saw Lesh and Timon, both looking apprehensive, perhaps in echo to my pain.

"The Hero of Varay is gone from us," Parthet said behind me. His voice wasn't loud, but the words seemed to hang in the air and reverberate.

Lesh was a soldier, but at that moment he was no more hardened to death than I was. Muscles rippled under the skin of his face as he fought to hide any display of grief. "We share your loss, lord," he said, and his voice nearly betrayed him. Timon cried openly, tears streaming down his face, leaving tracks in the dust we had all picked up along the way. He turned and clung to Lesh, who held his shoulders, hardly aware that the boy was there.

"What about the men he had with him?" I asked when I turned and saw that Mother had also come out of the cottage.

"The two soldiers fell with him," she said. "The squire survived. Harkane's duty is to see to Carl even in death, until he is properly laid away. I sent him on toward Basil as soon as we moved your father here and got the others buried."

"We didn't meet anyone on the road," I said.

"Likely he would have hidden at the first hint of riders," Mother said. "He was quite distraught, frightened. He was on foot, so he could hardly have reached Basil yet. I didn't know for sure that you would come. I couldn't be certain."

I shrugged to take some of the sting from my reply, but my voice left the bitterness in. "Perhaps if I had known something about Varay before this came up." I stared at Mother. She didn't say anything, but she didn't look away either. "What do we do next?" I asked.

"Take your father back to Basil, where he belongs," Mother said.

"We'll need a wagon," I said. I didn't want to just drape Dad across the saddle of a horse the way the old westerns used to show.

"There's a wagon and horse here," Mother said.

"What about the farmer? We can't just waltz off with his property."

"He has no further use for them. The Etevar's warlord laid a heavy hand around Thyme in his haste to draw your father. Dozens of people have been killed or taken as slaves. We thought there was just a small band of soldiers at Thyme, but the Etevar sent at least forty soldiers and his new wizard as well."

"Is he still here?" Parthet asked. I assumed he meant the other wizard. Mother shook her head.

"Lesh, will you hitch the wagon and bring it around?" I asked.

He bowed. "At once, Highness."

"Just back of the house, Lesh," Mother said. He bowed to her and left, taking Timon with him.

"You've learned of your heritage," Mother said to me.

"Some of it." I didn't want to talk about that yet. All it could was make me angry, and there wasn't time for that. "Can you tell me what happened here?"

"The telling takes time." We walked to a bench that leaned against the front of the cottage. Mother and I sat. Parthet stood facing us.

"We had the call for help some three weeks ago," Mother started. "Word had reached Basil that the Etevar had taken Castle Thyme again—a castle your father wrested from him once before. It was a direct challenge, a slap in the face. We knew it might be a trap, but your father left the same day. He had a good idea what he would do, what to expect. He *did* have more than twenty years' experience at this sort of thing. He knew how long he should be gone too. When he didn't get home or send word, I came after him. Only Harkane, his squire, was still alive. He had found this place and had started to carry your father here. They had been ambushed. Perhaps the attack on Thyme was staged just to draw your father, as we feared. The young Etevar held an old grudge over the death of *his* father. There were soldiers in Castle Thyme. Your father knew that, of course, but he didn't know that there were more lurking outside, waiting for him. The wizard shielded them. There was a long running battle, but time wasn't working right. That's the way Harkane explained it. The Etevar's warlord could bring out fresh troops from the castle and keep up the pressure far too long.'' Mother turned her head away from me.

"Are they still there?'' I asked.

"There's still a garrison. I don't know if the warlord remains, but the Etevar's new wizard left before I arrived.

"We've had rumors of this new wizard in Dorthin,'' Parthet said. "No one knows who or what he is, but the talk is that he's a completely new force out of Fairy.''

I wasn't sure what significance that might have, but I knew that my immediate future had been decided. Talking about it after the fact, it sounds like a moment of sheer stupidity, or some sort of cosmic hocus-pocus, but there was no time of considering options, no hesitation, and if it sounds like something from a bad movie script, I can't help that. Back at Castle Basil, everyone had talked about me as the Son of the Hero. The Hero was dead, though. I had a new trade now—short-term, at least. In fact, my entire future might be extremely short-term. High drama. Stirring music in the background. All that hokum. A certainty wrapped itself around me and squeezed like an anaconda. Louisville and Northwestern belonged to a past that could never be the same. For the present at least, I belonged in Varay. It wasn't even a matter of conscious choice. Maybe the decision would have been harder if there had been a special girl back home, but there wasn't, not at the moment. There were a couple I might miss from time to time, but that didn't matter. Nothing mattered outside Varay just then—at least, not outside the seven kingdoms. I had a score to settle, a *Mission* to complete.

One time, I asked my father why he had enlisted in the army on his eighteenth birthday. I had asked that question before. His usual response was that after years in an orphanage and in foster homes it was simply the fastest way out. This one time though, he hesitated a long time before he said, "I think I just OD'd on John Wayne movies.'' That made a lot more sense once I knew what he had been doing in the years since he came back from Vietnam.

When I got up off the bench and looked around slowly,

I think both Parthet and Mother saw the change in me, even in the new darkness. Parthet bowed almost low enough to push a peanut along the ground with his nose. Mother stood, straightened up, and nodded. Nothing was said. A few minutes later, Lesh led up the horse and wagon. The wagon was narrow and high, with a shallow bed set completely above the wheels. It looked as if it might tip over much too easily despite the reverse camber to the wheels.

"It's sturdy enough, lord," Lesh said. "It's been well cared for."

I nodded. "I'll need your help inside, Lesh," I said. It was too late to be starting out—twilight was gone, the night's early stars were out—but I had to make the start regardless. I wouldn't stay there, so close to the enemy. Lesh followed me inside. He knelt at Father's side for a moment, then we carried him out and set him in the back of the wagon and covered him with a light blanket. Mother brought her horse, a beautiful black mare, around from the side of the cottage. She didn't want to wait either.

"Uncle Parker, you'd better drive the wagon. If the enemy's still about, we need Lesh mounted, ready to fight."

"I'm ready for different bruises," Parthet said quietly.

"I want to put some miles between us and Castle Thyme before we camp. Are we going to be able to get that wagon to the road?"

"There's a path that keeps us out of direct sight of the castle, but it goes close," Mother said. "It's the only way."

"Then we'll have to chance it," I said.

Lesh led the way after Mother made sure that he knew the route. Parthet followed with the wagon. Glory was tied behind the wagon. I put Timon up next to Glory, or as close behind as he could get on the narrow path. Mother and I brought up the rear, with her moving ahead of me when the track got too narrow for our horses to ride side by side. We rode ready for trouble. Lesh had his lance. Mother kept her bow in her hand. I left the bottom two buttons of my shirt undone so I could reach my pistol quickly. Parthet had his staff plus whatever sorceries protected a wizard.

The path was narrow but might have been designed for the wagon . . . or vice versa. We rode for an hour before we reached what Lesh said was the main road and turned away from the castle and what was left of the village of Thyme. In the dark, we had to ride slowly. I gave Lesh my flashlight so he could pick our path through the trickiest stretches.

I concentrated on sounds, worried that the Etevar's soldiers might waylay us as they had Dad. We couldn't go on all night without rest, but every mile we covered took us that much farther from the greatest danger. We finally left the road and moved into a narrow valley. We couldn't get far from the road with the wagon, though. And there wasn't enough light for Parthet's camping magics, so we had to put up with the bugs. We kept watches through the rest of the night, one at a time except for Timon. We let him sleep straight through, better than the rest of us managed, I think. I hardly slept at all—again. Most of the time I stared at the sky and thought about times I had shared with my father, good times, generally. We had had a lot of fun together. All those memories . . . but he had concealed so much too. The secrets hurt, more as the night progressed. My parents had hidden an entire life, an entire *world*, from me.

When dawn came I was near exhaustion, but we got moving as soon as there was any light at all. The morning's ride was silent. As the wagon wheels dragged mile after mile under them, the danger decreased, but I remained too lost in my thoughts for talk. And I was so tired that I may have dozed off and on too. At noon, we ate the freeze-dried meals I had been carrying in my pack. They didn't go far among so many of us, but we weren't hungry enough for salted beef again. That afternoon, I brought down a small deer with my bow, so we had fresh meat for the rest of our journey. It took three days to get to Basil with the wagon.

After that first morning, I learned more of my hidden heritage. Mother seemed to have a need to talk, and I was content to listen.

The title Hero of Varay was as old as the seven kingdoms. Varay was named for Vara, a legendary superhero who brought the magic out of Fairy and held the land for its more mortal inhabitants as king and hero. Traditionally then, Varay's Heroes came from outside the kingdom. A Varayan might be King's Champion, but he was never given the formal title Hero of Varay. "That's one of the reasons we kept the truth from you," Mother said. "Your father wanted you to follow in his footsteps—if you chose to. But you remained an outsider, even though you are also heir to the throne. We stopped bringing you for visits when you were five."

"Why is it so important that I be both king and Hero?"

"The two have never been united in one man since Vara. Our legends promise a new golden age when one man can again hold both titles legitimately. It may be superstitious nonsense, but I don't know of another time when it's been possible to test it."

"More of the same kind of legend that makes the Etevars want to reunite the seven kingdoms under their rule?" I asked.

"Perhaps. But Varay has never sought to dominate the other kingdoms." Maybe not. Or maybe the Varayan storytellers were just better liars.

"What about the other magic doorways at home? Where do they lead?"

"All to places in Varay," Mother said. "To Basil, Arrowroot on the Mist, Coriander in the Battle Forest at the edge of Xayber and Fairy. They lead to most of the important places in Varay."

To the edge of Fairy but not to Castle Thyme? I thought, but what I asked was, "How is it done? How do you create a doorway?"

"The easiest way requires two members of the family, one at each end, linking their efforts through the rings, bringing themselves to each other. One can do it alone, but that takes longer. You have to go to each place and implant the silver, then you have to concentrate to take yourself back through the untried passage to make it permanent. Draining work."

"Where does the silver come from?"

"It's a seaweed that grows in the shallows of the Mist, along the shore of Xayber, in Fairy."

That figured. It wouldn't be anything convenient. "Do we have a stockpile of it somewhere?"

"No. The silver must be living when it's implanted in the doorway, and it lives for only a few months after being harvested from the Mist."

There were other items. Uncle Parthet was something over a thousand years old. There was nobody around who could say definitely how much over, and he tended to be vague on the subject. His first foray into our world was well before the First Crusade. Back then, according to him, there was little to separate the three realms—mortal, buffer, and Fairy. Technology was the distancing factor. Now, the mortal realms were slow poison for creatures out of Fairy and only reachable through potent magics for people from the seven kingdoms. And Fairy was consistently hazardous to the health of all outsiders. Even Mother was twenty years older than I had thought, nearing sixty-five. She could pass for half that, easily.

"We do live longer, and the middle decades pass more slowly for our bodies," she explained. "When you were a baby, Grandfather could still lead his soldiers in battle. His hair was black and full. He had the stamina of a teenager. And he was already over a hundred years old."

That led to another question. "What about me? I'm half one world and half the other."

"According to Parthet, the blood of Vara always proves true."

We didn't speak of any future beyond our return to Basil. Until Father was properly seen to, the future had to wait.

At Nushur, people lined the road. We stopped at the inn for only a few minutes. The innkeeper's lads brought out a small keg of beer as well as bread, carrots, and potatoes to go with our venison. The innkeeper refused payment. Dad's squire had been through the village. The news had spread. When I shook the innkeeper's hand and thanked him for his wares, he went down to one knee and seemed ready to cry.

On the road past Nushur, I asked why everything was

so medieval, why it was always like that in the books I read too. "What's so special about this stuff?" Mother didn't have a ready answer, but Parthet did.

"Many people have had glimpses of the truth, or memories of it. There was a time when the three realms were so intertwined that you could go from one to another as easily as you can drive from Louisville to Lexington today. For a long while, there were no obstacles. But people re-create their past every moment, just as surely as they create their futures."

"What's that supposed to mean?" I asked.

"You think that the past is rigid, unchanging history, right?"

"The interpretations may change, but the facts *have* to be the same."

"Not on your life, lad. *Both* change. The past is a fragile tissue of memories—'a lie everyone agrees on,' I think somebody in your world once said. That's very close. And when the memories change, the past changes. Some people have a greater control over their past and future than others do, but everyone participates to some degree. And the nonsense that grows out of people's heads! Your father once told me that historians now say that Richard the Lionhearted was homosexual and blame the centuries of war and distrust between France and England on a lovers' spat between Robin Hood's king and Philip of France. Nonsense! And I remember King Arthur and his queen. Arthur was no miserable warlord the way they make him out to be now. Camelot was real, and glorious."

"You were there, I suppose?" I asked, not even pretending to take *this* story at face value.

"Merlin was a valued friend," Parthet said, ignoring my tone.

"If all the worlds were one back then, what made it change, and *when* did it change?"

Parthet took a moment to think about that. "You've heard of Carolingian minuscule?" he asked. The term sounded familiar, but I couldn't place it. "The common script you write in, the lowercase letters at least. It was part of the revival of learning that the man you know as

Charlemagne fostered. That's where it started." He
laughed. "The pen *is* mightier than the sword."

People were waiting for us in the streets of Basil Town
also. Sad faces watched our cortege. I had a little trouble
dealing with the fact that all of these strangers were so
moved by the fact of my father's death. And everyone in
the castle was out and waiting in the courtyard, even King
Pregel. Dad was placed on a fancy wooden stretcher type
of platform and carried into the keep by four soldiers.
They took him to a small chapel dedicated to the Great
Earth Mother at the side of the great hall.

"At dawn," Pregel announced, "Carl Tyner, King's
Champion, Hero of Varay, will be placed in the vaults of
Basil with the rest of our heroes, to return to the Great
Earth Mother until he is needed once more."

A vigil continued through the night, mostly in silence.
I saw tears on more than one strong, rugged face. *These*
were my father's people, not the Hendersons and Mc-
Creareys back in Louisville. The people of Basil mourned
Dad as they would a brother, or their own fathers. Mother
sat next to the catafalque all night, her face nearly as
rigid as Dad's. I could see the pain in her eyes, though.
I could feel what she was feeling. I could almost view
the mourners through her eyes, and I knew it was a new
magic holding me, not just some trick of my mind.

Parthet and Baron Kardeen went off together for a half
hour about midnight. One or the other left now and then
through the night. Virtually no one could last the entire
night without at least one brief absence. The king didn't
stay, but he returned often. He would stand next to my
father, put his hand on Dad's shoulder, and look down at
the closed eyes and pale skin. Then he would take my
mother's hand and they would look at each other without
speaking. Once, the king came to me and clasped my
shoulders. His eyes held a terrible grief.

A bell tolled in the distance before dawn. Everyone
returned to the chapel dressed for the new day. Four soldiers carried the platform. Pregel and Kardeen led the
procession. Parthet, Mother, and I followed Dad. Lesh,
Timon, and Dad's squire followed us. Harkane was four-

teen, starting to fill out. The rest of the mourners fell into line as we followed a route marked by burning torches down steep stairs and along narrow passages below the great hall, through a cellar and down again to the royal crypt of Varay. Together in one long room the kings and heroes of Varay had their burial niches, the end of each occupied niche bearing a marble headstone with the name and dates of its occupant.

Dad's place had been prepared. The soldiers slid him into it, and a mason sealed the headstone in place. A purple banner was draped across the front. Pregel stood in front of the purple and looked around at the rest of us.

"Our Hero is dead," he announced, his voice echoing eerily in the catacombs, "but we have a new Hero at hand: Gil Tyner, Prince of Varay, heir designate, son of the Hero." He looked at me.

"Step forward and kneel before the king," Parthet whispered urgently. I did as he said. There was no time to think anything through.

"Son of my granddaughter, son of my Hero, king who will be," Pregel intoned. Baron Kardeen put a sword with jewel-encrusted hilt in the king's hand.

"Hold out your hands with the rings up," Parthet's voice hissed in my ear—even though he was standing back with my mother, ten feet away.

I held out my hands. The king touched me on each shoulder with the flat of the sword, then he touched the edge of the blade to each ring in turn, starting a burning in my hands. When he held the sword sideways and touched both rings simultaneously with the blade, sparks flew from the points of contact, as if the rings were the poles of a car battery. It *was* an electric charge: I felt it.

"May the magic of Vara sustain you. May the Great Earth Mother clasp you to her breasts. May your sword never know defeat. May your soul never taste shame. Rise, Prince Gil, Hero of Varay."

Pregel returned the fancy sword to Kardeen and then took my hands in his when I stood. There was an electric crackling through the crypt, a smell of brimstone, and it felt as if all the hair on my head and body was standing on end. Pregel's eyes burned into mine. Then he released my hands and hugged me—with considerable force.

"We have need of a Hero," he said aloud. Then he whispered, "We have need of *you*," close to my ear.

While we climbed back to the great hall, maybe eight or ten normal floors up, I could feel the magic settling in my body—it was as if new parts were being put into place.

It scared the crap out of me.

8

Basil

Going from the crypt to the breakfast table didn't blunt anyone's appetite, but it did make for a silent meal. The king presided over breakfast in the great hall, something Parthet said he rarely did. Both tables were full. The lower table was positively packed, with far too many people crammed along the benches. But there was no shortage of food. Servants brought in platters, serving bowls, and huge pitchers in relays.

I couldn't remember ever being so hungry, even though we had just buried my father. There was still no room in me for any outpouring of grief. It was just a thing that I knew would have to wait. Our meals had been rather skimpy on the road, and I had eaten very little after we got back to Castle Basil the day before—almost nothing through the twelve hours of the vigil and funeral. A memory, a series of memories, came to me while I ate. Dad always pigged out after his "business trips." The first couple of days after he got home he seemed to eat continuously. "Gotta have fuel for the furnace," he'd say, predictably. But the bursts of compulsive eating never made him fat. When he was on one of those binges, he out-ate me, and *I* was growing and keeping hyperactive all the time.

While I ate, I kept glancing at King Pregel, right next to me. He might be one hundred twenty-five years old, but he was packing in the chow as heartily as anyone

else. Pregel was as sedentary as he could be, but he was
still lean, almost gaunt in appearance. I couldn't recall
seeing any fat people in Varay. It started to puzzle me,
but I filed the question for future exploration. I had a lot
of questions about Varay.

When Pregel finished eating, he turned to me. "Bar-
ring great emergency it will be at least three days before
we return to the usual business of the court," he said.
"We have much to talk about, you and I, but not right
now. Take what time you need to yourself. See to your
mother. If you need anything at all, come to me or to
Baron Kardeen, any time of the day or night."

I nodded and thanked him. A moment later, he stood
and breakfast ended.

Timon had been at hand throughout the meal, serving
me, making sure I got food from each new platter that
was hauled in while the food was still hot. He knew more
about a page's duties than I did, but the attention made
me uncomfortable.

"Have you managed to get yourself anything to eat this
morning?" I asked when I got up from the table. Timon
didn't answer right off, so I assumed that he hadn't. He
certainly couldn't have found *much* chance. He had been
with me most of the time. "Then you'd better scare up
some food for yourself before it disappears. I'm going up
to the battlements."

"I'll go with you, lord," he said.

"Not until your stomach's bulging. It must be hell to
stand around and watch others eat when you're hungry.
You can come up when you're full. I won't fall off." He
still hesitated. "Go on, eat!" I said firmly. Once it was
a clear order, he seemed delighted to obey.

I wasn't sure how to get to the battlements of the keep,
but I knew they were up there—crenellations and smaller
towers at two of the corners. The logical thing was to go
out to the main stairway and climb until I ran out of
stairs, so that's what I did. Logic didn't always hold in
Varay, but that time I lucked out.

What I wouldn't have given for a castle like Basil when
I was nine or ten! Maybe it was no Caernarvon or Tower
of London, but it would have seemed like it when I was

a kid. The two watchtowers above the keep were the
highest points in sight, off to the mountains that dimly
wrinkled the southern horizon. I could see the sweep of
the forest away from the castle and town, the line of the
River Tarn, the patchwork greens of farms around the
town and off into the distance, blending into the forest.

I climbed to the top of one of the watchtowers. There
were crenellations, braziers, stands of weapons and piles
of stones, a guard walking his post—in desultory fashion.
The royal pennant flew on both towers, but below it flew
a black flag of mourning and the pennant of the Hero of
Varay. A mild breeze came out of the northeast. It wasn't
cold, but it was invigorating after the stuffy, smoky
warmth of the great hall. Maybe Shakespeare sent me
racing to the battlements, but there was a bright sun shin-
ing; it wasn't midnight and I didn't see any tattletale
ghosts.

Varay spread out in every direction. The only bound-
ary I could be certain of from my perch was the distant
line of the Titan Mountains to the south. Parthet had said
that they were unscalable, an absolute barrier. Not even
magic could take a person over or through them. The
Mist and the Isthmus of Xayber were too far north to be
seen from Basil. I knew how far east of the capital the
border with Dorthin was, also out of sight. Belorz was,
according to the map, more than twice that far to the
west. I wasn't overly confident that the map's scale had
been accurate, but Varay seemed to be about 250 miles
from east to west, somewhat more than that from north
to south. The actual borders were vague. Varay and Dorthin argued and fought over the line in the east. The
southern border depended on how far a person thought
he could extend it into the Titans. And in the northeast,
the border between Varay and Fairy fluctuated through
Battle Forest, even out onto the isthmus at times, de-
pending on how the fates or whatever were running. The
only borders that seemed fixed were the coastline of the
Mist and the line between Varay and Belorz. They were
separated by a dandy river that both kingdoms accepted
as a political divider.

If I believed the advertising, the kingdom would all be

mine someday—*if* I survived my term as Hero of Varay. Now *there's* a job title that could have been created by an ad agency. I could go back home and cash in on it for Saturday-morning cartoons, maybe a string of flashy movies starring some ex-musclebuilder or football lineman, license an entire array of toys, T-shirts, school supplies, and anything else that could carry a logo and fetch a price.

The thoughts and images went through my head, circled and danced, but I didn't see much humor at the moment.

I looked down at my clothes. I had switched my fatigues and chain mail for an outfit of local manufacture during the night—loose trousers, coarse-woven shirt, and leather vest. The Basilier equivalent of Sunday-go-to-meeting duds. And my weapons. The Hero of Varay was expected to be armed at all times. The pistol holster inside my waistband was chafing. A knife and my sword showed.

"Highness?" I hadn't heard Timon come up. I was staring toward the Titans, lost in my moody reflections.

"Yes, Timon. Did you get your fill?"

"Aye, lord, enough to last a week."

I doubted that. "What's going on downstairs?"

"Very little. Nearly everyone has gone to bed."

"You must be tired too."

"Not really, lord," he lied. I had seen him smothering yawns at breakfast and before. "Perhaps you should retire for a few hours."

"I couldn't sleep if I had to." I guess I was lying too.

"What will you do?" Timon asked.

"I don't know. Stand here until I get bored, I suppose. Maybe find a full barrel of beer and empty it."

"I mean, about . . . " He didn't have to finish.

"I don't know yet," I said slowly. My voice sounded tired even to me. I had another answer for Timon, but I censored it before it could get out. What would I do? Kill the Etevar and his wizard. Maybe it would have to come down to that kind of an-eye-for-an-eye revenge, but I couldn't fill the emptiness with a mad thirst for revenge at any cost. The Etevar has killed my father because *my* father killed *his* father. So I go off, kill this Etevar, and wait for *his* son to kill me? Madness, even though there were no police or law courts to run to for justice. This was so far removed from the society that I knew that I still couldn't make the mental leap—not standing on the castle's battlements, in a chilly breeze, not even just hours after we had buried my father. It all seemed so clear when I entered that dark cottage near Castle Thyme. No more.

"Everyone's sleeping, you say?"

"Aye, lord. There won't be much happening afore late afternoon, not even in the town."

"Did they stand the vigil with us?"

"Many did, I hear. He was everyone's Hero."

"Maybe I *should* try to sleep," I mumbled.

"Your chamber is prepared, lord." As a member of the royal family, I rated a private room, more than the overwhelming majority of the people in the castle could say. For the soldiers and servants, bed was often whatever piece of rush-strewn floor they could claim and hold.

The bedroom was the one my father had used in Basil. I recognized it because I had seen it through the doorway in my parents' bedroom in Louisville. Now it was mine. Mother had taken a different room somewhere else in the keep. I wasn't sure where. Lesh was sitting across the doorway to my room, leaning against the jamb, snoring freely. Timon woke him so I wouldn't trip or wake Lesh myself. Lesh came to his feet, forcing himself alert.

"Sorry, lord," he said.

"Never mind. A little sleep is what we all need. But you might as well come inside, out of the hallway."

"My place is at your door, lord." I wanted to argue, but I didn't think I could shake his sense of propriety without a long discussion, so I let it be.

"Come on, Timon." I propelled the boy inside. "Find a comfortable spot and get some sleep yourself." There was a bench piled high with cushions. I shoved him toward that and then I stripped off my weapons and collapsed across my bed. I guess I fell asleep almost immediately.

* * *

I found myself holding Yorick's skull, standing in his grave and declaiming how well I knew him while the skull told me to wake up. I tried to tell Yorick to shut up, that I had immortal words to say, but someone was shaking me. I opened my eyes and saw Parthet standing over me, his face nearly invisible in the shadows. I had slept through the day. The only light was coming through the open door from torches in the hall. While I pried myself up to a sitting position, Lesh brought in a lit torch and wedged it into a wall bracket opposite the foot of my bed.

"What time is it?" I asked around a heroic yawn.

"Two hours past sunset," Parthet said. "Quickly, lad, His Majesty waits."

That shortened my next yawn. "What's up? He said it would be three days before we got back to business as usual."

"This isn't business as usual. The Etevar has stolen those days from us," Parthet said. "Come on, lad. You'll hear it soon enough." He started to pull me to my feet with more strength than I would have given him credit for.

"Okay, I'm up." On my feet even. I flexed my shoulders and stretched. By the time I brought my arms down, Parthet and Timon were wrapping my sword belt around me. Protocol. The Hero of Varay *must* be armed.

It was a long walk, down from the mezzanine where my room was, through the great hall, up the main stairway on the other side, then back across to the king's private dining hall. A huge parchment map was spread across the table, the edges of the scroll held down with weights. The map was four feet by seven and appeared to show just Varay and Dorthin, in much more detail than the map I had been given before. Mother and Kardeen were already studying the map with the king when Parthet and I arrived. Lesh and Timon waited in the hall.

"Sorry we had to disturb you, son, but this is urgent," Pregel said.

I nodded and took the seat the king indicated, next to him.

"Our relations with the Etevars have never been

good,'' Pregel said. ''The ambush the current one set for your father was just the latest in a long series of provocations. Now it appears that the attack on your father was merely a prelude to something more ambitious. Parthet, tell him what you've learned.''

Parthet stood to achieve his meager height advantage. ''I was too restless to sleep this morning. I knew, of course, that the Etevar bore a bitter grudge against Carl, but I worried that there might be more to the scheme he used to draw Carl to Thyme. It had been troubling me for some time, but I couldn't put my suspicions together until this morning. So I decided to do a little spying.'' He paused to look around. Nobody questioned him. Obviously, the king had already heard the news; maybe the others had as well.

''I started by questioning Harkane at length with hypnosis and magic, probing for any clue he might have picked up at Castle Thyme, even subconsciously.'' Parthet shrugged. ''There was an aura of strong magic around his perceptions, but we already knew that the Etevar's wizard was involved in the setting the ambush.''

''What's the importance of that?'' I asked. ''Why did it take a wizard to set the ambush? I'd think any competent military commander could do it.''

''Part of the magic of the Hero of Varay is a considerably heightened perception of personal danger,'' Parthet said. ''Without a more powerful magic to conceal the ambush, your father would certainly have seen that there was more to the situation than it appeared, and been able to take his own measures.'' He waited for my nod before he continued.

''I do make a good spy. I'm old and crippled-looking. No one would guess that I'm more than that without the talent to spot my magics, so I visited Carsol, the Etevar's capital, and nosed around.''

''In one day? How did you get there?'' I asked.

Parthet looked to the king for permission before he answered. ''There is a passage from Basil Town to Carsol, one your father and I opened years ago, after your father defeated the previous Etevar.''

''You have a door into the enemy's capital but you thought it was too dangerous to have one into Castle

Thyme?'' I suppose I was as surprised as anyone at the anger in my voice. It just flared. A doorway into Castle Thyme could have put Dad beyond the ambush, kept him alive.

''The secret way into Carsol was a risk we felt justified,'' Pregel said. *''Now*, it's easy to see how things might have been different.''

''The Etevar's wizard would have looked for passages in Thyme,'' Parthet said. ''Even a poor wizard could spot a doorway, though it would take an extraordinary one to use it. The Etevar's new wizard might be that good.''

''He could find one in his own capital just as easily,'' I said.

''If he thought to search for it,'' Parthet said. ''That magic is much too passive to give itself away by chance. And this is the first time that passage has been used in years.''

Baron Kardeen cleared his throat. ''The doorway on this end is in a cellar that is kept flooded except when someone who is authorized uses the passage. The other end is in a much smaller cellar. Anyone who managed to open the doorway from the other end—anyone not authorized to—would likely drown.''

I held up both hands. ''Okay, okay. A justifiable risk.'' I turned to Parthet. ''So, you went to Carsol. What then?''

''There was an incredible amount of activity, people all over town. Part of it was celebration at the destruction of the king's greatest enemy.'' Parthet paused but wouldn't meet my eyes. He was talking about people celebrating Dad's death. ''But part of it was anticipation. The Etevar has called for a general levy of his warlords and all Dorthinis who owe military service. He plans an all-out invasion of Varay. With our Hero dead, he feels that he can't lose this time, especially not with his new wizard.''

''So what's so special about this new wizard?''

''No one speaks his name. To the Dorthinis, he is just 'The Wizard.' '' Parthet sounded miffed. ''They talk about him as a new arrival out of Fairy, perhaps a rebel there, but they claim that he is the most powerful wizard the seven kingdoms have ever known. They describe him as standing head and shoulders over the tallest Dorthini, which would put him well over seven feet—and makes him sound like an elf.'' That last was an aside to me. ''All sorts of impossible powers are ascribed to him. Magic is one thing, but some of the stories are clearly beyond any magic that could possibly work in the seven kingdoms.''

''How much time do we have?'' I asked.

''The levy is to assemble two weeks from today at Carsol. The army will need ten, more likely twelve, days to get from Carsol to the border. An army travels more slowly than a small party. Most of them will be on foot.''

''So we have a little more than three weeks to get an army to the border to meet them. Where will they attack?''

''They'll come by way of Castle Thyme, aiming straight for Basil across the middle of the kingdom. No other route would work.''

''That way will be slow,'' I said, more to myself than the others.

''Slow, but not impossible,'' Parthet said.

''It does give us time to get an army in front of them.''

''We have no army to put in front of them,'' Kardeen said. ''If we pull our men from the north, we'll be overrun by the Elflord of Xayber. He's a mad rebel against his own kind, but as long as he threatens the buffer zone and not other elflords, his people let him be.''

''Are you saying that it comes down to deciding *who* we want to lose Varay to?'' I asked.

''If it ever does come to that, there can be no question,'' Pregel said. ''Letting Fairy cut the buffer zone in half might destroy the fabric of our existence. Our only purpose is to separate the realms, Fairy and Mortal.''

''What options do we have, then?''

''I don't know. I only know that we have to find a way,'' Pregel said.

Picture a light bulb going on above my head. ''You mean that you hope *I* can find a way.''

''You are Hero of Varay,'' Kardeen said. ''We have

always relied on our Heroes in our greatest need, all the way back to Vara himself.''

"Hey, I'm the rookie here, remember? I don't have any miracles to pull out of a hat. How the hell can I take on an entire army single-handed?''

Nobody answered for a long time. But I kept my mouth shut, and eventually somebody *had* to speak. It was the king.

"Varay cannot fall while it is defended by a proper Hero.''

"Then I must not be a proper Hero,'' I replied.

"You are,'' Parthet said. "The magic is in you. You know that.''

I remembered the electricity when the king linked our rings, the sensation of power entering and surging through me, all of that. "I don't know what the magic is, how to use it.''

"You mother and I can help with that, some,'' Parthet said. "But more of the magic can only be known by a Hero. Your father would have explained it, but he didn't get the chance.''

"Because he was too busy getting himself killed trying to live up to your idea of the proper Hero?'' I asked. That caused another long silence. Mother broke this one.

"Your father did what he did because he felt it was right. He knew the risks. As you know them. He made his choice.''

"And don't I have the same right? Nobody ever asked me if I wanted any of this. Nobody told me what to expect, what I was going to face. You and Dad kept me in the dark for twenty-one years. I'm the son of the Hero. Does that rob me of the choice my father had?'' The grief I hadn't been able to express before was finally out in the open, but it came out more as anger than grief. I was boiling. All the little snits united at once. I got up and walked across the room while I tried to get myself under control. No matter how justified the anger, this was the wrong time and place for a show of temper. Except for Kardeen, we were all blood kin. The others grieved over my father's death as much as I did. But I had been lied to all my life, had had so much hidden from me, had been trained blindly for a role I was never told about. Everyone took it for granted that I would follow in my father's footsteps. And now they all blithely assumed that I would step right up and pull a rabbit the size of Alaska out of my Cubs cap. I fought with the fire inside, trying to contain it, without much success. A lot of it was pain, emptiness, but there was more, much more. My resentment was genuine and justified. It just picked a poor moment to all come out.

"Gil?" It was Mother, standing just behind me. I turned. We were alone in the room. The others had left, too quietly for me to notice.

"No one wants to rob you of free choice," she said. "If this hadn't come up when it did, we'd have told you all about Varay. We planned to bring you here to show you. Your twenty-first birthday. We thought you'd have all the time you needed to learn about Varay and make up your mind."

This time, she waited for me to break the silence.

"That still leaves a lot of years when you could have told me. My whole life's been based on a lie, and all I get is a note and 'we were were going to tell you soon.' It's not enough. It wouldn't have been enough if Dad hadn't got himself killed. All those *years!* Dammit, what the hell did you think you were doing with me? I've got plans of my own. I'm just six weeks short of a degree in computer science. I've got prospects of a good job as a software engineer, maybe a chance to strike it rich on my own with some innovative software. I'm good at it, damn good. Maybe live in Silicon Valley, find the perfect wife and beat the odds on divorce. I never made plans to be king of some hole-in-the-wall country no one ever heard of. How *could* I plan for that? Nobody told me that my great-grandfather is a king. Or that funny old Uncle Parker is a wizard, for God's sake. I'm nobody's damn puppet to jerk around." I ran out of steam. I was breathing hard, and I needed to slow it down. Mother just waited.

"I'm sorry about Dad getting killed," I said. "That hurts me just as it hurts you. But if I wanted to be a soldier, I'd have enlisted in the army back home." I walked past her, toward the door. Halfway there, I stopped and turned.

"Home. That's where I'm going. This isn't it. Unless I've completely lost track of time, I can still get back to Evanston before spring break ends." I waited for Mother to say something, but she just looked at me. Finally, I left.

I had spotted a number of doors with silver tracing in the keep, and I knew the door I wanted. I went back to my room and ditched Lesh and Timon. I told them to go down to the great hall, and I was still mad enough that they didn't argue. The doorway from the bedroom to the privy in the outer wall also led home. The castle didn't really have running water, but it did have sewer pipes. There was a wooden bucket to dump water down the toilet. I stopped just long enough to get my pistol from under the pillows on the bed, then I stepped through to home.

It was late Friday, early Saturday. I flipped on the TV to see what was on. Then I went upstairs and climbed in the shower for a long, hot soak, trying to wash out a week's dirt. I wished I could just wash out the week's events too—or a little more. I had the radio blaring in my bedroom, trying to exclude thought. It worked fairly well. When I came out of the shower I was relaxed and sleepy. I fell asleep almost at once.

But a person can sleep only so long, and I had slept most of Friday in Varay. It was four in the morning by the clock-radio when I woke, as alert as could be—no chance of getting back to sleep.

I got dressed, took Dad's Citroën, and found an all-night diner along the interstate east of town. I waded through two of their $2.99 breakfast specials, a half-dozen donuts, and four cups of coffee. I sat in the corner and watched other customers come and go. It was a long way from breakfast at Castle Basil, but I still had that insatiable appetite. I almost ordered a third breakfast, but the waitresses started giving me strange looks, so I paid my tab and left.

The night air was damp. Louisville had received a lot

of rain in the past couple of days. I overheard that in the restaurant. The air felt wet and chilly. Dad's car had a half tank of gas. On the way to the restaurant I had stopped at the bank and used my card in the all-night teller to get out a hundred bucks. Money was no problem. I had a trust fund. I had controlled the interest since my eighteenth birthday. Now that I was twenty-one, the principal was mine too. I had signed the papers before I left school and mailed them to the bank. Twenty thousand a year in interest—or I could take everything out and live like a king for a few years.

"Live like a king." Poor choice of words, I told myself. You saw how the king lives, the kind of life *you* could live.

"I should live so long," I mumbled. I realized then that my trust fund had almost certainly come from Varay. The source was another of the things my parents had never told me about.

I leaned on the steering wheel in the restaurant parking lot. I had a notion to start driving back to school. Nobody would say anything if I took Dad's car. I could drop a note in the mail when I got to Northwestern to let Mom know. If she even bothered to come home. It occurred to me that she might choose to stay in Varay now that Dad was gone. I started driving. I was across the Ohio River, heading north on I-65, before I changed my mind and turned around at the next interchange. The sun was up by then. I had no intention of returning to Varay, but I did figure to leave Mom a note at home, collect as much of my stuff as I could pack in the car, and stop the mail and newspapers. I'd make arrangements with one of the neighbors to look after the place. The orderly mind at work. School didn't resume until Monday, and I could make the drive in seven hours without pushing it. Even if I waited until Monday to go back, I wouldn't miss much at school, just three lectures. Nobody scheduled tests for the first day back from break—at least none of my professors did.

I stopped for groceries on the way home, deli pizzas, TV dinners, a couple of cartons each of Pepsi and Michelob. I stashed everything, then looked through the house, just in case Mother had come along to persuade me to return to Varay. She wasn't there, and that sort of surprised me. I was sure she'd hotfoot it home after me, or send Uncle Parker.

Maybe I missed something as a teenager, but I never had a real rebellious period. Dad and I had too much fun together. That's all I thought it was at the time. I didn't know that I was being bamboozled, secretly groomed to be a royal swashbuckler. Walking out of Castle Basil in a huff was my first real experience at rebellion. I wasn't sure what to expect. Sure, I was twenty-one, legally of age, financially independent, but I still expected Mom to come drag me off by the ear. *"You'll do what you're told, or else."* That was part of my anger at the whole situation, I guess.

I popped a pizza in the oven and turned on the big TV in the living room to catch the Saturday-morning cartoons—not the new gimmicky ones, but the good old ones. Wile E. Coyote was falling off a cliff when the network broke in with a big news special. Middle Eastern terrorists had been intercepted trying to attach a fifteen-megaton H-bomb below a pier in New York City's Hudson River. The bomb had been captured before the terrorists could trigger it. No one was saying how close the call had been. There was a lot of speculation that there might be other bombs planted in New York or other cities.

Panic time.

All the networks and cable operations were covering the story. Army units were on alert. Searches were "undoubtedly" under way for other bombs. There was a diplomatic flap as we consulted with our allies and with Soviet and Chinese officials. There were thinly veiled hints of massive reprisals against any country that could be tied to the bombs if one went off. One former secretary of defense intimated that such an offending nation would be wiped off the map—without nuclear weapons. There *are* other weapons.

Even with the buzzer on the oven timer, I almost didn't get my pizza out in time to save it. It wasn't *quite* incinerated, but it was the crunchiest pizza I had ever had.

Sitting in front of the tube, I managed to get most of that pizza, and a second one, down. It was midafternoon before the networks started repeating the interviews with their tame experts. I turned down the volume but left it loud enough to hear anything new.

"This can't be real," I said, getting off the couch. I was all set to get back to normal in the normal world. The last thing I needed just then was for terrorists to start playing with nuclear weapons at last.

Okay, you can add delusions of grandeur and paranoia to everything else, but I took it personally. I paced around the living room for a time, then stood by the picture window, looking out but not seeing much.

"Looks like once you go crazy, you can't come back," I mumbled. "It follows you." I recalled Parthet telling me how the different worlds were tied together, how events were reflected from one to the next. Disruption on one side led to increased strength on the other, and vice versa. Any major change hurt the buffer zone. All that mumbo-jumbo. It looked like it was starting. I wondered if it was because of Dad's death, or maybe even because I had walked off the job as Hero of Varay. It sounded farfetched, but not as crazy as the very existence of the seven kingdoms and Fairy.

A little after four o'clock, I gathered up my things, went up to the bedroom, and walked through the doorway leading back to the bedroom in Castle Basil.

9

Arrowroot

I didn't have any solid plans when I stepped back through to Castle Basil. I hadn't been consciously thinking about Varay's problems. At the start, I was too upset to worry about them, and later there was the bomb in New York to occupy my mind. But once I decided to go back, a few basic premises clicked to the front of my central processing unit. Maybe some of that training that Dad had insisted on over the years was finally taking over. I might be the rookie, but Dad had drilled all of that military nonsense into me. One thing was obvious. Hero or not, there was no way one man could handle a two-front war. I had to either make sure that the Varayan army only had to face one enemy or find a way to get that army back and forth between fronts fast enough to keep both enemies at bay without wearing out our troops. That's how the Saxons lost England to William the Bastard, among other examples. It may still be impossible for anyone to be in two places at the same time, even in a magical world, but maybe we could come close enough for government work. I had an idea . . . *one* idea.

There was no one in "my" bedroom in Castle Basil. I didn't see anyone until I entered the great hall. A dozen or so people were lounging around or working—including Lesh, who was draining a tankard of beer.

"Where's Parthet?" I asked loudly. That got everyone's attention. But nobody knew where the wizard was, so I went to check his room in the castle and then headed for Baron Kardeen's office. Lesh stayed with me, but I moved too quickly to give him a chance to ask the questions I could see he wanted to spring.

Parthet was just leaving Kardeen's office when I got there.

"We need to talk right now," I said, "somewhere private. And we need that big map."

Parthet nodded. "Kardeen has the map." We got it and went up a circular stairway to a room above the chamberlain's office in the tower. I told Lesh to stay at the door and make sure we weren't disturbed by anyone but Kardeen, the king, or my mother. I couldn't have excluded them if I wanted to.

Inside, Parthet unrolled the map across a table that was much too small for it. The ends of the map drooped toward the floor.

"First off, I need to know more about the magic doorways," I said. "Can I take other people through them?"

"Once you open the way, anyone can use it—while you hold it open."

"How do I open a new passage?"

"First, you line the doorways on each end with sea-silver. If there are two of us available—and there are only four of us who wear the twin rings now—one stands at either end of the passage, rings on the silver. Then we have to concentrate on each other until the connection opens and we're face-to-face. It usually only takes a few seconds, or seems like it. If you have to open a passage alone, you line the first door with silver, then look through the way you'll see the room or whatever from the other end. Fix that scene firmly in your mind while holding the rings against the silver. Then you have to go to the other end—the hard way, I'm afraid—line the door there, put the rings against the silver, and concentrate on the room at the other end until it appears. Then you step through to fix the passage."

"Where do I get the silver and how do I attach it to the door?"

"Getting the silver is the snag," Parthet said. "It grows only in the Mist, off certain beaches along the Isthmus of Xayber." He pointed out several locations near the top of the map. The map showed only the nearest portion of the isthmus—I guess the part that sometimes became part of the border or something. "There are probably other areas, but those are the ones I know of, the nearest ones."

"Behind enemy lines."

"Yes," Parthet agreed. "But once you have the weed, attaching it is simple. Start at the floor with one end and press it in place. If the first strand isn't long enough, just overlap the ends the least little bit. The sea-silver adheres easily. You just have to make sure that it remains wet from the time you harvest it until you use it."

"I don't suppose there's a doorway leading to one of those beaches?"

Parthet shook his head. "It's unlikely that this magic would work in lands dominated by Fairy anyway."

"What's the nearest point to those beaches that I can reach by doorway?"

"Castle Arrowroot at the edge of Battle Forest and the Mist, where our north shore meets isthmus."

"How long will it take me to get to the silver and back

to Arrowroot?'' One day, I would have to ask why all the castles were named after spices, but not right then.

"Eight days if everything goes perfectly, and *nothing* ever goes perfectly for mortals inside Fairy. Ten days is a more realistic minimum, and two weeks is yet more likely—if you can make it in and back at all. That's never certain even in peacetime. And the Elflord of Xayber will know when you enter his lands.''

"Tell me about him.'' I studied the map while I listened to Parthet. The map was almost devoid of detail for the isthmus, not much help at all.

"There's little enough I can tell,'' Parthet said. "He's an elflord, quite literally larger than life. No one in the seven kingdoms knows his real name. Likely no one outside him immediate family has ever known it. Like most creatures of Fairy, he considers his name his most closely guarded secret, lest it be used to conjure spells against him. He is apparently something of a rebel in Fairy, even by their loose standards, refusing to acknowledge the authority of their king—the Elfking. But they take no action against him unless he raids the domains of other elflords. That's pretty standard for that lot—'I don't give a damn what you do as long as you don't do it to me.' Xayber has a motley army of human renegades and fairy creatures. Freebooters, brigands. Xayber has powerful magics at his command and a deep hatred for all the people of the seven kingdoms, even the turncoats who serve him.''

"Can we get him to leave us alone for a time? Will he agree to a truce?''

Parthet snorted. "The only way you could get him to leave us alone would be to kill him, except that he probably can't be killed, not by a mortal. The only thing that might deflect his attention from us even for a short time would be an attack on his lands by another elflord, and that is unlikely.''

"How long would it take to ride from Arrowroot to Castle Thyme?''

"Four days if you ride like a host of demons is at your back. Four and half, maybe five, if you want to make sure your horse survives the ride.''

"I'd be better off coming back here to start the ride."

"Or here." Parthet stabbed his finger at the map. "Castle Coriander, inside Battle Forest. It has part of our army too, and you could make it to Thyme from Coriander almost as quickly as from here."

I continued to stare at the map, focusing hard. I don't have a photographic memory, but I wanted to absorb as much of the map as I could. Parthet waited patiently. There *might* be time, if I could do anything right in the north.

"Can you get a message through to the Elfking with your magic?" I asked. Something Parthet had said a couple of minutes before had given me a second idea—if it was worth anything.

Parthet had to think about it. "I'm not sure, but it may be possible. I've never tried to communicate directly with anyone in Fairy."

"You have a pen and paper?"

He dug out the pad and pen he had used at the inn in Nushur. I wrote large, thinking of Parthet's poor eyesight, and used several pages of the pad to finish my note.

"The activities of the Elflord of Xayber are already causing major disruptions in the mortal world beyond the buffer zone. His assaults on the seven kingdoms threaten the stability of your realm also. He seeks this chaos to make possible his usurpation of your throne. Gil Tyner, Hero of Varay."

I gave the pad to Parthet, and he read it with some difficulty, moving his arm in and out until the letter focused for him.

"Is any of this true?" he asked when he finished reading.

"Most of it, I think." I told him about the nuclear bomb. "The rest seems likely as well, don't you think?"

"It's possible, perhaps possible enough to start something."

"If you can get the message to the Elfking."

"I'll do what I can."

"Now, suppose we reconvene the meeting I broke up yesterday."

* * *

I didn't say anything about my abrupt departure or the reasons for it. I did tell everyone about the nuclear bomb in New York and my guess that it was related to events in the buffer zone. The others all nodded. Even King Pregel seemed to understand the implications of nuclear weapons. There might not be TV or radio in the buffer zone—not even a newspaper as far as I knew—but that didn't mean that the elite was totally ignorant of our world. They couldn't afford to be.

"I'll try to get the Elflord of Xayber off our backs, if just for a few weeks, so we can concentrate on the Etevar," I said. "I've given Parthet a message to send to the Elfking. I'm going after sea-silver. If I get a chance, I may spend a day or two pretending to be the army of some other elflord marauding in Xayber." That last was a throwaway, a chance thought that came while I was talking. It sounded pompous as hell, but nobody even blinked.

"If I can sidetrack Xayber, so much the better. We can use the sea-silver to move the army east to meet the Etevar. If I can't sidetrack the elflord, the silver becomes even more important. We'll set up passages from Arrowroot and Coriander to Thyme so we can move troops back and forth to cover both fronts. When I get back from the isthmus with the sea-silver, I'll set up the doorways at the northern castles, then ride to Thyme, to that cottage in the orchard, to set up the other end. With me there and either Parthet or Mother handling the doors in the northern castles, we can keep the passages open for the troop movements." I gave them a moment. There were no questions. *The Hero* was speaking words of salvation. They were eating it up. It gave me a sick feeling.

"In the meantime, it might be wise to strip the rest of the kingdom of every possible fighting man and move them east."

"It sounds risky, but it's the only chance we've seen that offers any hope at all," Pregel said when I paused again.

Heaven help us all, I thought. But I took it as a go-ahead.

"Mother, there's one thing you need to do while I'm

gone. First thing Monday morning, take Uncle Parthet—
hog-tie and drag him if you have to—to Louisville. Take
him to one of those one-hour eyeglass places. Get his
eyes tested and buy him a half-dozen pairs of unbreak-
able, unscratchable glasses with those neck chains to keep
him from losing them off his face.'' Parthet looked embarrassed, more so when the rest of them laughed.

"Uncle," I said, putting my hand on his shoulder,
"we need you at your very best for this. We may need
every magic you know before it's over. And since you
need to see well to do your magics, cracked eighty-year-
old glasses just won't cut it."

"You're right, of course," Parthet said sheepishly. "I
should have done long ago, but I never find the time."

"Is there anything else we need to do right away?"
Pregel asked. His willingness to defer to my plans so
easily, so completely, gave me mixed feelings. It was
heartening that he trusted me, but it was also discour-
aging, to say the least. If the wild ideas of a novice were
the best Varay could manage, we were in deep trouble.

"People, weapons, and food," I said. "As much as
we can start moving east, I'd say. And whatever author-
ization I'm going to need to get things moving in the
north. Those people don't know me."

"I'll prepare a warrant for the royal seal," Kardeen
said.

"You go with the full authority of the crown," Pregel
added.

A damn blank check. That gave me more chills. But
there wasn't much more to be said right then. I went off
with Mother and Parthet to learn what I could about the
inherent magic of being Hero of Varay. They couldn't
tell me much. There was the greater awareness of danger
that had been mentioned before. The magic was also supposed to convey something of the strength and skill of
Vara, first of the line, the mystical hero-king whose
golden age I was supposed to bring back.

"Your father was secretive," Mother said in answer to
my complaint. "He told me that he couldn't explain most
of the magic, that it might weaken it. You may be able
to pull off your deception in Xayber. It's a guess, but

from hints I picked up over the years, that magic may deceive an elford at a distance. For a time. Not forever.''

"The magic grows on you, with you," Parthet said. "That is the ancient wisdom, and your father said it was accurate.''

It wasn't much. I decided to go to Arrowroot in the morning after a couple of good Basilier meals and a night's sleep. When I got to my room, I found that my entourage had grown. Harkane, Dad's squire, was waiting with the others. When I entered the room, Harkane came to me and went down on one knee.

"I would be honored to serve you as I served your father," he said. There was no way to refuse—especially after Lesh told me that the king had sent Harkane.

We all went to the great hall to eat, and when we got back upstairs after we finished—about two hours later—I told my people what we were going to be doing for the next couple of weeks. "Timon, you'll be okay here while we're gone," I added.

"My place is with you, lord," he said.

"Not this time. We ride to war, to Fairy and Dorthin. It's no place for a boy your age." He argued longer than Lesh or Parthet would have. Even when I made it a flat order, Timon sulked.

"You did right, lord," Harkane said when we were more or less alone. "Your father always left *his* page behind when the danger was greatest also." I felt that it was a presumptuous remark for a squire new to "my service," but I was glad he'd made it. Varay was still strange to me. I thought that by local standards. Timon might be right, that he did belong with me, even on such a ridiculously dangerous mission. But there was no way I was going to haul a kid his age along on what might be as suicidal a quest as my father's last one.

I lay awake for a long time that night, second-guessing my decision to return to Varay, and trying to put together a more solid plan for its defense. But no matter how I stirred the mix, I was going to have to ad-lib most of it, and that didn't feel very smart to me. The algorithm was full of bugs. After midnight I got up and headed down to the crypt. Alone. I managed to get out of the room without waking the others by taking the scenic route. I stepped back into my parents' bedroom in Louisville, went down to the basement, and stepped back through to a different part of the castle. Some of the rigmarole was sinking in. I took my sword and knife along. I strapped on the belt almost without thinking. The Hero of Varay *must* be armed.

The route to the crypt wasn't as brightly lit as it had been for the funeral procession, but there were occasional torches along the way, even one inside the burial chamber—fresh, so someone took care to keep a light burning there.

I don't think I went down there to *communicate* with the dead. I never believed that was possible. I'm not sure why I headed almost instinctively for the crypt that night. Maybe *Hamlet* was working on my head again. A stonecarver had been at work, preparing the headstone on the new niche. Dad's name was finished, but not the dates. I put my hands against the stone. Cold marble. In my mind, I talked to Dad, told him what I was planning to try, confessed that I was scared, that I didn't see how I could possibly pull it off. No matter what kind of front I put on for the living folks upstairs, I still didn't know what I was doing, I was scared, and I wanted to run for home and try to forget the whole nightmare.

Dad didn't answer.

It was appropriately chilly in the crypt, and I got hungry almost at once, as ghoulish as *that* might sound. But I didn't leave. I was in no real hurry to get out of the crypt, and that surprised me.

It was eerie. The slightest noise echoed over and over, forcing me to pay attention, to look around me almost constantly, as if someone might sneak up on me down there.

I looked at the capstones on the other niches. There were a lot of them. The dates weren't A.D. or B.C., so I couldn't place them absolutely, but the numbers ranged from a high of 3713 down to a death date of 177 on the stone labeled Vara, right in the center. Looking at the wall, it was kings to the left and Heroes to the right.

Something happened. I don't have any idea what it

was—something just inside my head, I think. I hope. I got so frightened, though, that I almost chickened out and ran for home again. When I could control the panic, I forced myself to stand there and look at the wall of burial niches again. I wondered where they would put me when the time came, if I served as both Hero and king. Which end would be mine? Or would they start using the other wall and put me in the middle opposite Vara? Gloomy thoughts in a gloomy place. Of course, the odds looked good that the question wouldn't arise. I might easily end up in the vault before Pregel. I assumed that that would put me next to my father, or just above him.

Gil Tyner, King of Varay? It sounded crazy, absurd. There was a surrealistic air about the entire situation. That feeling was as dangerous as the Elflord of Xayber or the Etevar of Dorthin. Maybe I hoped that standing in the crypt where we had buried the last Hero would help etch the reality in my mind. How *can* you prepare for mortal danger, make it feel as real as it has to feel? I didn't have a drill sergeant to scream at me, or banner headlines in newspapers and network anchormen wailing about a war. No jingoistic propaganda, no visible evidence of the danger but that stone on my father's burial niche.

I guess I spent a couple of hours there, standing before the rows and layers of dead kings and heroes while my mind drifted wherever it wanted to go. Part of the time I thought about things Dad and I had done together. At times I could almost hear him talking to me—memory-talking, not spirit-talking—bits of lessons he had taught me, even some of the corny jokes he liked to tell just to hear people groan. I tried to come to grips with my resentment over the secret life my parents had led. Maybe all parents lead lives their children don't know about, but this was something more than a teenager's shock at learning that his ''ancient'' parents still enjoyed sex.

There was no way to recover the years of lies, no way I could change my own past to include Varay—despite Parthet's philosophy of history. Maybe I couldn't even extinguish the resentment I felt, but I couldn't let it fester. Forgive and forget? Not exactly. I wasn't ready to tell

Mother, "That's all right what you did to me," because it wasn't. And I certainly didn't expect to forget.

I was as trapped as any of the people in those burial niches, and I was still alive to suffer the frustration of the trap.

Finally, I climbed the stairs back to my room. I even slept for a time, and this time there were no dreams. After a hearty breakfast and a round of farewells, I opened the passage to Castle Arrowroot and stepped through with Lesh and Harkane.

My war was about to start.

10

Annick

The waters of the Mist lapped at the curtain wall of Castle Arrowroot, a constant background music. The castle sat at the angle where the coast bent north to form the Isthmus of Xayber. A broad moat wrapped around two-thirds of the fortress and connected with the sea, making the castle an island, all to itself. Castle Arrowroot wasn't overly large, but its walls were high and thick, a weapon of war guarding one of Varay's most vulnerable border areas. Our point of entry was in a corridor leading from the outer battlements to the keep. Lesh knew the layout of the castle and headed us toward the great hall. The first person we met was a garrison soldier. Harkane announced me in a drill-field voice, and got through the spiel without a crack in it.

"His Highness Prince Gil, Hero of Varay, wishes to be shown to Baron Resler, Castellan of Arrowroot." Even though Harkane's voice wasn't solidly sunk into its adult register yet, he sounded fairly impressive.

The soldier bowed his head toward me and said, "At once, Your Highness." Then he led the way.

Baron Resler was still at the table, eating breakfast with fierce determination, a scowl apparently glued to his face. The garrison soldier announced me with a flourish.

Everyone stared for a moment. Resler stood and made a formal bow and greeting. He was about five foot six, built wide and solid but without visible fat. He was a military man. That was clear in his face and in the way he moved. His face was weathered, his beard trimmed, his hair rough-cut but shorter than most men wore it in Varay. Bushy eyebrows were separated by the deep vertical furrows of a perpetual frown that had nothing to do with his mood.

"Will you breakfast with us, Highness?" he asked.

"We ate before we left Basil, but perhaps a morsel or two, and coffee." I saw a steaming pitcher on the table. "Don't let me interrupt you."

Resler took me at my word. He seated me at his right and went on eating while a page brought me a platter and utensils, and poured coffee. I had to remind the boy not to give me heaping portions, just a sampling of everything. Eat, eat, eat, etiquette and need—a need I didn't fully understand. Lesh and Harkane found seats lower on the table. They showed no reluctance at shoveling in another full meal even though they had eaten at least as well as I had at Basil.

"We don't have time for social graces here," Resler said around his chewing. "We plunge right into the business at hand, even in the midst of a meal . . . if you have no objection."

"No objection at all, Baron." The coffee was stronger and more bitter than the usual brew at Basil. If you weren't expecting it, that coffee could cross your eyes. "I need the three best horses you have, this morning, and you need to get ready to move virtually all of your men to Castle Thyme about two weeks from now. The reasons for that will have to wait until we're alone." I took out the warrant that King Pregel had signed and sealed. Resler wiped his hands on his wool robe before he took the document and read it.

"The wizard was here two days ago," he said when he finished. "I knew your father, of course. I grieved to hear of his end. You look a lot like he did when he was younger." Resler's voice was gravelly, even when he spoke softly.

"The grief has to be postponed for now," I said. "We have to worry about all of Varay."

Resler nodded solemnly. "Perhaps we should go to my apartments to discuss what needs to be discussed."

At Arrowroot, meals didn't end when the big shots got up. I doubt that anybody even noticed when we left. Once Resler and I were alone, I told him the essentials of my plan.

"I know of the doorways, of course, but I never considered that they might be used to move an army," he said.

"That depends on my being able to get fresh sea-silver out of Xayber." I reminded him, not sure that he knew about the weed or its use. "That's why I need your best horses for my men and me."

"You'll get them. When will you leave?"

"As quickly as possible. You know the situation here far better than I do. What's the best time and route? What will give us our best chance to avoid the elflord's forces?"

"There's no certain time or road." He lowered his head and thought about it, holding up a hand for silence when I started to speak. "I think I'd best give you some idea what we face here first," he added.

'I'd appreciate that." The views of the man in charge at the scene had to be better than what I'd gotten at Basil.

"Things get powerful confusing. This isn't a proper little war at all. There are just two main routes from Xayber into Varay. Arrowroot guards one. Coriander sits astride the other. Any large force, any *army,* has to take one or the other—or come by sea—but there are dozens of paths and trails that a small raiding party could take. We have to patrol the coast and halfway to Coriander."

"With how many men?"

"Never enough," Resler said, predictably. What commander ever thinks that he has enough men, supplies, or support? "Right now, I have about four hundred and fifty men. Ten times that wouldn't be enough to do a thorough job, even if we only faced steel and not elfin magic."

"What about Coriander?"

"Baron Dieth has a more vulnerable castle, fewer men, and as much ground to cover."

I knew that manpower was spread thin throughout Varay. By any "modern" demographic standards, the country was more underpopulated than some deserts back home. People had moved to other kingdoms over the centuries. Many had left the buffer zone altogether, fleeing to Fairy or to our world. Varay was too often in the way of invaders.

"Attackers come at any point of our border," Resler said. "When the elflord is feeling particularly strong or cross, he sends his army against the castles and towns. But he's never been able spring a strong enough magic to cut us off from resupply." I understand that he was talking about the magic passages. "More often, though, he just sends raiding parties to attack our villages, burn crops, steal livestock. Usually, the raiders come out of Battle Forest from the isthmus. More rarely, a dragon ship comes out of the Mist to ravage a coastal fishing village and escape before we can respond."

Resler shrugged. "It could be worse. Vara's magic protects us somewhat. The elflord's offensive magics always seem to go awry when he hits us with them. Outside Fairy, those magics aren't always reliable for Fairy folk."

The way Varayan magic didn't work in Fairy or the way my lighter wouldn't work even in Varay, I thought. I wondered if my pistol would work either place. Dad had carried firearms, though they hadn't been with his body, and guns hadn't saved him. It was something else to ask Parthet about when I got a chance. In the meantime, I just had to remember not to count on my gun.

Baron Resler walked to a window. It wasn't glass, but a skin that had been scraped and oiled until it was translucent, then stretched and tacked to a frame. He opened the window and looked out at the Mist.

"I've spent most of my life fighting forces out of Fairy," he said. "Oh, there are months, even years at a time, when the elflord makes no trouble, but we can never be sure. We can't stop our patrols. We never know until our people spot his, or until he attacks. He never tires of it. Over and over your father put his mind to the problem without success." Resler turned to look at me again.

"You can't imagine how weary I get of the fighting, how I long to see the old prophecies come true."

"What prophecies?"

"That we'll have us a new golden age when the same man is both Hero and King of Varay."

I thought, Oh shit, not again. But I just said, "You think that will stop the attacks out of Fairy?"

"How could the age be golden if this warfare continued?"

I didn't try to answer that.

"We've lived a long time on hope," Resler said, turning to the window again. I shook my head. He was another True Believer who though that a vague legend could do what all his years of experience couldn't. I waited, and the melancholy mood seemed to lift from him.

"You were wanting suggestions for your route," he said. He strode across the room to me. "There is no certain way, but your best chance is to stay in the forest, fairly close to its edge, near the Mist. Any force traveling the western side of the isthmus would take the open road along the beaches and bluffs. You might chance upon a patrol in the forest, but perhaps not. Speed is essential. The elflord knows when outsiders trespass in Xayber. You may have one other problem. Lately, we've had two dragons flying south out of Xayber to hunt. They haven't raided right around here yet, thank the Great Earth Mother, but dragons are nothing if not unpredictable."

"That's all I need," I muttered. "We'd better get started, unless it's safer to start after dark."

"Light or dark means nothing to creatures of Fairy, so there's no call to wait on that account. Come, Highness, we'll find you horses and such food as you can carry."

It didn't take long to outfit us. Lesh and Harkane chose lances from the castle's stock of weapons to go with their swords and knives, and Lesh added a wicked-looking battle-axe. I had my own weapons, all of them. The horses were excellent by appearance, a coastal breed with long hair. They were smaller than Gold or his ilk, but they looked strong, and the chief groom said they could stand the greatest rigors of a campaign. Resler told the groom that we were to have the best in the stable. The groom chose them, and Lesh signaled his satisfaction. I accepted Lesh's judgment, because I didn't know enough about horses to contradict him.

When we headed for the main gate, the portcullis was down and the drawbridge was up. Resler took no chances of being surprised. While we waited for the gate to be opened, I glanced up at the ramparts between the gate towers and saw a young woman staring down at me. Her long blond hair blew freely. She was dressed in dark green with a thick leather belt around her waist. I smiled. She nodded, so slightly that I though I might have imagined it.

"You know the lady above the gate?" I asked Lesh softly.

He glanced up. "What lady?" I looked again and she was gone. I described her, and Lesh shook her head. "I don't recall anyone like that, but it's years since I was here last."

The portcullis went up, the drawbridge went down. We walked our horses across the rough-hewn surface of the bridge.

There was a large, open plaza between the castle and its town. Built at the shore, Castle Arrowroot didn't have the advantage of height that helped protect Castle Basil. The near edge of the town was two hundred yards from the moat. The buildings were lower than the curtain wall as well. The plaza and streets were paved with stone. The houses and shops seemed considerably more substantial than those in Basil Town, and the roofs were of timber or slate rather than thatch. Arrowroot had a different feel to it than Basil Town. Basil was open and friendly. Arrowroot was closed and suspicious. There were no open shopfronts, no tradesmen plying their crafts in full view of passersby. Apart from the three of us, there weren't any passersby. The lower stories of the town were made of stone, and the doors looked formidable. Living under the immediate threat of attack left a mark that I could almost feel as we rode through the silent streets.

"They don't take much to strangers," Lesh said.

I grunted, too nervous to speak. I looked around all

the time and wondered if the feeling of—almost—dread was natural or perhaps enhanced by the elflord. That feeling could be a mighty weapon.

We had to wait at the town gate. I thought that the gatekeepers were going to insist on a pass from the baron, but after Harkane made a loud fuss, the gate was opened . . . and quickly closed behind us.

Beyond the town wall—another difference between Basil and Arrowroot—the farm fields provided another clear zone, three hundred yards or more from the walls to the trees. This early in the spring, the crops would offer no cover and little incentive for a raider. Halfway across the cleared acreage, I reined in my horse. I stared at the forest ahead, then turned and stared back at Arrowroot. I felt an equal sense of foreboding in each direction, as if Arrowroot was as dangerous as Battle Forest and Xayber.

"There's magic at work here," I whispered. "Resler said that the elflord's magics fail outside Fairy, but there *is* magic working against Arrowroot."

"How can you tell?" Lesh asked.

"I can feel it, can't you?" Then I realized that he couldn't, that this was my first experience of the heightened awareness of danger that was supposed to belong to the Hero of Varay. "Trust me, Lesh. There's as much danger behind us as there is in front of us."

"Aye, lord, I'll take your word." Lesh looked back. Harkane didn't say anything, but I thought I saw a smug look sneak across his face.

As we started riding forward again, I tried to analyze the feeling of danger, but that didn't help. Danger in front, danger behind—equal. I couldn't localize the feeling or tell what the source of the danger was back in Arrowroot. Or who. But I didn't question my awareness. It was firm knowledge, not nervousness. Once we reached the forest, the danger felt one-sided. The threat from Arrowroot had faded—just a little. Battle Forest was rife with danger. But the sensations still weren't specific. I only knew that there was danger, and I hardly needed the extra sense for that.

Battle Forest was as different from Precarra as Arrowroot was from Basil. Battle Forest felt immeasurably old. The trees were mostly huge firs, some of them hundreds of feet tall. The bark was a dirty gray, cracked and scarred. There were signs of old fires that had burned out the underbrush without killing the trees. In some places, gnarled vines had grown around the trunks. The oldest vines, as thick as my thigh, squeezed the trees, forcing them to grow between the garroting loops. Impenetrable brambles isolated huge tracts of forest, defining the possible routes by their absence.

Nerves made it easy to feel an evilness about the forest, no matter how illogical that feeling might be.

The three of us rode bunched close together. The road was wide and level, and the lowest branches were well above our head, but we bunched up anyway. Whether or not they were conscious of it, my companions must have felt the danger on some level. The horses, more sensible than many people, were clearly uneasy, skittish, unsatisfied with a walk. I didn't want to press the animals, though, certainly not right at the start. If we had to rely on speed once we crossed into Fairy, I didn't want to squander the horses' strength.

A little more than a mile into the forest, we heard the sounds of a horse galloping behind us.

"Off the road," I said. "Lesh, that side. Harkane, here with me." I took my bow from my shoulder and nocked an arrow. Lesh and Harkane had their spears ready, aimed back along the road. We weren't perfectly concealed, but if our horses stayed quiet, we might not be noticed by a racing rider until he was too close to avoid us.

He? It was the blonde I had seen on the battlements of Arrowroot. She reined her horse to a stop before she could possibly have seen us.

"Prince Gil?" Her voice was clear and sounded like a child's. I moved my horse to the middle of the road and eased the tension on my bowstring. Harkane followed me, but Lesh didn't come out until I told him to.

The blonde couldn't have been older than eighteen, if that. She had a sword hanging from her belt and an unstrung bow tied to the side of her saddle, under her right leg.

"Who are you?" I asked.

"My name is Annick." It sounded like *an-neek*. "I live at the castle."

"Why did you follow us?"

"I need to go with you into Fairy. I may be your only hope of getting back alive." I let a beat or two pass. Lesh and Harkane restrained any burning need to inject their opinions.

"I think I need more of an explanation than that," I said.

"My mother is Baron Resler's younger sister, though he hardly admits to that since I was born. That was nine months after a raid during which the elflord's forces briefly occupied part of Arrowroot Town, including the house where my mother lived. She was raped by an elf warrior. That makes me halfelven. Having me along is the cloak of invisibility you need. Xayber won't spot you, at least not as quickly as he would without me."

"Send her back, lord," Lesh advised.

I took the arrow from my bow and returned it to the quiver. I understood that Annick wasn't talking about literal invisibility but about being able to deceive the elf-lord about our identities. I stared at Annick while I tied my bow to the saddle, under my leg, the way she carried hers.

"Why is it so important to you to go with me?" I asked. "Not why I should think it's important. And how do you know where we're going?"

"There's no other place you could be going from here," Annick said. "And since it can't be a friendly visit, you must intend something against the Elflord of Xayber. Why do I want to do?" She snorted and made a face. "Whenever my mother looks at me, she wants to kill herself in shame. She had tried to kill herself, over and over. She blames herself for what that beast did to her. When she sees me, she's reminded of him. My uncle took me from her when I was a baby for fear she would harm me. While the beast who sired me lives, neither my mother nor I will know any peace. And if I can't get to him yet, maybe I can at least help you foil his master's ambitions to conquer the seven kingdoms." It was an impressive speech, full of passion. I wondered if a single word was true.

"Lesh, do you know anything of this?" I asked.

"No, lord."

"Of course not!" Annick snapped. "It's not the sort of tale one spreads."

"It's also not the sort of tale that can be hidden easily in a place like Varay," I said. Servants would talk. Repeated suicide attempts by a lady of note would be hot gossip, even without tabloids and their video sisters. The intelligent decision would be to follow Lesh's advice and send her packing, but I didn't feel any particular danger from her, and if she was by some odd stretch telling the truth, she might be the edge I needed.

"There are no proofs that will open a closed mind," Annick said, and I nodded my agreement.

"I think perhaps you are telling the truth, part of it anyway," I said.

"Your confidence overwhelms me, lord." She didn't try to subdue the sarcasm.

"I don't give a rat's ass whether I overwhelm you, underwhelm you, or just bore you to tears," I said. "If you've changed your mind about wanting to accompany us?"

"I should, but I won't. My quest is too important to me."

Whatever that is, I thought. "Then we've wasted enough time here. Shall we go?"

The four of us rode on through the forest. I hoped I wasn't putting too much stock in my allegedly heightened perception of danger. In any case, it would be easier to keep an eye on Annick if she rode with us than if I had to worry about her tagging along.

11

Xayber

The border between Varay and Xayber was as unmistakable as the Berlin Wall, despite the talk of fluctuations. There was no fence or any other physical barrier, no signposts saying: "You are now leaving the mortal sector." you couldn't *see* any difference, not at first, but we all knew precisely when we crossed the border. Even Lesh felt the change and understood it. The air seemed charged, ionized like just after a vicious thunderstorm. The breeze carried a trace of rotten-egg smell like sulfur water. The forest *felt* sinister. The calls of birds, the rustling of branches and leaves, seemed muted, deadened. The footsteps of our horses seemed to change tone, become hollow. All the scene lacked was the eerie telltale soundtrack music of a killer about to strike to fit right into a mad-slasher movie.

Better get used to it, I told myself. You could have two weeks of this creepy shit.

"You know where we're heading?" I asked Annick after we crossed the border. It was more an attempt to distract myself than a burning curiosity.

"Just that you're invading the realm of the Elflord of Xayber."

"We're going north, staying close to the western edge of the forest and the isthmus."

"Then you must be after sea-silver. There's no other reason for such a journey." She sounded very sure of that, but she sounded very sure of everything she said.

"Do you come into Fairy often?" I asked.

"Only once before. When I was fifteen, I came looking for the beast who raped my mother. I didn't find *him*, but I slit the throats of three of the elflord's soldiers." She talked of killing with a cool passion, the way I might have described a hot date in college. It was chilling.

Our horses needed no urging to pick up the pace. If

we had asked them for a hard gallop, they would have willingly pounded away until they dropped. As it was, we had to check them more often than urge them on, varying the gait to what I hoped was an efficient combination. Our breaks were few and short that first day, taken when we spotted a place where we would be concealed from anyone passing along the road—not that it was much of a road inside Fairy. We had crossed the main coastal route almost as soon as we entered Battle Forest and went on to this track that was obviously little used.

I looked at Annick a lot, when I thought she wouldn't notice. She was attractive, but I wasn't at all attracted. She would fit in a TV commercial easily, maybe playing volleyball in a skimpy swimsuit on a beach full of beautiful people, but she talked like the Count of Monte Cristo justifying his long quest for vengeance. While we rode, Annick braided her hair, then coiled the braid and pinned it so it wouldn't blow in the wind. She rode with the casual assurance of someone who lived in the saddle. I didn't doubt that she could use her weapons with deadly efficiency. Hell, even though she didn't set off my danger signals, she scared the crap out of me. Slender, soft-looking, no more than five-three, she scared me. Not the kind of thing to tell my college chums. Annick seemed to change physically once we crossed into Fairy. It was subtle, like the changes in the air, in the feel of the land. There was something a trifle fuzzy about her outline once we were in the land of her father, something that made it hard to focus on her. Her skin looked whiter, almost ghostly. Undoubtedly, a lot of it was my imagination—*that* was running amok. But she *was* quite different. I was there partly to avenge the death of my father. She was along, according to her, mainly to find and murder *her* father. She was half Fairy and half Varay. I was half Varay and half Kentucky. Maybe the antipathy was unavoidable.

On the map, the Isthmus of Xayber looked like a tornado, a long, narrow funnel touching down on the north coast of Varay. According to the map—and what little anyone back at Basil seemed to know about it—the isthmus was over four hundred miles long, widening as it went north, gradually at first, then more rapidly as it reached what Parthet called the blackheartland of Fairy. Along the stretch that I expected to see, the isthmus varied between thirty and seventy miles wide. Most of it was heavily wooded, and there was a hilly spine to the isthmus, with the hills becoming mountains farther north.

Except for infrequent snatches of conversation, we rode in silence. Lesh rode point. Annick rode beside me, when possible. Harkane stayed close behind. The only alarm of the day came about two hours before sunset. I can't be more precise because my watch stopped when we entered Fairy. I felt danger approaching, a strong signal that I couldn't possibly have missed.

"Off the road," I hissed while I looked southeast. "Dismount. Hold the horses still."

Nobody questioned my orders. Perhaps even Annick believed in the mystique of the Hero of Varay. The feeling of danger grew stronger, but it was several minutes before I found out what had triggered it. I sensed the approaching shadow and was looking in the correct direction when the shadow finally came into sight.

"A dragon," I whispered. I couldn't see the creature, but its shadow was clear. We held our breath while the shadow passed and went on north. I only caught the briefest glance of the flying reptile, a hint of the body eclipsing the sky. When it was gone, I waited for the feeling of danger to fade and disappear.

"Okay, he's gone." I took a deep breath and looked around at my companions. Lesh and Annick looked impressed, Lesh more than Annick. Harkane had his annoying smug look wrapped around his face again. It was almost as if he were a teacher watching me discover what I could do.

We mounted and rode on.

"For being between two warring armies, this forest seems awfully damn deserted," I commented, wondering mainly what Annick might say.

"The armies are there," she said. "The Elflord of Xayber doesn't need a wall of warriors along his frontier. My uncle's troops never cross it."

"We're riding an established trail. *That* should be guarded."

"Perhaps the elflord wants intruders to get far enough to let him play with them," Annick said. "He's totally evil. If he finds us, he'll toy with us as a cat toys with a mouse before she kills it." She stared at me, her eyes almost purple in the late-afternoon light.

"How can you live with such hate?" Harkane asked from behind us. I was surprised to hear him say anything like that.

Annick didn't bother to look back at him. "It's the hate that keeps me alive," she said.

"Then you're the loser, no matter what happens," Harkane said.

"Enough!" I said before Annick could fire another salvo. "Let's start looking for a place to camp for the night." Without Parthet along, we couldn't find a place like the thicket that had sheltered us on the way to Castle Thyme—barely a week before—so we would just have to do the best we could.

We left the road a few minutes later, picking our way through the trees to the right, deeper into the forest. When I could no longer make out the line of the road, we dismounted.

"At least nobody will stumble over us by accident here," I said. That was the only good thing about the site. There was no water and scant grazing for our horses. We got the animals unsaddled, tethered to a picket line, and tended. They couldn't wander far.

Supper was salt beef and bread with a few radishes and onions. I made a mental note to stock up on junk food the next time I got to Louisville. A Milky Way would have tasted great right then. We didn't even have coffee to ease the meal, not that I would have dared a fire.

"We'll take turns standing watch," I said at dusk. "I'll start and wake Annick." I looked at her. "You wake Lesh and he'll wake Harkane. If it's still dark when you get tired, Harkane, you wake me."

We made up our bedding. Harkane set his closer to mine than I liked, but I didn't say anything. Lesh set up by a tree a few yards away. Annick separated herself from the rest of us as much as the glade permitted. When she lay down, she unsheathed her sword and slept gripping the weapon. That may have been as much for our benefit as against the possibility of outside attack.

Darkness came quickly. There was no trace of a moon that should have been past the first quarter, and no stars were visible. Stars shone on the seven kingdoms, even if the constellations weren't always the ones I knew from Earth. With the dark came new sounds in the forest. I recognized the call of an owl, but none of the other sounds. None of the noises were particularly close, and nothing stirred my danger sense. That was idling. I felt danger, but nothing imminent. It was just a constant background, something to remind me that everything about the isthmus, about Fairy, was dangerous.

I sat with my back against a tree trunk, facing the road, and checked my pistol to make sure there was a round in the chamber. That was just something to do with my hands. I didn't really expect the gun to work in Fairy. The actions reminded me to ask Harkane what had happened to my father's guns.

Harkane. I wasn't sure how to relate to my father's squire, my squire now. He was part of the life that my parents had hidden from me. I resented him for sharing that life. And I resented the way he seemed to measure me against my father all the time. He had recovered quickly from his shock and fear at Dad's death. Once I accepted him as my squire, he perked up in a hurry. If a Varayan squire had the same functions as in medieval England—and I wasn't completely certain of that yet—he was supposed to be my weapon bearer and apprentice, learning how to become a knight or whatever. The apprenticeship system applied to the military elite—page, squire, knight. Harkane needed to fill out a little to be a top-notch warrior. He looked as if he ought to be a freshman in high school, dishwater-blond hair cut in what I once heard called a Prince Valiant cut, faded blue eyes.

Lesh was easier to understand. I had been comfortable with him from our first meeting. He was a veteran soldier, stoical, willing to take on anything, as long as there was someone to tell him who to fight and when. Without ever seeing him in battle, I trusted him. Maybe his reflexes wouldn't be the fastest, but there are other considerations that are important.

Now there was also Annick. After a day of concentrated thought, I still didn't know what to make of her. The flaming hatred she made no effort to conceal disturbed me as much as it did Harkane. I glanced her way in the dark but couldn't see her. When I first spotted her on the battlements of Castle Arrowroot, I noticed how good-looking she was, but the hatred and anger she wore turned me off faster than an icy shower. God help the man who tries to rape her, I thought.

I got up and stretched after a while, then walked around a little, being careful to avoid getting disoriented in the dark. After the first flurry of sounds, the forest got unnaturally quiet. The animal noises got rare and farther away, except when our horses moved around. When one moved, they all did, since they were tied together on the picket line. There was no way to gauge time. When I figured that two hours had passed, I took a couple of steps toward Annick and whispered her name. She came awake at once, or she was already awake, and answered. She stood and moved close enough for me to make out her silhouette.

"I'm going to bed," I told her, still whispering. When I got wrapped up in my thermal blanket, sleep was a long time coming.

Sleep. I've always had trouble getting to sleep, even when I was a little kid, but once I do get to sleep, I can be almost as hard to wake as the dead. That's what it was like in my world. In my apartment in Evanston, I used two alarm clocks and a clock-radio to make sure that I wouldn't oversleep and miss classes, and *that* wasn't always enough. Things had been different in Varay, generally. I still had trouble getting to sleep most nights, but I woke fast—except for the evening after the vigil for my father. I had gone so long without sleep before that that I was just out of it. Slight noises could wake me now, like this night. I woke when Annick called Lesh and when he woke Harkane, and a couple of other times. But it wasn't until sometime after Harkane took the watch that my danger sense started screaming and I woke already jumping to my feet and drawing my sword.

"Up!" I shouted. Annick was on her feet almost as quickly as I was. Lesh wasn't much slower despite his age and size.

"What is it?" Harkane asked, startled by the way I'd sprung up. The night was almost gone. There was the feeblest gray light, enough to let me see my companions and our horses, but not much more.

"Listen." I heard something new, a crashing through leaves and small branches. "In the trees." We all heard a brief crunching noise then, closer, louder. I got my bow, then bent over to pull an arrow from my quiver. Annick had to string her bow first.

The next crashing sounds were almost directly overhead. I barely got my bow up in time before the thing dropped on us. *On me.* I pulled back the string and let fly. The creature dove right into my arrow. Annick's shaft caught it from the side. The thing veered and pulled up, climbing back through the trees. But it didn't leave. I turned, looking into the dark of the tree foliage, trying to home in on the creature, whatever it was. All I knew then was that it was damn big for a bird.

It came in low for the second attack, bulleting along head-high, weaving around tree trunks. I let go a hurried arrow that missed, then dropped my bow and drew my sword. I scarcely had time to set my feet and get a good grip on my sword. Again, the beast came straight at me. I held my blow as long as I could, then hacked at the beast's neck as I ducked under its wing. Maybe that wasn't the smartest way to do it. My blade bit in. I was holding on too tightly for the sword to be yanked from my grip, so I went over backward. My butt hit the ground and then my head. The creature nosed into the dirt just behind me and I ended up flipping before I finally figured out that I had to let go of the sword. Before the beast came to rest, Annick's blade and two spears pierced it. The lances pinned the creature to the ground despite its continuing struggles. I got to my feet and retrieved my sword.

"Finish cutting off its head," Annick said. I didn't ask

questions. I was short on air already. I kept hacking until the head rolled forward and came to rest a foot from the neck.

"What is it?" I asked as soon as I could. The wings were still flapping weakly, the body twisting. I wiped my blade on the moss and grass.

"Some creature of Fairy," Lesh said—as if that were all that mattered. No one rushed to be more specific, so maybe that *was* all that mattered.

I got out my flashlight. Looking at the creature in light didn't help me identify it. The face was a grotesque parody of a human face. Thick, wiry hair reminded me of a picture of the gorgon Medusa. The wings were leathery and ended in distinct hands—long, six-fingered hands with claws that were four inches long. The chest and shoulders were thick and heavily developed, but the body tapered off quickly behind the wings. Annick spitted the head on her sword and held it up. The jaw fell open to disclose a herd of pointed teeth. Annick studied the face for a moment, then used her sword to flip the head off into the forest.

"Best to get that as far from the body as possible," she said, bending to clean her blade. "Some of these creatures can put themselves back together if they're given the chance." I looked at the still-twitching body and fought back a rush of nausea. I turned off my flashlight and put it away. I had seen enough . . . too much.

"We'll leave as soon as it's light," I said. I backed away from the body just as its nearer hand made a weak grab for my ankle. I hopped farther away, in a hurry.

"What do we have to do, burn the son of a bitch?" I asked. My voice may have been a little shaky.

"That might help, or it might just rise whole from the ashes," Annick said "There's no way to know for certain."

"Leave it to me, lord," Lesh said. He went back to his stuff and got his battle-axe. He chopped at the creature, and I was glad to leave it to him. I turned away and started getting ready to leave. The sounds of Lesh's butchery kept my stomach on edge. I guess the others felt queasy too. Nobody suggested breakfast before we got back on the road.

It was a day for strangeness. The forest turned weird early on. Crazily deformed trees first showed up as an occasional oddity, then became more common until most of them were bent in strange shapes. Some were knotted like pretzels. Others rose a few feet, then bent parallel to the ground, with most of the greenery on the top half and squat branches below supporting the weight. The leaves and needles became gray-green. A bird with a call like a mocking laugh followed us through much of the day but stayed out of sight. The laugh was perhaps the eeriest sound I've ever heard. The trees and the birds— those weren't the only problems. The streams were far apart and never more than a trickle. Our horses wouldn't drink from the first three we came to. They sniffed at the fourth for minutes before they decided to chance it, and they had to be awfully thirsty by then.

Twice that day we left the road to hide from approaching soldiers, coming down from the north. The second band had nearly two hundred riders. We were close enough to hear talking but not what they said.

"Baron Resler's in for a rough go," Lesh said as we mounted up again after the second group of riders were out of sight. "A lot of new soldiers heading his way."

"My uncle won't have the rough time," Annick said. "It's the men he'll send out to fight. *He* hasn't left Arrowroot in years except to attend banquets at Basil, and then somebody always opens a passage for him."

For our second bivouac in Fairy, we found a place near the stream the horses were willing to drink from. A horizontal tree with heavy foliage was between us and the road. There were enough other trees around to shelter us from the eyes of anyone riding by or flying overhead. Sleep was harder to come by that night. Memories of our visitor of the previous night intruded. We kept the same rotation on our watches. Annick was on guard when I finally dozed off, but the last thing I remember thinking was that it must be about time for her to wake Lesh.

When my danger sense flared, I didn't leap straight up. There was nothing so compelling propelling me this time.

The extra sense was more discriminating than a burglar alarm. I woke, listened for a moment, then got up on one knee. "Lesh? Harkane? Annick?" Lesh and Harkane answered right away. Annick didn't.

"Annick?" I whispered, a little louder. There was still no answer.

"Who was on watch?" I asked.

"She was, I guess," Lesh said. "She never woke me."

"I didn't hear anything," Harkane added.

I was sure that more than a few minutes had passed since I fell asleep. I had been dreaming, though I didn't recall the substance of my dreams, simply that they had been there, plural, apparently extending over some time. I felt rested, as if it were time to get up for the day.

"Annick?" I called, louder still. I got to my feet with my sword drawn. The feeling of danger was persistent but not immediate.

"Her horse is here," Harkane said.

"We can't look for her in the dark," Lesh grumbled. "Pardon my stubbornness, lord, but I did say you should have sent her back at the start."

I got out my flashlight and used it within the little nook where we had set up our bedrolls. Annick's bedding, saddle, and pack were there, but her weapons were gone.

"Maybe she heard something and went to investigate," I whispered—without any great conviction. "If anything had dragged her from camp, we would have heard the commotion." And, I would have known if anything like that had happened so close . . . at least, I *thought* I would have.

Lesh grunted. We waited in silence, for perhaps an hour, before we heard anything. My danger sense picked up a bit, but I had my sword in my hand, so there was nothing to do but wait—until Annick crept back into camp.

"Where the hell have you been?" I asked when I was sure it was her. My flashlight showed blood on her tunic, but there was no hole in the fabric.

"There's a patrol camped nearby," she whispered. "I became aware of it after you fell asleep." She bared her teeth. "They never heard me. I killed two of them and got away without waking the rest."

"The rest? How many others?" I asked.

"Three. I'd have done them too, but one was stirring." She cackled softly. "I wanted to kill all but one, let him wake to find himself the lone survivor. That would have boiled his brains down to molasses."

"We'll have the elflord down on us for sure now," Lesh said. He didn't have to add another "I told you so" for my benefit.

The elflord or somebody. "You pull another stunt like this while you're with me and I'll throttle you myself," I told Annick. I meant it, though I didn't fully realize that until the words were already out. "Lesh, Harkane. We can't leave survivors to spread the news. Annick, you'll have to lead us back."

"They left a fire burning. You only need to go fifty paces north to see it." But she turned and started walking that way.

I snagged up my bow and quiver, and we all followed her. I shoved the flashlight in a pocket and concentrated on staying right behind Annick. She picked out the trail without difficulty. Baron Resler had said that creatures of Fairy wouldn't be hindered by the dark. Apparently his halfelven niece had inherited that eyesight. The rest of us stumbled now and again. Things got easier once we spotted the campfire. As we got closer, we could see the ground more clearly, as much because of the approach of dawn as for the puny fire.

"They're all human, after a fashion," Annick whispered. "Renegades from the seven kingdoms, mostly from Varay, no doubt. Traitors."

It was easy to see which were already dead. The bloodstains looked black in the dim predawn light and fire glow.

"Lesh, Harkane, work as close as you can to the nearest man. I'll take the farthest and Annick the one in the middle. With your bow," I added in an aside to her.

The job was necessary but not pleasant. I had never aimed a weapon at a human before. The bow wavered in my hands for a moment. It wasn't until Annick loosed her arrow that I was able to shoot my man. Then Lesh got the third. It was over in seconds.

This time, I *did* puke.

12

The Swamp

My rage had a life of its own. For a time, the fury was so consuming that a part of my mind could only stand back and watch in astonishment. For the rest, I had to fight to hold back my temper—a rage far beyond anything I had ever experienced before. We got back to our camp without trouble and hurried to get packed and to saddle our horses. By the time the sky was light enough for us to guide our horses to the road safely, I had been stewing for a half hour. Standing on the road, ready to mount, I finally felt—almost—confident that I could speak my mind without losing control completely.

"I want you to know," I told Annick very quietly, "that I meant exactly what I said about what I'll do if you pull another stunt like that. Either do things my way or get the hell out of here right now." I had to bite off the next sentence that wanted to come out: *I've got no use for mad dogs.* Annick and I stared at each other for a full minute or more before she replied.

"I won't do anything like that again without your approval." There was nothing meek or repentant about her promise. I couldn't even be sure that I could trust it. I could only hope that my danger sense would warn me before she did anything else rash. But as the morning wore on, I noticed that Annick seemed much less tense than she had been during our first days on the road, as if the killings had satisfied some deep addiction—at least for the moment.

It was a little different for me. No, make that a *lot* different. No matter what else happened—*ever*—I would never be the same. I had killed another human being, intentionally, "with malice aforethought." I had stood there in the dark and killed. Simple as that. And blaming Annick for the need didn't get me off the hook. It was my choice, my decision. I had killed and I had ordered my companions to kill.

You *can't* turn back from that.

There was fog that morning. It started patchy, not far north of our camp. At times, our heads were above it, making it look as if our horses were swimming through the clouds. As we moved on, the fog got thicker, totally enclosing us finally, until we could scarcely see fifty feet. For a couple of hours, the road—trail—was particularly rough and hilly as it skirted the line of hills that defined the isthmus. On the high ground, we sometimes rose above the fog. Then the road would drop almost to sea level again, plunging us back into the damp fog. The map at Castle Basil had been woefully shy of detail for the parts of the isthmus it showed. The swamp came as a complete surprise. We reined to a halt as a road dwindled to an uncertain track through the first bogs.

"Did you come this far before?" I asked Annick. She shook her head.

"We could cut over to the coast and follow the beaches," Harkane suggested. "Wc'd make better time and it would be safer riding."

"Until we met the first patrol," I said. I took a childish pleasure in seeing him lose a little of his habitual smugness. "We're not here to fight, at least not until we've got the sea-silver."

"How about we bear east for a bit?" Lesh suggested. "We get back to higher ground, it should be dry."

I flirted with the idea. It was tempting. But I finally decided against it. I didn't want to stray too far from the west coast while we were outbound. I could only find sea-silver along that shore, and I had to have that.

"We'll try to follow what's left of the trail," I said. "The swamp should cut down on the number of patrols we have to worry about. With better routes around the swamp, I doubt that anyone'll be in it—unless they're looking specifically for us." I gave Annick an annoyed glance at that. Far from giving us a "cloak of invisibility,'' her deadly excursion might draw the elflord's forces down on us faster than ever.

The swamp. It was the first one I had ever been in. My expectations came straight out of movies and books. I don't suppose that I was disappointed. Mucking through a swamp offers few attractions for anyone but a masochist. The only good thing about it was that the path never completely disappeared. There was always a safe way, if we were careful. At times I couldn't tell solid ground from mud soup just by looking. The vegetation wasn't even a sure guide. Some of it floated on goop that could almost pass for solid ground. And there were vast pools of algae-filled water, slimy mud pits, pockets of gas that erupted with a stench as a hoof pierced them. Eventually, I had to more or less rely on my danger sense to pick a path through the worst stretches. And even that couldn't keep a horse from an occasional misstep on a narrow track. Moss-draped trees and ground mist complicated matters. But the worst part was the swamp's fauna. We saw sawed-off dragons like the ones I saw when I first arrived in Varay, larger crocodilians gliding through stagnant waters—one of those had to be fifty feet from snout to tail. A four-legged reptile that Lesh called a snake scuttled into a pond as we approached the rock it had been sunning itself on. I *hate* snakes, even if they have legs.

''I'll warrant there's worse in this swamp,'' Lesh said after I mentioned my distaste for snakes.

''Much worse,'' Annick said. ''Any creature of the elflord could be here, and some as are even older— web-footed wolves, lowland trolls, maybe even a full-sized dragon come to wallow in the stinking mud.'' From the prickling of my extra sense, I knew that Annick was right about those other hazards.

Finding our way took all of my attention in the swamp. In a way, I guess that was a good thing. I couldn't dwell on the dead men we had left behind. I knew they would be missed sooner or later. And when the bodies were found, we would have a lot of people and other beings looking for us. Sure, I hoped to cause a bit of confusion for the elflord along the way, but I wanted to get my sea-silver first. Anyway, slitting the throats of sleeping men wasn't the kind of confusion I had figured on spreading.

We didn't take specific rest breaks. Finding safe pathways gave us plenty of idle minutes. Our progress was maddeningly slow. I doubt that we averaged even one mile an hour all day. The sky remained heavily overcast. Three times we were raked by short but furious rainstorms. I decided fairly early in the afternoon to grab the next substantial piece of solid real estate to make our camp for the night. I was exhausted and felt so cruddy from the swamp that I couldn't stand it. We were all dragging.

The solid land we found wasn't much, but no one argued when I said that we were done for the day. The ground was wet after the rain, but it was firmer than most of it we had seen.

We had just started to settle in when I heard a sound that made me think of a pig running from the butcher, and my danger sense kicked into high gear. I got out a quick warning and drew my sword. Then we had a pack of wild pigs grunting and squealing around us—only they weren't quite pigs. Compared to this batch of creatures, Miss Piggy is the beauty queen she thinks she is. The faces were vaguely porcine, down to the flat noses, but on bodies that looked like something dredged out of a really bad science fiction movie. Hairy, bloated bodies with obscenely muscled arms and legs: call it *Attack of the Mutant Body Builders* and show it in 3-D and Smell-ovision. They seemed equally adept at moving upright or on all fours. Standing erect, they weren't too much shorter than me, but they could scratch their knees without bending over. They looked and smelled as if they bathed in outhouses.

Somebody yelled, "Trolls!"

I don't suppose that was the most critical piece of information just then. I already had my sword out. When I saw the trolls, I pulled my knife as well. None of us had much chance to get set before they were on us, rising right out of the muck that surrounded our little patch of terra firma. What followed wasn't at all pretty. The fight wasn't one of those precisely choreographed battles that you see in the movies, where every move is planned and rehearsed down to the last detail before the cameras roll. There were no niceties of fencing technique, no elegant combinations. We couldn't drive the creatures off. They wouldn't retreat, not a single step. All we could do was kill them and try to keep them from returning the favor. Butchery. Slaughter. But it wasn't as simple as working in a charnel house. The trolls carried long knives, hatchets, and clubs. They could fight back—and did. But all they seemed to know of tactics was to run straight at one of us, screaming and waving their weapons. Maybe they thought they were ugly enough to scare us to death. No sense of order or tactics at all. Not much sign of intelligence either. They just charged out of the swamp screaming insanely, right into our weapons.

When they *did* get to us, they did fight, viciously, insanely, on the attack every instant. If there had been just a few more of them, they might have succeeded in putting us on their dinner menu. That, Annick assured me afterward, was exactly what they would have done. Annick did show that she could handle herself against enemies who weren't sleeping, though. She was a berserker, howling as rawly as the trolls. Teeth bared, a blade in each hand, she waded into the fray as if she had been looking forward to it all year—like the prom. Maybe I looked like that too. There were no mirrors handy. Once I crossed blades with a troll, my training—and that strange directional itch that was the proprietary danger sense of the Hero of Varay—took over.

There's really no way to fully convey what a fight like that is like to someone who hasn't experienced it. It's running into an airplane propeller with a blade of your own and hoping you'll come out the other side in one piece. It's a riot of food blenders, and if you make a single mistake, you come out puréed. It's something Americans haven't faced since Vietnam—hand-to-hand combat, deadly face-to-face fighting, win or die. The only alternative to gut-wrenching fear is insanity. You're no longer a civilized being. You're either a feral carnivore or you're dead. Your mind and senses either get hyper-

active, flooding you with sensory input, or they short out
completely, leaving you to fight on mere instinct . . . or
on training drilled in so thoroughly that it's become automatic. Blood and sweat abound in incredible quanti-
ties. The smells become overwhelming. You wield your
weapons. You try to look in every direction at once,
watching for the next possible threat, the next blade or
club coming at you . . . and you try to get your blade
there first.

Hack and lunge. Knee an enemy in the groin, kick him
in the shin, step on his foot, spit in his eye—whatever it
takes to give you that little extra advantage, the millisec-
ond or two you need to get a blade in to finish the job.
Feel the tug of resistant flesh as your blade skewers a
living being—but don't think about it, not then. Drag the
blade free. That can be difficult. Sometimes you have to
brace your foot against the body to drag your sword loose
of clinging flesh. The hafts of your weapons get slippery
with sweat and blood. Your fingers cramp. The steel of
your blades runs red. The ground gets treacherous
underfoot.

The four of us met the blind charge of the trolls. Harkane and Lesh stayed close together, back to back, covering each other. Annick and I were more widely
separated, so our "formation" was almost a triangle,
with the corners just far enough apart that our swords
wouldn't catch on each other's. We fought for an eternity
or two—maybe ten minutes. When it was over, there were
ten dead trolls on our little patch of land and at least two
more had fallen back into the morass they had come out
of. Even more may have dropped back into the swamp.
There was no way to be certain.

When the fight ended, the four of us could do no more
than stand where we were while we caught our breath
and while the adrenaline of our battle frenzy faded from
our systems. There was a numbness that came up behind
the insanity to cuddle us, a paralysis that was more mental than physical. If there had been another wave of the
trolls just then, I'm not sure that we could have defended
ourselves. But there wasn't. Slowly, we came out of our
trances and looked around at each other, verifying that

we had all survived. Everyone had minor cuts, scrapes, and so forth—though they almost escaped notice at first in the general bloodiness. We were all exhausted, especially Lesh, the oldest of us. After grappling with the trolls we were all covered with blood and sweat, and smeared with the muck that had coated them. We smelled at least as bad as the trolls, and there was no clear water around for us to wash in—not nearly enough.

Lesh looked around and found a piece of ground that wasn't covered in gore or bodies and plopped down. "I hope there's no more waiting their turn," he said. "I don't think I could handle it."

"With a little luck," I said, having trouble getting even that much out. I hobbled over to Lesh and took his spear. "Harkane, let's dump these bodies." Harkane nodded. We used the long weapons to lever the dead trolls back into their muck. Those dam trolls sank like lead, even in the thick gumbo of the swamp. We tried to push the bodies away from our tiny shore, but they sank too fast.

And one of them wasn't dead.

I had already rolled three or four bodies into the bog— slow work. I was wedging Lesh's spear under the next troll when he made a grab for my leg. My danger sense didn't warn me soon enough to sidestep him. Maybe the exhaustion that came after battle was responsible for that. And I was a bit off-balance. I fell backward heavily, and the troll was on top of me before I could do anything. The spear fell away and I couldn't get at my sword or knife soon enough. At least the troll wasn't armed either.

He was strong, insanely strong, and heavy. His arms weren't simply as long as a gorilla's, he had the strength of a great ape too. he swung at my head, and even though I twisted away enough to keep him from connecting solidly, his fist scraped my face so roughly that it felt as if he had ripped the cheek off. I took a swing of my own, but I couldn't get much oomph into the punch while I was on my back. His head was out of reach, and beating on his chest didn't seem to affect him at all. I bucked, and we rolled to my left. I got a little freedom and managed to put a little force behind a knee to his groin. He grunted but swung at my head again. This time he stunned me with the blow. My vision went fuzzy and I started to flop over on my back again. The troll went for my throat, but he never got there. The point of a sword emerged from his neck as my eyes cleared. Annick was behind him, leaning forward.

When Annick pulled her sword free, blood gushed from the troll's neck, over my face, clouding my vision again. I may even have blacked out for an instant. I know I was unsteady when I got up, and it was several minutes before Harkane and I could return to the work of dumping the rest of the trolls. But once burned was more than enough. We went around and made sure that the rest of the trolls were dead, poking them with the business end of the spears to make sure that we didn't have any more possums.

After that chore was finished, we did what little we could to get the crud off us, particularly around our cuts. We didn't need six kinds of infection.

13

The Mist

None of us slept much that night.

A bugle call at dawn heralded our next threat. The call was barely audible, smothered by another heavy fog. We got on the trail and pushed on as fast as we could, making more mistakes with the footing in our hurry. We heard horns several more times, tooting sometimes intricate melodies. One horn would answer another. It didn't take too long to deduce that it was more than standard military calls. The music was a telegraph system, and I had no way to read the messages. I assumed that they were about us.

We aimed as close to north as the terrain permitted. If my dead reckoning was working, we would be level with the first of the beaches where the sea-silver grew early that afternoon—if we weren't held up too long by the swamp or by the patrols looking for us. Every time I heard the horns, I cursed Annick silently. Once in a while, I couldn't restrain an angry glance her way. She didn't seem to notice.

Despite the inconvenience they caused, the persistent fog and intermittent drizzle may have helped us, may have concealed us from the hunters. The rain certainly washed off some of the stink remaining from the swamp and the trolls. We continued to hear horns, quite close a couple of times, but we got through the morning without seeing any of the musicians.

Near noon, a new force entered the hunt, a *presence*. It had to be the elflord himself, casting a magic eye about for us, quartering the land to find the intruders who had killed his minions. The first time I felt the probe, I tried to think a blanket of invisibility over us. We stopped, and I concentrated on making us the little people who weren't there. Maybe I couldn't put up an actual shield like Parthet, but I didn't have anything to lose by trying. I felt the probe pass. My danger index lowered fractionally. But I didn't know whether or not we had been spotted.

"Someone's using magic to find us," I told my companions.

"I felt it too," Annick said.

"We may have escaped detection, but we can't count on it," I said. Annick nodded. She seemed almost tranquilized. Perhaps it was just that she was as worn out as the rest of us from fighting the swamp and the trolls, but I still felt that it was the killing that had relaxed her. "I'm going to start looking for a path over to the coast. We should be almost far enough north to find the sea-silver. We may have to hide in the swamp until dark before we cross the beach, though." I stopped when Annick shook her head.

"If the lore is right, sea-silver can't be seen in the ocean at night. We have to harvest it during the day." When it was most dangerous—but it wasn't something I could argue. Annick might be wrong, but she probably wasn't.

"Then we'll have to make do," I said. "We'll get

lined up near a patch of the silver and wait until the coast
is clear.'' The phrasing was accidental, but I had never
heard the cliché used so literally before.

We started bearing left whenever the swamp offered a
choice. It was still slow going, especially since I knew
that we might hit a dead end at any time. There was no
way to swim our horses across open water in the swamp.
Even the most placid-looking ponds were inhabited by
the giant crocodilians and other nasty beasts. Once I
judged that we were heading just a little north of west, I
tried to keep us as close to that heading as possible. The
sky cleared about noon, so I could get a better idea of
the time and our course. The last of the ground fog evap-
orated. The temperature climbed. We continued to hear
horns now and then, but farther off. And finally we heard
the sea.

The sounds of surf hitting the shore drew us on like a
magnet. We hit a long stretch of firm clay within the
swamp and then picked our way through a final marshy
patch. The trees were smaller, pathetic-looking, all bent
east, away from the sea breezes. We stopped in a tight
copse of the dwarf trees and dismounted. Looking
through the grayish greenery, we could see the Mist. Just
then, it looked beautiful.

Beyond our trees there was a narrow stretch of grass
and hard-packed dirt. The line of a wide trail road was
visible, wagon tracks and signs that many horses had used
the trail—recently. The beach beyond the road was of
dark gray sand that stretched off in an arc in both direc-
tions. The beach was wide, maybe an average of five
hundred yards. It went south as far as I could see, but
ended a mile to the north. A massive outcropping of rock
rose two hundred feet above the sand and stuck out into
the Mist like a swollen thumb. Sheer bluffs dropped to
the sea. The waves weren't hitting the beach itself, but a
sandbar farther out. The water near the beach was rela-
tively placid at the moment, but from the driftwood scat-
tered higher on the shore, I could see that it wasn't always
so serene.

The sun came out from behind a cloud and set shards
of crystal in the sand to sparkling in an almost blinding

display. Far out over the Mist we could see a weather front coming in, a line of thick, dark clouds that towered from sea to sky. But in the middle, I could see the silver seaweed gleaming in the lagoon, a thick band of bright silver that followed the arc of the beach from almost directly in front of us north toward the cliff.

Annick pointed. "That's what you came for."

"That's what I came for," I agreed. I looked at the sky and guessed that we had a little more than two hours of good light left. "It would be nice to get a full night's sleep and collect the silver in the morning, but if that storm front keeps coming, the surf may be too rough in the morning." Parthet had told me that the sea-silver grew in water between four and twelve feet deep, allowing for rather modest tides. Even staying at the shallow end of the patch, it wouldn't take much surf to complicate our harvest.

"I don't think we can chance it now, either," Annick said. "Look at the headland." Her eyes were sharper than mine, but I did catch a glint of light on metal and saw tiny figures moving. The movement must have been horses. At more than a mile, I don't think it was the riders.

"There must be a dozen or more of them," Annick said, squinting for a better look.

"Let's get comfortable," I said, suppressing a sigh. "Maybe they'll leave." If not, we would wait till as near sunset as possible, then try to sneak across the beach to get our silver. I slipped my pistol into a saddlebag and took off my sword belt.

"Harkane, help me strip off this tin shirt. I can't wear twenty pounds of metal in the water." We got the mail off. It was a relief. I felt almost light enough to float away. Harkane rolled the mail and strapped it behind my saddle. I put my sword belt back on.

We watered the horses, using the last of the water in the two oversized bags that I planned to carry sea-silver in. When I cut the weeds, I would fill the bags with seawater. Parthet had said that salt water would keep the silver usable longer, but that fresh water would do in a pinch. Since replacing the sea-silver would mean another trip like this one, I wanted to keep what I got in top shape.

The riders came down from the headland and rode our way, spread out across the beach in a loose skirmish line. They weren't riding very fast, so I thought that it might be just a routine patrol, not an attempt to catch us. A long horn call sounded just before they passed our hiding place, but I didn't hear any reply. There were fifteen riders. The one in the center looked like a giant. He wore a long two-handed sword like a claymore, sheathed across his back. I held my breath, but the riders went by without a second look our way.

"Their leader is an elf, or at least halfelven like me," Annick said after the riders were well past us. I assumed that she meant the big guy. One of the bits of lore I had picked up in Varay was that real elves weren't cute little fairy-tale creatures who made shoes at night or any of that nonsense. The elf warriors who rode out of Fairy were neither cute nor little. Parthet had suggested that three hundred pounds spread over seven and a half feet of height was a good average. "None of it fat," he had added.

"Mount up," I said. "If they keep going south, we'll ride for the sea, about halfway to the headland. I'll go in for my silver and we'll get out of here as fast as we can."

"I'll help in the water," Annick said. I just nodded.

We watched the riders. They rode at a slow trot, casually scanning the beach ahead of them. We waited until they were just dots, almost invisible in the distance, before I started riding toward the water. The others followed. On the sand, I prodded my horse into a canter, aiming for the section of shore I had chosen. After the tortuous going of the swamp it felt good to let the horses stretch out for a moment. Breeze in my face, the sea ahead. The horses seemed to enjoy the change too.

"Keep a sharp watch," I told Lesh and Harkane when we dismounted at the water's edge. "Give us all the warning you can if they come back." I handed Harkane my sword and its sheath. They would just get in the way in the water. I kept my knife to work with.

The near edge of the seaweed bed was thirty yards out.

The top of the sea was brilliantly reflective. The silver gleamed like polished metal. Even when the sun ducked behind another cloud, the sea-silver gleamed. Annick and I each carried a water pouch. She had taken off her sword too.

"Ready?" I asked. Annick nodded. We waded in.

The water was frigid. Cool would have been a blessing, but the Mist felt like ice. We waded and floundered toward the sea-silver, moving slowly in the lash and recoil of the current. The undertow threatened to drag our legs out from under us at every step. By the time we reached the seaweed, my knees felt ready to buckle from the strain.

"Cut as low as you can," I told Annick. I pulled my knife, took a deep breath, and dropped beneath the surface.

The cold seemed less pressing once I submerged. I could see well enough, though the salt water stung my eyes badly. I needed a few experiments to find the best way to reap the silver. Then the harvest moved quickly. I gathered in an armful of silver and crammed it into the mouth of the sack, then cut the weed as close to the roots as I could—up for a quick breath and a glance at the shore, then down to gather the next sheaf. It didn't take long. Annick and I finished and were standing there catching our breath when Lesh whistled and pointed south. The patrol was returning.

Annick and I tried to hurry back to shore, but that made it more difficult. We stumbled and fell. Maneuvering the filled pouches of sea-silver and water complicated matters too. We had to keep them submerged so we weren't carrying all that extra weight, forty pounds or more per bag.

Lesh had the two largest horses, his and mine, ready for the pouches. All of the paraphernalia those animals had been carrying had been transferred to the other horses. We got the bags of sea-silver tied behind the saddles and covered with blankets. Harkane returned my sword. I didn't bother with the chain mail. There wasn't time and I didn't want the weight over my wet clothes anyway.

The fifteen riders in the south were clearly visible against the distant sand, but they were still a few minutes away. We mounted and I stared south for a moment, discouraged at the chances of holding our own against so many . . . or escaping from them. I was surprised when my extra sense signaled closer danger from the other direction, but I turned quickly. Another half-dozen riders were coming toward us at a gallop, down from the headland, and they were a lot closer.

I pointed at the six and said, "Head for them," and we did, spurring our horses to a gallop. I drew my sword. I had no intention of wasting arrows trying for an impossible shot from horseback. Annick did try one shot, and her arrow pierced the shoulder of the nearest rider. Luck, blind luck. No archer can guarantee that result once in ten tries when archer and target are both galloping hard at each other. Annick must have realized it too. She didn't try a second arrow. Lesh and Harkane had their spears tucked firmly under their arms. They weren't the fancy lances of medieval movies but they would be effective weapons—sharp metal points on the end of ten-foot long hardwood shafts.

We had no choice but to fight the closer riders, and unless we disposed of those six—five after Annick's lucky arrow—damn fast, the fight would give the larger band time to catch us on the beach. There were simply too many in that group. I wouldn't have been happy with four of us facing just the elf warrior who led the group. His claymore could slice through spears and shatter our smaller swords. The only realistic chance I could see was to get to the swamp and hope that we could lose the elf and his cohort.

Only one of the first five riders looked less than human. His grotesque face looked akin to the swamp trolls, but this one was wearing clothes and armor. Annick skewered him as our groups collided. He wasn't nearly as fast as she was . . . or maybe he just didn't have the motivation. That evened the immediate odds, but none of the others were so cooperative.

It was something more than paranoia that made me think that these riders, like the swamp trolls and the weird flying creature we met on our way north, were all aiming specifically at me. You're paranoid if you think "they" are out to get you and "they" aren't. Well, you may still be paranoid if "they" *are* out to get you, but it's not a delusion then. It's real. I wasn't wearing a sandwich board that said "I'm the Hero of Varay" on one side and "Come and get me" on the other, but I didn't have to make any great mental leap to decide that these creatures of Fairy must somehow be able to sense that I was the one to focus on.

The four riders who were left after Annick got rid of two of their comrades certainly seemed determined to reach me. My companions were just a distraction—though a deadly distraction. But we were evenly matched, thanks to Annick, so I only had to face one enemy right off.

I had never attempted fencing on horseback. A gap in my education as a swashbuckler. And all of those years of learning what to do with my feet and body while I parried and feinted and lunged, all the wild language of formal fencing, were wasted when I crossed swords on that beach.

Maybe that's going a bit too far. The situation was novel, but I did manage to get my sword up to block the blade that was swung right toward my nose. The other guy might not have known from *quarte* or *sixte,* so we started out fairly even. He was more a hacker than a fencer, and I don't mean that he played with computers. All I had to do was keep getting my sword in the way of his until our horses danced around enough to let me get past his guard. I didn't worry about style either. And I didn't wait to see him fall. As soon as I pulled my blade free, I kneed my horse and pushed past to reach Harkane. He was in trouble.

Harkane backed away as I caught his opponent from the side. There was no trouble with elegant form this time either. My first swing bit about halfway into my foe's upper arm. He turned toward me but couldn't do much to defend himself. He managed to block my next blow, but not the lunge that caught his throat after that.

I didn't waste time looking south for the other group of riders. I didn't need to look. I could feel the elf warrior and his band getting closer, and, near the end of my second duel, I could feel something more deadly than a host of elf warriors.

Harkane and Lesh combined to dispatch the last member of the small patrol. I looked south and then up finally . . . and saw death overtaking the elf's band. An immense shadow drew my eyes upward. A dragon was swooping down toward the galloping riders.

"To the swamp!" I shouted at my companions. We raced northeast, but we kept looking back over our shoulders toward the group pursuing us and the dragon pursuing them. The elf drew his six-foot sword, looked back, and kicked at his horse's flanks, looking for more speed from the already-overtaxed steed. The elf's head turned left, then right. Maybe he was shouting at his men. He was still too far away for me to be certain. His men spurred their mounts on, hardly needing encouragement, trying to outrun the flying death behind them.

It was an impossible flight.

"Hold up!" Annick shouted behind me, after we had crossed about half of the beach. "The dragon chases motion."

I reined in quickly. There wasn't time for a round-table discussion on the subject, but it made a certain kind of sense. We dismounted and moved to our horses' heads to hold them as still as possible. The horses weren't happy about sticking around.

I saw a large blob fall from the dragon.

"What's it doing, bombing them?" I asked softly. It wouldn't have surprised me.

"Just lightening up, I expect," Lesh said. "Dropping a load of crap from his last meal." Lesh's snort wasn't quite a laugh. "I've seen dragon droppings. Must drop more'n ton at a time. One of those turds hits you, you've had it." He was serious. That was obvious, but the image he conjured up almost sent me into hysterics. I managed to hold back the laugh that was trying to get past my fear, but it was a struggle. Still, there was nothing at all funny in what was going on.

The dragon struck. There was nothing the four of us could do but watch. At the moment, that dragon was saving *our* bacon, but I couldn't help but feel for the men—and even the elf—that it was attacking. Each massive front talon grabbed a horse and rider. The dragon's jaws opened and bit off the top half of another rider as it pulled out of its dive. The elf stood in his stirrups and took a full swing at the beast. He connected with the dragon's shoulder, just in front of the left wing, but the blade bounced back and the elf nearly tumbled to the sand. He might as well have tried to slice the wing off a 747 with a Swiss Army knife. The dragon climbed quickly. One of the men in its grasp fell, still on his horse. That was from about two hundred feet up. Then the dragon dropped the rest of his grisly cargo and dove again. And again. Each time, he got one or two riders and horses, until only the elf was left.

The elf jumped off his horse and slapped its rump to run the animal off. I couldn't guess if he hoped that the dragon would chase the animal and leave him alone or if he just wanted to get the horse out of the way. The dragon circled and dove again, not at all distracted by the panicked horse racing north. The elf faced the dragon, his claymore out in both hands, ready for his last stand. It couldn't be anything but a last stand. The dragon came low, then climbed and circled again, surveying the carnage he had already caused. He eyed the elf, then climbed to make another power dive, pulling up just as he reached his target, stalling to a stop.

As they met, the elf sliced at the bottom of the dragon's jaw and black blood spurted down on him. As far off as we were, I heard the thud of the blade biting into the dragon, the rushing sound of blood gushing out—like water from a fire hose. The dragon reached out with a talon that was bigger than the elf . . . and the elf sliced it off cleanly. More blood spurted. I wondered how sharp that blade was. It seemed incredible.

The dragon folded his wings and dropped on the elf. I figured that that was the end of the affair, since the dragon had to weigh hundreds, maybe thousands, of tons. But after a long moment of the dragon thrashing about, we saw the elf crawl out from under one wing. The wing flailed and knocked the elf face first into the sand—*hard*.

Almost at once, the elf started crawling forward again, dragging himself a few feet farther from the dragon. The reptile was still thrashing, its head weaving like a cobra rising from a snake charmer's basket. Thunderous groans came from its slack jaw. It was hurt, but still very much alive.

Incredibly, the elf was also still alive. Somehow. He got to his knees slowly, in obvious pain. I shook my head, marveling that anyone could take that amount of abuse and not only survive but be able to get to his feet afterward. But the elf couldn't walk. He stumbled and fell back to his knees and crawled toward his sword. He had to inch his way, and he collapsed twice before he reached it. The dragon started waddling after the elf, moving just as slowly. The missing foot was hampering him, I guess, as much as the blood he had lost.

Without warning my companions, I mounted and kneed my horse, aiming him toward the combatants and giving him a slack rein. Annick and the others followed as soon as they saw what I was doing. They were as captivated as I was by the duel. Even our horses had lost some of the fear they had displayed before.

The elf used his sword to help him get to his feet, though it was a clumsy crutch, digging into the sand. When he picked up the sword to hold it out toward the dragon, he swayed, obviously unsteady, but he managed to raise the sword over his head, and he sliced forward, biting into the dragon's snout—but that snout butted the elf and hurled him and his sword away. The blade stuck in the sand, a cross to mark its owner's grave . . . but not yet. The elf crawled toward the sword again, determined and somehow able to move, however slowly. But this time, he just couldn't make it all the way. He collapsed eight feet short of the mark. His face flopped into the sand. Then he lifted his head a little and looked at the blade, a hopeless distance away.

But the dragon wasn't ready to continue the fight immediately either. Its head was also down in the sand, one open eye watching its quarry while it tried to gather strength to finish the battle.

I reached the elf and dismounted a few feet short of

where he lay sprawled. My plan was to carry him away from the dragon, do what I could for him. After the fight he'd put up, I didn't want to leave him to be part of the monster's supper. The elf warrior was fair of face and hair, his skin as pale as Annick's, his eyes the palest blue I had ever seen. Mortally wounded, he still looked like a movie star. I knelt down to him in unconscious homage to his valor. I could feel his magic. He could feel mine.

The elf opened his eyes and looked up at me. "Take my sword, Hero," he said, struggling with the words, "and slay me this dragon that I may die in peace."

I looked from the elf to the sword that was as tall as I am, then on at the dragon that was the size of an airliner. Sure thing, I thought. I recalled hearing someone say that dragons couldn't be killed by a mortal, and Parthet's inability to name one who had. But when I looked at this dragon, I thought that—maybe—most of the work had already been done.

"If I can," I told the elf as my companions arrived.

"Highness . . ." Lesh started, but I waved him quiet.

I pulled the claymore from the sand. It was the largest sword I had ever held, but it didn't feel nearly as heavy as I'd expected. I had handled a couple of claymores once, but I'd never had the chance to practice with them. I held the blade straight out in front of me and walked back to the elf. If he was concerned that I might use it on him instead of on the dragon, he didn't show it.

"A deep thrust, straight through an eye," he said. The words came out singly, labored. A little blood flowed from the corner of the elf's mouth. "Aim for the middle of the back of its head." I nodded. The elf closed his eyes for a second. As I stalked closer to the dragon, though, the elf lifted his head to watch.

The dragon was also watching me. One amber eye stared, tracking my movements. The head waggled weakly. The dragon couldn't raise its head out of my reach, though it tried. Its wings fluttered weakly. It tried to turn away, tried to interpose a wing between us, but it couldn't move fast enough to avoid me. I hoped it was too weak for one last burst of defiance.

This all seemed to be happening in slow motion. I

guess my mind was running a little faster than usual. But stalking from the elf to the dragon, I had more than enough time to consider that the dragon's relationship to the reptiles of the real world had to be pretty ancient, if there was any direct link at all. It had a huge bloated body and a head that looked positively puny in comparison. A pinhead. Still, that head was big enough to cause problems without half trying.

I slashed at the dragon's snout when it opened its yap—a gaping food hole that I could have walked into without bending over. The mouth slammed shut again.

An eye was going to be quite a reach for me. Maybe the dragon had a pinhead in relation to his size, but the head was still bigger than an elephant. I moved around to the side. The eye, about the size of a soccer ball, looked down at me from just above the top of my own head. I took a deep breath and tightened my grip on the elf's sword. Behind the head, the dragon's thin neck curled back to a body that was taller than a two-story building. The head tilted my way, bringing my target a little closer. I stepped forward and thrust the sword into the eye with every bit of my strength (and whatever "strength of Vara" being Hero of Varay was supposed to give me), leaning into the hilt with my shoulder, pushing until the dragon's renewed thrashing around pulled the sword out of my hands—and out of my reach. I backed off fast, almost tripping over my own feet in my hurry to get out of the way. Black blood and purple goo spurted from the eye. The dragon flopped and twisted for minutes before it was finally still. The head lolled over, the wounded eye staring blindly into the sand.

"I think it's dead," I mumbled—too softly for anyone to hear, I think. Then I pulled the sword out of the eye, cleaned the blade in the sand, and carried it back to the elf.

"Well done, Hero," he said. Then his eyes closed for the last time. I knelt and felt for a pulse in his neck. Nothing. It was strange—not that he was dead, but the way I felt. Not long before, I had been ready to fight him, but now I was mourning his death. I looked up at Annick as I stood.

"He wasn't your father by any chance, was he?" I asked.

Annick shook her head firmly. "No, he can't be. I'm sure I would know if we met."

I wasn't about to get into a discussion about *that*.

"I guess we should bury him," I said instead.

"Even *I* wouldn't dishonor him so," Annick said. "An elf warrior belongs out in the open air." I wasn't going to argue. I knew zip about elf customs and I wasn't at all sure I wanted to learn.

"Whatever you say." I felt tired suddenly, fatigue just trying to swallow me whole. I stabbed the claymore into the sand at the elf's head. "I wish I knew his name. He was really something fighting that dragon." A true hero, I thought. I looked down. The magic I had felt from him before was gone. A supposed immortal had found that he wasn't, not by a long shot. I shook my head and started to walk toward my horse.

"You're not going to leave his sword, are you?" Harkane asked. His voice actually sounded pained.

"Why not?" I asked.

Annick answered. "To leave an elf warrior's sword would be disaster. It would return to kill you."

"Why? I didn't kill him."

"It will seek you out if you abandon it, though. That is the way of such weapons."

Again, I couldn't argue the point. I didn't know what I was talking about. I pulled the blade from the sand. Harkane pulled loose a heavy sash from the elf's body. The claymore hadn't been in a normal sheath. Two spring-loaded C-clamps closed over blade and guard. I strapped on the rig and tried it. With proper pressure, the clamps freed the blade—very smartly.

There were a bunch of fancy characters etched high on the flat of the blade, above the blood channel, near the guard. Annick looked at them and said, "The runes name this sword Dragon's Death." For one dragon at least, I thought. I looked at the runes, traced them with my finger. I had thought that the translation magic was supposed to handle writing too—I had been able to read that *Chapbook* once I got to Varay—but I couldn't make out anything at first. But when I looked closer, I could read the inscription. The script was just very convoluted, worse than my mother's handwriting.

With the sword in my hand now, I could feel its magic.

14

Elflord

We chased our shadows away from the Mist after we washed off the gore of battle. Despite the continuing risk of being discovered along the beach, all four of us went into the sea to get clean. The salt water stung our minor cuts from the fight with the swamp trolls, but I figured that that was all to the good. It might clean them out, lessen the chance of infection. We headed northeast then, deeper into Fairy. At first, I aimed that way just because it seemed to be the fastest route away from the carnage on the beach. Then it seemed right for a couple of better reasons. Most important, any pursuit would look to the south if anyone suspected that we had come up from Varay. And going north might actually give me a chance to sow some of that confusion I had bragged about, my wild idea to make the Elflord of Xayber think that one of his peers was raiding his territory.

Sunset caught us before we had traveled far, but we kept going as long as we had enough light to navigate by in the open. We stayed clear of the swamp and even avoided the gnarled forest as much as possible. After two hours of riding, we found a sheltered area away from the road that looked decent. There was fresh running water for everyone, and plenty of grass for the horses.

I didn't tell the others that I planned to keep going deeper into Fairy until we camped for the night. There were no objections. I hadn't expected any. Lesh and Harkane would obey orders, and Annick was delighted at any chance to hurt the Elflord of Xayber some more. Going farther into Xayber's territory was a gamble—and quite possibly stupid. I had no way to know how powerful the magic of the elflords was. I didn't know a *lot* about Fairy and the seven kingdoms. But I did know that we were going to have to take some real risks to have any chance to stand off both the elflord and the Etevar.

I took the first watch again and sat with the two-handed elf sword in my lap. Dragon's Death. The blade felt sharp enough to shave metal with but so strong that it couldn't be nicked or damaged in a fight. Even after seeing the blade in action, I thought that it was an impossible combination. The hilt of Dragon's Death was designed for larger hands than mine, but I could hold it. I might even be able to wield it in a fight—but not a marathon. It was a magic blade. I was still new at all this magic hocus-pocus, but I could *feel* the sword's magic in my mind, and that's something else that is hard to explain. On the simplest level, it was something like the static electricity discharged when two sets of the family rings touched, an aura, or maybe a physical field. I wished that I knew what the sword's magic was, precisely, how it might help or hurt me. Maybe Parthet would be able to puzzle it out when we got back to Varay. Using a magic I didn't fully understand could be dangerous. I had no trouble thinking of magic as a weapon—a weapon with all the potential of a gun or a sword. Of course, I was already using a lot of magic I didn't really comprehend—the magic of the Hero, the magic of the doors, the magic of the land itself.

It all needed a lot of thought, and I was too tired to do it all that night. I hadn't had a full night's sleep since leaving Varay, and our last night in the swamp had been almost sleepless. An exhausting day had followed. *Gil Tyner—Dragon Slayer.* Another ludicrous title to add to my collection. Fortunately, my danger sense didn't kick up all night. I woke Annick and went to sleep. When Harkane woke me just before dawn, I felt rested enough for another day in the saddle.

We crossed the spine of the isthmus early that morning and turned north between the main ridge and a line of lower hills to the east. The paths were narrow, often steep, but at least we didn't have the swamp or low-hanging branches to worry about. After the past couple of days, it was almost a picnic. No one had any idea how far we might have to go to find a village or town to harass. I had a rough idea of racing through some sleepy little burg and setting fire to a few buildings before we turned around and scooted south. I didn't want to skulk around slitting throats in the night. Maybe I would face the warriors of Fairy in battle someday, but I had no taste for the kind of action that Annick seemed to delight in.

Since my danger sense remained quiescent—just barely ticking over—we didn't push our horses while we headed deeper into Fairy. I wanted to save their speed for our escape. Late that afternoon, I used my bow to bring down a miniature mountain goat after Lesh said that they made good eating. There was a sheltered dent in the hillside nearby, and Lesh assured me that he could make a smokeless fire, so we made camp early and got ready for a hot meal. We hadn't seen anyone on the road all day, hadn't even heard any horn calls.

Lesh did the cooking. Harkane tended the horses. I climbed the ridge to get a better view of the countryside. Annick followed me.

"You don't think much of me, do you?" she asked when I stopped just below the crest, maybe 150 feet above our camp.

I peeked out over the top of the ridge, careful not to stick my head up too far. There was nothing special to see, just more country like that we had been riding through. Then I sat on a rock and looked at Annick. I couldn't, *wouldn't,* come out flat and tell her that I thought she was a bloodthirsty bitch. But I wouldn't lie to her either.

"You get too much pleasure out of killing," I said. I kept my voice as neutral as possible.

"They were our enemies—*my* enemies, at least."

"What you did that first time wasn't an act of war. It was something private and dirty—murder, nothing more."

"Vengeance is my right!" She flared the way I had expected her to. Maybe vengeance was her right, in Varay. Maybe, in the skewed logic of the buffer zone, it was even her duty. But . . .

"That's not the point. What I said is that you enjoy it too much. In my world . . ." I shook my head. "Let's just say that the standards of my world and yours are considerably different." I didn't want to get into an argument with her. I was afraid that it would get out of hand.

"I've never seen *your* world." She didn't sound as though she had much interest in it either. "All I have is my world. Why are you here?"

"Damn good question. I wish I had a good answer," I said, still hoping to avoid an argument. It was a question I had asked myself often enough. I still wasn't sure. "I guess I'm here because I'm the son of my parents." I told Annick, as briefly as I could, how I had learned about Varay and why I had come, and the rest of the story up to my arrival at Arrowroot.

"You're here because it's your duty to be here," Annick said—with some force, as if she were trying to emphasize a point won in a debate.

"That's what everyone seems to think," I conceded.

"You do your duty. I do mine. Is it so wrong to want to do what you're bound to anyway? To enjoy fulfilling your destiny?"

I didn't continue the argument—ah, discussion—because I could smell supper, and if Annick and I went on any longer I'd ruin my digestion if not my appetite. It was time to take another quick look over the ridge, then climb back down to camp.

Lesh did a bang-up job on supper. He had roasted the meat with the last of our onions stuffed into small cavities he had carved into the meat, and had collected the drippings and heated them with water to give us juice to spoon over the meat and to dip our hard bread in. It tasted like a feast after the days of dried, salted beef. All that was lacking was the beer. The four of us ate about twenty pounds of meat, and there was enough left over for breakfast and lunch the next day—that much longer before we would have to return to our jerky.

"It do fill the nooks and crannies," Lesh said, slapping his belly after Annick and I each complimented him on the meal.

The night was surprisingly chilly. While I was on guard, I walked around to keep warm. The air was clear, the sky studded with a wealth of stars for a change, giving me enough light to avoid tripping over my companions. I stayed on duty as long as I could keep alert, then woke Annick. As on the other nights, she woke instantly, immediately alert. She was still on guard when I woke again, sensing imminent danger. I woke the others with a word while I tried to pinpoint the threat. Before, the sense had always been strongly directional. This time the danger seemed to surround us.

Annick got her bow ready and stood in the center of our camp, turning slowly, peering toward the top of the rises that concealed us. With her elven night sight, she was the only one who could see clearly. Our starlight suddenly seemed inadequate. I focused on the narrow entrance to our cul-de-sac. The weapon that came to hand when I first jumped up was the elf sword. I held it in front of me at an angle, ready to spring into the fight I knew was near.

But it didn't come. After a time, I lost the edge of my danger warning, but it didn't fade completely. The danger was still there, close. We settled down and waited. For an hour or more, the feeling of danger ebbed and flowed.

''There's someone out there,'' I whispered. ''They're either trying to catch us off-guard or they're trying to screw up their courage to attack.''

''This isn't the best spot to be in, I'm thinking,'' Lesh said. ''We're in a jug, and all they've got to do is cork it.'' We could have gone over the top, but that would have meant leaving our horses behind, and we were much too far from Varay for that.

''We'll have to make do,'' I told Lesh.

''A quick charge out in the dark?'' he suggested.

''Not unless we have to. But let's pack everything up.''

''I don't feel magic out there,'' Annick whispered. ''It must be trolls.''

''Then they're smarter than the trolls in the swamp,'' I said. I was still having trouble with the nuances of language, even with the translation magic. It wasn't nearly as unnerving talking in the dark, when I couldn't see that everything people said was out of sync with their mouths. The difficulty seemed to be that the translation magic wasn't as sophisticated as it might have been. For instance, it lumped together a lot of different creatures under the generic "troll." Like lumping together humans and the great apes as primates. Maybe personal introductions aren't essential, but it would be nice to know what kind of diner I was going to give gas to.

We made noises packing up. That must have made the difference.

I yelled, "Here they come!" as the awareness swept over me—an almost intuitive knowledge that bypassed the normal thinking processes. I had slung the claymore rig over my shoulder again while we were getting ready to leave. The claymore was the weapon I reached for, and I can't explain why. My own sword was at my waist, and I had years of practice with it. And the Smith & Wesson was within reach. But I went for that six-foot cleaver as if it were my customary weapon.

It was the proper reflex, however it came about. As I brought the elf sword over my shoulder, it bisected one of the mountain trolls jumping down from the perimeter of our hole in the wall. I hardly felt a strain. The blade went through that troll like empty air—bones and all. I don't know if it was that "strength of Vara" that initiation as Hero was supposed to confer or if it was some magic of the sword, or a combination. I just know what happened.

The blade glowed in the dark once it had tasted blood. I found myself whistling a strange melody while I wielded the sword. The third surprise was that the elf blade felt almost weightless in action.

There was something else. We were fighting in the dark, but even though I could only make out vague shapes, mostly when they moved, I knew exactly where everyone was all the time. Throughout the engagement, I was aware of positions. Lesh and Harkane were at the exit from our campsite, keeping any trolls from coming in that way. Annick was at the back of the depression with her sword and knife, working hard to stay out of my way. I ranged through the rest of it, moving toward trolls as they came over the top—sometimes anticipating their appearance. I couldn't see well, but I didn't have to. I *knew* where everyone was.

And I knew more. Dragon's Death wasn't leaving wounded trolls to pop up and cause trouble later. The elf sword sliced too thoroughly. We got a little more light in the cul-de-sac as the fight progressed. Blood flowing on the blade of the elf sword made it glow more brightly. That happened fairly quickly. By the time I sliced into my fifth or sixth troll, the blade was as bright as a Jedi light saber. The trolls could see me clearly enough. And I could see the trolls that came close enough for Dragon's Death to reach.

The fight went on for a few minutes more—not long, really. I heard words that I couldn't understand and can't duplicate—the first failure of the translation magic. Then a guttural voice shouted, "The elf was masked!" Those trolls who could escape did. A fair number couldn't. The glow of my elf sword faded quickly. My danger sense idled again.

"They're gone," Lesh said.

"Let's get out of here before they come back," I said.

"They won't be back," Annick said. She sounded very confident. "They think you're an elf warrior because of the sword and the song. How did you know to conjure with that?"

"I didn't, and they may discover their mistake, so let's move."

I used my flashlight to make sure we didn't forget anything. That also gave us a chance to take a better look at our attackers. They were as ugly as the swamp trolls, but not as dirty or vile-smelling. They didn't look *exactly* the same, but the differences could only interest another troll.

We rode north again, deeper into Xayber's lands. Just after sunrise we found a pass through the lower line of hills and turned east. Beyond the hills, the land was gently rolling, tall grass with occasional wooded stretches. These trees actually looked fairly normal—not the haunted-forest type of trees we had seen farther south along the isthmus. We rode from one copse of trees to the next, worrying more about cover than roads or speed.

We stopped once when I felt that unseen presence probing again. It passed, then returned and passed again, more slowly the second time.

"He's closing in," I muttered. It had to be the Elflord of Xayber. I couldn't hope to evade him forever. The others looked at me. Nobody questioned my awareness of someone searching for us with magic. My companions took my magic sense more for granted than I did.

"If we can't find somewhere to strike at the Elflord today, we head back to Varay," I said. "The deeper we get, the harder it'll be to get out in time to meet the Etevar's army, and right now, he's a greater threat to Varay than Xayber." I stared at Annick for a long moment, but she didn't speak.

We found our target before noon. We came through a wooded draw between two low hills and saw a riot of bright colors a half mile off.

"Pull up," I said, turning my horse as I spoke. We moved back around the side of one of the hills, away from the bright colors, out of sight. "Let's climb the hill for a better look." We dismounted and led our horses partway up the gentle slope. Lesh and Harkane stayed well below the crest with the animals. Annick climbed to the top with me. I didn't argue. Her eyes were sharper than mine.

"Tents, pavilions, six in all," she reported slowly. "People. It looks like some sort of picnic outing."

"A picnic, nor a war party?" I asked.

"Not a war party with women in party gowns."

"How many people?" I could see movement around the tents, but I couldn't see well enough to take a reliable count.

"I can't see inside the tents," Annick reminded me. "Not more than a few dozen people, though, judging from the horses and wagons."

It looked like just the kind of target I had been hoping for.

"We're not going in to see how many we can kill," I said. "Rip a few tents, scatter the horses, scare anyone we can. We don't fight unless we have to fight to get out."

"We'll have to fight," Annick said, meeting my eyes. "It's not all fancy ladies, and some of the ladies of Fairy might be more than a match for you at that." If Annick was any point of comparison, I could believe it.

"Let's get going," I said.

It looked as if we might be able to get within two hundred yards of the tents before we lost our cover if we were careful and took a wide arc to the left, around the hill we were on. I didn't want to be out in the open any longer than necessary. That would give our targets too much warning, and *The Charge of the Light Brigade* wasn't at all what I wanted to stage. I pulled my Cubs cap down tight and drew the claymore. Using the elf sword one-handed *and* on horseback would be awkward as hell, I knew, but it would be a hell of a lot more impressive than my own sword. And I *did* want to impress the locals. That was the whole point of the exercise.

"When we get close, make a lot of noise," I said as we came out of the trees and charged the tents.

Once more, the horses that Annick's uncle had provided stretched into a willing gallop, racing toward the tents. So far, the only thing that had managed to unnerve the animals was the dragon, and that had the same effect on humans.

A few of the revelers at the Fairy picnic looked like civilized versions of the trolls we had seen, more like the one troll soldier on the beach. There were also tall, fair folk who had to have elvish blood. There were squat dwarfs, and normal humans. Most of them were sporting weapons. Even the ladies all seemed to wear long, thin daggers at their waists, and some had bows or swords as well.

As soon as I saw weapons—not drawn, just there—I knew that we wouldn't get through the encampment without violence. Annick shot two arrows as soon as she saw a raised sword—a good fifty yards off. After that, all I could hope for was to get in and out as quickly as possible, before the locals could organize any real defense.

We headed directly for the center of the camp. Lesh cut picket lines and tethers and chased off horses. Harkane did some fancy stunt riding, leaning way over to grab several hunks of burning wood from a bonfire in the middle of the camp—hardly slowing down at all. Then he circled around to use the brands to fire all of the tents and open pavilions. The silk, or whatever it was, burned fast.

A few of the Fairy folk stood ready to meet us—apparently not at all discomfited by the change to their schedule. The four of us were well separated by then, so everything happened as a series of individual duels. Annick went into her berserker mode again, chasing down locals, forcing them to fight. Lesh and Harkane paid more attention to my instructions. They concentrated on causing confusion and damage, only fighting when they had to defend themselves. Me, I had my hands full for a few minutes.

An axe-wielding dwarf jumped out in front of me and tried to chop my horse out from between us. I jerked hard on the reins and the animal reared and came down hard toward the dwarf, forcing him to back off. By the time he stepped forward again, I had my horse turned so I could meet the dwarf with Dragon's Death. The claymore quickly shortened the dwarf by a head. I noticed that I was whistling again, the same eerie melody I had whistled while we were fighting the mountain trolls. Although the elvish sword didn't glow as it had in the night, I had no trouble handling it, even one-handed. There was no nonsense of the sword doing its own fighting regardless of me, or dragging me along with it. I was always in control, but that sword proved to be as easy to use as a reed wand.

Just after I cut down the dwarf, something hard hit me in the back. The impact pitched me forward. If I hadn't managed to get my left arm hooked around the neck of my horse, I would have been thrown over his head. The pain in my back was like being hit by a pitch—a hard fastball. My vision blurred for a moment. I fought to push myself upright in the saddle again and puffed, trying to get my breathing in order. I hadn't seen what hit me, but I assumed that someone had thrown a spear—with one hell of a lot a force behind it. The lance wasn't sticking out of me, so I knew that my chain mail had turned the shaft aside. The spot where it hit was—well, "sore" doesn't begin to approach an adequate description of how it felt, but I couldn't stop to check the extent of the damage. The thrower—one of those tall, pale types that I assumed had elven blood—ran at me, drawing his sword. He was on foot and his blade was just a normal broadsword, but he didn't see at all intimidated by my longer weapon.

We didn't play games. My back hurt so badly that I had to grit my teeth against the pain. My only thought was to end this duel as quickly as possible. I parried his swing, then my sword whirled around full-circle, whistling through the air, and took off his sword arm above the elbow. I kicked out to knock him back. The shock went all the way up my leg to the pain in my back. But the guy did go down and he didn't bother to get back up.

I left him lying there and backed my horse through a circle, looking for the next threat. The Fairy camp was a shambles. Every tent was burning, and so were two of the wagons. Quite a number of revelers were down, dead or wounded. Their horses had all run off, except for one with a broken leg. That horse rolled on the ground and neighed in panic and pain. We had done everything we could hope to do.

"Let's go!" I shouted. I waved my sword above my head until that aggravated the pain in my back too much to continue, then led the way out of camp, due south. The others closed up quickly behind me. Even Annick broke off right away. Maybe she thought I would leave her there if she didn't. Maybe I would have. None of the arrows that followed us came close, and there was no immediate pursuit, not without horses. But we rode as if the posse were right on our tails. The horses might return, or someone at the picnic might have the magic to contact others to hunt us.

I could feel my eyes tearing up from the pain in my back, but I couldn't take much notice of that yet, not until we had some space between us and the people we had just attacked. When we were not quite out of sight of the burning tents, we cut right sharply. I hoped to leave the impression that we were going northwest, that we had simply made a tiny little error, turning just a couple of minutes too soon. Then, when I was absolutely certain that none of the elvish folk could still see us, we turned south again and drifted back to our original course. It was another hour before I dared to stop and dismount so we could rest our horses and check out my back.

Getting my chain mail off brought new agony. I lay down on my stomach—almost fainted and fell—and Annick and Lesh both checked out my wound.

"There's a puncture, not too deep," Annick said. "A very dark bruise around it, bigger than both my fists together."

"There may be a broken rib or two, lord," Lesh said.

Annick poured water and did what she could to clean the wound. Her touch was surprisingly light, but that didn't stop every new touch from adding to the pain. "There's not much else we can do here," she said when she finished.

"Look in my pack," I said. "I think there's a roll of gauze and some tape. If I've got a busted rib, it needs to be bandaged as tight as possible." I didn't remember seeing anything like aspirin. Mother wasn't likely to think of something like that.

The process of bandaging hurt so much that I almost passed out again, but when it was finished, I did feel a little better. The pain wasn't nearly so acute. The tight gauze girdle exerted pressure all around my middle. I got my shirt back on, but not the chain mail. I didn't even want to think about putting all that weight back on, even though the armor had undoubtedly saved my life.

I sat on the ground for a few minutes after the tape was secure, then got to my feet gingerly. I could feel sweat beading up on my face, but we had to press on.

"We'd better get moving again," I said, my voice low as I tried to get by without breathing very deeply.

"We head for home now?" Lesh asked. I nodded. "Back to Arrowroot?"

"That's where Parthet is due to meet us." I recalled

the feeling of danger there, but I had to go to Arrowroot. "We'll stay on this side of the isthmus as long as we can, try to get south of the swamp before we turn west." The elflord might be confused further by that—assuming that we had confused him at all. Dorthin, Varay, and Xayber all met at the southeastern corner of the isthmus. If we couldn't convince the elflord that we were an enemy out of Fairy, maybe he would think that the Etevar were feeling him out. Setting Xayber against Dorthin couldn't hurt Varay.

We had been stopped long enough getting me taped up that the horses had cooled down and Harkane had watered them. Harkane helped me back into the saddle. The pain was still there, but I thought that I would be able to deal with it. I had to. We rode slowly for a time. The pain didn't go away, but it abated a little—or I simply became used to it. I could breathe a little more easily.

Trusting my danger sense a little more—and worried about what riding the rough terrain of the countryside would do to my back and ribs—I didn't try to keep us concealed. We rode the main road south, bold as could be. I shoved my Cubs cap in a hip pocket. Annick unbraided her hair and let it blow free. At first glance we might appear to be a young lord and lady of Fairy out with servants.

Shortly after we started riding again, I felt the questioning presence again, but more lightly than before. The elflord hadn't yet identified us as his irritant. I forced my mind as blank as possible, like before, and the presence passed.

A little later, Harkane moved his horse up next to mine. "You've made it past the dangerous stage," he whispered softly. "You have the magic of the Hero working to mend your wound. By the time we get home, it should be only a memory."

"I hope you're right," I said. "And I hope we don't come up against anything serious before then." We had a lot of Fairy to cross before we could reach Varay and even temporary safety.

Near sunset, we left the road and moved into the hills to find a campsite that would shelter us but not bottle us in. I settled on a flat ledge halfway up a gentle slope, with trees on three sides. There was running water below. We refilled our drinking bags and let the horses get their fill before we moved them up to the campsite. We didn't unsaddle the animals, though, and we unloaded only what we absolutely needed for the night. It was too likely that we would be on the run before morning.

Despite the way I was hurting, I might have felt less nervous riding by night and hiding by day if not for the warning that darkness couldn't hide us from elves and the corroborating evidence that even a half-elf like Annick could see almost perfectly in the dark. Giving ourselves the inconvenience without the advantage was pointless.

Annick was full of vigor when we made camp. Her eyes and face had an excited look that might have seemed feverish in other circumstances. She looked younger, fresher. I wondered if she got some tangible physiological benefit from killing, if the addiction was physical as well as psychological. I had intended to complain about the way she had acted during the fray, but I held back. It's not just that I didn't feel up to an argument. I guess I had given up. She gave no indication that she was looking for reformation, so the aggravation would have been pointless.

"What will you do when this fight is over?" she asked me. Harkane and Lesh were already settling down to sleep. I was sitting propped up against a tree trunk, as comfortable as I was likely to get. The pain did seem to be fading somewhat. Maybe Harkane had been right. In any case, I wasn't feeling quite as bad as before.

"Which fight? We haven't started the real battle yet," I said. Dusk hadn't quite fled into darkness.

"After you beat the Etevar."

"I haven't started to think past that. I know what everyone expects, that I'll stick around and play prince and occasional Hero. Become King of Varay someday." That was a gloomy thought. I wasn't stodgy enough to play Prince Charles or loose enough to be randy Andy. But I couldn't see going home to play with computers at the moment either. It was difficult to think of computers as real just then. "I don't know what I'll do. Maybe go back to my world and do some traveling."

Annick stared at me. I was uncomfortable about it, especially knowing that she could see me better than I could see her in the growing night.

"What will *you* do when you've killed all the people you've spent your life hating?" I asked.

She shrugged. "I'll find something if that time ever comes."

"You think it'll be that easy?"

Annick didn't answer.

The attack came while I was still awake, still on sentry, but that didn't help. For once, my danger sense didn't scream soon enough. The Elflord of Xayber had finally located us, and the gap between my danger warning and his assault weren't enough to let me do any more than whip the claymore off my shoulder and get it out in front of me. It was pure luck that I was already on my feet. I had decided that I had better get up and move around a little to keep from getting stiff. Then it came.

There was no direct physical attack.

My mind was suddenly in the grip of an incredible power—a psychic bearhug. There was intense pain at the start, worse than the pain in my back had been at its worst, and then a feeling of utter helplessness. I struggled against the force and the void behind it. I fought to open my eyes, scarcely aware that I had closed them in the first onslaught. I blinked and found myself standing on a featureless plain that was unbroken to the horizon in every direction. It was a gray nothingness. There wasn't even real ground beneath my feet, just an unidentifiable, almost undetectable surface. I was standing alone with just the elf sword. I turned slowly, sword at the ready. My back didn't hurt—I noticed *that* right away— but my danger sense was running up and down my spine. The general message was something like: *Holy shit, are you in for it now!* As if I needed a prompter to tell me that.

"Okay, Xayber, come on out and let's get this over

with. Time for all good rats to come out of their holes.''
Bravado. Also a poor choice of words. Huge rats started
rising right out of the ground—something like Clayma-
tion. The rodents were the size of the goat I had killed,
and nearly transparent, their innards right there for me
to see. They came at me as if I were the pie-eyed piper.
All I could do was hack at them with the elf sword and
hope that I ran out of rats before I ran out of strength.
My back didn't hurt, but I didn't feel particularly chipper
either.

''Okay, what's the next act?'' I asked when the stream
of rats finally dried up.

A giant face appeared in the distance, in what passed
for a sky in that gray void. It was an oblong face with
pale complexion, black hair, thin mustache, and short
goatee, haughty-looking beyond words. I don't suppose
the resemblance was really all that close, but it made me
think of that three-view portrait of Cardinal Richelieu
that seems to be in all of the history textbooks. The face
stared at me. When the mouth moved, I heard the words
as if they were spoken right in front of me.

''You're the one who dares challenge me? What a dis-
appointment. I had hoped for something more divert-
ing.''

''Divert your head up your ass where it belongs,'' I
said. And, for a moment, that's exactly what I saw. When
that image faded, it was replaced by a more complete
version of the face atop a normal-looking body—as normal as any eight-footer *can* look. The elflord was only
ten feet away from me, and armed much as I was. His
claymore fit him better than mine fit me.

''Okay, you got that trick down pat,'' I said. ''Now
try this one. Drop dead.''

He didn't oblige this time, though. It was too much to
hope for. I moved my sword back and forth in front of
me and started whistling that strange melody again as I
advanced toward the elflord. There was no place to run,
so I decided that I might as well act as if I weren't unduly
worried about the elflord. The music seemed to give him
an instant's pause before he brought his sword up and

came to meet me. The battle tune he whistled was different from mine, but it was just as eerie.

I didn't know what the connection was between the whistling and the elf sword, but I *had* figured out that they were linked.

The elflord made the first attack, bringing his sword overhead as he stepped forward—stomp the lead foot ahead, then drag up the other foot. I met his blade and pressed to his left. We disengaged and came at each other the same way again. I pressed to his right this time, trying to feel him out. There were a few more tentative, probing passes, then the fight shifted gears rapidly, heating up in a hurry.

This time it was real fencing, not the hurried hackwork my earlier encounters had been. The practiced routine brought its own sort of comfort. We fought at reach. We fought *corps à corps*. The long swords smashed into each other in combination after combination, at every possible angle, the shock of impact jarring my wrists and sending signals of pain all the way up arms that soon started to feel like lead weights. That was different from my earlier fights with Dragon's Death too. Before, the sword had seemed almost weightless. After a few minutes this time, I could feel the full weight of the claymore. Maneuvering the sword, parrying the elflord, got harder. I met each of his attacks with less leeway, less leverage. It wasn't hard to project the outcome. Soon I would miss a parry and the elflord's blade would slice through me the way I had sliced troll and dwarf with Dragon's Death.

I had to find an edge if I wanted to get out of the duel alive. I would have liked to slip a hand grenade down the front of his tights, but I didn't have a grenade handy and I couldn't be sure it would work if I did.

Something.

I followed a parry with a quick step toward Xayber, and our blades locked at the guard.

Surprise! Xayber hadn't been expecting me to close like that. He could have rested his chin on top of my head . . . if he had leaned over a little. He was that much taller than me. His sword pressed in and down on mine. His weight pushed forward, trying to force me to step back. He had the weight, but my being two feet shorter gave me a slight advantage in leverage the way we were locked together.

Then the elflord disappeared from sight. I could still feel the pressure of his sword and body, but I couldn't see him. I *could* still see myself, an image of myself, standing a little beyond, holding the elf sword at an angle, hilt on the ground, point angled toward my gut. I saw myself fall on the blade, saw the point spring out of my back—about where I had been injured before—at the center of a fountain of bright red blood. The vision multiplied until I could see hundreds of copies of myself in all the phases of committing suicide. Miniatures, drive-in-movie-screen size, everything in between, over and over and over. Then the pictures started to strobe—again, over and over. I squeezed my eyes shut and pressed against the invisible elflord. When I opened my eyes again, he was back—grinning. He gave way and we went through another short passage at reach. I didn't feel quite as drained as before. The sideshow had given me time to catch my second wind.

Then the elflord changed himself into a copy of me and I dueled with myself. The absurdity of that gave me a lift.

"Gee, I even get to costar with myself," I said—or grunted, one word at a time. "Think of all the movie stars who never got to try a dual role."

The elflord returned at that, but he wasn't grinning any longer. We continued to fight, going one way and then the other. My whistling got louder, more intense. So did his. It seemed to give us both new strength. Seeing him nonplussed did me worlds of good too, but that and the "new strength" were both relative. The fight was beginning to get to me.

"So. You're more than you appear to be." Xayber forced a disengagement and stepped back out of reach of a lunge. I brought my sword up in a salute and tried to spread a grin across my face. From the reaction I got, I guess it worked.

"You don't recognize my magic?" I don't know what brought that comment out of me, but I loaded it with obviously mock surprise. "You must be slipping. Shall we have another go? I think it's time Xayber belonged to a lord more fit to hold it." I took two quick steps toward him and lunged at his throat. He backed out of reach again, brought his sword up to his face, and vanished. The gray and the light went with him.

I collapsed across Lesh.

15

Coriander

Lesh woke noisily when I fell on him, and that woke the others. I was so wiped out that I couldn't move, not even an arm. Limp, exhausted, turned inside out, I could scarcely mumble answers to the questions that Lesh and Annick fired off. On top of all that, my back was hurting again—worse than ever. Falling across Lesh hadn't helped.

Annick guessed what had happened. "He's been caught by the elflord. We've got to get him away from here as fast as we can."

That sounded good to me, but the three of them had to do all of the work. It's a good thing we had unloaded only the essentials. I was baggage, useless, as if I didn't have a bone or muscle left—Dorothy's Scarecrow with his stuffing ripped out. The others even had to hoist me into the saddle and tie me in place. When we rode out, Harkane was at my side to make sure I didn't fall. He held the reins of my horse.

Annick led the way with her night vision. Harkane and I were close behind her, and Lesh rode rear guard. For the first hour—maybe longer; time was a nebulous abstraction for me just then—I was scarcely conscious, maybe not even "scarcely" part of the time. There wasn't much difference between being unconscious and being whatever it was the rest of the time. Perhaps there was less pain while I was completely out of it. But memories of my duel with the elflord haunted me constantly, nightmares that weren't stilled by waking, and it wasn't until later that I started to make any sense of it at all.

The duel with Xayber was real. I could have died during it even though I never physically left our camp and the elflord never physically entered. That was why my wound didn't hurt during my duel. My *body* wasn't physically involved. It must have remained just standing in place while the fight went on. *I could have died* wore at my mind through the night. There was no question whose magic was more powerful. In my short time as Hero of Varay I had come to rely on my new ability to sense danger, but the elflord had almost completely negated that puny talent as an offhand prelude to his attack. His magic had barely begun when mine ended. The elf sword was a bonus, pure luck. It as the only thing that let me survive the duel. The sword had its own magic, and drawing the weird battle tune from me was only a small part of it.

"You did right good, lord," Harkane whispered— sometime during that blurry night ride. "You survived the elflord. That means you beat him. Your father never faced a duel like that inside the elflord's domain, where he's most powerful."

I didn't feel like a winner. At that point, I wasn't even sure that I felt like a survivor.

I puzzled over the suicide sequence at length, once I started spending more time conscious than not. The only explanation that came close to making sense was that the elflord didn't think he could kill me by magic alone, and since he wasn't physically present, all he could hope for was to make me kill myself. I was guessing on insufficient evidence, though. I didn't know *why* he might have thought that his magic alone wouldn't suffice—because he thought I was an elf or because he knew I was Hero of Varay, or whatever. There was a chance that he wasn't certain just who I was. But if he caught me again, his ignorance probably wouldn't matter. He'd come close enough the first time.

Gradually, I started to get my wits back. Instead of feeling totally sapped and snapped, I just felt exhausted. The pain in my back and side settled into place again, throbbing as steadily as my heart. We stopped to rest the horses. I *think* it was the second time, but it was the first that I was really aware of. I almost managed to dismount by myself. When we got ready to ride again twenty minutes later, I didn't have to be tied to my saddle. But Lesh and Harkane did have to help me mount.

"What happened?" Annick asked after we started riding south again. She rode at my side long enough to hear my semicoherent tale. I needed quite a while to tell it. I ate a little beef jerky and drank a lot of water along the way. That helped.

"I was right, it was the elflord," Annick said when I finished.

"We have to be out of Fairy before he comes for me again. There's no way I could survive that a second time."

"I think we'll be south of the swamp by dawn," Annick said. "Do you want to turn east and try to stay hidden in the forest again?"

"Trees won't hide me from him." I may have shuddered at that. We rode on for a few minutes before I continued talking. I had to do some thinking, and rational thought came hard.

"Let's just make the best speed we can, straight south—unless he sends troops after us. And we're not going straight to Arrowroot. That's too dangerous." Particularly with me useless for combat. "We'll try Coriander instead. We can get in and out of your uncle's castle quickly from there." Or from Basil, if it came down to that, I thought. I told Annick about the feeling of danger I had had when we first left Arrowroot, before she joined us. I didn't want to head into that without knowing what was behind it.

"I guess I should react to that," Annick said. "My mother and my uncle are there." She paused, then added, "But I don't feel any of the things I should. Does that shock you?"

I didn't say anything.

"There'll be fighting at Arrowroot, right?" she asked.

"Probably. The elflord has obviously found some magic that works inside Varay, at least as far as Arrowroot.'' That was another complication. If Arrowroot was under active attack, I wouldn't be able to take soldiers from there to fight the Etevar, and the entire foray into Xayber might be wasted.

"Coriander faces Xayber too," Annick said. "The danger might be there as well."

"Maybe, but maybe we won't be expected to head there.''

We rested for a couple of hours just after dawn, near the edge of the forest. I managed to sleep most of that time. When I woke, I felt stronger even though my back and side still hurt. Annick rebandaged my wound and said that it had been bleeding again.

"Probably from when I fell on Lesh after the duel with the elflord,'' I said, and she nodded.

When I had new tape on, I managed to get up and walk around a bit. I wasn't up to anything strenuous yet, but I thought I would be able to take care of routine. Annick had caught several plump fish while I slept. I've never liked sushi, but I ate my share of the raw fish. There was no time for a fire, and I wasn't ready to chance even one of Lesh's "guaranteed smokeless" fires yet.

We rode almost continuously for another two days and the night in between, resting only when we had to. By sunset the following day, people and horses were all dragging. I'd like to say I was feeling a lot better by then, but the best I can honestly manage is that I didn't feel any *worse*. The back of a horse isn't all that conducive to recuperation. With the burst of hard riding, though, maybe the pursuit (if there was any pursuit) would be too far behind to matter. That was the hope, why I was willing to keep going even though I was hurting. Anyway, we saw riders only once, and we were able to get under cover before they spotted us, thanks to Annick's eyesight and my returning awareness of danger. I didn't feel any probes from the elflord.

Luckily.

Eventually, we had to make a longer stop, spend the night in one place. We followed a small stream deep into the forest, wading two miles upstream. We were in place well before sunset. Harkane and Annick caught fish and a few tidbits that looked like crayfish. I let Lesh start another of his smokeless fires—but said that we had to douse it before it got completely dark, even though our campsite was so isolated. Harkane went off into the woods and came back with his helmet full of berries that looked like raspberries and tasted like peaches.

"The way we've been going, another day and a half might get us to Varay," Annick said while we were eating. "Or a day and a night."

"I don't want the horses dropping under us in the stretch," I said.

"You think we'll have trouble close to the end?" Annick asked—almost meekly, and that surprised me enough to give her a long stare.

"I'd almost bet on it," I said. "If the elflord's armies are really on the attack, we may have to go through them at either Coriander or Arrowroot." Usually, my guesses don't work out, but I might have been a card-carrying prophet with that one.

We had a quiet night and a peaceful ride the next day. The quiet night especially helped me. Then, after sleeping for half of the following night, we got an early start for our last day on the isthmus. Of course, we were also nearing the area that the chamberlain's map labeled "Here there be dragons," but I didn't take that very seriously. It's not that I felt cocky after administering the *coup de grâce* to one dragon—I knew that didn't qualify me as a proper dragon slayer—it's just that dragons didn't seem to tie themselves to any one spot. They didn't have to. They were arguably the "meanest SOBs in the valley," so they could go wherever they damn well pleased.

I knew we were getting close to Varay because I could feel the danger in front of us increase slowly, mile by mile, as we headed south. It was like a chronic ache rather than a sudden pain, and I had experienced enough of both kinds of pain lately to know the difference. That last night that we camped in Fairy—the half-night—I slept like the dead, not fully recovered from my duel with the elflord or from my physical wounds. I intended to take my turn as sentry to show the others that I was really recovering, but my companions vetoed it. Not that I argued very hard. A good Basilier meal would help. I found myself thinking about food a lot. I was looking forward to a chance to pig out again—too much of too many kinds of food too fast, washed down with about a barrel of beer. I think food was on everyone's mind.

"I ran a trotline all night," Annick said when she woke me near dawn. It had been well past midnight before we camped. "We have loads of fish." Nearly three dozen. Lesh already had them over a fire. We had been on thin rations the last few days, and even three dozen plump little fish wouldn't completely fill the empty spots.

The others stared at me while we ate. I couldn't read minds, but I could guess what they had to be thinking. They had to wonder whether I would be up to any kind of fight when we reached Coriander. I was wondering the same thing myself.

"I don't know," I said, and none of them asked what I meant. Lesh raised his eyebrows. Maybe he thought I *was* reading minds.

"We'd better get moving," I said without enthusiasm when the last of the fish were gone. The lethargy was more than a remnant of my duel and my wound. It was also an expression of my danger sense. It seemed that there was no place in this crazy world as safe as right where I was sitting, that any movement in any direction was toward peril.

"Are you all right?" Annick asked.

"Still tired, still aching," I said. I forced myself to my feet. "I'm not looking forward to more fighting either."

"Sometimes it's the only way," Annick said.

"Sometimes, but I'm still not thrilled with the prospect." End of conversation. Annick took it as a put-down and spun away from me.

The feeling of danger quickly got strong enough to scratch. The way ahead of us was blocked, a line clear across the isthmus from the way I felt. It was so strong that the pain in my back and side seemed to fade in comparison. We stopped for a few minutes fairly early that morning while I tried to judge how far ahead the danger was, but I didn't have the experience for that kind of fine-tuning. Drop a threat on my head and I could react, but this was too subtle.

"There's a whole damn army out there," I muttered, thinking out loud.

"Can we get around them?" Lesh asked.

I hesitated, then shook my head. "We can't afford the time to try. Besides, we'd probably have to steal a boat and sail around them, and I don't know anything about boats."

"Neither do I," Lesh said. Harkane shook his head.

"I do," Annick said, "but we'd have to cross to the other side of the isthmus and go back who knows how far to find one. So, unless you can fly us over this army, we have to go the way we are."

"Be ready to hightail it at the drop of a hat," I said when we started riding again. Maybe it was the wrong signal at the wrong time, but I chose that moment to pull the Cubs hat from my pocket and clap it on my head.

We saw two hunting parties, not much later. At least one of the groups spotted us, but they didn't give chase.

"An army takes a lot of feeding in the field," Lesh said after we angled out of sight of that group. "If their orders are to get food, that's all they're going to worry about." When they didn't break off to chase us, I had to agree that Lesh seemed to have it right.

By noon we were close to the Eastern Sea, almost *in* it at times, but just because the road angled that way, not because we sought the ocean.

"That's Dorthin, off across the water," Harkane said. "We're almost to the border." We were nearly to the base of the isthmus. The land stretching east wasn't just a headland, it was the mainland, the northern coast of Dorthin. Xayber extended no farther south than a line from this corner of the isthmus across to Arrowroot. Dorthin came right to this same corner—not more than a couple of miles from where we were sitting.

"Where's this Fairy army then?" Lesh asked.

"Already inside Varay, probably ringed right around Coriander and Arrowroot by now," I said. "Maybe with patrols deeper into the kingdom."

"We can't be five miles from Coriander right here,"

Harkane said. "I've been on that beach right there in the curve at the base of Xayber."

"Things could start getting hairy any second now, folks," I said. It was time to lay out my grand plan for getting past the elflord's army and into Coriander. Snag was, I didn't have anything like a real plan.

"A lot depends on how tight the siege of Coriander is, if there is a siege," I said, thinking out loud as much as "informing" my companions. "We need to get through Xayber's army and up to the gate, and hope to convince the gatekeepers to let us in before the elflord's people reach us." I thought about the static we had gotten trying to get past the gatekeepers on the town wall at Arrowroot, and we were trying to get *out* then.

"I have your pennant," Harkane said. I didn't know that I *had* a pennant. "It was your father's." He dug the strip of cloth from a saddlebag and held it up for me to see the familiar crest from home, the pennant I had seen flying over Castle Basil after Dad's funeral. "I'll wear it on my lance, as I did for your father."

"Okay, that's one problem solved." I hoped. "But keep it furled as long as you can. I don't want to tell Xayber's people who we are too soon. Until we're challenged, we'll just ride toward the castle as if we've got every right to be there. Coming out of Fairy, maybe nobody will question us if we look like we belong. Maybe we can get close enough to make our mad dash for the gate once we are challenged. The last thing we want is to get bogged down in fighting now. Once we stop moving, we're dead." That warning wasn't just for Annick. It was for all of us. Annick nodded like the others. I couldn't tell how she took it.

Castle Coriander sat atop a low man-made mound in the center of a mile-wide clearing—also man-made. The village was at the southwest edge of the clearing and even smaller and more primitive-looking than Nushur. This was just a couple of dozen rough cottages. The castle had one refinement I hadn't seen before. The outer wall was lined with long barbed spikes, a nasty complication for anyone trying to scale it. The castle had no moat, not even a dry ditch, so it needed *something*.

The besieging army was there all right, at the edge of the clearing and in the village. The circle was complete. The Fairy army could move to intercept anyone coming out of the castle . . . or trying to get in.

We rode in a tight group, keeping Annick in the middle. Her hair was braided and under the hood of a forest-green cape. We didn't want to advertise that we had a girl with us. That might look fishy in a combat zone. And I had removed my Cubs cap and replaced it with the steel pot that Harkane had brought along for me. I also had the mail shirt on again, despite the way it hurt me. We followed the road leading toward the castle gate, past hundreds of soldiers—men and those troll-like creatures—but only a few people who looked as though they had elvish blood. No one showed much interest in us at first. If the soldiers noticed anything, it was the elf sword hanging over my shoulder. I was acutely conscious of the sword myself. I had to fight the urge to draw it. I started whistling the sword's melody under my breath, and that was no conscious choice. I couldn't help it. As we neared the front lines, at the edge of the clearing, the number of Fairy soldiers increased. Finally, a mail-clad soldier blocked our path and held up his hand for us to stop.

"Go," I whispered. It would have been too much to hope for to think that we could get all the way through without a challenge. We put our heels to our horses. I drew Dragon's Death, and the soldier jumped out of its path. More soldiers came at us from the sides of the road, but not quickly enough to get in front of us. And then, after we were out in the clearing, archers started aiming for us.

"Unfurl that pennant," I shouted as an arrow skidded along my arm, ripping the fatigue shirt and sparking on the mail beneath it. The arrows kept coming. Somehow, we avoided any serious wounds, though we all received minor cuts in that first flurry. I had a nick taken out of my right leg. Two horses were also hit, but not badly enough to stop them.

Harkane waved my pennant. Lesh bellowed my identity as loud as he could, over and over, starting long before anyone inside the castle could possibly understand what he was shouting. Halfway there, I looked over my shoulder. Several dozen soldiers were chasing us, about half of them on horseback. They couldn't head us off, but we wouldn't have time to dicker for the gate to be opened. If it wasn't open when we reached it, we would have to fight—if our pursuers risked coming that close to the castle wall.

Fifty yards. I saw people above the gate, but no movement that suggested that they were ready to open up. Harkane kept waving the pennant. Lesh kept yelling. Then there was finally some movement on the parapets. I heard a creaking start. Then I looked over my shoulder again . . .

. . . and something happened.

I don't know exactly what the cause was, but my horse stumbled and I went headlong over him, rolling and tumbling when I hit the dirt. I went down hard, ending up on my back, and that sent such a shock of pain through me that I nearly passed out. My horse jumped over me and kept going toward the castle. I rolled over and found that I still had the elf sword in my hand. Getting up proved to be nearly impossible. I only managed to get as far as my knees by the time Lesh and Harkane got back to me. Annick had her bow out and she was doing her best to slow down the pursuit. I pulled myself up to my feet, using Lesh's leg and stirrup to help support my weight. Together, Lesh and Harkane managed to get me up on the horse behind Harkane. I was too shaken to do anything but hold on. Somewhere during this time, Annick stopped shooting arrows and chased down my horse. It carried one of the sacks of sea-silver.

We got to the gate with about a half second to spare. Archers on the battlements turned our pursuers back. More armed men waited for us inside the gate. There were plenty of hands to help me down from behind Harkane—and to support me afterward. I would have fallen without help. Harkane was too shaken by the accident to make his usual announcement of who I was, and Lesh was too busy trying to see to me, so I ended up introducing myself.

"I'm Gil Tyner, Hero of Varay." I left off all the jazz

about being prince and heir that Harkane would have added. "I need to see the castellan at once."

"I recognize your companions, and I see your father in you," one of the soldiers said. I had lost my steel pot when I fell. "I'm Baron Dieth, Castellan of Coriander." Nothing about his dress distinguished him from the men around him.

"Let's go inside," he said. "You all look to be in need of a meal." That drew a weak smile from me and a noisy smacking of the lips from Lesh.

"We need to talk, Baron," I said. I could hardly recognize my own voice. "But first I've got to check our cargo." As I feared, both of the sacks holding sea-silver had been pierced during the fusillade. At least Annick had managed to catch my horse after it threw me. We still had both bags of seaweed. "We need to keep this stuff wet—new pouches filled with water. And I'd like to save as much of the seawater that's left in here as possible."

Baron Dieth gave orders, and two of his men carried the leather bags of silver seaweed into the keep, doing what they could to slow down the leakage. We followed. Lesh and Harkane half-carried me. I was too wobbly to navigate on my own.

"I was your father's first squire when he became Hero," Dieth said. "I still grieve at his death."

16

To Sleep

Coriander had been built strictly for its military function, and it was only barely adequate for that. No thought at all had been given to the comfort of its garrison or to style. Coriander was small, smoky, and horribly crowded with people, animals, and bugs.

Servants were beginning to haul in supper when we reached the great hall, but supper had to wait a few minutes for my companions and me. Dieth and one of his people worked to clean and tape the new cuts we had all received running the gauntlet to get into the castle. Then, at Annick's insistence, my back had to be looked after.

"Not good," Dieth said after he had looked and prodded about a bit. "I picked up some first aid from your father. I'd say the lowest rib is definitely broken, the one just above *may* be, and there seems to be infection in the wound. I can help some, but you really need more attention than I can provide here. Parthet or your mother would be better qualified." He turned away from me and shouted across the great hall. "Aerbith, I'll need a poultice of rimeweed and the flask of number." He pronounced the last word *num-mer*, not *num-ber*. From "numb"—at least, that's how the translation magic gave it to me.

The poultice was bandaged over the wound on my back and stung worse than iodine or Mercurochrome ever did. I squirmed and twisted until Dieth made me drink about a jigger of a bitter green liquid. I can't begin to describe that, but it was the vilest taste I've ever experienced. Still, by the time I sat up and started to put my shirt back on after my ribs had been taped again, the pain in my back was almost gone.

"Better," I said—cautiously, trying a few easy movements.

"That should take care of you for a few hours, time enough to get through supper at least," Dieth said.

Dieth put the four of us at the head of the single trestle table with him. There were loads of food and plenty of beer. Coriander might be under siege, but the magic passages made siege a poor weapon against Varay. An enemy would have to ring every possible supply point for siege to work, as long as there was someone around to open the passages. The entire country would have to be under the domination of an invader, not to mention a certain house in Louisville, Kentucky. As long as there was a family member to open the doors, Varay could resist—unless a greater magic could block the passages. I didn't know if that was possible, but after my run-in with the Elflord of Xayber, I suspected that it might be.

"We haven't been able to send out our usual patrols

for ten days now,'' Dieth said once we were at the table
and starting to eat. "The elflord's had us corked up
tight."

"Ten days? It's just been six or seven since we saw all
the men heading south," I said. I dug right into the food
as if I hadn't eaten in weeks. At least the number made
it possible for me to shove food in without pain.

Dieth shrugged expansively. "Then they've simply
thrown another coil around us, not that they needed it.
If Arrowroot's near as hard pressed as we are, there won't
be a man available to send against the Etevar."

"You know the situation, then?" I asked, talking
around a mouth full of food.

"The Wizard Parthet was here a week back, on his
way to Arrowroot. He briefed me. But when he saw the
elflord's army outside here, he said he didn't know how
it would affect the campaign."

"A week ago? What was he doing, riding?"

"Of course not. He came and went by the doors, the
way he always does. Maybe it was even nine or ten days
ago. I'm not positive anymore. It's been too hectic here."

It didn't make sense. Parthet wouldn't have gone to
Arrowroot to meet me that far back. It couldn't have been
ten days before. We had left only *nine* days ago, and he
wouldn't have started out just as we were leaving. Maybe
he was inspecting, or maybe he was just moving closer
to Fairy to better cast my message to the Elfking. With
the doors, Parthet could flit around Varay at will.

"You'll stay the night?" Dieth asked somewhat later.
The pace of eating had slowed down a little. I still had
an appetite, but I wasn't cramming it in quite so roughly.

I shook my head and took a quick gulp of beer to wash
down food. "I have to get to Basil and tell the king and
Baron Kardeen what we've managed. But even before
that, I need a quick peek at Arrowroot." While I was
still free of pain. "You'll show me the doors?"

"Of course, lord."

I stopped shoveling food in for a moment and looked
at Dieth. "You were my father's squire?"

"Many years ago, when I was just a lad."

"When this crisis is over, I hope we have time for

many long talks. I never knew of my father's life here. A few weeks ago, I didn't even know that Varay existed.'' Something about the drug Dieth had given me must have mellowed my mood as well.

Dieth nodded. He did seem pained by Dad's death, even in the middle of his own nasty little war.

After taking in a little more food and beer, I collected my people. We got back into our war gear and went for the doors. The passage to Arrowroot was in the cellar of Coriander's keep. The door to Castle Basil was on the floor above the great hall.

''Have your swords ready when I open the way to Arrowroot,'' I said. ''I don't know how close the danger will be.'' The rest of our weapons were back in the great hall, except for my pistol, and I had pretty much discarded that from my thoughts. I stood in front of the door and stared at the silver tracing.

''You know where in Arrowroot this opens?'' I asked Dieth.

''I've never been down here when it was open,'' he said. ''It doesn't get much use. The old doorway opened into a gate tower on the Mist side of the castle, but your father set up a new passage after I left his service.''

''We going straight through?'' Lesh asked.

''Depends on what happens when I open the way.'' My palms were sweating. I couldn't have been more nervous if I were about to stick my hand into a snake charmer's basket. ''Ready?'' I looked around at my companions.

''Aye, lord,'' Lesh said. Annick and Harkane nodded.

I stretched my hands toward the silver. I remembered the sense of danger from that first day, and I had seen enough evidence of the danger sense since. I closed my eyes while I took a deep breath, then opened them again.

''Here goes.'' I touched my rings to the silver. The passage opened to a door on a blank corridor. I didn't see anyone, any clue to what might be happening there, but a wave of such deadly peril engulfed me that I stepped back in a hurry and broke the connection.

''What is it?'' Everyone asked that, more or less in unison.

"The worst I've felt." Everyone understood what I meant, even Dieth, since he had once been Dad's squire.

"You think the elflord's taken Arrowroot?" Dieth asked.

"Or worse." I wasn't sure what I meant, but I didn't have any doubt that the elflord could find *something* worse.

"What will you do now?" Dieth asked.

"Go to Basil and see if they know anything about it there. Then I think I'll probably still have to go into Arrowroot." I was the *Hero,* after all. Any solution was going to have to come from me, no matter what the problem was.

"If you'll open the way here again, I'll go through and start whatever needs doing," Annick said.

"I don't think so," I told her.

"If you know what the danger is, you can prepare for it better," she said.

I shook my head. Maybe Annick could do the spying, but if the elflord's army *had* taken the castle, there was a good chance that she would just start killing and keep at it until somebody killed her. I didn't want to give Xayber any more warning than absolutely necessary.

Dieth showed us to the doorway to Basil after we collected the rest of our gear and the new pouches with the sea-silver.

"Thanks for your help, Baron," I told him. "We may be back this way or go straight on to Arrowroot from Basil." I opened the passage—not a hint of danger at Basil. Annick, Lesh, and Harkane stepped through while I held the way open.

"Until we meet again, lord," Dieth said as I got ready to follow my companions. He touched his hand to his head in salute. I nodded and went through the door.

We came through in one of Basil's gate towers and headed across the courtyard for the keep and great hall. It was late evening. Supper was over, but a few men were still at the long table drinking.

"Lesh, check Parthet's room and workshop. See if he's around." If he wasn't at Basil, I'd have to pop through to his cottage, but I wanted to check the castle first. "I'm going to look for Kardeen. Harkane, find Timon. Maybe he knows what's going on here.''

"What about me?" Annick asked peevishly.

"You'd better stay with me. You may have answers I don't.''

Kardeen's chambers were a floor above the king's, close enough whenever His Majesty might want him. I banged on Kardeen's door and waited until he called out—not too happily, I thought. The room was dark, so I took a torch from the hall with me. When Kardeen saw me, he got up fast and pulled on a fur robe.

"We were afraid you were lost," he said as he hurried across the room, knotting the belt on his robe.

"Why?" I cocked my head a little to the side. "It's only been nine days. Parthet said he didn't think we could get back in less than ten, that it would probably take even longer than that.''

"Nine days?" Kardeen shook his head. "It's been twice that.''

It was my turn to shake my head. "Impossible. Four and a half days going north, four days coming back." I looked at Annick, who had stopped right in the doorway. "Nobody said I lost that much time during my struggle with the elflord.''

"It couldn't have been an hour," Annick said. "But time does strange things in Fairy. I've never heard of it running *that* much faster, but time *is* different there.''

I started to protest instinctively. Time is time. All parts of a solid world *have* to rotate in the same period. It was an outrage to the laws of physics to think otherwise . . . but then, there was a lot about the buffer kingdoms that seemed to have little relation to the laws of physics—magic doorways, ethereal duels, dragons. Those dragons had no more business flying than Wrigley Field would. But the protest never got out of my mouth.

"Where's Parthet?" I asked instead.

"At Arrowroot, waiting for you. He wouldn't stay here.''

"Have you heard anything from him?"

"Not for a week. Why?" I told him about the intense

danger I felt from Arrowroot and about the siege of Coriander. He knew about Coriander.

"Your mother has been handling their resupply, opening the way," Kardeen said.

"How much time do we have to meet the Etevar?"

"Little enough to intercept him at Castle Thyme, at the border. If you opened a passage at Arrowroot this minute, then rode your horse to death, you might barely have time to reach Thyme ahead of the Dorthini army. And you say there's trouble at Arrowroot and Coriander."

"There is. When I ride east, I'll start from here. I've been over that route before. Does that buy me enough time?"

He nodded hesitantly. "It should, a day or two. But we can't abandon the northern castles if they're under siege."

"Did you send any other men on toward Thyme?"

"We have six hundred men near there now. That's not nearly enough to hold the Dorthini army."

I closed my eyes to think. There could be no help from either of the northern castles unless the elflord backed off, and if he already controlled Arrowroot, I didn't see any way to make him back off. "I guess I have to go into Arrowroot first," I said. "Find out just what's going on there. Can you find me a half-dozen soldiers?"

"We'll find them. When will you go?"

"Before dawn, when most of the people there should still be asleep, whether they're ours or Xayber's. Maybe we can raise a little hell."

"We can do that!" Annick said. Kardeen looked at her.

"You're Resler's niece?" he asked. She nodded.

"We picked her up on our way into Xayber," I said. "She's been a help." Somehow, I managed to get that out without choking—probably because Dieth's drug picked that moment to start wearing off. I guess I grunted at the return of pain.

"Are you all right?" Kardeen asked, concern immediately appearing on his face.

"Not completely," I admitted, "but I don't have time

to worry about that. Baron Dieth had a foul brew for pain. It worked. Would there be any of it here?''

"Number," Annick said, and I heard the same *nummer* pronunciation as before.

"I'm sure your mother has some around here somewhere," Kardeen said. "You'd best have her check you out right away. What happened?''

"A spear took him in the back," Annick said. "He has a broken rib, maybe two, and the wound may be infected. Hadn't been for the armor, he'd have been skewered for proper.''

"Let's get you attended to," Kardeen said. He took my arm and led me out of the room.

I learned something new about my mother that night. *Another* something new. She was something of a doctor— and I don't mean witch doctor. I was guided back to my room. A page went for Mother. There were twenty minutes of her fussing over the injury. I got my pain medicine, and it tasted just as vile the second time. Mother smeared some kind of jelly over the wound. This preparation didn't sting the way Dieth's poultice had. It felt warm but not hot, soothing.

"The one rib *is* broken, but the other may not be. I can't be sure without X rays," Mother said. "You shouldn't have any real problem with it now, but you need to stay flat for at least forty-eight hours.''

"No chance," I said, and Mother didn't argue.

"I have to tell the king that you're back," Kardeen said then. "He left standing orders that he was to be told instantly of your return, and I'm already late. You'd best get a few hours rest before you leave.''

"As long as someone wakes me three hours before dawn," I said.

"I'll see to it," Kardeen promised.

Timon managed to promote a few gallons of hot water, and I took the time to get cleaned up. With a fresh dose of painkiller in me, I managed to get it done without help. Then I dropped across the bed like a dead man. Annick ended up in my mother's room. I slept without dreams. I had no sensations at all until Lesh shook me awake. Waking was difficult, almost impossible. The last thing I wanted to do was abandon sleep. At least there was no pain yet.

"The cooks sent up breakfast and coffee," Lesh said. A table had been set up in the room and loaded with food. I hadn't heard any of the preparations. Timon and Harkane helped me dress. They did most of the work. My mind was still somewhere closer to sleep than waking.

Mother came in with Annick while I was chugging my first cup of scalding, bitter coffee. From the glance Mother gave me, I could tell that she didn't approve of Annick—which meant that she had completely misread our relationship. I had seen that look before when I dated girls Mother didn't like.

"I'm worried about Parthet," Mother said while she took another look at my back. "If the elflord captures him, it won't go well. The lords of Fairy take harsh measures against the wizards of the seven kingdoms when they can."

"You mean they'd kill him?"

"Eventually. Parthet is old. It might not take him long to die under the treatment he could expect." Then she handed me a silver flask with the family crest and some extra designs worked into it. "This is the painkiller. Only take a single capful at a time, and don't take it at all until you feel the pain. It *should* be longer each time."

"Nobody warned me how screwy time is in Fairy," I said. I was getting used to things like that, people forgetting to mention things that were too "obvious" to need mentioning—*if* you knew enough about the land to start with. "Not that it would have made much difference. I still had to go," I added. But I wouldn't have taken the extra time to go farther north and raise hell after I got the sea-silver. And then I wouldn't have taken the business end of that spear in the back.

"How did you get the elf sword?" Mother stared at it. I told her, very briefly. I was too busy eating to weave the full tale.

"Be careful. Such weapons can cut the hand that holds them."

"So can everything else around here."

"Grandfather wants to see you before you leave," Mother said.

"Getting waked up twice in one night has got to be hard on him," I said, hoping to get out of a pointless formality. There wasn't much time, and I didn't see what good it could do.

"No matter, he sleeps lightly," Mother said. "He's been worried. You were gone so long."

I nodded—simple punctuation. "We'd better go see him, then."

The meeting was short and not as gloomy as I had feared. I introduced Annick and said what a help she had been. It was easier to say this time. Pregel thanked her and asked about her mother. Annick's bitter reply was the most painful part of the ten-minute meeting. It embarrassed everyone but her. The king had been informed about my injury. He asked me how I felt and then asked Mother for her medical opinion. She told him that I really should be flat in bed for two days but that I would likely be okay anyway as long as the injury wasn't aggravated, that I appeared to be healing lickety-split the way my father always had. I was starting to feel pain again, but I wanted to wait until I got away from Pregel to take my next swig of that awful elixir.

When the audience was over, Baron Kardeen had my extra soldiers and everyone was armed and armored. I left my shield behind—I hadn't found a use for that yet, despite my initial enthusiasm for it—but I did wear a helmet. Harkane had scared up a new one for me. The fact that I wore a tin pot willingly should give some idea how nervous I felt about the expedition. My Cubs cap was in my pocket, the blue bill sticking out. One bag of sea-silver was brought to the doorway that led to Arrowroot. We wouldn't take it through until Arrowroot was secure, though. If. The other bag was taken to the door leading to Coriander and put under guard. If I succeeded in Arrowroot, I would pop over to Coriander, set up the door there, then return to Basil to start my mad ride to Thyme. I didn't expect to need the second bag, at least not until I reached the other end, if then, but I wanted it handy, just in case.

Annick had an arrow nocked when I opened the way to Arrowroot. My bow was over my shoulder. I moved to the side and held the passage open with one hand while Lesh and the other soldiers hurried through to take up positions on the other side. Annick, Harkane, and I went through last. We left Timon behind again. He still wasn't happy about being excluded.

Once more, the sense of danger was overpowering as soon as I opened the passage to Arrowroot. Danger flowed through the doorway like heat out of an oven. But I was ready for it this time. I gritted my teeth and moved on into Arrowroot, Dragon's Death out and ready.

There were no torches burning in the corridor we entered. There were no watchfires on the battlements. Castle Arrowroot was silent but for the lapping of the Mist against the outer wall.

"Which way?" Lesh asked softly once we had a couple of torches burning.

"To the great hall, but carefully. We don't know what's waiting for us," I said.

We had trouble skulking—ten of us in chain mail and toting metal weapons—but it didn't matter. There was no one in the corridors, and everyone in the great hall was sound asleep. Underscore the *sound*. The volume of the combined snoring was incredible. A twenty-one gun salute might not have wakened men who could sleep through that din.

"These are Resler's people," Lesh said after we got a few more torches lit along the walls. Annick confirmed it.

"Hey, Kobe!" She prodded one of the sleeping men with her foot, roughly. His snoring changed tone for a moment, but he didn't wake. Annick pushed his shoulder again. He still didn't wake. Neither did anyone else. I whistled, as loud and shrilly as I could. A few men rolled over or interrupted their snoring for an instant, but that was all.

"Let's find your uncle," I told Annick. She led the way to his room. There was no answer to my first knock, so I bashed on the door with the hilt of Dragon's Death and shouted for Resler. There was still no reply, so I went in anyway. Resler was in bed, snoring as lustily as any of the men downstairs. We got lights going and went to work at waking the baron. It took ten minutes and two pitchers of water over his head before he even started to stir, another five minutes to get him sitting up with his eyes open.

"Morning already?" Resler asked, staring blankly. He didn't notice that he was sopping wet, or who was in his room, or anything. He yawned wide.

"What the hell's going on?" I demanded, almost shouting in my effort to shock his brain awake. It didn't work.

"What's going on?" he asked back, dreamy. His eyes started to droop shut again.

"Lesh, see if you can find coffee. Or whiskey if there's no coffee brewing." He nodded and left.

"Wake up, Baron." This time I did shout. Annick shook her uncle. Resler looked from me to Annick, then back at me. Something finally seemed to be getting through to him.

"What's going on?" he asked, a little more coherently.

"That's what I want to know," I said, still speaking loudly. "Why won't anyone wake up?"

"I don't know. I was sleeping so peacefully." Resler seemed to be speaking at about half speed, and running down. He raised his hands and started to rub at his cheeks and eyes. He looked as if he hadn't shaved since I left to get sea-silver. Finally, he looked up at me, more closely.

"You're back already? We thought it would take another week."

"Another week? I've been gone almost three weeks now!"

Resler shook his head slowly, then stopped. His eyes opened a little wider. "It can't be more than three or four days."

I was getting confused. First I was told that I had been

gone twice as long as I thought, then that I had just left. I watched Resler as he continued to come awake. It was incredibly, impossibly slow going.

"Where's my uncle, the wizard?" I asked when Resler looked as if he was finally getting his act together.

Resler's eyebrows moved toward each other. "We have a problem," he said slowly. "Something came over us." Very slowly now. "It hit the town first. The elflord . . ."

"What about Parthet?"

"He was—he was trying to find a way to fight—to fight the sleepiness." Resler started to sag, falling asleep again almost in the middle of a word.

"Wake up!" I screamed. His eyelids rose. He stared at me bleary-eyed.

"I wasn't." He blinked several times. "I was." He stood, moving like an arthritic scarcely able to bend his joints.

"What about Parthet?" I asked again.

"He's here somewhere." Resler started pacing slowly. "I can't think. My head's all fuzzy."

"Harkane, find Parthet. Take one of the men with you." Our six soldiers were standing in the hall outside the Baron's room. I sent four of them to the great hall to start waking the garrison. I warned them how hard it would be. I kept the last soldier at the baron's door.

All of the assurances that the elflord's offensive magics didn't work well outside Fairy weren't worth dragon's crap. Xayber had at least one dandy trick that was working all too well. Why worry about killing your enemies in battle or frying them with lightning or whatever if you can just put them to sleep and waltz in to slit their throats at leisure? That thought ripped a growl from my throat and a quick glance at Annick, but I didn't say anything. Xayber didn't even have to bother with finishing off sleeping soldiers if he didn't want to. He could just leave them to the Rip Van Winkle routine until they were irrelevant. Could. My immediate worry was that he might prefer to do a more thorough job, that the grim reaper's barbers might be on their way in at any minute. I wondered why they hadn't moved in already if the castle had been like this for a week, maybe two.

Annick and I kept at her uncle, trying to keep him awake. Lesh arrived with a bottle of whiskey—Johnny Walker Red Label scotch at that.

"There's nobody awake in the kitchens either," Lesh reported. "Cooking fires are stone cold. Rotten meat hanging in the larder. Looks like they've been snoozing for ages."

"No coffee?"

"I started a fire and put coffee on to boil. It'll be ready soon, but I thought this'd help." Boiled coffee. No wonder it all tasted so bitter.

Annick poured scotch down her uncle's throat. He gagged and sputtered, but it did seem to help. Then Harkane came screaming back.

"I found the wizard! On the battlements, standing like a statue, arms up, staring at the sky!"

I started running.

17

Perchance to Dream

Parthet wasn't alone on the battlements of the keep. There was also a sentry walking his circuit, a soldier who wasn't completely asleep, though he did seem to be in a trance, sleepwalking. The sentry didn't even notice the bunch of us who charged up the stairs and surrounded Parthet until he had walked another complete circuit, and even then he scarcely reacted. He simply detoured around us.

Parthet looked in bad shape. He *was* rigid, "like a statue." He was standing with his feet spread, head tilted back, arms extended upward at full reach, not even trembling—like Charlton Heston holding open the Red Sea before Yul Brynner could catch the fleeing Israelites. When I touched Parthet's shoulder, I got an electric shock and a fleeting glimpse of an unmistakable face.

"He's locked in a duel with the Elflord of Xayber," I said. That was all the explanation the people who had been with me in Fairy needed.

I had to do something. The idea of butting in and facing the elflord again turned my stomach. I was scared, and I couldn't hide that, not from myself. But I couldn't hesitate either. I took the elf sword in hand, got in front of Parthet, and touched my rings to his. There was another surge of electricity and I felt the hair on the back of my neck stand up. My teeth ached and I felt as if the skin on my face had tightened up about three sizes. Parthet slumped and disappeared from my view.

And I was facing the elflord on that featureless gray plain again. This time, I didn't wait for him to start the game.

"You try my patience!" I said, with genuine anger and all the phony confidence I could muster to hide my fear. "This man is mine, and this place. Leave while you may."

It was all bluff and bluster. I don't think I've ever felt half as arrogant as I tried to sound. I held Dragon's Death between us and took a couple of steps toward the image of the elflord. The face that looked back at me showed no emotion. I did have one advantage, maybe a couple. First, there was little chance now that I would be vulnerable to anything like the fall-on-your-sword ploy. I had seen it before and I wouldn't be taken by surprise again. Just keep a tight rein on your head, I told myself. And the second advantage: I was outside his realm now. I wasn't quite as certain of that one.

I also wasn't sure how long I could maintain this bluff. I brought my hands together so the rings touched, closed my eyes, and turned my back on the elflord. When I opened my eyes, I was back at Arrowroot. I took a deep breath and let it out slowly.

"Are you all right?" Annick asked.

I looked around the battlements while I felt myself out. "I think so. Where's Parthet?"

"Lesh and Harkane carried him downstairs. He's in trouble, Gil." There seemed to be real concern in her voice, and that surprised me. It was also the first time she had called me by name. "Was it really the elflord?"

I nodded. "There was no duel this time. I broke the contact." Okay, I was bragging a little, but more than that, I was wondering what was in the painkiller I had been taking to give me that kind of gall. "How long did it take?"

"Only a couple of minutes."

Long enough for Lesh and Harkane to carry Parthet off the battlements, at least. "See if you can learn anything from this guard," I said. He was still walking his post, paying no attention to anything but getting one foot in front of the other. "I've got to get downstairs to see to Uncle Parthet."

Lesh had ousted Baron Resler's chief functionary from bed, literally, to make room for Parthet. The steward didn't seem to mind. He was sound asleep on the floor, out of the way. I checked Parthet over. His pulse was weak and erratic, his face pale but sweating, and I could scarcely see any movement of his chest as he breathed. He needed a top-notch urban trauma center—with a resident witch doctor.

"Lesh, stay with him. If he stops breathing . . ." That took some time. I had to demonstrate artificial respiration. There wasn't time for a primer on CPR. I hoped it wouldn't come to that.

"Harkane, come with me. I'm going to open the way to Basil. Find my mother. Tell her what's happened to Parthet and bring her back with whatever she can find to help him. She can open the passage back."

"I know," Harkane said. He appeared rather shaken.

I was gone only three or four minutes. Parthet looked the same when I returned. "Lesh, get that scotch from the baron's room, if there's any left."

I had taken several first-aid courses while I was a teenager and I knew that whiskey wasn't the wisest choice of stimulants, but it was all we had, and I was afraid that unless I did something fast, I was going to lose Parthet. And his new glasses. The pair he had on when we found him had huge square lenses with heavy black frames— owl glasses with lenses thicker than the bottom of a dime root beer mug. They were on the nightstand next to the bed now. I looked through them but couldn't see anything but a blur. After I wiped off the dirt, water spots, and bird droppings, I still couldn't see through them.

Mother arrived quickly. She had an old black doctor bag with her, the kind that went out of style when house calls did. She gestured me out of the way and examined Parthet. She lifted his eyelids to check his eyes, put a hand to his chest to check respiration, then took a stethoscope out of the bag and listened to his heart.

"Put the blood-pressure cuff on him," she said then. I pulled the gadget out and set it up.

"Harkane told you how we found him?" I asked while the air hissed out of the cuff after Mother finished. She nodded. "He may have been like that for a week or more."

"I think he'll be okay." Mother took off the stethoscope and put it back in the bag. "He's tougher than a ten-year-old rooster. Did you give him anything?"

"About a tablespoon of scotch." I pointed at the bottle.

Mother helped herself to a long swig. "It won't hurt him. You don't realize how hard it is to kill a wizard."

"I'm beginning to get the idea," I said dryly. "I've even got a damn good idea what the elflord put him through. I've been there."

Mother's eyes narrowed. "You've lost weight."

"We didn't eat all that well in Fairy."

"We'll discuss your adventures when there's more time." She said that the way she used to say, "Just wait till your father gets home." I guess she was still fuming about Annick. I didn't feel any burning urge to correct her impression.

"Right now, I think Parthet needs another stimulant," she said. She administered this one, a larger dose. "Is the kitchen working?"

"Nothing's working. Most of the garrison's so deep asleep that it's impossible to wake them. The rest are in a trance, sleepwalking."

"The baron was sleeping again when I got the bottle," Lesh said.

"I think that's what Parthet was trying to fight on the roof," I said. "Obviously, he wasn't successful. I'm surprised that the elflord hasn't already sent his army in to set up housekeeping."

"He has," Annick called from the door. She was out of breath from running. "They're coming across the plaza with a siege tower now."

"I'll take care of Parthet," Mother said. "You'd better go evaluate the threat."

Yeah, and I thought I'd better check it out too. We all went except Mother. Annick and I had our bows. Maybe we could pick off a few of the enemy and make them think that the elflord's magic had failed. If they thought that the garrison was awake, they might not press the attack. I sent Lesh to round up the rest of the soldiers from Basil while the two I had with me accompanied Annick, Harkane, and me to the curtain wall.

There were more than three hundred men advancing across the plaza. Half were pulling on ropes, dragging a wooden tower—a framework with stairs and a drawbridge at the top. The near side was covered with wood and hides. A few more soldiers were behind the machine, pushing. The rest advanced in ranks, keeping station on either side of the tower.

"You ever shoot a flaming arrow?" I asked Annick.

"A what?" was quickly followed by, "Oh, I see. No, but am I right in thinking that this is a good time to start?"

"Yeah. Try to set the tower on fire." I took matches from my pocket. "These are supposed to be waterproof. They may work, if you can find anything flammable to tie to the heads of the arrows."

I got busy with my bow while Annick went into the guard shack. She came back with lamp oil and a bunch of rags to tie around her arrows. I needed a couple of shots to get the range—it can be tricky shooting down at an angle—but once I did, I scored hits. After the last of my aluminum arrows were gone, I found a crate of the local wooden variety by the weapon racks. They weren't quite as accurate, but they did help slow down the elflord's army. They weren't expecting fire either. Annick started a half-dozen small fires on the tower. Neither the leather nor the wood had been wetted down. They had no water handy to put out fires. I guess we *were* a complete surprise. Their leaders must have assured the soldiers that Xayber had taken care of the garrison.

The tower quit moving. Men scrambled to knock away the flaming arrows and tried to beat out the flames while others ran off to do the Jack and Jill routine. I wished them the same luck, but wishing didn't do any good.

Lesh showed up with ten men, the rest of ours and a few of the regular garrison who seemed to be awake finally. Two of our Basiliers claimed to be decent archers. I sent them for bows, arrows, and rags and told them to help Annick with the arson. With a little luck, I hoped we could set more fires than the enemy could extinguish. But once the attackers started pouring water on their contraption, fires were harder to start. After twenty minutes, we quit trying and concentrated on picking off soldiers. Four archers could only slow them down a little, though. They had the numbers, and once their leaders put some backbone into the grunts, they'd come on. And once they got the siege tower in place, it would be just a matter of time before they overwhelmed us.

"Massey, wake up!" Lesh shouted. I turned. Massey was one of our Basiliers. He stirred and shook his head.

"I don't know what happened," he said. "I got so sleepy."

"It's working on us," Annick said. "Are you okay?"

I shrugged. "I don't feel sleepy. You?" She shook her head. Lesh and Harkane seemed alert—most of the other Basiliers as well. But one, Tebber, was yawning fit to split his head open. The locals were nodding too, off and on. The magic was still working.

A gust of icy wind made me turn to look out at the Mist. There was heavy fog on the sea, maybe a half mile out and coming closer. I hoped that the breeze would help keep us awake at least.

"If that fog rolls in, we won't be able to see our targets," I said.

"Then we'd better get as many as we can now," was Annick's practical reply. She started letting off arrows as quickly as she could nock and aim. For once, I didn't feel like curbing her instincts. Extra speed didn't seem to hurt her accuracy either.

Riders were moving around the edges of the group of soldiers in the plaza now, urging them on. I saw three swords like Dragon's Death, elf swords on elf warriors, officers in the army of their lord—the elvish equivalent of knights, I suppose. The foot soldiers pressed forward, dragging and pushing the tower. They weren't breaking any speed records, but soon they'd be able to move archers to the top and keep us busy. Once we lost the height advantage, our job would be a lot more dangerous. And, almost as I thought that, the archers did start climbing and the tower's speed decreased a little more.

"What about that metal thing you carry under your shirt?" Annick asked.

The gun. "It probably won't work here," I warned, but I drew the pistol and flicked off the safety. It was as good a time as any to find out for sure. I set my bow aside and took a two-handed grip on the pistol. I aimed and pulled the trigger, expecting nothing.

Bang. "I'll be damned," I muttered. But I hadn't hit anyone. I took more care the next time and saw one archer tumble from the siege tower into the men who were pushing it. The next shot wounded another archer in the arm, putting him out of action. Then a click. I worked the slide to eject that cartridge and tried again. Another click. I pulled the trigger again, then cocked the gun by hand and pulled the trigger once more. No luck.

"Well, it was a good idea while it lasted." I holstered the gun and picked up my bow again.

I glanced north. The fog was definitely closer. South: so was the tower. Lesh and the other soldiers with us had started testing their strength with spears. There were bundles of wooden lances with fire-hardened tips. With a little oomph behind them, they could pierce padded leather and take the air out of a man in mail . . . as I knew from experience. They also gave us a few more chances to try firing the siege tower. Those spears could support more fire than the arrows. Not enough to make a difference, but it did slow the attackers again.

"We've got ten, maybe fifteen minutes before they get that tower in place," I said, loud enough so that most of the people on the battlements could hear. "I'm going down to see how Parthet's doing. I'll be back."

I've never gone in for jogging, but that wasn't the time for a casual stroll. Parthet was awake, but flat on his back and not moving much. I didn't expect him to be up dancing jigs. I recalled how I felt after my first set-to with the elflord, and that had lasted only minutes, not days.

"What's it like out there?" Mother asked calmly.

"They've got a siege tower almost in place, with the men to use it. On the other side, we've got the heaviest fog you ever saw racing in off the Mist. And the men I brought from Basil are starting to fall asleep."

"How did you free me from the elflord?" Parthet asked weakly.

"I broke in on your connection with the rings and told him he was starting to bug me." Parthet smiled, just a little. "What were you doing squaring off with him, anyway? I thought you were going to send a message to his king."

"I did. At least, I think it got through. Then, when people started dropping off to sleep here I had to try something to help." Parthet was quiet for a moment, gathering strength. "You were overdue and there was no one else to turn to."

"You wouldn't by chance have a quick spell for overturning a siege tower, would you?" I asked.

"Not a quick one, and I'm too weak to use the slow one I do have."

"Can I use it?"

"No, lad, not even if I had time to teach you the words."

"Mother, if I open the way, can you get Parthet through to Basil?" She nodded. "Okay, let's go. We don't have much time. If there are any men left to send to help us, get them here fast or it'll be too late." I picked Parthet up and carried him. He wasn't very heavy, but heavy enough to put a noticeable strain on my back and ribs. I gritted my teeth and followed Mother out of the room. After I got them both transferred to Basil, I raced back to the outer wall.

The siege tower was within a dozen feet of the moat,

but it wasn't moving very quickly at all now. There were no pullers left, just pushers. The odds were too heavy in front of the rig. The fog had arrived, though. It already hid the northern wall of Arrowroot.

"That can't be natural," I said as I started using my bow again. Annick didn't bother to answer She was still shooting arrows as fast as she could, concentrating so fully that she didn't seem to notice the blood on her fingers from the constant chafing of the bowstring. The muscles at the side of her neck stood out each time she drew the string back to her cheek. The fog kept coming toward us, a wall as straight as any ever built by a construction crew, catching us from behind and moving across the moat toward the tower. I could barely see Annick, and she was only six feet from me.

I heard muffled shouting below—command tones.

Here they come, I thought. I put down my bow and drew the elf sword, moving toward the spot where the siege tower's drawbridge would come down. We waited in the isolation of that fog, listening to an occasional muffled noise coming from beyond the wall. I could feel my back starting to ache again, so I grabbed a quick sip of the painkiller.

Wood creaked finally, but there was no thump of the drawbridge coming down, no sudden surge of my danger sense.

"What's keeping them?" Annick whispered.

"Something's happened," I said, an understated expression of the surprise I felt as the feeling of danger started to wane for the first time since our arrival in Arrowroot. I took a moment to try to probe with the sense—and I wasn't even sure that I could use it that way.

"I think they're pulling back," I said after a moment.

I heard a loud yawn inside the castle, then a thick "What the hell's happening? Where'd this blasted fog come from? Where am I?" One of the garrison soldiers, fresh from his long nap. Lesh answered him, and, also inside the castle, somebody started blowing a horn.

"That's the alarm!" a new voice shouted.

"Where's the trouble?" another asked.

"Settle down," I said, not quite in a shout. "We'll

know what's going on soon enough. Watch for the siege tower outside the wall.''

That brought another assortment of comments from garrison soldiers. There were running feet inside the castle, in the courtyard, and on the stairs, as men raced to their battle stations, a week or two late. They were stumbling into each other and over obstructions. The fog was so thick that I couldn't make out my own feet unless I moved them.

"Somebody bring Baron Resler here," I shouted. "This is Gil Tyner." I didn't add titles, but I heard a distant-sounding voice say, *"The Hero of Varay."*

"They're all waking up," Annick said, her voice closer than before. "Did you scare the elflord off when you challenged him?"

"I couldn't scare Xayber off with the 82nd Airborne behind me," I said. Let her puzzle over that for a while, I thought with a chuckle.

"The fog's passing," someone said from the north side of the keep. Other voices took up the refrain and got clearer. A few minutes later, the tail end of the fog crossed the parapet where we were waiting. It was another perfectly straight line, fog on one side, clear air on the other. The fog moved across the moat, toward the town, picking up speed once it was clear of the castle. The siege tower was standing right at the edge of the moat, but there were no enemy troops in sight . . . except for about a dozen bodies left sprawled in the plaza.

The tower and the bodies were surprises to the soldiers who had been sleeping. "Where the hell did *that* come from?" was a popular question.

The fog bent toward the east like an echelon movement in a parade. There were no live soldiers in the plaza, no elf warriors waving claymores, no trace of any enemy but the dead.

"They used the fog to pull out," Harkane said.

"They've run off!" one of the Basiliers added.

Annick dropped her sword. I turned when I heard metal clatter on stone.

"Great Earth Mother!" she swore. "You've beaten the elflord *again*."

18

Doors

I knew that it wasn't that simple—it couldn't be—but I was so astonished by Annick's reaction that I couldn't correct her mistake just then. Maybe the way I faced the elflord contributed to his decision to pull back from Arrowroot, but I couldn't be the main reason. Xayber and I hadn't come to our main event yet. I wasn't looking forward to that. No, something else must have convinced the elflord to call off the siege. Even if he thought I was a hotshot elf warrior out to make life difficult for him, Xayber had a bunch of elf warriors in the attacking force. This had to be Parthet's victory. His message must have reached the Elfking and started something in Fairy, behind Xayber.

Soldiers finally came through from Basil. Maybe the barn hadn't burned down first, but that was only because somebody had blown out the match. It took time to sort out the confusion in Arrowroot. Resler got patrols out to check on the town's residents, to make sure that the elflord's army was really gone, and to see to the dead that had been left behind. I went to Basil to check on Parthet. He was in bed, propped up, awake and eating. Mother was confident that he would recover.

"It'll take time, though," she told me in the hallway outside his room. "At his age, he can't spring back the way he once would have."

"Do what you can," I said. "We're going to need his magic when we meet the Etevar. He's certain to have his wizard along."

"I don't know." Mother shook her head doubtfully. "Three days? He may need that many weeks."

"We don't have weeks. Unless there's another qualified wizard lurking around that I don't know about."

"There isn't. Uncle has never trained an apprentice."

"Well, one thing anyway. You can be my link to open

the new doorways. I'll set up one in Arrowroot, pop over to Coriander, and set one up there—with a little luck, maybe the elflord has abandoned that siege too—then come back here to start my ride to Thyme.'' Mother nodded. I stared at her for a moment. Our roles had changed drastically since I arrived in Varay, and I was just becoming aware of that. ''You can handle a passage when we transfer the troops too, I guess.''

''I might as well, since I'll be there to open them.''

''Yeah. I don't want to try it solo if I can avoid it. But once the army comes through, we have to have Uncle Parthet.'' There wasn't the slightest doubt in my mind of that.

''I'll do what I can.''

There wasn't time for much more. I wasn't even sure that I would have time to get the doorways set up and make the ride east before the Etevar's army crossed the border. Mother and I set up schedules for when I'd want somebody at the new doorways. We couldn't synchronize watches or get on the telephone, or anything like that. We would try just before sunset the next day, in case I managed to get to Thyme that fast—though Mother and I both knew that it would take Kentucky Derby racing the whole distance to make it—and then the morning after that, beginning at first light and continuing for as long as it took. I picked up one of the pouches of sea-silver and stepped back to Arrowroot. Annick was waiting for me.

''How's your uncle?'' she asked.

''Eating. He'll recover. Where's *your* uncle?''

''The last I saw, he was in the great hall, trying to organize a meal.''

He was still there. I interrupted his work for my own. ''I'm going to open new passages, one from here and one from Coriander. Then I'm going to ride to a place just this side of Castle Thyme to put the other ends of the passages. When I've got them open, we'll bring through every soldier we can to meet the Etevar.''

Resler started to nod but checked his head in midgesture. ''Just what do you mean, 'every soldier we can'?

How many men do you figure to leave to guard my castle and town?''

I had never really gotten down to thinking about those details, but I hesitated for only an instant. ''We don't leave a single soldier behind. This has to be all or nothing. If we don't stop the Etevar, the elflord is *his* headache. If we do stop him, we can ferry your men back here as quickly as we move them out.'' Resler nodded, but with obvious reluctance. ''I'll put this end of the passage at ground level, through an outside door so we can transport horses.'' For a moment, I thought that Resler was going to demand confirmation of my orders by the king, but he didn't.

''The northwest tower might be best then,'' he said. ''It's nearest the mews. You open the way. We'll be ready.''

I grinned. The hoopla of being Hero had *some* benefits. Resler was plainly unsatisfied with my decisions, but he wasn't going to argue. ''There is that problem yet,'' I admitted. ''I've got to get cracking.''

''So do I,'' Resler said. ''I'll see you in a couple of days.'' His face was grim as he nodded and walked off. He did have a lot of work to do before he could be ready to move his garrison out. There were people missing from his town, though most of the locals were okay now that they were awake again—just scared. Food had to be found, which meant hunting parties. And there was a siege tower to dismantle.

''I'll show you the door he means,'' Annick said after Resler was gone. She hadn't said a word to her uncle. She had held back as if she didn't even want him to notice that she was around.

''I thought you'd want to get out and join the hunt for stragglers,'' I said, but not harshly—*carefully*, not harshly.

''No. I'm sticking close to you until this is over. You've hurt the elflord more in a couple of weeks than I have in a lifetime.''

''And one of these days the elflord will do whatever it takes to even the score,'' I said. I didn't care much for this new Hero worship. In some ways, I preferred the old bloodthirsty, rebellious Annick. Especially since I knew how misplaced her awe was. When the letdown came, she would be more bitter than ever. And there *would* be a letdown. Few of the Heroes in the vault below Castle Basil had died of old age.

The sea-silver seemed alive and active, animal rather than plant, when I pulled the first strand from the water bag. When the silver completed a circuit between my rings accidentally, I felt an itchy tingle in both hands. I got to an end of the strand and applied it to the bottom corner of the doorjamb. The silver grabbed at the stone the way iron filings grab a magnet. I was able to stretch the weed in place as fast as I could slide my hands along the jamb. By the time I got halfway up the first side, the silver seemed to be leaping ahead, racing to attach itself, leeching to the stone. The first strand reached up the side and across the top. A second completed the circuit. When I was done, I couldn't even make out the joins between the two strands, even though I knew precisely where they were.

"Stand inside the tower, behind me," I told Annick. I didn't want any avoidable distractions while I finished my work.

I stood in the doorway the way Parthet had told me to and reached out to touch the tracing on either side with my rings, igniting that soft tingling again. I stared out at the courtyard, not focusing on anything in particular, simply trying to set the entire scene firmly in mind, what I would see from the other end of the passage. People crossed the courtyard. Some turned to look at me, others made a point of looking away. I tuned them all out, as best I could. I didn't know how much effort I had to put into this memorization for the magic to work, but I couldn't afford to come up short after making an insane marathon ride across nearly half the kingdom. Sure, I hoped to have either Mother or Parthet on this end when I opened the way, but I didn't dare count on that absolutely. I had to be ready to try the job single-handed if it came to that. And if my first shot failed, I wouldn't have time to ride back to make a second attempt. I scanned the lower parts of the curtain wall to my left, the keep directly across the courtyard, the pavement stretching away from the door. I stood there and soaked in the view until I could close my eyes and see it all almost as vividly as with my eyes open before I took my hands from the tracing and did a lot of blinking.

"That's one," I told Annick as I bent over to pick up the water bag with its sea-silver. "Now for Coriander."

Baron Dieth was almost bubbling over with excitement when I arrived. Xayber's army had simply packed up and left. "They just melted back into the forest," was how Dieth put it. He had been in no hurry to order a pursuit—a wise decision as far as I was concerned. The elflord's soldiers had taken a few villagers with them, presumably as slaves, but most of the local peasants had been safe inside the castle, so losses weren't as serious as they might have been. I told Dieth what we were going to do, in more detail than before. He nodded and suggested a suitable doorway. Annick watched while I lined the doorway and did my memorizing. Then we returned to Basil.

Parthet was sitting at a small table in his bedroom with a platter of food and a pitcher of beer—and he was making them disappear the old-fashioned way, without magic.

"You did a bang-up job at Arrowroot, lad," Parthet said, without slowing down his intake. "If you hadn't come along, I think the elflord would have kept me hanging there until I shriveled up and blew away." His voice sounded a lot stronger, he seemed to be in good spirits, and he didn't even appear to be nearly as stooped over as he had been before. His encounter with the elflord seemed to have actually done him some good.

"I still don't understand all of it, but we can puzzle it out later if we have to," Parthet said. "Don't waste time worrying about me, lad. You get yourself over to Thyme and set up the doorways. I'll be ready to do my bit on this end." He stopped eating long enough to take off his glasses and wave them at me. "You know, these are really marvelous. I'm seeing things I haven't seen in a thousand years."

I smiled. It was a tremendous relief knowing that Parthet was recovering, and not just because I wanted him beside me when we faced the Etevar's army. I told him exactly where I had put both new doorways and where I would put the ones in the east, and then I left him to his meal.

Next I had to face what almost became a mutiny among my "entourage" when I told them that I was going to make the long ride east alone.

"Every extra rider will slow me down that much more, and we don't have any hours to spare if we're going to get our army in place before the Etevar marches into Varay," I told them.

I couldn't see pulling a ride that might turn out like the one in *The Three Musketeers* with everyone falling by the wayside in one trap after another, leaving only the hero (small *h*, please) to finish the ride and quest. My promise that they could be the first ones through the doorways didn't help much, but there was a limit to how far they would press the argument. I *was* the Hero of Varay, after all. The only person who could overrule me was the king, and none of my people thought enough of their chances to make that appeal.

Then there was Annick. She waited until we were alone.

"*I'm* going with you no matter how many high-and-mighty pronouncements you make," she informed me, and then she made her arguments in a hurry, before I could blow my stack and order her locked in a dungeon or something—and I didn't even know if Castle Basil had a dungeon.

"You try making this crazy ride alone and you're liable to lose the whole kingdom," she shouted—right in my face. "You're going to ride day and night, you said, racing as fast as you can to beat the Etevar. Why, if it wasn't for that number you're swilling, you couldn't even stay upright that long. And what happens if your horse stumbles or steps in a hole? You're in the middle of nowhere without a ride. You won't be able to travel far or fast on foot with that busted rib and that hole in your back, no matter how much painkiller you drink. By the time you find yourself another horse and finish your ride, it's too late. The Dorthini army is inside Varay. They've destroyed the men already waiting for them and it's too late to get the rest of our soldiers in front of them. Ride at night? You're blind in the dark. I'm not. You'll travel faster with me, not slower. And if one horse is injured, we still have a second.''

My first reaction was anger. With Annick, it had to be anger. But I couldn't refute her arguments and I wasn't stupid enough to let my anger get in the way. I could take a second horse, switch back and forth to spread the burden, but handling two horses might slow me too. I had never tried riding one horse and leading a second. My back? Who could say what a day and a half, almost two full days, of hard riding would do to it? And Annick was certainly right about night vision. She did have that useful bit of elvish heredity. I didn't even sputter. I kept my mouth shut until the anger faded.

''Then let's eat and get out of here,'' I said.

Pushing ourselves and our horses for all we were worth, I thought that we might reach that cottage in the orchard near Castle Thyme in thirty hours. Since it was well past noon when we left Basil, that meant sunset the next night, or later. Earlier would be better, but earlier was unlikely, despite the arrangements I had made for either Mother or Parthet to be ready to open the passages before dark. I needed light to complete the passages, and if there wasn't enough light to work by when we arrived, I might have to wait until the next morning when I would have Parthet or Mother waiting to help with the final connections again. I didn't know if torchlight or a fire in the cottage's fireplace would be enough for me to do the job alone. The hard part of the magic was already done, I hoped. With someone on the other end, maybe firelight *would* be enough. Maybe.

Most of the ride was a blur. Annick and I concentrated on our horses, willing them to greater speed, and we watched the road for holes or rocks that might twist a horse's foot and lame it. I was swimming in sweat within an hour and developed a monumental headache from the futile mental effort. I kept putting off taking more painkiller as long as I could. It was so powerful that I thought it might easily be addictive. I didn't want to take any more of a chance on that than I absolutely had to. Even when I did take a sip, it didn't completely erase the pains of riding or of my mending injuries.

Fields and forest passed on either side of us. Annick and I pushed our animals to their limits, almost beyond reason, stopping only when it was absolutely essential and resting for no more than a few minutes at a time when we did. My headache stretched down my spine and linked up with the pain in my back early in the ride. Then those pains connected themselves to the cramps in my legs and the throbbing of a butt too long in the saddle. While it was light out, Annick and I rode side by side, or I rode just in front of her when the road narrowed. Once dusk started to congeal into night, Annick took the lead and I concentrated on keeping my horse, Gold, close to hers, just a little behind and to the side so we wouldn't collide if Annick had to stop suddenly.

We rode through the village of Nushur in the dark. I toyed with the idea of stopping for fresh horses, but decided against it. We probably wouldn't have found very good animals, and waking the place for remounts would have cost us too much time. At least, I was afraid that it would. So we rode on through the night, into morning and a sun that stabbed deeply into our sleepless eyes.

Our horses started stumbling on dust and air. Their pace fell way off. Their chests heaved as they fought for air, sweating, trying to keep up with our demands. Long before noon, it was obvious that we had to give our animals at least a couple of hours to recuperate. If we didn't, Annick and I would both be walking before long. But we pressed on, ''a little farther, a little farther,'' until we nearly waited too long. We finally pulled up along a decent little stream and a grassy bank that allowed us to get away from the road. The animals would have to wait to drink, but they could rest and graze while they were cooling off.

When I dismounted, I could scarcely stand. My knees were jelly. The rest of me felt as if I'd been repeatedly bashed with baseball bats—the kind that players tamper with to give them more action. I tried to take a few steps to work out the kinks, but I could hardly move. My back and ribs almost escaped notice in the general achiness. I took a sip of the painkiller anyway. Annick seemed to have almost as much trouble moving as I did, so maybe the rib was pretty far along in its mending. As soon as we *could* move around with some ease, we drank our fill of cool water from the stream and refilled our drinking skins.

"I'm going to soak off some of the sweat and dirt," Annick said. It sounded like a good idea, but I wasn't prepared for the casual way she stripped. The tunic came over her head. She dropped her trousers and stepped out of soft boots. That was all she was wearing. She draped her clothes over a branch, "to let the wind blow some of the stink out of the them," she said when she turned to me.

Despite the way I felt about Annick, seeing her naked roused me quickly, fully. Her skin was milky white from forehead to toes. Against that almost albino pallor, her nipples looked purple, twin wine-colored birthmarks. Her pubic hair was as blond and fine as the hair on her head, and so sparse that it scarcely blurred the skin beneath it. When she moved, the muscles in her arms and legs flexed smoothly, strength without bulges. She stepped down into the water and moved away from shore, sinking until only her head showed. Then she turned toward me again.

"Aren't you coming in?"

"I'm coming," I stuttered, and I almost made a bad pun of it. I took off everything but my jockey shorts and turned away from Annick when I got that far. I didn't want to show her how she affected me.

The water was cool, but not cool enough to deflate me. I went under and swam a few strokes downstream, then back. We swam and washed for twenty minutes, maybe half an hour, letting the water clean and relax us. As much as possible, I avoided looking at Annick, but that didn't help much. The look I'd had before was imprinted as deeply in my mind as the doorways I had prepared at Arrowroot and Coriander. I was still in the water when Annick climbed out—slowly, temptingly, her backside wiggling gently. I ducked underwater again as she cleared the top of the bank and stayed down nearly a full minute before I got out.

"I never expected you to be bashful," Annick said when I got to the top of the bank and started stripping loose water from my skin. "You're going to be mighty uncomfortable riding with wet drawers."

"We don't have time for anything but bashful," I said, trying to concentrate on getting rid of water. "Aren't you afraid you'll burn?" She sprawled on her back in a sunny patch of grass, arms and legs stretched out—like a snow angel. But there was no snow and she was certainly no angel.

"I never burn," she said. I shook my head. With skin that pale, a candle ought to pop freckles out on her, but she didn't have a single freckle visible. More of her elvish heritage, I assumed.

I didn't have to worry about the misery of riding with wet shorts, though. I had a change of socks and underwear left in my pack. I changed, keeping my horse between Annick and me. When I had everything but my shirt on, I took both horses to the stream for their drinks. Annick flipped over to dry her back in the sun. She spread her hair out to the side. Not a single freckle anywhere.

I stayed with the horses while they drank and grazed a little more. They had every right to expect a long holiday from work, but the work wouldn't be done until we got to that orchard and cottage, set up the doors, and pulled the army through from Arrowroot and Coriander. If then. When I finally led the horses away from the stream, Annick was dressed. I had her pull the old, wet bandage off my back. When she said that the wound was scabbed over nicely, I decided not to bother having her put another gauze patch over it.

Annick ran a hand up and down my spine, and when I spun around to face her, she gave me a teasing little smile that added a painful twist to my groin. I almost told her about groupies. Almost. Another time, another place, I might want to take advantage. After all, you don't have to be *completely* pure at heart to be a Hero.

* * *

By midafternoon, it was obvious that we weren't going to reach the cottage before dark. Even with the rest, our horses couldn't maintain anything like their full speed. We had to pace them as best we could, just to keep them moving at all. A little before sunset, we turned off the road and started moving cross-country, the way Parthet, Lesh, Timon, and I had the first time out. I wasn't completely certain about this part of the route, but it seemed safer than parading right past Castle Thyme. I described what I remembered of the route to Annick, since she would soon be picking our path.

We were close to the orchard—near the end of the low hills—when we stumbled across the army that Baron Kardeen had sent on ahead by road. *Army*—a few hundred men who were waiting for the promised reinforcements. They were glad to see us, but they would have been happier to see a lot more.

"There are Dorthini patrols everywhere between here and the border," the commander, Sir Hambert, said.

"Any sign of the main Dorthini force yet?" I asked.

"The last scouts who made it back said that they couldn't reach Castle Thyme before noon tomorrow—probably a lot later."

I closed my eyes in relief for a moment. We had made it in time. If it mattered. After the long ride I couldn't help but think that it might still come down to simply bringing more people through to be mowed down by the Etevar's army. I didn't share my gloomy misgivings, though.

"Be ready to move up right after dawn," I told Sir Hambert. "I'll open the passages then and we'll bring the rest of the army through." I asked about the orchard and cottage, if Dorthinis were using the place.

"Not that I know of," Hambert said. "None of my scouts has reported any activity around there."

"How many Dorthinis in the main force?" I asked.

Hambert hesitated. "I don't trust the numbers my scouts give me," he said. "They've reported as many as five thousand. I hope that's an exaggeration. My own guess would be half that." I tried to tot up the rough numbers I had. Even if the Etevar had only twenty-five hundred men, he would still outnumber us nearly two to one. And he had Castle Thyme. That might be worth another thousand soldiers if he used the advantage wisely. I didn't count on him to be stupid.

"Annick and I will go on to the cottage tonight," I told Hambert. "Bring your men up at dawn."

"Two miles, that way." Hambert pointed just north of east.

Annick led the way. We rode slowly, giving our horses a chance to cool down. Since darkness had already fallen, we had all night to wait.

"We'll have to wait for dawn," I told Annick. "With Dorthini patrols around, we can't show a fire for me to try to finish the passages tonight."

"That's still plenty of time, isn't it?"

"If those scouts were right about how far off the Dorthinis are."

Riding at a slow walk gave my aches a chance to make themselves felt again, and when I took a nip of painkiller—the flask was getting low—exhaustion flowed over me. Off and on, I had dozed a little in the saddle coming east, but you can't get much rest that way. I looked forward to some real sleep, but at the same time I was afraid that Annick and I might both oversleep, snore on through the morning while the Etevar got closer and our men fretted at the delay. I mentioned that worry to Annick.

"I wake at the first hint of dawn, no matter what," she said, waving her hand in a dismissing gesture. "It *never* fails."

I hoped that she was right, even though part of my mind was trying to remind the rest that we would have Sir Hambert and his men coming up to the cottage at dawn, that *they* would certainly wake us, but when you're as tired as I was then, irrational fears seem saner than logical thought. I even got to the point of *Perhaps my danger sense will keep me from oversleeping with the enemy so close,* with the nervous tag *but it might not wake me until the cottage is surrounded.*

We reached the orchard and dismounted to lead our horses the last stretch. They were near the end of their endurance. Even Gold seemed hard put to keep up with my own slow walk. There were no lights on in the cottage, no sign of people or horses already there, but we checked the cottage and orchard out thoroughly before we put our horses in the tiny attached stable, unsaddled them, and brought in water and hay for them. Then we carried our stuff—and the sea-silver—into the cottage.

There was no real bed, just the hard bench where my father's body had been. I had no intention of sleeping there. Ghosts had been in my mind all too much lately. I got my thermal blanket and my saddle and found a spot on the floor where I thought the morning sun would get me in the face, just in case. The night was a trifle chilly after the heat and sweat of the long ride. I shucked my weapons and boots and settled myself in, wrapping the blanket around me. I had my elf sword close—and my own regular sword. I took a couple of deep breaths and started to drift off, doing a fairly good job of not thinking about Annick and the way she had looked naked earlier. I was much too tired to let my mind cook over her.

I thought.

I yawned, relaxed, sliding down the incline. Sleep was waiting to jump all over me for a change. There would be none of the long tossing and turning that I usually have to wade through to reach slumber. I could hear Annick's soft movements, but they didn't bother me—until I sensed that she was very close.

When I opened my eyes, Annick was kneeling right over me. There was enough dim light filtering in to let me see milky white skin as she came down and kissed me. Her hair slid forward off her shoulders and covered my face. Then she was in the blanket with me, pressing her body against mine.

Tired as I was, I couldn't ignore her. I could feel both our hearts beating, not in time. Between us, we got my clothes off. Annick had stripped before she came down on me. Passion replaced exhaustion, and we went at each other as though it were a contest, a joust—bruising kisses, frenzied groping, inarticulate grunts and moans. We seemed to be all over the cottage, rolling around, bumping into things, rolling back. Annick eventually straddled me and reached down to join us. Locked together, we continued to roll around the floor like wrestlers. The build-up was maddening, the climax explosive. I felt almost as drained as I was after the duel with the elflord. My back didn't waste much time reminding me that it wasn't completely healed yet, but even that wasn't enough to slow us down.

Afterward, when I fell asleep, Annick was half on top of me yet—not on my injured side luckily. She had collapsed, as spent as I was, but still holding on. Neither of us could have found the strength for an encore.

19

The Congregation of Heroes

I guess I slept soundly through most of the night—what was left of it—but it wasn't a peaceful sleep. I had a long dream, very detailed. It seemed so real that I never realized that it was a dream until after I woke, and even then it didn't fade away the way dreams normally do.

It started with a long walk down the stairs leading to the burial crypt below Castle Basil. I was alone on the stairs, not part of a procession. My footsteps echoed. I looked around almost constantly, as if I were trying to tie the echoes to someone else. There was a nervous knot in my gut, but my only companions were the multiple shadows I cast in the torchlight.

When I reached the doorway to the crypt, I hesitated for a long time, or so it seemed, before I entered. I didn't want to go into that chamber. I felt a powerful dread.

A long table had been set up inside, parallel to the burial wall. The capstones of the burial niches for all the Heroes of Varay were missing. The dead Heroes were sitting along one side of the table, my father at the center. They all stood and raised golden goblets in toast when I appeared in the doorway. They looked as though they belonged in a reunion picture of victims from slasher movies. Dad's wounds were all open, gaping, both the wounds that had killed him and those that had scarred over long before—the scars that had once made me believe that he was a spy like James Bond. All of the other Heroes sported similar wounds. There was no blood—just open gashes in skin and clothing.

The man standing next to Dad at the center said, "Hail the Hero of Varay," and then he took a long drink from his golden goblet. The rest of the Heroes echoed his toast and drank. Then each introduced himself—in chronological order, I think. The one who had offered the toast called himself Vara. Dad was the last. I caught a few other names in between that I recalled seeing on the missing capstones back in Basil.

Even Dad introduced himself formally when it finally came down to his turn.

"We've been waiting for you, son," he said after he drank his toast. He raised his goblet again. "I had hoped that the wait would be much longer, though. Your mother and I had such great dreams for you. Come, your place is waiting."

I didn't move from the doorway. I *couldn't* move. I was frozen in place. Moving would mean—at least in my mind—that I was accepting this . . . this *verdict*, and I wasn't ready to do that. I held on to the doorjamb.

"What's this all about?" I asked. My voice echoed over and over, so thickly that the words were almost obliterated by the interference. None of the other voices had raised even a hint of an echo.

All of the Heroes but Father and Vara sat down. Most seemed to busy themselves refilling their goblets from a row of decanters. Father looked to Vara. Vara spoke.

"My dying vow was that no other Hero of Varay should ever die alone," he said. *No echo.*

"I haven't died," I said.

"We will be with you," Vara said.

"I see." I shifted my gaze to my father. "At the same place you died?" He didn't answer. He looked away from me. I had little choice but to look to Vara again.

"Does this mean that you can see the future?" I asked.

"There is no time on our side," he said, which wasn't an answer at all. "Come in and have a drink with us." He pointed at the one empty chair at the table.

I stared at the chair for a while—I can't even guess how long. Finally, I closed my eyes and shook my head. "I don't think so," I said, opening my eyes to focus on Vara. "It's too soon. I can't give up yet. I've still got a job to finish." I looked to my father again. "Your job." He acknowledged that with a nod.

"I'm leaving now," I said. And then, I wasn't sure that I *could* leave. I experienced some kind of split-existence thing. My *mind* had me turning around and walking back to the stairs, but my *body* wasn't responding. It took a moment before I figured it out—a dizzying realization. My hands gripped the jambs of the door yet and I had to consciously relax my grip and remove my hands.

I'm leaving now, I told myself, and this time I did. Movement still wasn't automatic. I had to concentrate on every step, watching as I moved each foot out in front of the other. I seemed to be sweating profusely by the time I got to the stairs and started up, and it wasn't over even then.

I climbed those stairs forever. Now, the stairway leading from the crypt back up to the living levels of Castle basil *is* extremely long, but no stairway could be as long as the one I climbed in that dream. I climbed and climbed, and when I looked back down, I had scarcely gone a tenth of the way. I climbed some more, making a little progress, but not as much as I should have. I counted my steps over the next stretch and looked back down when I reached fifty. It looked as though I had actually made it up about a dozen.

I kept climbing.

I woke to find that my body had started without waiting for me. I wasn't climbing steps now, though, and I couldn't remember getting to the top of that stairway.

But this was no dream now. Annick was on top of me again. I'm not even positive that *she* was fully awake when we started making love the second time—near the tag end of the night. While our lovemaking lasted, my memories of the congregation of Heroes in the crypt were pushed aside, out of focus but not completely out of mind. Afterward, Annick and I lay together, neither of us ready to sleep again. Memories of the dream—nightmare—flooded back over me. For some minutes, all I could do was relive the scene below Castle Basil. To get that out of my head, I tried to focus on the battle that was coming, the fight that I would be one nexus of by necessity—and that Annick would certainly be in the middle of by desire.

The night had nearly ended. Annick and I got up, cleaned up as best we could, and dressed. There was a trace of distant morning visible outside, a glow that let me see well enough to move about in the cottage. As soon as there was enough light to *work* with, I had to complete the passages. Soon after that, unless something went drastically wrong, our private arena would be the staging area for the complete armed might of Varay—as pitiful as that might me.

Annick hugged me and rested her head on my shoulder for just an instant. She was warm, pliable for a change. She kissed my cheek and whispered, ''I needed that.''

I brushed the hair away from her face. ''I think I did too.'' I returned the hug and we broke the clinch. There was neither the time nor the desire for another round, not then, maybe not ever. Despite the vigorous intimacy of the night, we were still worlds apart, in many ways. We looked at each other but found no words. I couldn't ask Annick what she was thinking, because I couldn't share my thoughts in return, not a cold appraisal of how little we had in common. After more minutes, the spell was broken, quickly, like the snap of a crab leg.

''I don't suppose that we'll see much of each other after the battle's over,'' Annick said.

''That's possible.'' Her words brought my dream back to the fore. If the dream was true, I wouldn't be seeing much of anyone. Back home, I would have dismissed the nightmare without too much thought. But, *in Varay,* I couldn't be so sure that there was nothing to it but nocturnal fear.

''You have your duty and I have mine.'' Annick kept her voice low, but the determination was still there. ''I won't forsake my vengeance for anyone.''

I shrugged. That was safer than words.

"This night is one to remember, but not to relive," Annick said.

"I think that's best." I took her hands in mine, just long enough to give them a squeeze. "I don't think we could ever recapture the moment." I tried to keep any relief out of my voice. "But the paths of our duty may cross on occasion," I added, releasing her hands.

"We'd better get our horses saddled," Annick said. She turned away, and we had enough to occupy us until I could start on the doors.

Sir Hambert and his men were just moving into the orchard when I decided that I had enough light to work. I used the cottage's front door for the link to Arrowroot. I applied the sea-silver and stood looking into the cottage when I reached for the tracing so the men and horses would be coming out of the cottage as they arrived. It would have been incredibly stupid to get *that* turned around. The actual connection came quickly with only slight effort and a sudden twinge of hunger. Parthet was there, his hands touching mine, his face looking up and grinning.

"Your mother is at Coriander," Parthet said. "We decided that that would be faster than me popping over there after we did this door. I've got Resler and his soldiers here, ready and waiting. I'll hold this way open while you do the other." He looked quite his old self, fully recovered.

"Right." I grinned back at him.

I used the stable door for the second passage. There wasn't much choice, but this door wasn't much wider or higher than the cottage's front door. Even Parthet could have spanned it without difficulty. Lining two doors and opening the passages took less than twenty minutes. Not bad, I thought.

When the men started coming through from Arrowroot and Coriander, I had new responsibilities. The biggest "command" I had ever held was captain of a tug-of-war team in high school. And all that meant was that I got to hold down the tail end of the rope and get dragged across the line last when we lost. We always lost. But now, I had the entire army of Varay to command, and the stakes were enormous, more than just getting dragged through the mud. I would have help, but everyone would look to me for a battle plan and for any tactical decisions. After all, *I* was the hotshot Hero, whether I was qualified for anything or not. Barons Resler and Dieth came through with their men. I expected Dieth to be helpful, but I wasn't sure about Resler. Annick didn't think he was worth much. And Parthet came through with the last of the men from Arrowroot. So did Baron Kardeen, with another score of Basiliers. And I had Harkane, Lesh, and even Timon with me again.

Kardeen set up a headquarters for us in the orchard close to the cottage. He had a large-scale map of the area right around Castle Thyme, both sides of the border, showing considerable topological detail. Kardeen took care of administrative details too, finding out just how many men we had—mounted and on foot, archers, lancers, that sort of thing. He was damn efficient. In thirty minutes he had messengers running and we were getting organized. I told him that we needed to find out where the Dorthini army was and how many men were coming. He got word to Baron Dieth and scouts were out in five minutes.

"How do you do it?" I asked Kardeen.

"Experience. I've been making sure that things get done for twenty-five years."

"You should be running this show instead of me."

He shook his head quickly. "I'm an administrator, not a general. But you tell me what you want and I'll find a way, or find the people who *can* find the way. If there is one."

I nodded. "Right now, a lot depends on how far off the Etevar's army is. If we've got time, it would be nice to get inside Castle Thyme before his main force arrives." I shrugged. "We probably won't have that kind of time, but just in case we do get the chance, it would help to know the layout inside the castle."

"Give me ten minutes and I'll have the floor plan."

Kardeen laughed. ''That's an easy one. Try something harder.''

''Okay, how about a simple way to get inside?''

''That's military. I'll have to find you someone who knows the castle for that.''

There was a commotion at the edge of the orchard, and I went to see what that was about while Kardeen went to find someone who knew Castle Thyme. One of our patrols had surprised a Dorthini patrol and taken a couple of prisoners. No one had escaped to carry the news of our presence back to Castle Thyme or to the approaching Dorthini army.

Our scouts didn't get back until midafternoon, and by then I was ready to start swinging in the trees I was so nervous. The early reports that the Dorthinis would reach us somewhat after noon hadn't been borne out, but I still thought that our scouts should have had time to find the enemy and get back . . . if any of them were going to get back. When the scouts did return, they brought both good news and bad news. The bad news was that the Etevar had four thousand soldiers. The good news was that they wouldn't reach Castle Thyme until the next morning. They were moving slower than expected and the only logical place for them to bivouac for the night would leave them with three hours' marching to reach the castle.

I went looking for Parthet and found him just returning from Arrowroot.

''Let's put together a think tank,'' I told him. ''I want to find a way to get inside Castle Thyme before the Etevar gets here.''

Parthet nodded, and we gathered the three barons, Sir Hambert, and two soldiers who had once been garrisoned at Thyme. My people were all there too, but only Parthet took part in the conference.

''I want to take Castle Thyme before the Dorthini army arrives, and I don't want the Etevar to know that we've done it,'' I started. ''We get part of our force inside the castle and put the rest around it as if we have it under siege. The army outside retreats from the approaching Dorthinis tomorrow. Once the Etevar's army moves past the castle, we move the men inside out against the rear of the Dorthini army, put the Etevar in the middle.'' Turn the ambush idea back against him.

Everybody claimed to like the idea even though it didn't alter the fact that we would still be outnumbered by about three to one when the main Dorthini army arrived. A practical way to get inside Castle Thyme was harder to find. I was counting on Parthet, but his reaction to most of my suggestions was ''I've got to be able to see what I'm doing to do it,'' and we had to make our move against the castle during the night.

''Other than you climbs the wall,'' one of the soldiers who knew the castle well said, ''they's jest two ways in, the main gate and the postern. The gate's gotta drawer-bridge and por'cullis. Postern's jest a thick door. When they's fixin' to use that, they shoves a plank acrost the ditch or jest climbs down through it.''

''The postern, it's a wood door?'' I asked.

''Aye, wood a foot thick wi' a wood bar and leg-sized metal hinges.''

I turned to Parthet. ''If we get you close after dark, you think you could conjure us something to get us through that postern fast? Something like an explosion or a cutting torch?''

''Gots to be real fast,'' the soldier said. ''That door's hard by the guards' room. They hears anythin' faster'n the Great Earth Mother can scratch her grabber.''

''No light at all?'' Parthet asked.

''We can't afford much,'' I told him. ''No more than my flashlight, with some kind of shield over it.''

He took a long time thinking. He shoved his glasses up on his nose. His eyes moved around as though he were studying the rims. ''A flash fire,'' he muttered. ''Once it starts, I've *got* light.'' His voice trailed off, but his lips kept moving. After a couple of minutes of that, he looked at me and nodded. ''It may be possible.''

''What then?'' Kardeen asked.

''We probably won't be able to get a lot of men up to the postern in advance—too much chance of discovery—but once Parthet forces the door and we get inside, we'll need reinforcements in a hurry. Any idea how large the garrison is?''

"No, but we have a couple of prisoners who might be persuaded to talk," Kardeen said. I thought about splinters under the fingernails, hot branding irons, that kind of thing. I doubt that I would have objected to them, which bothers me now that I've got time to brood on it.

"I'm sure we can persuade them to chat," Parthet said before I could put in any comment. "I've got a jim-dandy truth spell that'll get all the answers we need."

There were thirty-two men left inside the castle. The patrol we had intercepted would be missed when they didn't return by sunset. Their orders were to get back before then, and orders weren't disobeyed lightly in the Dorthini army. The garrison had been drawn from the Etevar's personal guard, the men he had trusted to waylay and kill the Hero of Varay. My father. There were always three sentries on duty on the battlements, relieved every two hours during the night. The rest of the garrison was quartered in the keep, and there was always a sentry on duty there during the night as well. He would hear any commotion when the postern blew.

We spent the rest of the afternoon getting ready for the night's foray and the morrow's battle. I picked a dozen hard types to go with Lesh and me in the first "team" that night. Dieth furnished the men to wait in position to reinforce us as soon as the postern was open. We went over the plans of the castle that Kardeen provided. The layout was simple, straightforward, utilitarian. The keep was a small inner circle tangent to the larger outer circle of the curtain wall. A tiny courtyard. A dry ditch around the castle. We put together several ladders to speed our way into and out of the ditch.

Thanks to Kardeen's efficiency, we had a hot supper, all thirteen hundred and more of us, even though I wouldn't let anyone light fires that might give away the fact that we were around. The kitchen people at four castles did the cooking. Mother and Parthet tended the doorways while the food was carried through. The meal wasn't as plentiful or varied as the repasts at Basil, but it was a decent enough meal, in both quantity and quality.

After supper, we went over the plans for the assault on Thyme again. Lesh, Hambert, and I would be the first through the door—underscore the *I*. Two men would escort Parthet to safety as soon as he blew the postern open. If he could. More soldiers would pour into the castle as quickly as possible, fanning out to meet the garrison. It was a nice, simple plan—put the spearhead in, then hurry to overwhelm the defenders through sheer numbers—provided it worked. As soon as the postern blew or burned, the rest of our army would surround the castle, first to make sure that none of the defenders escaped and second to put our phony siege in position.

Then there was just the waiting. We didn't want to move until we could expect most of the garrison to be asleep. I tried napping, but I was too keyed up to stay down for long, and anyway, every time I closed my eyes that dream from the night before was ready to jump out at me. I certainly didn't need *that*.

We didn't have a lot going for us in the coming battle against the Etevar, and if we didn't grab the castle, the odds would be insane . . . well, more insane. But taking Castle Thyme was no guarantee of success—not by a long shot. There was no way that one man, even a regulation *Hero,* could make up for all the numbers unless he had a few rabbits in his hat and a lot of luck. The Etevar had a better-trained and much larger army, and a better wizard. Parthet was the first to concede that.

"Let's get started," I said—somewhere around eleven o'clock. Keeping track of time was still a hassle. My watch had started running again after we left Fairy, but it acted strange. Once it had even run backward for an hour.

We walked from the orchard to the castle. Horses would only be a giveaway on this raid, and our army didn't have many horses to start with, only about three hundred. Most of our fighters were foot soldiers, infantry. We moved as quietly as you could expect several dozen men in armor to move. Annick picked our way through the woods. I hadn't included her in my plans for the raid, but she dealt herself in and silently dared me to try to keep her out of the fight. I didn't try.

The castle was also silent. I didn't expect to hear carousing. A drunken debauch would have been asking too much of luck. Lurking in the shadows forty yards from the ditch, we watched one of the sentries walk his post on the parapet, visible only when he passed one of the crenels. The postern faced west, the main gate south. Two of my men scurried across the open stretch with ladders while Annick and several others covered them with bows, just in cast the sentry caught on. He didn't. In twos and threes, the rest of us crossed the clearing, timing our moves with the sentry's tour on the wall, then we jumped down into the dry moat. *Dry?* There was muck and mud a foot deep in it. The smell left no doubt as to what we were wading through. Castle Thyme didn't have a sewer system.

Getting our people up near the postern wasn't all that easy. There was only a narrow ledge at the base of the wall, not wide enough for safety, let alone for comfort, and no one wanted to fall in the crap below.

Parthet had to go at one side of the door, close enough to work his hocus-pocus. I was at the other side so I could charge in first when the door opened—my "right" as Hero. Annick had wormed her way right behind me, even ahead of Lesh and Hambert. Altogether, there were eight of us up on the ledge. A dozen more soldiers waited in the bottom of the ditch or on the ladders, and about the same number crouched on the other side of the ditch, trying to look invisible. The rest of our strike force was in the trees, forty yards away, with a rough plank bridge to throw across the ditch as soon as we were inside keeping the defenders from dumping their end of the bridge into the crap.

"Okay, Uncle. Your show," I whispered.

He grunted. "You have that flashlight?"

"If you need it."

"I need it. There's not enough starlight to conjure a good fart. Play the light along the hinges, slowly, while I get started."

I had fitted a half-shield of leather to make the light

harder to spot from above. I turned the light on and moved the beam the way Parthet directed. The hinges were large metal strips that extended almost the entire width of the door. Smooth rounded boltheads were visible, but there was no way to dismantle the hinges from the outside.

Parthet chanted softly. I couldn't understand a word of it. Either magical formulas were exempt from the translation magic or it was just gibberish Parthet used to psych himself up. As he continued, he got louder, making me worry that the sentry would hear. But before I could work myself up to shushing Parthet, the top hinges started to glow a dull red and I smelled wood burning— like old railway ties. Then the second hinge started to glow and the first got brighter, and hotter. I turned off the flashlight and stuck it in my hip pocket when the metal was light enough to see by. Tiny flames became visible around the metal, then large streaks of the door charred visibly.

"Put your shoulder to it," Parthet said. "A sharp rap." I edged sideways. Bashing into glowing metal didn't seem very smart even though I had leather and chain mail to protect me, but we had to get inside, and the longer I hesitated, the more chance there was that the sentry would see us.

My shoulder scarcely touched the door before it popped inward, hinges and all, so quickly that I almost fell into the castle. I caught my balance against the far wall, getting my hands out before my head could slam into the stone, before I could hit hard enough to jar my bad ribs. I drew Dragon's Death and turned toward the guardroom and great hall of Castle Thyme, where we expected the first challenge. I didn't have much room to swing the elf sword in the hallway, but it would make life problematic for any defenders who tried to get too close to me.

Lesh and Annick were in the corridor with me by the time I got set, before the first defender appeared. He shouted an alert, then charged, even though my sword was twice the length of his and he couldn't get close without opening himself to the bite of Dragon's Death.

But I was limited too. All I could do was keep prodding, making short jabs at him, forcing him to back off while I looked for swinging room. The guard tried to stall me long enough for his help to arrive. When he was nearly back to the room behind him, he made a desperate attempt to get past my blade. His maneuver didn't work. I sliced at his head, backhanded, and he went down to stay.

After that, it was one short duel after another until all of our strike force got into the fray. I had to fight two more Dorthinis, but the encounters were nothing to write home about. Against these enemies, Dragon's Death was once more almost weightless. At need, I could handle it with one hand, as easily as I could swing my own smaller sword.

Then the fight was over. The rest of the garrison surrendered when it was obvious that we had the numbers. These Dorthinis were all good soldiers. There was no "fight to the last man" nonsense. Just as well. I had no stomach for a massacre, not even of the men who had ambushed and killed my father. But I didn't waste any grief on the Dorthinis who died before the surrender.

Once we had accounted for every member of the garrison, we lowered the drawbridge so our reserves could come in with the horses to wait for the Dorthini army to arrive and pass. The rest of our troops moved into their phony siege positions. We raised the drawbridge again well before dawn.

When the first Dorthini scouts arrived in the morning, they saw the Varayan army besieging Castle Thyme. We sent a cavalry patrol to chase the Dorthinis, with instructions to make sure that they didn't catch them. We *wanted* the Dorthini scouts to escape and carry the news of the siege to the Etevar. We had our slim surprise primed . . . if we could make it count.

20

The Dance of Ghosts

We left the Dorthini flag flying over Castle Thyme, seven gold lilies—stylized like the French emblem—on a black field. Harkane had my pennant ready to replace the Etevar's when we "announced" ourselves. I slept for a short time, but managed to wake myself when I started to slip back into the dream that had captured me the night before. I was walking down the steps to the crypt and, somehow, managed to stop and wake before I found myself in the company of all my predecessors again.

I didn't try to sleep again after that.

The morning dragged on. The van of the Dorthini army was two hours away, then one hour. Parthet used some of the sea-silver to open a passage between the castle and the cottage in the orchard so we could keep abreast of the news . . . and so we would have a bolt-hole in case of disaster. A small band of our cavalry skirmished with Dorthini outriders a couple of miles from the castle, then retreated in good order. We wanted to harass the enemy just enough to keep them from trying to make contact with the castle garrison. Castle Thyme was our Trojan Horse, and we couldn't afford to give away the secret too soon.

Parthet didn't know of any Dorthini magic comparable to the doorways, but he couldn't rule it out either. Since the Etevar had the new-and-improved-model wizard, anything was possible. We patrolled every corridor and passage of Castle Thyme, watched everywhere.

From dawn on, I stayed on the parapets, under cover of a shed that had been erected to give sentries a place to get out of the weather. Parthet stayed with me, except during his brief excursions to the orchard for the latest news. The rest of "my" people also stayed close through the morning.

The Dorthini van was in sight before the Varayan forces

"besieging" Castle Thyme started their slow withdrawal across the road into the rolling countryside toward the orchard. Dorthini cavalry came forward to engage, to try to keep our army from settling into strong defensive positions before the Dorthini infantry caught up. Our people had to keep the area around the castle hazardous enough to justify "Dorthini" defenders keeping the drawbridge up and the gate closed. We had replaced the postern door; it at least *looked* normal.

There were no surprises in the early morning. Everything went right according to plan. I could even be detached about it, recalling battles that Dad had made me study while I was a teenager, looking for comparison—or for any tip I could dredge out of those memories to help us. I didn't have any crazy urges to get out into the fighting right away. I felt no guilt at being safe while others were fighting and dying. I knew that my turn for danger would come soon enough. The only problem I had was with memories of my crypt dream. I *heard* Vara talking to me again, reminding me that he had sworn that no Hero of Varay would die alone as he had, telling me that they would all be with me when my time came.

Are there real ghosts here? I asked myself many times that morning. More and more, I was starting to believe that the answer was probably *yes*. Vara's voice seemed to be too real to be simply my imagination.

It was almost noon before the Etevar arrived with his personal guard and the bulk of his army—the infantry. My pulse picked up while the armies went through the motions to set up battle lines—movements that appeared to be a lot slower than they really were. It was almost a ballet, a dance of death. Our people stayed close enough to the castle to justify the defenders leaving the drawbridge raised. My danger sense started going full blast—and I could see thousands of reasons.

Then the armies seemed to become static for a few minutes, with just minor movements behind the front lines on both sides—like two immense football teams waiting for the opening kick-off. Our army surged forward toward the Dorthinis. Baron Resler was in charge down there on the "field," pending my arrival. The fighting—the bleeding and dying—started in earnest. There would be no whistles blowing to stop *this* warfare every few seconds, no flags thrown for unsportsmanlike conduct.

I was above the battle, if only in a strictly physical sense. In the first minutes, I could see the entire field clearly. It wasn't like moving markers on a sand table to recreate a battle. There was no mistaking this for a movie war either. I didn't have any trouble remembering that this was real. There was the flash of sunlight off blades. Dust rose from thousands of feet and hooves, gradually obscuring the view. There was blood—gallons of bright red blood—all over. There was screaming.

And there was death.

"The Heroes of Varay are waiting for me to join them," I told Parthet without taking my eyes off the battle.

"What are you talking about?" he demanded, grabbing my arm, turning me toward him.

I told him about the dream, briefly, and kept looking back down at the battle. The two of us were alone on the parapets of Castle Thyme for the moment. My other companions had joined our reserves, all cavalry, in the courtyard. The men stood by their horses, keeping them as quiet as possible, crowded in between the walls. My horse, Gold, was down there too. Timon was holding him for me—as close as the boy was going to get to any fighting. I hoped.

"Don't let the dream get to you, lad," Parthet said when I finished my narrative. "Dreams can't be trusted."

"I'm not sure it was only dream," I told him.

"Best put it aside like a dream, lad," he said.

I shrugged and concentrated on the battle. I couldn't put the dream aside that easily.

"I hope you've got a few tricks up your sleeve," I told Parthet as the time for my sortie approached.

"I can make a show, lad. There, you see the Etevar?" Parthet pointed into the mass of men south and just barely east of the castle, at a pennant like the one flying over our heads. "The two men in black there. The Etevar is the shorter one. The other is his wizard. I can feel his magic, and he's not even using it.''

I saw the men Parthet was talking about, but they were too far off in the rising dust of the battlefield for me to see any details of their appearance. Tall, dressed completely in black, and riding black horses. And, new glasses or not, Parthet could hardly have made out any more.

The Varayan army started to give ground slowly and in good order, luring the Dorthinis on, making sure that the Dorthinis paid a price for every inch, and making sure that there were no inviting gaps in the Varayan line. The last of the Dorthini army moved west of the castle, following their prey. At any minute, a royal messenger might ride up to the gate and demand entrance. It was time for my act. I hugged Parthet before I went down to my horse and my troop.

''Take care, Uncle,'' I told him. ''We don't want to waste all those new eyeglasses.''

''And you, lad.'' Parthet grinned and shoved me gently toward the stairs. ''Remember what I told you. Don't pay attention to dreams.''

Easier said than done.

The sixty-odd members of my troop mounted up when they saw me coming down to the courtyard. I climbed on Gold and waved at Parthet. Once we left the castle, he would be in an exposed position. We weren't going to leave many people with him—just Timon to run my pennant up the flagpole once we started fighting, and two men to operate the winches for the portcullis and drawbridge. Castle Thyme was sealed up again as soon as we rode out. That would give Parthet and the others time to scram through the portal back to the cottage . . . unless the Etevar's wizard could negate that magic.

The battlefield didn't look like any I have ever seen in the movies or in my mind. There was no colorful medieval pageantry, no bright tunics and pennons, no brilliantly reflective armor to catch the sun in blinding moments. Once the armies started fighting, it was all earth colors—dust and blood. Blood red was the only bright color around, and even the blood faded as it soaked into the dirt.

We trotted toward the center of the Dorthini line. They didn't react to our approach at once. They must have assumed that we were their comrades, eager for a taste of the anticipated slaughter. That was what they were supposed to assume. It was the whole point of the charade. Then there was a commotion in the knot of warriors around the Etevar and his wizard. I could make a shrewd guess at what had them stirring. Someone who didn't have to take his boots off to count past ten had figured out that too many of us had come out of the castle, more men than the Dorthinis had quartered there. Or maybe someone had spotted my elf sword. I hadn't drawn it yet, but I did then, and extended my arm to point the blade at the Etevar. That was the signal for my troop to charge, and for our main force to stop their slow withdrawal and push forward again.

That eerie tune started to come out of my mouth again, the same tune that the elf sword had drawn from me every time I used it, but louder and more intricate than ever. I led my sixty people directly toward the Etevar. He had been commanding his army from just behind the center of the battle line.

Urging our horses to a gallop once the Dorthinis figured out that we were Varayan, I hoped to reach the Etevar's tight little group before any other Dorthini contingents could interpose themselves. I figured that if I could get rid of the Etevar in a hurry, that would stop the battle. It didn't work, though. Dorthini troops seemed to flow into the space in front of us as easily as marchers on a drill field, and once the fighting started on our side of the main battle, our progress slowed to almost nothing. I kept pressing toward the Etevar but couldn't get any closer.

Even though I didn't manage the shortcut to end the fight quickly, our rear attack did surprise the Dorthinis. Homer's Trojan Horse was still a workable concept. Trying to face threats on both sides of the line sapped the effectiveness of the Dorthinis to a greater degree than I would have dared hope. The confusion was something.

Although our sortie didn't significantly alter the immense manpower advantage the Dorthinis had, the time they lost regrouping to protect the Etevar from my band stopped their advance to the west and let our main force take the offensive. Then we sprang one more surprise. Baron Dieth brought his cavalry in from the north, another 150 men, putting pressure on the Dorthinis from three sides.

It wasn't easy to fight my own battles and try to keep track of the fray as a whole at the same time. My first priority had to be to keep myself from being folded, spindled, or mutilated. Or anything else. I seemed to have Vara and my father at my side, more as vultures than as protectors, waiting to collect me when I fell. I hoped that it was just combat jitters, but I was having trouble believing that.

Right at the beginning, my elf sword moved most of the Dorthini soldiers away from me. It must have convinced them that the better part of valor was to let somebody else deal with me. Maybe they thought I was an elf and way out of their league. But then I started to feel static electricity around me and I knew that I was the focus of hostile magic. The Etevar's wizard was trying to reach me. His lack of significant success made me think that Parthet must be doing something to interfere. I heard distant thunder and guessed that it was Parthet's.

I couldn't afford to give the interplay of magic too much attention, though, because a pair of Dorthini riders chose that moment to come at me together, one on each side. If it hadn't been for Lesh and Harkane, the ploy might have worked. As it was, I deflected the first Dorthini to my companions and concentrated on the second.

We didn't fight just with our swords. Our horses became weapons too, and the Dorthini was more adept at that part of the job. Maneuvering animals took more concentration and effort than swinging blades. The horses had ideas of their own, and they didn't always agree with the riders'. Horses sometimes have more sense than people. The only thing these animals wanted to do was get away from the melee.

With the longer reach Dragon's Death gave me, I could

have cut the Dorthini's horse down, but I was loathe to attack any animal that didn't have its own designs on my health and well-being. That inhibition dragged out the fight—almost as if it tied one hand behind my back. The Dorthini had a good hacking sword, with a blade nearly as broad at the hilt as my elf sword. I couldn't snap his blade, and he was good enough to keep me fully occupied for several minutes.

More Dorthini riders pushed in toward us. For a moment, the press of numbers forced my troop back a few paces in the direction of the castle. Then I got a clear shot at the Dorthini who was trying to get right in my face. I flashed a one-handed slice across, skipping my blade off the tip of his. Dragon's Death caught him solidly between helmet and eyebrows. Blood welled out like red wine overflowing a mug before he fell and dragged his horse down with him.

I had a little clear space in front of me. Through a break in the dust, I saw the Etevar's wizard staring at me. At the moment, he looked to be no more than a horse's length away. I knew it was a trick of perspective or magic, though, since he was actually fifty yards or more from me. But I could see him as if he were right there. He had a pale face and black beard and sideburns. A single eyebrow covered both eyes, a thick black line that looked as phony as Groucho Marx's greasepaint mustache and eyebrows. The wizard grinned, and toothpaste-ad-white teeth showed in the middle of the beard.

There was no time to think it through. I spurred Gold toward the wizard, impatiently cutting two Dorthini foot soldiers out of my way with a single swing of Dragon's Death. The battle couldn't end until I got rid of either the wizard or the Etevar, maybe both. The dust closed in again as I forced Gold between the panicked horses of two men I had just wounded, who were trying to escape. I lost sight of the Dorthini wizard, and when I spotted him again—after I sparred inconclusively with several more soldiers—he was farther away, as was the Etevar, a rougher-looking man, swarthy-skinned, with hair as black as his wizard's.

The battle flowed toward the castle again. My troop

had to give some ground, but we had shown enough power that the bulk of the Dorthini army broke around us. The drawbridge of Thyme was up, so the Etevar couldn't reclaim the castle as a quick refuge—though why he might look for refuge when he still had us vastly outnumbered didn't occur to me at the time. I had my hands full, trying to keep my people together and dealing with those Dorthinis who couldn't avoid us.

One encounter in that phase of the battle will stick with me through eternity, I think. A Dorthini foot soldier, armed with a long spear and a short sword like a Roman legionnaire, came running at me. His face was distorted as he screamed some battle cry or oath, making him look almost like one of those troll soldiers out of Fairy. Defending myself was instinctive by then. I whirled Dragon's Death left and right, cutting the spear into three pieces. The Dorthini threw the remaining piece of his spear at Gold's face and drew his sword while he rolled under my horse and came up on the other side—too close for me to finish him off quickly. I turned and brought my sword down, but it was my fist that hit his head—his helmet. I kicked out, moving the Dorthini back, and brought my sword down again. He got his short blade in the way but couldn't parry the full force of my blow. Dragon's Death skidded along the side of his head, knocked his helmet off, sliced off his left ear, then bit into where his neck and shoulder met.

He couldn't have been any older than Harkane—fourteen, maybe fifteen. Blue eyes opened in wide surprise. The muscles in his face relaxed. Blood spurted from his neck and he died. For a moment, all I could do was stare down at him. He was just a kid. I gagged and almost threw up.

I backed Gold around, trying to see how things were going around me. Horns sounded near the Etevar, and his army moved farther east, clear of Castle Thyme. The Dorthinis marched into what little was left of the village's spring crops. Suddenly, the Etevar and I were in the open, between our armies, with only our own guards to support us. I spurred Gold forward again, knowing that I had to take a chance to reach the Etevar before he got behind another wall of soldiers—and before the Dorthinis could cut me off from *my* support.

Then my danger sense went berserk, and so did my horse, but the Dorthinis weren't the cause. It was a distant shadow, first in my mind and then in the sky, and a cry like metal ripping in an auto wreck. A familiar feeling, a familiar shadow. A dragon—a mother-*huge* dragon—was heading straight for me.

While I fought to control Gold, the two armies moved farther apart—and away from me—as though I had just broken out with the stigmata of every infectious disease ever known or imagined. Even most of the troop right with me decided that they belonged somewhere else. All I had left were the people I would have bet on to stay— Annick, Lesh, Harkane, Hambert—and a very few others. Annick sheathed her sword and got out her bow. She dismounted when I did. So did Lesh and Hambert. Lesh had his battle-axe. We passed our reins to others and got ready to meet the new threat.

This dragon was coming specifically for me, just like all of the threats in Fairy. My danger sense was very definite about that, and there was more. The Etevar's wizard loomed in my sight again, appearing much closer than he actually was. His hands—delicate-looking, with long, pointed fingers—grasped a broad medallion that hung from his neck on a heavy gold chain. I could see each link in the chain, but his hands covered whatever device the medallion bore. The Dorthini wizard squinted, concentrating on me. I saw his mouth move as he chanted, flashes of white teeth and almost purple lips and tongue.

This is it, I thought. I looked around for Dad and Vara and the rest of the congregation of Heroes. This dragon was much larger than the one the elf warrior had died fighting on that beach by the Mist. Even if I somehow managed to drop this beast, I had to expect to go the way of the elf. And there was nowhere to run.

I stepped several paces in front of my companions to get room to swing the elf sword. Dragon's Death—a meager hope. My mouth was moving too. The whistling that came when I used the long blade got louder and louder until there were almost words to it, a magical chant of the incoherent sort I had heard Parthet use. And Annick was humming some kind of counterpoint as she raised her bow. The air fairly crackled with all the magics. I wondered if they were subject to static, interference, the way radio signals are.

What did the elf think about when he faced this? I asked myself. The dragon was coming on fast, but I still seemed to have plenty of time. There was even time for me to feel amazed at how calm I felt. I accepted the outcome . . . as long as I could reach it with the fortitude that the elf warrior had shown.

"Steady, lad. Keep your wits about you," sounded right next to my ear. It was Parthet's voice, but he was still standing on the castle wall. I glanced that way. The same sort of alteration of perspective that had made the Dorthini wizard appear close let me see Parthet up close too. Then I recalled—from our first ride east—that Parthet had said that there had been so much magic used around Castle Thyme that it was unpredictable.

"Put on a good show, Uncle," I whispered. He nodded as if he heard me. I turned and stared at the Dorthini wizard and made a short cutting gesture with my sword— something like drawing a bow sharply across a violin— as my whistling reached a peak. The Dorthini wizard frowned and clutched his medallion tighter. I felt a trickle of exhilaration. I *could* reach him, touch him. I remembered that Parthet had suggested that I might have some gift toward wizardry. And there were the magics of the sword and the Hero that I still didn't know everything about . . .

. . . in an arena where magic wasn't predictable anyway.

What do I have to lose? I asked myself. The answer was an easy *nothing*.

I attempted to use magic that I didn't know I had—that I didn't know that *anybody* had. While the dragon folded his wings for a fast glide, I concentrated on the Dorthini wizard, trying to superimpose my image over his, hoping to confuse the dragon and deflect it toward the wizard who—so far—appeared to be controlling it. The wizard fought back, stabbing deeply into my mind, loosing a flash of light in my head that made him invisible for a dangerous moment.

I blinked over and over. There were spots in front of my eyes . . . spots large enough to hide a dragon. I looked up quickly, squinted against the light and the sky.

The dragon wasn't deflected even for a second. It swooped toward me, suddenly appearing to be as fast as a jet. Its talons were stretched open, its jaws gaping wide. It had all its weapons ready, just like the dragon in Fairy. I thought back to the way the elf warrior had met that dragon's attack. I replayed it in my mind—except for the way it ended for the elf.

And then the dragon was on me.

I swung Dragon's Death and dove to the left, rolling and coming back to my feet in time to take a whack at the dragon's tail. I connected with its hide both times but didn't do much damage. Lord, was that sucker *big*. It made the one on the beach look like a runt.

No mortal can kill a dragon and live! Those words burned themselves into my mind the way the hinges had burned into Thyme's postern. *No mortal can kill a dragon and live!* The Etevar's wizard showed his face—and a malicious grin—behind the words.

As I turned to keep facing the dragon, I beamed, *I have killed one dragon and lived!* straight at the Etevar's wizard with all the force I could muster. I felt Parthet strengthening my boast. The Etevar's wizard wavered in an instant of doubt. *And I turned the Elflord of Xayber out of Varay!* I added.

The dragon's second pass was a carbon copy of the first. Dragons didn't seem to have a very wide repertory of offensive moves. This time I saw an arrow blossom from the dragon's forehead, so I knew that Annick had found the range. But the arrow didn't weaken or deflect the beast any more than my first swipes had. I slashed at the snout and jumped right this time, while the dragon's jaws snapped toward the other side, where I had gone the first time.

Odds and evens.

Something new came over me then. I'm not sure I can

describe it. Maybe it doesn't need any more than to say
that I became fey—deathbound and crazy with it, manic.
A new power seemed to settle in me, or waken. I felt as
if I were growing inside my skin, but I wasn't turning
into the Incredible Hulk or anything like that. It was all—
I don't know—just a sensation within my mind. I moved
a few steps toward the watching Etevar and his wizard. I
drew the wizard's eyes to me again, somehow *forced* him
to meet my stare.

I am Vara returned! my mind screamed at him.

I had no idea at all where that boast originated, certainly not in *my* brain. Sure, I had been told that the
magic of Varay's Hero was supposed to include some of
Vara's strength and skill, but I hadn't been idling away
at that kind of musing. With a dragon coming at me? The
boast just sprang from my head. I didn't even have time
just then to look around to see if Vara and Dad were there
with me.

When the dragon dove at me this time, I planted my
feet and held my sword at full reach over my head—just
the way I had seen the elf warrior do it. I didn't duck to
either side this time either, and that was sheer madness.
I just brought Dragon's Death straight forward with all
of my strength, and then some, I guess, as if I seriously
thought that I might be able to split that dragon fore to
aft.

The shock of the collision could hardly have been
worse if I'd been hit by an out-of-control semi. The
dragon knocked me down, dragged and bounced me
along the ground, and finally ripped the elf sword from
my hands. I didn't even have the wit to let go of the
sword. As soon as I slowed down enough to get some
control over my own movements, I rolled left, *fast,* to
get out from under the collapsing body of the gargantuan
beast. Pain stabbed at me from every part of my body.
The dragon's wing and leg pummeled me. I felt skin and
muscle tear, *my* skin and muscle. The wing's trailing edge
bounced me forward again and finally pinned me against
the dragon's flank for a moment before I bounced clear—
butt over brains.

"We're here, son." I heard Dad's voice as plainly as

I had ever heard any sound in my life. I couldn't move. For a time, I couldn't even get my eyes open.

Am I dead yet? I wondered. Mentally, at least, I shook my head. I hurt so much that I had to be alive. My heart was still pounding. I inhaled. That added to the pain.

It won't be long, I decided. If I wasn't already mortally wounded, the dragon would finish the job soon enough.

"We're here, son," Dad's voice said again. "We're waiting for you."

More than anything, that was what forced me to keep trying.

I got my eyes open. They burned. I saw sky above me . . . and dragon to the side. I was flat on my back. I rolled over on my side, facing the dragon. Everything seemed willing to move, though not without complaint. My chest hurt. More than one rib had to be broken now. My arms were both bloody, but I could make fists with both hands. I could move the fingers.

The dragon didn't fly off for another go-round. That didn't feel like much of a victory, though. The damn thing was a mountain next to me. The tail was moving from side to side, not all that fast, but enough to keep anyone from coming close. The neck and head were swaying too—not as much as the tail.

I didn't see any people, just dragon.

The feeling of power—or whatever I had felt before— had deserted me, been dragged out of me. I had to finish rolling over, onto my stomach, before I could start to get up. I got up on hands and knees . . . one knee. My left knee didn't want to bend in the middle. And the foot felt as if it had been crammed into a boot that was only half as big as it needed to be. I tried to reach for my hip pocket to get the silver flask that Mother had given me, but the flask was gone. So was the pocket. No painkiller.

I retched, threw up. No blood in it, I told myself. I thought that might be a hopeful sign.

The dragon bellowed in what I hoped was intense pain.

"Get up," I told myself. "Get up and finish the job while you can."

Dreamer, another part of my mind said, laughing at me. Why not lie back down and wait?

I wouldn't do that.

Instead, I fought my way to my feet. With a leg that wouldn't do much of anything but throb, getting up was difficult—and agonizing. I stood and limped toward the dragon's head, making a wide circle and watching it closely. It was slow going. I had to step forward with my right leg and then drag the left leg up into place. The leg would hold me, but I couldn't do much else with it.

I had to stop and fight back the waves of pain every few steps. I had never dreamed that so much pain was possible.

For the first time, I got a chance to see just how damn huge that dragon really was. I don't think I could possibly exaggerate its size. You could have put a football field on its back and left room for cheerleaders. The neck and tail were each longer than the back. Its thighs were like those old redwood trees with roads cut right through their trunks. A circus could have used one of its wings for its big top. The teeth were big enough to serve as headstones. It was as tall as a four-story building. New York City and Chicago could have met for a barbecue with steaks for everyone from its meat, with enough leftovers to stuff the entire NFL.

Big. Maybe a quarter mile long.

I don't know how long I stared at the dragon, running those stupid comparisons through my mind. It probably wasn't nearly as long as it seemed at the time. I started walking again, coughing dust and retching. Every time the pains got together and squeezed, strange things happened to my head and gut—none of them pleasant.

Eventually, I got around in front of the dragon. My elf sword had split the top of its snout from between nostrils the size of basketball hoops to between eyes the size of hula hoops. The eyes were open, though the fletching of one of Annick's arrows protruded from the pupil of the left eye. I couldn't reach Dragon's Death. I stretched as far as I could, but my fingers fell a good eighteen inches short of the sword's hilt. Finally, I leaned against the dragon's snout, put my good foot on the corner of its lower lip—gingerly—and got up just far enough to reach the elf sword. I pulled on Dragon's Death and fell backward when it came free.

The dragon moaned and moved its head from side to side, just a little.

"I hope you're hurting as much as I am," I said, *very* softly. I rubbed a sleeve across my eyes. They were watering constantly from the pain. Getting to my feet again was as painful as the first time, and just as slow. I stood there—ten feet from the dragon—and looked up at it. Its eyes were definitely out of reach, even with Dragon's Death, as long as I was on the ground.

I came close to giving up then. The only way I would be able to reach this dragon's eye to put that long thrust into it would be to climb up on top of the snout. Even if I could manage that, all the beast would have to do was toss its head to throw me far enough to finish the job of killing me.

Static electricity started to pop and crackle all over me again. I got hot—roasting. The wizards were dueling over me again. I glanced toward the battlements of Castle Thyme. Parthet was still there. He didn't seem to be looking at me, but somewhere past me, past the dragon. I turned my head and spotted the Dorthini wizard. I didn't have an up-close-and-personal view this time, so I couldn't see the expression on his face, couldn't tell if he was nervous or ready to gloat.

The Etevar was next to him, holding his horse quiet, watching.

I advanced on the dragon again, slowly, still dragging my left leg, using it only as a prop to hold me up. When I got right up to the dragon's bleeding snout, I was temporarily out of his sight. I rested there a moment, in the shade, trying to gather my strength, and my nerve. With only one good leg, I was going to need both arms to climb, so I slipped Dragon's Death into its clips on my back. Then I got my toehold at the corner of the dragon's mouth and scrambled for the top of its snout.

The head rolled to the side. I held on to a couple of knobby wartlike projections until the rolling stopped. Then I got up—on one knee with the other leg trailing behind—and drew Dragon's Death again. The whistling started immediately. I rammed the point of the elf sword into the dragon's uninjured eye and leaned in and down, uncertain that the blade could even reach *this* monster's brain. I pushed and twisted, and the dragon bucked and tried to roll its head again. For an instant, I was dangling from the sword's hilt, holding on desperately. The dragon flapped its wings a couple of times but couldn't generate enough lift to get off the ground. It couldn't even get its chin more than a couple feet of the ground.

When the beast quieted down again, I maneuvered back into position. This time, I put all of my weight behind the sword until the guard was sinking into the eyeball itself.

And then the eyeball popped like a gigantic zit and foul-smelling crud gushed all over me, topped by gallons of black blood. It came so hard and fast that for a moment I thought I was going to drown in it. I choked and gagged and retched so hard that I almost lost my grip on the elf sword. My hands were deep in what was left of the eyeball now. The dragon moaned, then screeched and gave one last violent shake that tossed me and the sword to the ground. More blood—barrels of it—spurted from the wound and poured down on me. It was all I could do to get my face free of the flash flood.

As the dragon died—with a noisy death rattle that sounded like someone dropping a junkyard on a tin roof—the line that no mortal could kill a dragon and live through it also died a final death . . . or would if I somehow managed to get up and limp away. There would be a new old wives' tale. *Only a mortal who* has *killed a dragon* can *kill one.*

A big if: I wasn't at all sure that I would be able to get up and move away from the dead dragon. Only my continuing pain convinced me that I wasn't already dead. Unless death didn't end the pain—not a very comforting possibility. I got my hands and arms under me, and rested my head on an arm to keep my face out of the pool of blood. I was soaked, covered in blood and gore and goo and dust—stinking, rancid. Father and Vara seemed to call to me again, and I had to bite my lip to keep from saying, "I'm ready. Carry me off."

It wasn't just the pain, though a new throbbing in my head was so severe that it almost eclipsed the roster of other pains through my body and left leg. I was groggy with the pain, probably delirious—or near it. Retching, vomiting, came in cycles and kept me weak. There was also exhaustion and a sudden fear that I could never escape the smell of death, the stink of the dragon's blood and innards.

The smell of the goop I was lying in was what finally made me fight my way to my feet. The slippery footing made it harder than ever. I needed the elf sword as a crutch now, and that is one thing that it wasn't very good at. The damn think kept sticking into the ground. I swayed so wildly that I thought I was going to fall again. I don't know how much time passed before I even thought to look for the Etevar, his wizard, and his army. I can't even say how long my fight with the dragon lasted—probably not half as long as it's taken me to tell the story.

I stumbled away from the dragon, looking for dry, solid ground, trying to get out of the shadow of the damn thing before I collapsed again.

21

The Eyes of Thyme

The two armies were still facing each other. Apparently, the war had taken a time out for my halftime entertainment with the dragon. With the dragon dead and me back on my feet—at least for the moment—the Varayan army started moving forward again, slowly, almost too slowly for it to be real.

My companions came back to me—all their faces as pale as Annick's normal complexion. Harkane had my horse. Gold was still nervous about getting close to the dragon, but he wasn't fighting the reins. Lesh and Hambert supported my weight while Harkane wiped as much of the sludge off me as he could with a large wad of rough cloth. Then he dried the hilt and blade of Dragon's Death.

"Are you all right?" Annick asked, her voice sounding almost fearful.

"No," came out as a hoarse croak. I coughed and spit. "I'm not in much better shape than that goddam dragon." It was a stupid question, but I didn't have the energy to point that out.

"Look, lord," Lesh said, nodding off to the southeast. He turned me so I could see the Dorthini reaction to my victory.

The Etevar's army was coming apart at the seams. Groups of soldiers, some large and some small, were breaking away, running. I guess that seeing their wizard and his dragon defeated was enough for those deserters. But it wasn't a general rout by any means. The Etevar was busy, rallying as many as he could. Warlords were trying to keep more detachments from running off, sometimes even whipping men back to face us.

"Mount up, lad," Parthet's voice said in my ear. "You've got to finish the job." I looked around, but Parthet was still on the battlements of the castle. The distant-whispering was still spooky.

I looked up at Parthet. His eyes were on me. "You've got to be kidding," I said.

"You have to, lad. It's the only way."

I couldn't. There was just no way. If it hadn't been for Lesh and Hambert at my sides, holding ninety-five percent of my weight, I couldn't even have stayed on my feet.

"It's your duty," Annick said, a blank look behind her eyes. She stared at me, past me, daring me to get angry with her again.

Hell, that was probably the only thing that could have got me moving.

I didn't have much strength to draw on, even for anger. I didn't see how I could possibly handle any more fighting. But I had to try. I looked around. Gold had calmed down a little more, but there was no way I was going to be able to mount alone.

"Lesh, I'm going to need help," I said. He nodded. "You may have to tie me in the saddle again."

"If we have to, lord," Lesh said. I wondered what I

looked like. Even Lesh sounded as if he was about to lose control of his emotions. He boosted me into the saddle, and Harkane was on the other side to make sure that I didn't fall off there.

"We'll be right at your side, lord," Lesh said. Someone brought Lesh's horse over for him. I held on to the pommel of my saddle. Tie me in the saddle? My head started playing tricks again, something about El Cid winning a battle after his death, leading his army into battle—a corpse tied to his horse . . . or was that just another Charlton Heston movie?

"We're ready, lord," Lesh said. I opened my eyes and looked up. Most of the people I had led out of the castle were back, mounted and ready to go into action again. Annick didn't even look at me now. She had her sword out and she was staring at the Dorthini line.

"Uncle Parthet, if you've got any way to prop me up through this, you'd better get busy," I whispered, looking up toward the battlements. His face seemed to zoom in and he nodded . . . but the look on his face was grimmer than anything I had ever seen. His mouth was moving rapidly, but I couldn't hear anything. I hoped it was a potent spell he was weaving.

I looked back to our army. Barons Dieth and Resler were out in front with the cavalry. They were looking to me. Our battle plans hadn't made any allowances for halftime intermission, and there wasn't time for a huddle. I reached up past my shoulder to make sure that Dragon's Death was still in its clips, but I didn't draw the weapon.

It was time for the final scene, but for a moment I just sat there, hunched forward, my eyes on the back of Gold's neck—looking for the energy to do anything at all. I couldn't even have fallen on my sword right just then. Finally, after what might have been almost as long as it felt like, I straightened up and looked around.

"Let's do it," I said. If I could have come up with any alternative, I would have grabbed it in a second, but my mind was damn near blank—at least as far as useful ideas were concerned. All I could do was try to project one step ahead at a time. I clucked at Gold, and he started forward, toward the enemy. I led my troop on an oblique line so we could move into position in front of the center of our army. Keeping track of the Etevar and his wizard didn't take any effort at all now, even when I wasn't looking in their direction. As on that night in Fairy with the mountain trolls, I knew where my enemies were.

We trotted away from the dragon, back out into the afternoon sun. The sun was behind us now, in the eyes of the Dorthinis. Before I turned my troop directly toward the center of the Dorthini army, I gestured for the rest of the Varayan army to advance again.

I must have been burning with fever on top of all the injuries, with delirium hovering nearby. There can hardly be any other rational explanation for the fact that I got on my horse and rode at the enemy again despite the extent of my pain. I didn't even have it in me to wonder, What the hell am I doing here? It just wasn't important any longer. As far as I could tell, I was already so far gone that it didn't matter whether I lay down and waited or kept going until the congregation of Heroes yanked me off. But at least it made the pain fade a little.

You have your duty and I have mine.

The sight of me advancing at the head of the Varayan army sent a few more detachments of Dorthinis running. I was too dragged out to get much of a boost from that. I wouldn't have had the energy to cheer if their whole army had turned tail. I was barely aware of *Who's Afraid of the Big Bad Wolf?* lilting past my brain.

The two armies had been more than a half mile apart by the time I finished off the dragon . . . and the dragon nearly finished off me. The Dorthinis still weren't doing much to close the gap. They were just waiting—maybe even drawing back a little, postponing the second clash. I was out in front of our force, my continuing "right" as Hero, but Lesh and the rest of my companions were so close that you'd need a photo-finish camera to see that I was in the lead. The survivors of the troop I had led out of the castle were just a little behind my companions, fanned out so they had fighting room. Dieth and Resler brought their cavalry right up behind that group, and the infantry—the bulk of our army—advanced in two ranks behind them. At the rear, a few dozen archers and maybe sixty riders completed the tally.

On the Dorthini side, the cavalry was split between the center and both ends of the line. In the center, just behind the infantry, the Etevar and his wizard had a hundred mounted soldiers right around them.

That's where I aimed.

My danger sense was a futile throbbing at the back of my head, barely able to make itself felt over the other pains. I knew where the danger was, and I was heading for it intentionally. I kept my eyes on the black-clad figures of the Etevar and his wizard, looking for some kind of signal from them, some way to escape more fighting. I hoped that the fact that I had just killed the wizard's dragon and walked away—more or less—might make them eager for peace terms. With more than a third of their army running east and most of the remainder wishing that they were, it seemed a smart idea for the Etevar to try for a truce.

That's what *I* thought anyway.

As we closed to about eighty yards, I pulled Dragon's Death and looked back for an instant. Our cavalry was a tight wedge with me at the apex now. Any second, I figured, the Dorthini wizard would come up with some new trick to try to stop me. I was mildly surprised that he hadn't hit me with everything he had while I was still groggy from my fight with his dragon. It wouldn't have taken much at all to finish me then.

I raised my sword and made a feeble pumping motion with my arm, then moved Gold into a modest canter. Behind me, our cavalry kept pace. Out in front, the center of the Dorthini line held firm . . . although people were still fading from the flanks.

"Let's get them," I said. It wasn't nearly a shout. I started whistling the sword's battle tune. I drew strength from that, maybe even from the sword and from whatever Parthet was doing to help prop me up. My brain went into combat mode. That's how I thought of it at the time.

"One last battle," I whispered through the sword's song.

I aimed directly for the standard of the Etevar, slamming us right into the center of the Etevar's best troops. I didn't get much chance to fight there, though. With my companions shielding me so tightly, only a couple of Dorthinis got close enough for me to even feint at them.

That was enough at the start. And when the crowding got closer and more Dorthinis came within reach, Dragon's Death bit into soldiers and horses, falling as if it had the weight of a dragon on top of it. The Dorthini elite started to break around us, and then the Etevar and his wizard were right in front of me.

This time it was no illusion. The wizard was staring straight at me, not ten feet away, but his eyes were blank white. There was no color in them at all.

"His eyes were with the dragon," Parthet's voice whispered in my ear. "Ignore him. He can no longer harm you."

I needed a moment to absorb that. The Dorthini wizard had been directing the dragon with his eyes, seeing for it, seeing *through* it. Annick had blinded one eye of the dragon with an arrow. I had finished the other eye with my elf sword.

A *blind* wizard! He couldn't see to do anything.

The Etevar wasn't blind, though—except with rage. He charged me, screaming. His horse's reins were draped around the pommel of his saddle. The Etevar had a sword in one hand and a mace in the other. He led with the sword, and when I parried that, he tried to dent my head with the mace. I ducked and pushed, since I couldn't get my sword back fast enough to use it. When the Etevar swayed back, off balance, I leaned over to the side to try to finish the fight quickly. I lost my balance too, though, and the best I could do was push off Gold with my one good leg and jump the Etevar. We went to the ground and rolled.

There was plenty of room around me now, too much. The fight with the Etevar's elite had opened up the formation.

I hung on to the Etevar as if he were a life preserver. I knew that if I let go, he'd be able to get to me before I could get up. So we got to our feet together. I don't think the Etevar realized that he was doing most of the work for both of us. With my bum leg extended a bit behind us, I pushed the Etevar away and got Dragon's Death between us. Facing sword and mace together didn't worry me particularly. It may have helped me more than it helped the Etevar. He couldn't use both weapons to full advantage simultaneously.

He charged, swinging the mace first this time. The handle was metal, not wood, so I couldn't slice head from handle. His follow-up was an underhand lunge with the sword, toward my groin, below the mail shirt. Dragon's Death rebounded from mace to sword, moving both away from me. My blade came back up, reached for the Etevar's face. He leaned back, sidestepped, and came in again.

All I could so was shuffle along or pivot, and that handicapped me. For a time it was sword against sword, with the Etevar holding his mace back—a balance and a threat. His broadsword was longer and heavier than most, but it still wasn't in the same league with Dragon's Death. If I had had two good legs under me, and even an ounce of strength, I could have ended the duel quickly, without trouble.

The Etevar gritted his teeth and fought without speaking. I didn't have the air or the energy to talk. Chat during a duel may sound good on the movie screen, but it has no place in real life—not unless you're completely tired of living.

The Etevar had to realize that I was gimpy by then. He started moving in a slow circle around me, forcing me to turn and drag my bum leg as he tried to get me off balance so he could get past Dragon's Death. The circling wasn't comfortable, but it did let me keep track of what was going on around us. I had to know if any of the Etevar's people came close enough to help him. I was beyond relying exclusively on my danger sense.

I made the first mistake. The routine lulled me. The Etevar crossed his weapons and caught the blade of Dragon's Death coming down, using the head of his mace to pin my sword against his. Then he pushed in toward me, lowering his head as if he planned to butt me to the ground. I stepped back, and my bad leg forced me to pivot. The Etevar brought his weapons through and the sword scored a long cut along my left arm. I pivoted back toward him and brought both arms down, slamming my fists and the hilt of Dragon's Death into the back of his neck as he tried to step past. He went down, though not for a long enough count to let me take advantage. But in his rush to get back to his feet, he left the mace behind.

He charged again right away, though—apparently maddened with rage. He came at me as if he planned to bowl me over with just his anger. When Dragon's Death came straight down, his sword wasn't enough to keep it off. The elf sword bit into his shoulder. I dragged it off to the side and made a home-run swing, aiming for the most vulnerable target, his neck.

The Etevar's blade dug into my side, but his head was off before I got out, "For my father."

And then the darkness claimed me.

Raucous music. Old Teutonic drinking songs seemed to alternate with modern pieces like "Another One Bites the Dust" and "Bohemian Rhapsody." I fancied that I could smell blooming lilacs and wondered if I had somehow found my way home to Louisville. The pain was gone, so I assumed that Dad and Vara had finally come to collect me. It didn't seem to matter. I had finished the job I started out to do. I told myself that I didn't really want to be King of Varay anyway.

What comes next? seemed to be more important at the moment. I was curious, but mostly in a distracted, intellectual sort of way. *What is death? Who runs things here?* And *Where the hell* is *"here"*?

"Come back, lad."

At first, I didn't notice the voice. I was lost in the void of eternity, trying to deal with that.

"Come back, lad."

It was Parthet's voice. It's over now, Uncle Parker, I thought. But my peace was becoming more and more disturbed. The emptiness suddenly had borders. I felt pressure on my head. A tingling nibbled at my skin. This wasn't an electric tingle, more like the nibble of a fish on your toe while you're swimming.

"Hang on to my voice, lad." Parthet again. Then I heard one of his mumbo-jumbo chants. It started as a whisper that I had to concentrate on to hear, and it built until it forced my attention.

I'm not dead, I realized, and I wasn't sure whether to be relieved or disappointed. The pain returned—not so great as before, but still more than I really wanted to endure.

"His eyes are open!" That was Lesh's voice. I assumed that he was talking about me, but I didn't know that my eyes were open. I tried blinking. There *was* some light, not much. Dusk, I thought. The rest of the afternoon had gone, and the early evening. There were forms in the hazy twilight around me, forms that took shape as the light seemed to strengthen. Parthet and Lesh were both leaning over me.

"You're going to be all right, lad," Parthet said. I thought that I heard relief in his voice, but everything was still hazy. "We'll get you inside now. I couldn't let them move you before."

I didn't answer, but Parthet didn't seem to expect me to. He stood and spoke to other people. The words were simply too slippery for me to hold on to them, whatever they were. After a moment, I felt myself being lifted—on a stretcher or something.

"Into the castle," Parthet said, his voice farther off but stronger. I managed what felt like a deep breath and let myself be carried. Lesh stayed at my side, talking, telling me about the rest of the day's events. The battle was over. The Etevar was dead. His soldiers were either dead, fled, or under guard. His blind wizard had been bound and hooded.

It is over. I squeezed my eyes shut for a moment. When I opened them again, my vision had improved. I saw Annick standing up on the snout of the dragon, retrieving her arrows. She stared down at me from that vantage, then climbed down the other side and got on her horse. The last I saw of her, she was riding west—into the sunset—alone.

When my bearers carried me through the gate of Castle Thyme, King Pregel was waiting to greet me.

"It's over here," I told the king, or tried to tell him. I'm not sure if any words actually came out. I closed my eyes again.

I must have slept. When I opened my eyes the next time,

there was bright light around me. *Sun*light. From the look of it, I guessed that it had to be around midday, which meant that I had slept fifteen hours or more . . . maybe *days* more. Pregel was sitting on a chair next to my bed.

"I've been here since the start of your battle," he said. "You certainly are my proper heir."

From the strength and joy in his voice, he wouldn't be needing an heir anytime soon, which was great with me. Even assuming that I would someday be physically up to anything again, I wasn't ready to commit to a century or more of his job. I had serious reservations about keeping the job I had. Silicon Valley was looking better and better. I'd rather face my dragons on a game screen any day.

"How badly am I torn up?" I asked, surprised that my voice was understandable.

"You're mending nicely," Pregel said, avoiding the question. "Parthet said that you'd be able to get up and try walking for a few minutes after your breakfast."

"How long have I been out?" I asked.

"A few hours short of two days." Parthet. I looked back—off behind me. He was standing there, looking quite pleased with himself.

"I was almost dead," I told him.

His grin got a little sheepish. "Well, I can see what I'm doing now." He touched the frames of his glasses. Then his face turned serious again. "I'm really not sure that I can take much credit. It was close the first night. You were babbling, talking to your father and Vara."

I didn't remember that.

"Enough talk," Pregel said. "Let the boy have his meal." I tried scooting myself up in the bed, found that it wasn't nearly as painful as I had feared, and then had plenty of hands helping me. Mother came in with three pages who were loaded down with food and pitchers.

Wonder of wonders, I even had an appetite. Pregel and the others gave me a long time to eat without interruption. No one spoke until the pace of my eating slowed down.

"Well, boy," Pregel said. "It's seems you have your first crown."

I still wasn't thinking one hundred percent clearly. At first, Pregel's statement drifted right past me, and then when it did register, it derailed what thinking processes I did have working.

"What do you mean?" My danger sense started to prickle.

"Dorthin is yours now, boy," Pregel said. "You've slain the last Etevar. He has no heirs."

"Wait! Time out. I don't want Dorthin."

"It's yours, by right of conquest if nothing else," Pregel said. "Something must be done to keep the surviving warlords from warring among themselves for it. The winner would turn against Varay as soon as he could."

"Give it to someone else!" I said.

"You don't understand. It's not mine to give or take," Pregel said. "It's yours—do with it what you will." He sounded a little miffed by my attitude.

I looked around the unfamiliar room—somewhere in the keep of Castle Thyme—more panicked by the thought of getting stuck with Dorthin than I had been by facing the dragon. I kept looking around. No one offered any suggestions.

"I can give it away?" I asked, turning back to Pregel and Parthet.

"You can give it to someone to hold for you," Parthet said.

I let out a noisy sigh of relief, not catching the subtleties of Parthet's phrasing. An idea popped into my head. I knew just where to look this time. Baron Dieth was standing over by the door. I turned and got my legs out of bed. Pregel had said that I was supposed to be up to walking. I had help standing, but when I got to my feet, I didn't have any trouble staying up. While I took a moment to wonder at *that* miracle, Harkane put a robe on me. His face looked gaunt, worried.

I could walk. I limped quite noticeably, and walking was slow going, as much because I was afraid of falling as anything else, I think. And there was still pain—all over—but nothing compared to what I had experienced before. One cautious step at a time, I walked over to Baron Dieth.

"You were my father's first squire," I said. "Will you hold Dorthin for me?"

He went down on one knee. "To the death, High-ness," he said.

"Then it's yours." I figured that it would take some-thing more formal to make it firm, but I would let Baron Kardeen worry about that.

"Such a post calls for a dukedom at least," Pregel said. "It is your honor to bestow."

And Kardeen was there to coach me on what to say and do.

"While we're at this," I said when I finished with that, "Lesh, you've been with me from the start. I couldn't have made it without you. It's time we made you Sir Lesh." But I still looked to Pregel and Kardeen to see if I was doing the right thing. Neither of them objected. Finally, at my recommendation, King Pregel raised Sir Hambert to the barony and gave him Coriander in place of Dieth.

"You might want to take a few steps out to the bal-cony," Parthet said then, "as long as you feel up to it."

There was something in Parthet's voice that made me think that he had a specific reason for his suggestion. I started to ask, then changed my mind and just nodded. It wasn't a long walk, only a dozen steps, and there were people at either side of me, ready to catch me if I started to fall. I didn't. I made it all the way to the small balcony that looked down on the courtyard of Castle Thyme. The open space wasn't all that large, but there were several hundred people down there, looking up at the keep. There was a cheer when they saw me.

Tears ran down my face. I waved and tried to smile. All those people waiting to make sure that I was really recovering. I started to understand at least part of what had bound my father to Varay for all those years.

Then the sky darkened. There were no clouds. It was as if someone had put a polarizing filter over the sun. I looked up. So did Parthet. I guess that none of the people down in the courtyard saw the magic. The image of the Elflord of Xayber appeared in the sky, scowling fiercely enough to turn Medusa to stone. There were no audible words to his message, but the gist was something like *Sooner or later, upstart, your ass is mine.*